Seven Days in May
Convention
Night of Camp David
Vanished

All of Fletcher Knebel's many best-selling novels have dealt with major themes of national importance.

TRESPASS

is no different.

Here is a chilling yet compassionate portrait of real people caught up in an American tragedy that could too easily become tomorrow's reality.

TRESPASS was originally published by Doubleday & Company, Inc.

TRESPASS

FLETCHER KNEBEL

PUBLISHED BY POCKET BOOKS NEW YORK

Lines from *The People, Yes* by Carl Sandburg, copyright, 1936, by
Harcourt, Brace & World, Inc.; copyright, ©, 1964, by Carl Sandburg.
Reprinted by permission of the publisher.

TRESPASS

Doubleday edition published October, 1969

Pocket Book edition published November, 1970

4th printing.........March, 1971

This *Pocket Book* edition includes every word
contained in the original, higher-priced edition. It is printed
from brand-new plates made from completely reset, clear, easy-to-read
type. *Pocket Book* editions are published by Pocket Books, a division
of Simon & Schuster, Inc., 630 Fifth Avenue, New York, N.Y. 10020.
Trademarks registered in the United States and other countries.

L

To Theodore Lewis

"Get off this estate."
"What for?"
"Because it's mine."
"Where did you get it?"
"From my father."
"Where did he get it?"
"From his father."
"And where did he get it?"
"He fought for it."
"Well, I'll fight you for it."

Carl Sandburg

THE PEOPLE, YES

TRESPASS

Chapter One

She glanced at the house, high on the green slope, as they
turned off the Great Road, and she knew at once that
something was amiss. The thought hovered, a fitful
nagging.

He saw the house the moment she did, but the sight
evoked only a familiar and perplexing mood. There was
the pressing weight, the tug of things past, and the mild
despair. In recent months the sight of Fairhill seldom
buoyed him as it once had. Rather, he could see his life
stretching from Fairhill to infinity on a ribbon of paper on
which nothing is written. He was bored.

She leaned involuntarily against him as the Jag con-
vertible, top down, swung into the long asphalt driveway
which curved toward the house. She righted herself, tilting
away from him, back into her own tight little space that
she had marked off and barricaded since they left the
Brethertons' and the Saturday evening drinks on the
patio. He had been irritating—"profoundly shallow" was
her phrase for it—as he often was after a few drinks in
any company where he felt comfortable with his kind. She
knew he was aware of her self-imposed isolation, and he
was driving too fast because of it, that male thing again.

Air stirred by the car swished through the birch trees,
three or four slim, white trunks to a clump, which lined
the drive. The immense lawn rolled gently upward like a
green swell of sea. Dogwood trees, pinned to infant shadows, framed the house. The brave oak, a huge, solemn
boulder of a tree, stood in silence, no leaf trembling.
Fairhill, serene and confident, commanded the countryside in the twilight of early July.

It was all so still, so stamped in certainty, as though
Fairhill were a print of Princeton in the summer, as
though this quiet end of day were fastened timelessly to
the house and lawn and to the tangle of woods which hid

the creek on the far side of the hill. She was never of two minds about her home. She loved its strength, its grace, its imperturbability. Fairhill overlooked lesser estates along the Great Road with a kind of majestic detachment, mellowing with the years. Or did she impute some of the attributes of her marriage to the place where it was arbitrated? Tim lacked the grace of Fairhill, but he did have its strength and durability. She would grant him all his sturdy qualities, but often, as this evening, they added up to a very heavy piece of furniture. At the Brethertons' he had been so judicious, so rational, so persuasive. The only trouble was that his premise was wrong because he really did not know what he was talking about. Her husband was one of the most logical, unperceptive men she knew.

Liz looked again at the long, white house, patches of red brick showing beneath the weathered paint, as Tim turned onto the spread of asphalt before the three-car garage. Yes, something was wrong, a bothersome detail upstairs. And then she saw it.

"Why did you raise the shade in our room?" she asked, and was promptly conscious that Liz Crawford, the apostle of the free spirit, was also Liz, the finicky homebody. Some corners of herself would always vex her.

Tim braked to a stop, switched off the ignition, and looked upward without interest. The humoring of a wife could be a chore.

"What an eye!" Tim saw that a shade at one of their bedroom windows was raised perhaps five or six inches above mid-frame. All the others, both upstairs and down, met the center line in agreeable conformity. "Wasn't me. I never touched the damn thing."

"Well, I certainly didn't," said Liz. The reproof, as thin as foil, intimated that they both knew who the culprit was. She was displeased with herself for promoting such trivia to a matter of moment. But it was Tim's fault that she was testy. He had been insufferably dreary after the fourth gin and tonic.

They walked apart, not speaking, toward the front door which, in the Princeton custom, had been left unlocked. The small, pillared portico was flanked by azaleas, the blooms of early May long since powdered away. Liz looked up again at the shade, then shrugged.

The foyer was muffled in shadow as were the long living room to the left and the dining room to the right. They walked stiffly, as if by appointment, past the wide, half-spiral staircase and down the hall to the library. Liz stepped to the right, kicked off her buckled shoes into her sewing room. It was an act of assertion of their separate identities. The "sewing room" was a jumble of Liz's roving interests, a desk with a portable typewriter amid a clutter of papers, a half-finished canvas, and the scatter of tubes and brushes on shelves and floor, tennis rackets, skis, several piles of magazines, and, in a corner, a hooded sewing machine. Her shoes belonged here, and if she had worn stockings today, they would have been shed here too. As it was, she padded in bare feet to the library, Tim's room.

They both sensed the coming scene. Tim knew that a single word could unleash her pent irritations. At least the skirmish would be fought on his territory, but the thought gave him little comfort. He lacked the energy for bickering, and he wished she would go off quietly somewhere and read a book. He sighed inwardly, knowing the hope was a futile one. Although it was still light outside, Tim switched on the bronze desk lamp. The battleground was illuminated: the forest-green rug, deeply and roughly tufted, the bookcase crammed with its wares from floor to ceiling, the casement bay window, the tidy desk, the oak-paneled walls, and the two leather easy chairs. The terrain was totally masculine, and Tim surmised the fact titillated Liz. She would be fighting on alien ground.

Tim pulled off his summer-weight sport jacket and threw it on the ledge by the casement windows. He loosened his tie and eased into the chair nearest the fireplace. Timothy Rush Crawford, Jr., at home. Scotch ancestry, mostly, charted back to colonial days by an aunt who doted on genealogy. She had discovered years ago that a Crawford fought with General Washington. Tim had light brown hair, a bristling thatch of it, which he let curl about his ears in tentative concession to the current vogue. His face was long, angular, and the chin a trifle sharp. He registered his eyes as blue on all the forms, but actually they were so indistinct in hue that old friends could not name the color. He was a tall man, six feet one, still trim for his thirty-eight years. Tim jogged in the morning, played weekend tennis through three seasons, and skied in the winter. He tried to keep fit, but he knew he drank too much, a prisoner of this aimless, inchoate boredom.

He eyed Liz, coiled vigilantly in the other easy chair. A man became accustomed to beauty in his wife even if she had the kind of luster which, if not instinctively denigrated by the owner, arouses envy in less-favored women. The features he knew so well were orchestrated as though for a symphony to the WASPs, the eyebrows widely spaced, nose straight and unobtrusive. She was tallish, once a bit bony, but now ripe and edgeless. She had worn her black hair a dozen ways over the years. Now it fell straight to her shoulders, flared upward at the bottom. A white band held the hair tight from her forehead in a perfect arc. Liz, Tim knew, could have been the show horse of Princeton's young matron set, but she stubbornly exposed abrasive facets of herself as though to proclaim Elizabeth Faircloth Crawford as flawed as the next woman. Tim supposed that he and Liz could qualify as beautiful people, but Liz fought the dubious accolade. "Liz would really like to be a bit of a bitch," her friend Peggy Abingdon once said, "and sometimes she almost makes it."

"Drink?" asked Tim. He unhitched himself from the chair and walked to the bar, a converted antique washstand with marble top.

"No," said Liz, "and you don't need one either. You've had four."

"Thanks for counting. It's Saturday night, remember?" He poured gin over ice in a tall glass. The tonic hissed under the bottle opener and sprayed his hand.

"Oh, all right," she said. "Make me one too. If it's going to be wet out . . ."

"Just damp, Puss."

Very adroit, thought Liz, trying to disarm her by use of her nickname. In a skirmish, she was always Liz, in the rare battle, Elizabeth. Tim intended to detour the confrontation. She felt a welling of quiet indignation at his tactics.

He handed her the drink. It fizzed slightly, a slice of emerald lime floating with the ice. He sat down, faced her with an ingenuous smile.

"I like your hair that way," he said.

"I don't care to discuss my hair."

"Oh." He sipped his drink, searched her for storm signals, saw new ones, and retreated to neutral ground. "What time are the kids coming home?"

"About nine-fifteen," she said. She held her tiny, oblong wristwatch, discreet gold with a gold band, up to the desk light. "It's eight now. Peggy's bringing them."

The children, Scott, five, and Holly, a year younger, had attended a birthday party at the home of a Montessori classmate, Peggy Abingdon's daughter. Ordinarily they would have been accompanied by Vivika, the live-in Swedish maid, but Vivika had gone to Stockholm for a month's vacation. It was the beginning of vacation time at Fairhill. Fred, the gardener, had his first week off. Only Dora, the five-day cleaning woman, was working. She would be on duty Monday morning. Dora never missed a day.

"After nine's a little late for the kids," said Tim. The thought had not occurred to him earlier.

"This is the first time," she replied. "It won't hurt them."

Tim held his glass vaguely in her direction. "Nice dress or whatever. Is it new?"

"Tim, I've worn this at least ten times." It was blue denim with large, stitched pockets, hem cut an inch above her knees. It was casual, simple, and she had paid $185 for the understated look at a new Italian boutique on 64th Street in New York. "And I don't want to talk about clothes."

"Okay, Liz." He raised his glass defensively, peering at her over the rim. Obviously the wrangle was not to be postponed.

"Tim, I can't understand why you insist on undercutting everything I believe in when you get in that pseudo-profound mood of yours. I think it's petty."

"Now what are we talking about?" He was resigned but wary.

"You know exactly what I mean. We're talking about your little thing at the Brethertons'." She took a quick, unintended swallow of the gin and tonic.

"Oh, you mean about skin-deep liberals?"

"Did you talk about anything else? It was all a very pointed but clumsy picture of your wife, and I did not, repeat, did not appreciate it."

"I wasn't talking about you. I was talking about all the joiners, the critics, the talkers who don't know what in the hell they really believe."

She sniffed her dissent. "You mentioned Planned Parenthood. That's me. You mentioned, oh, so patronizingly, United World Federalists. That's me. To say nothing of Equality Now. In case you hadn't heard, that's me again. . . . Tim, if you want to debate me, let's do it face to face, instead of you sneaking around under the cover of generalities in front of other people."

"But you do believe, so I couldn't have been talking about you, could I?" He admired his own adeptness and forced a smile. "I specifically said I meant the emoters who go along for the ride."

"You and your sophistry," she said in a rush. "Everyone there knew you were putting your wife down. I suppose you just happened to pick what I belong to? . . . And besides, what's so terrible about emotion, anyway? If you want to know what I think, Tim, I think you're afraid to show some honest feelings. You're afraid it might poke some holes in that very proper cardboard we call Timothy Crawford."

If it was cardboard, thought Tim, it was soggy and crumpled. Did she know that he ached for an excuse to put two months and ten thousand miles between himself and Fairhill? He thought momentarily of Ginny, surprising himself. He had not thought of Ginny in months. But the battle game could not be evaded.

"Calm down," he said flatly. "You're not attractive when you screw your face up like that."

"I'm not trying to be attractive." She flicked self-consciously at her hair. "I'm trying to talk sense to a man who prides himself on being rational. If you're so rational, why don't you try reasoning with your wife, instead of using a public forum to criticize her?"

"It wasn't a public forum, and I wasn't criticizing you." The color rose in his cheeks. She was partially right, but she didn't understand what had impelled him—that wish to chuck the whole deal for a couple of months, Fairhill,

Princeton, the Brethertons, the law firm. Oh, hell. What was the use?

"You know you're lying," she said.

"You're hell-bent on making a scene, aren't you?" He placed his glass on the broad arm of the chair, rose awkwardly, and walked to the stone mantel. "I could use a cigarette."

He reached without looking toward the corner of the fireplace ledge, fumbled a moment, then surveyed the length of the mantel. "That's funny."

"I'm glad you find something amusing."

"I left a pack here when we went out." He turned, frowning.

"Well, don't accuse me." Liz had not smoked in a year, and although she never alluded to the months or weeks, her abstinence stood as a silent rebuke to his lack of will power.

"I'm not," he said hastily. "Really, Liz. It's just—"

"You probably smoked the whole pack at the Brethertons'." She could not suppress the edge of triumph in her voice, yet almost at once she chided herself for scoring battle points on an irrelevant issue.

He stepped back to his chair and took his drink again. He shook the ice slowly as he stood looking toward the windows, concentrating. Tim's talent for sudden absorption, the self swiftly transported, always unnerved her. It was as unnatural as falling sound asleep during a jet take-off. She felt a twinge of envy.

"You smoked more than you thought. So what?"

"No." His tone became judicious. "No. I took the pack off the mantel, then remembered I had some in my pocket, so I put the pack back on the mantel." He smiled, disconcerted at revealing his secret struggle with nicotine. "That was the last thing I did before I left the room."

"You could have put it somewhere else," she said. But she said it without conviction. They both knew Tim's memory was phenomenal and that he seldom bothered to dissemble on small matters.

"No, I remember that spot of green on the mantel, right where I left it." Tim's brand came in bright green packs. "I'll get some from the carton in the pantry."

Liz swung a crossed, bare leg while he was gone. She

thought of the raised bedroom shade, connected it tentatively with the misplaced cigarettes, then dismissed the idea. This interruption annoyed her. She wanted to have it out now with Tim.

"Damned odd." He returned with a lighted cigarette in his hand and a pack bulging at the breast pocket of his shirt. If there was to be renewed combat, Tim came equipped with his defensive armament.

She attacked. "If you weren't talking about me, why did you use Planned Parenthood as an example?"

"Look, Liz. Let's knock it off, huh." He settled back in his chair. "If I offended you, I apologize."

"Then you admit you were talking about me?"

Damn marriage, he thought. Why must they forever pick at each other like children confined too long indoors? "No, I don't. Maybe I did it subconsciously. If so, well, please skip it. I promise it won't happen again." But who could pledge his subconscious to anything? "Okay, Puss?"

With his return to "Puss" he could see her tension ease somewhat. She was realizing that her anger had placed her at a disadvantage.

"All right, I'll skip it. . . . But honestly, Tim, why can't we talk out our differences? If we don't, they'll keep driving a wedge between us." She paused. "People who don't talk to each other wind up talking to their lawyers."

"Puss, there isn't an attorney in Mercer County, including me, who could unravel us. You know that." He studied her, a blend of challenge and tenderness. He had been snotty at the Brethertons', but how could he explain this nameless restive feeling that came over him so often in recent months? "We are different. I know you think I'm too rigid. I suppose, to yourself, you call me stuffy. That's my way. I can't help it." He was conscious of the words distorting his thought even as they formed. That was not what he meant at all. "You're, well, kind of a free-floater. But look at everything that binds us, the kids, Fairhill, thirteen years, tennis, bed, friends. . . . Hell, it would take a magician to untangle us."

The list annoyed Liz. Why couldn't Tim talk straight just once? He had dropped "bed" so indifferently, between tennis and friends, when they both knew it was the most binding part of their marriage, at times a tight ban-

dage for their mutually inflicted wounds, at times a rich
and closely knit cocoon. Without it, she knew, they might
be lost.

And he hadn't even mentioned the bonds, those 200
government bonds, $5,000 par each, given them by her
father who groaned ceremoniously over the gift tax. It
was the fiscal glue of their marriage, inscribed to "Timothy Rush Crawford, Jr., OR Elizabeth Faircloth
Crawford." Steve Faircloth admired his son-in-law as
much as he loved his daughter, and he had planted the
pair of them on financial flypaper, one million dollars'
worth of sticky, gummy adhesive, a legacy of trust—or
was it subtle distrust?—in their union. That tiny word
"or" was a conjunction of infinite complexity, far more
glutinous than "and." Legally either of them could cash
one or more of the bonds without consulting the other,
but who would dare—or want to? Old Steve might as well
have spelled it out: "You are both free, honorable adults,
and you are both enmeshed forever in your freedom and
your honor." So neat and yet so ethically inextricable.
And so different from Fairhill, the 65 acres once known
as Oak Farm and renamed in her honor by Tim. The estate came directly to Tim from Tim, Sr. Fairhill, where
Tim had been born, where she and Tim returned after his
father's death, and where both Scott and Holly were conceived. Big Tim had none of the deft, if inscrutable, in-
tentions of Steve Faircloth. He left the estate to his son,
period.

"Untangling us would be a mess, except for Fairhill,"
she conceded, "which is all the more reason to talk about
us. Tim, tell me frankly, do you think I ought to chuck
some of my projects? How about Planned Parenthood?
Do you really think it's all a liberal 'catharsis' as you
called it, just a social hour masquerading behind a cause
or something? I forget your exact words."

"No." He inhaled slowly and washed the smoke down
with gin and tonic. Liz had overlooked nothing. She
would shake this bone until it was dry. "No, I think
you're sincere. But Jesus, Puss, look at the rest of that
crowd at Pretty Brook or the Present Day Club. Peggy
Abingdon, always yammering about fewer babies when
she's got five kids of her own. If they're really serious,

they'd knock off that silly name and call it—" He hesitated, searching. "Call it 'SCOFF.'"

"I suppose that's some kind of devastating acronym?"

"Yes. As a matter of fact, it is."

"All right. I give up."

"SCOFF—Screw Only for Fun."

"My, aren't we clever tonight." She limned her stare with acid. "Tim, you have about as much social conscience as a flea."

"Well, that's what they mean," he insisted. "And how about the hypocrisy of those volunteer clinics in the Trenton black neighborhoods? Is it more blacks they're afraid of? If they're so dedicated, why don't your friends set up shop along the Great Road and stop all those explosions of white kids who get enrolled in St. Paul's or Foxcroft the day they're born?"

"I stopped at two, thank you." She leaned forward, shaking her glass at Tim like a gavel. "You pretend to be so rational, and yet you blame me for the faults of others. Guilt by association. That's not logic. That's being devious."

"All right. Take your feds." He knew his nickname for the United World Federalists would enflame her. "A gaggle of people who want to settle the problems of the world when they couldn't even stop a brawl in the neighborhood gin mill. Most of them wouldn't know a gin mill if they saw one. . . . It isn't five thousand miles away."

"That's not only third-rate sarcasm, it's utterly simplistic. You really mean that because I want a world of law instead of anarchy, I'm a softheaded idealist, just another naïve female." She was fully embattled again. "That's what you really think of me, Tim. . . . Well, let me tell you something about you. You don't read enough, you don't know enough, and you're ignorant of what's going on—plain, old-fashioned ignorant."

"Thank you, Mrs. Crawford." He was feeling his drinks now, and he spaced his words, dropping them like shoes. "Wife of the town illiterate."

"I didn't say illiterate. I said ignorant."

"Okay, then. Proud wife of the village idiot."

"You're impossible." She drained her drink, went to

the bar in angry strides, and put the glass down with a clink. Then she walked to the door.

"Now where are you going?" He slurred the words. The gin had brought a flush to his face.

She wheeled at him, a soundless maneuver on her bare feet. "To the kitchen for a drink of water. Water! You might try some."

Liz padded down the hallway, through the dining room to the enormous, tiled kitchen with its copper hood over the stove, copper pots strung on the walls like trophies, and the huge bronzed refrigerator and freezer, officiating in opposite corners as the president and chairman of the culinary corporation. She walked to the sink.

"Tim! Come here—please."

He ambled in after a moment, drink in hand and a pleased expression on his face. No domestic skirmish could survive the cry of a lady in distress. He was needed.

"What's the matter?"

"Look." She pointed at the drainboard. It was empty save for an upended glass. "Just before we left, I took a drink of water and then put the glass in the drain."

"So?"

She pointed to another glass on the counter. "That wasn't there. I had to get my glass from the cupboard. When we left, there was only one glass by the sink. Now there're two. Did you get some water when you were out here?"

He shook his head. "Maybe the kids forgot something and Peggy brought them back."

"And took your cigarettes and raised the shade in our bedroom?" She also shook her head. "Tim, somebody has been in the house."

He leaned against the counter. This new development intrigued him. "Yeah, it looks that way, doesn't it? Maybe Fred or Dora."

"Dora wasn't here today and Fred's on vacation. Besides, Fred doesn't smoke, and he never goes upstairs except to change the storm windows and screens. And Dora would never enter the house unexpected without leaving a note."

Tim drank slowly while he considered. "You may be

right." The prospect of an unknown intruder somehow cheered him. At the least it augured a marital cease-fire.

"I wish we'd gotten a new dog," she said. It was her first confession of the evening. When Mac, the elderly German shepherd, had died in May, Tim and Holly had wanted a shepherd puppy, but Liz and Scott contended Mac's memory should be honored for a few months. Liz *is* upset, thought Tim.

"Somebody has been here," she said. She fetched her drink from the cooler, which held a jug of mountain-spring water. "I'm sure of it, Tim."

"Let me have a look."

He prowled through the downstairs, whistling as he opened closets and peered behind doors. They met in the hallway and returned together to the library. Dusk was settling, etching the light from the desk lamp. A new breeze stirred outside. It would soon be dark.

"Everything looks okay."

"Did you look at the silver?"

He grinned. "Yeah. All snug. So are we. . . . Drink?"

She declined with a motion of her head. "And I wish you wouldn't, Tim. If somebody . . . well, suppose, they're still here?"

He looked at her in surprise. "What makes you think that?"

"I don't know. I haven't felt right since we turned in the drive. That shade upstairs . . ."

He relaxed in his chair, relieved that her new concern had turned her from conjugal warfare. She was right about his behavior earlier, he knew. He had been describing Liz as he lolled in the wicker chair at the Brethertons' and talked in flowing generalities of the country, stultified institutions, and the bankruptcy of the liberals, but in reality he had depicted Liz. Why? Why the oblique assault on his wife? Was it because he was fed up with his own endless conferences, at the law firm, at the Harvard Board of Overseers, at that meaningless commission in Washington which nibbled at his time? Tim Crawford, establishment lawyer, impeccable credentials, sound man, thinks things through. What bull. He was Tim Crawford, the time-marker, the uncommitted, and, in secret, the aimless seeker. Jesus, what a dreary round of nothing.

And so, did he envy those displays of emotion that shot like geysers from some deep well of vitality within Liz? Was it a deadness within himself that mocked her enthusiasm? He slumped on his spine. He felt empty and futile. Five gins were over the mark. He had better take an aspirin and scramble some eggs or he would go through Sunday with a dull headache.

He studied Liz. She was perched on the edge of his desk, one bare leg dangling and her dress stretched tight across her thighs. He knew that hundreds of men envied him those long legs, toasted a delicate beige by the spring sunlight on the Fairhill tennis court and now richly tanned because she lounged beside the pool in late afternoon when she had exhausted her interests for the day. Exhausted? He smiled. Liz's passions never flagged.

She was beautiful now, absorbed in thought, the slightest of frowns on her high forehead. She swung one leg, her heel thumping against the desk. Tim could feel flickers of sensuality, and he wished Holly and Scott were home in bed. He looked at the ship's clock, ticking quietly on the stone mantel. Eight forty-five. The children would be here in half an hour.

"Tim."

He started, fearful of a summons to another round of spiny truth. Or, he thought, put us on Channel 10 on the 11 A.M. slot and we could be an unending soap opera, *Social Register* division. He braced himself mentally.

"I just thought of something. You remember that phone call night before last? When you answered, there was just breathing and then a click?"

"Yes."

"Well, this noon, a man's voice asked for Archie. When I asked Archie who, the man hung up."

"Could be coincidence, Puss."

"I know, but— Tim, I think someone is in the house right now. I can feel it."

"Could be." But the possibility seemed remote to Tim. After all, the house had gone unlocked for years without incident. Some years ago, after the first rash of riots in Jersey cities, he had begun to bolt the doors, but each time he turned the key he felt ridiculously cautious, the

Mr. Milquetoast of Great Road, and he soon abandoned the undertaking.

"I suppose the upstairs ought to be looked at," she said.

"Sure." He started to hoist himself from the chair, found it an effort.

Liz shook her head. "No, Tim. Don't go." Her frown deepened.

"Say, you are scared, aren't you?" His surprise was unfeigned. Liz was quick to battle but slow to alarm.

"Not for us," she replied. "I was thinking of Scott and Holly. They're always seeing monsters anyway."

"Well, then, I'll case the upstairs. You're imagining things, Liz."

She leaned toward him. "No, no, Tim. Stay here." Her voice fell to a whisper. "I think you should call the township police." She motioned toward the desk phone.

"Oh, come on, Liz. That's going pretty far."

He was watching her face to gauge the depth of her intuition when suddenly she tensed. Her foot, which had been swinging nervously, stopped dead against the desk. She froze, a look of amazement on her face, then cried "oh," a gurgle of sound. She snatched at her dress, pulling the hem lower. She was staring at the doorway.

Tim looked.

At the door stood a black man. He was framed in the funnel of light from the desk lamp, and he leaned easily against the doorjamb in a half slouch. His dark face was impassive behind a drooping mustache and a clump of goatee. His hair, cut in the Afro style, resembled a lump of black coral. He wore dark green dungarees and a black turtleneck sweater over which dangled a medallion from a long silver chain. He looked from Liz to Tim and back again, unsmiling.

"Forget the police," he said. The voice was matter-of-fact, confident, with the faintest of drawls. "The phone line's cut."

Chapter Two

Silence fastened on the room, suspending them in time like moving figures halted in a photograph. Outside the dusk melted into night, blotting the lawn's firs, red maples, and hickorys against the sloping woods beyond. Tim and Liz sat immobile save for one small movement when Liz again smoothed down her dress on the exposed thigh. The black man did not shift position. Three persons remained fixed, a mute triangle, twelve feet on a side. In the distance could be heard the wheeze of tires on the Great Road. The ship's clock ticked off the seconds, measuring the silence. The hands marked eight fifty-two. The last minute had become an hour.

The black man moved. He reached in his dungaree pocket and withdrew a green pack of cigarettes and a book of matches, lit the cigarette, and squinted in the first spume of smoke. He stepped forward and dropped the spent match in a large copper ashtray that stood on a stand beside the vacant chair. He held up the pack.

"Yours," he said to Tim. "I forgot mine."

Tim stared at the speaker. The words loosened the grip of shock. Tim glanced at Liz. A curiously slack expression had frozen like a flower in sudden frost. She was terrified.

The black man nodded toward the empty chair and said to Liz: "Maybe you oughta sit down." The voice was low, easy, controlled.

Liz gulped, a convulsion that dismayed her. She shook her head, pressing her lips together to ward off trembling.

"Okay. If that's the way it is." The black man flicked his shoulders dismissively, lowered himself into the leather chair, and stretched his legs. He wore black moccasins and white wool sweat socks. He smoked without speaking, looking first at Liz, then at Tim. The silence pulled taut again. Another minute passed. For the black man it was one of methodical inventory.

"That was a very refined family fight," he said. "Lots of fancy words." The faint drawl had a leisurely cadence, but Tim found the meaning ominous. A stranger had eavesdropped on Fairhill's private flagellations. It was as though an unknown interloper had caught Liz in the act of disrobing. Tim saw that Liz was gripping the edge of the desk with oddly prominent knuckles.

Tim waited, but the black man offered nothing further. Was there contempt in the small smile, half hidden by the wreath of mustache and the goatee? Tim could not be sure. Again the unnerving quiet. They were being tested by the ticking of the ship's clock.

"I'd like to ask a question," said Tim at last. He was glad the sound of his words did not convey his unsteadiness.

The black man nodded. His authority in the room had been acknowledged. "Go ahead, Crawford."

Use of his name startled Tim. Although he should have expected it, the name bespoke knowledge, preparation—adding a quick new dimension to their triangle.

"What's this all about?" he asked.

The black man gazed straight at Tim, dark brown eyes holding washed blue for a moment, then he surveyed Tim from head to foot as though checking visible resources against an unseen list. The silver medallion—Tim noted that it held the embossed head of a man—shone against the black sweater.

"My name is Ben Steele," he said, as if a name explained a world.

"Oh." Liz gasped. She stared at him in unmasked fear and fascination. "February Twenty-first?"

"Yeah," said Steele. "A deputy. As you probably know, our commander, Daniel Smith, is in exile—they say."

The name struck Tim like a hammer blow. Anyone allied with Daniel Smith was bad news, very bad news, at Fairhill. Dan Smith. February Twenty-first, the day some years ago when Malcolm X was assassinated in—where was it?—Harlem? Smith's new armed movement, Blacks of February Twenty-first, named for the complex, powerful, messianic hero of the ghettos, Malcolm X. Tim could see Smith's narrow, severe face with the pointed beard, the guns, the headlines, the TV montages of rebellions, marching blacks. He felt a quick pang of alarm for Liz, for Holly and Scott. The children would return home in a few minutes.

Tim started to speak, found he had to swallow. He cleared his throat, too loudly. "Look, Steele. I repeat the question. What's this all about? You barge in here uninvited, you—"

"Uninvited, huh?" Steele cut in. "Wait'll Perly hears that one."

"Perly?" asked Liz. Her voice was newly small, like that of a child.

"Perly Wiggins," said Steele. "He's our law man. Draws up writs, affidavits, deeds. You dig? . . . Just like Crawford."

"Oh."

The exchange of glances between Liz and Tim was swift, furtive, as though all communication between them had been forbidden. Steele traced the covert trade, his expression one of amused superiority. Liz felt a rush of indignation through her fear.

"Do you have a gun?" asked Tim.

Steele stubbed out the cigarette and cocked his head. "No. But the rest of 'em do."

"There are more of you?" asked Tim. "How many?"

"In the yard or in the house?"

Tim felt the jolt through his whole body. Were they surrounded by an army? He pressed his palms together, trying to contain the surge of mottled rage which thrust through his fear. Hold it down, he counseled himself. He spread his hands on the arms of the chair, rubbed the leather, and found that his palms were sweating.

"I'm the only one in the house," said Steele without waiting for an answer. "There's Perly and two others outside. That's four for four—when the kids come home. We're just as glad it's vacation time for some of the help, or we might need more. Of course, we got reserves all over." He waved his arm vaguely toward the window.

"How many guns?" asked Tim.

"That's our business, Crawford, but I don't mind tell-

ing you. Let's see. Some thirty-eights, a rifle, two shotguns. That's it, I guess."

He said no more and silence welled about them again.
After a few moments Liz slid slowly off the desk to her
feet. Her legs felt shaky as though a first, timorous move
had been made from a hospital bed. She supported herself
with both hands planted on the desk.

"I think I would like to sit down," she said to Steele.

"Sure." He got up. "Take the chair."

They changed places, Liz stepping self-consciously to
one side to avoid contact. She dropped into the armchair
and her back sought the haven of the familiar leather. Her
bare feet felt unshielded. She tried to hide them behind
the stubby chair leg, a futile move that grazed an ankle.
Steele hoisted himself to the desk with easy grace. He was
a tall man, well over six feet, perhaps two inches taller
than Tim. He had powerful shoulders, huge hands, and
large feet.

"Is this some kind of ransom thing?" asked Liz.

Steele concentrated on her. The medallion swung free.
"No. Our deal is a lot more simple. Perly will explain it
later, after the children are in bed. . . . First things first,
and first I'm going to tell you about the kids."

He slid off the desk and stood with his thumbs hooked
in a wide black belt which centered on a buckle made of
brass. His hands were enormous, thought Liz.

"Who's this Peggy who's bringing the kids home?"

"Peggy Abingdon," replied Liz. "Her daughter had a
birthday party."

"Oh, yeah." Steele grinned at Tim. "The dame from
SCOFF? Right? That wasn't bad . . . huh, Crawford?"

"You listen closely," said Tim. The thought was a
harsh one.

"Yeah, it pays to listen." Steele's face hardened. "Now
dig this, Crawford. I want you to meet the car when this
Peggy drives up. Just thank her and send her on her way.
And speak up. I don't want any whispering. Understand?"

"That may not be easy," said Liz. She thought of
armed men in the dark, of Holly and Scott. "You see,
Peggy's the sort who usually likes to come in for a nightcap."

"Oh, one of those," said Steele. "All right, then, you meet the car, Liz."

She was shaken by the abrupt use of her familiar first name. It had a rude sound on the voice of a dark intruder.

"Make up something," Steele continued. "I don't want that woman in this house. Hear? Now you speak up loud. We'll be listening."

"Then what?" Liz was appalled at the thought of leading Scott and Holly into the house, tiny hostages—for what?

"You introduce the kids to me, we'll talk a little, and then you put them to bed." Steele's manner softened slightly. "Don't worry. A visitor, a black one, at that. The kids will like it. They can meet the others tomorrow."

"You're staying . . . all night?" asked Tim. Steele's cool posture of command stunned him. Fairhill occupied? Fairhill, only three miles from downtown Princeton, not much farther from state police division headquarters? It was preposterous.

Steele addressed Tim as though he were a subordinate. "Maybe forever. But that's for later, after you hear Perly and me." He turned to Liz. "Right now we're dealing with this Abingdon broad and the kids. Have you got it straight, Mrs. Crawford?"

She nodded. The "Mrs." somehow tamed her fear. She had expected him to call her something insolent; just what, she did not know.

Steele faced Tim again. "Where your guns?"

"There's not a gun in this house," said Tim with unexpected truculence. "There never has been."

"I know that."

"Then why ask?"

"Testing you. For truth, man. I think I know you, Crawford. But I got to be sure."

A sound of tires on the driveway began thinly, then fattened. Steele motioned to Liz. She arose and walked to the hallway. Steele was right behind her.

"Speak up, now," he warned. "I'll stand by the door. I want to hear you. . . . And Chili's in the bushes by the garage."

Chili! Liz walked out the back hallway and into the

night as though a pistol were pointed at her. And for all she knew, there might be a gun protruding from the shrubs beside the garage. She looked in that direction, trying to discern movement in the darkness. Headlights probed the night, grew larger, painting all three garage doors in stark light and throwing a small shadow ahead of the Jaguar, which remained outside, top down, where Tim had left it. His carelessness bothered her momentarily, then was forgotten.

The flagstones felt rough to her bare feet. She stepped off into the grass, walking quietly, a prisoner watched by invisible guards. This was all too absurd. She felt that she was about to betray the children and that she should make some dramatic move, perhaps leaping into the car and telling Peggy to drive off swiftly, turning across the lawn, speeding back to the safety of the Great Road. But who was Chili and where were he and his gun?

A long Chrysler station wagon halted on the asphalt apron. Peggy, her hair scrambled by the wind despite a protecting kerchief, waved from the driver's seat. Beside her sat two teen-age girls whom Liz recognized as the children's swimming instructors. Scott's mophead was thrust from the open window behind Peggy. "Hi, Mom," he called. His voice stabbed her, like early love. Liz waited on the grass at the corner of the garage near the garden hose, which was coiled as usual in neat, green loops on its bracket.

Holly squeezed past Scott to be the first one out of the rear door. She rushed at Liz, grabbed a bare leg, and hugged it. Scott, two steps behind, seized the other leg. The children held her captive for a moment, then released her amid a joint clamor. Their high spirits at this hour distressed Liz. They didn't realize.

"Scott won a pander," shrilled Holly, "but he cheated."

"I did not," Scott cried. "Holly's lyin' again."

They faced each other in solemn passion, intent on accusing before they forgot why they accused. They were framed in a cross of light from the house and the car's headlights. They're so small, so unaware, so madly exuberant, thought Liz. Their high-pitched voices raced like a blender at high speed.

Peggy stepped out of the car holding a large stuffed

panda, black and white, with a pink ribbon at its bulky neck and glass eyes staring with sly wisdom.

"Here you are, darling," said Peggy. "Scott won it for the pool jump. You can carry it."

"Hello, Mrs. Crawford." Bunny Jeffers was a girl with long, prayerful, blond hair, a Princeton University faculty daughter. She was seated beside her friend Eileen Duncan, a Negro whose father was a postal employee. The girls, both thirteen and recent high school freshmen, taught swimming to small fry who gathered Wednesday mornings at the Pretty Brook Tennis Club. Scott and Holly were zealous pupils.

"Hello Bunny . . . Eileen." Liz stood uncertainly with the panda under her arm.

"The girls were wonders this afternoon," said Peggy. "I'd have died without them helping me."

Peggy stepped back toward the station wagon. Liz knew she was about to turn out the lights preparatory to a nightcap for herself and soft drinks for Bunny and Eileen. Liz followed her, grasped her bare arm. Peggy was a dumpling of a woman, always convivial and occasionally erratic.

"I'd love to have you all in," said Liz loudly, "but we can't tonight."

Peggy turned, surprised.

"It's Tim," explained Liz in an unnaturally high voice. "He's not feeling well." The excuse sounded limp despite the emphasis. "So you'd best not."

"Oh, I see." Peggy Abingdon obviously did not. She hesitated, and Liz, taking her arm, moved her as imperceptibly as possible toward the open car door.

"You're sure you're all right?" asked Peggy.

"Of course, dear." But she suspected Peggy would construe the high pitch for embarrassment and assume that Tim was in some foul mood. Their friends had recently remarked on the volume of his weekend drinking.

Peggy climbed in the car and inspected Liz doubtfully as she started the motor.

"See you Wednesday morning, kids," called Eileen to Holly and Scott. They waved good-by.

"Thanks, Peggy," said Liz. "I know Scott and Holly loved it. Were they good?"

"No worse then the others we had. And we had, my God, twenty-four." She waved, backed the car around, and then, as she drove off, her head tilted up to scrutinize Liz in the rearview mirror. She probably imagines that Tim is raving, falling-down drunk, thought Liz. The station wagon rolled toward the Great Road, headlights flashing among the birches and the two red dots of the taillights pinned to the night like punctuation marks.

From Liz's subconscious loomed Steele's face, dark and stern. She had forgotten for an instant. She knelt beside Scott and Holly in a sea of concern.

"We have a surprise for you," she said, remembering to raise her voice.

"What?" Holly was instantly alert and curious.

"Nothin' to eat, I hope," said Scott from his native skepticism. "Ick. I'm full."

"No. Visitors." Liz tried to sound a festive note. "A Mr. Steele and some friends. The others are asleep, but Mr. Steele wants to meet you."

"Grown-ups in bed already?" Holly was incredulous.

"Come on." Liz bundled the panda under an arm, grasped Holly's hand, and walked toward the house. The grass was chill, and Holly's small hand was lost within hers. Liz could feel dampness at her eyes. The children were too young for this.

Steele was leaning against the fireplace mantel when they entered the library. Tim rose awkwardly from his chair. Scott and Holly huddled instinctively close to Liz but stared at Steele with bright anticipation. Liz stood the panda on its four fat legs. It teetered but remained upright.

"Mr. Steele," said Liz, "these are the youngest Crawfords, Holly and Scott."

Steele came forward, bent over, and put out his hand. "Call me Ben," he said gently.

Scott moved closer to his mother. Holly frowned, inspected Steele's face briefly, and fixed her gaze on the medallion. Liz wondered what Steele thought of their miniature size, inches shorter than their friends of the same age. They were the Lilliputians of Fairhill and, like Fairhill, now so vulnerable.

"Mr. Steele came to visit us," said Tim.

"Shake?" asked Steele.

Scott, overcome by shyness, merely smiled, but Holly reached out, clutched Steele's fingers for a moment, then pointed at the medallion.

"Who's that?" she asked.

"Frantz Fanon," replied Steele. "He was a famous black man."

"Did he play football?" Scott's voice had its familiar squeaky rhythm, and Liz knew the boy's shyness had evaporated.

"No," said Steele. "He was a psychiatrist, a thinker, and a writer."

"Oh." Scott lost interest.

"Scott won a pander," Holly announced.

"What's his name?" asked Steele.

"He hasn't got one," said Scott. "We're going to let Peter Wilson name him."

"And who is Peter Wilson?" Steele looked at Liz with accusing concern.

Scott and Holly eyed each other in veiled, shared mystery, then broke out in giggles. Holly's tiny face, her eyes glittering like blue beads, bunched in a proud grin.

"Peter Wilson lives upstairs," said Liz, then explained hastily: "He's a mythical character they invented."

"You mean we made him up, don't you?" Scott's protest was sharp, but his face crinkled in glee.

"Peter Wilson has food an' everything," said Holly. "He'll feed the pander."

"Which room does Peter live in?" asked Steele.

The question plunged the children into another swirl of merriment. They laughed and wriggled in their private world, oblivious of the three adults.

"Peter Wilson doesn't sleep in a room," said Scott with mock disgust. His thin face was suddenly solemn under the mop of curly black hair. "He sleeps in the hallway all night—standing up and everything."

Holly spluttered over this audacious fib, but in her joy she studied Steele intently to see whether Scott had succeeded in deceiving the stranger. Of course Peter Wilson did not sleep standing up like a horse. He stretched out on a rug outside her room. This was the first moment of truth for the tall, whiskered, black man.

"Peter Wilson died once," said Holly gravely, "but Scott made him live again."

"I put a new heart in him," boasted Scott, "just like on television."

Boy and girl stared at Steele, grinning, alertly measuring his reaction. Would he scoff? Would he pretend, like Daddy and Mom, would he try to curry favor with them by agreeing, or would he truly believe? Fred Jenkins, the gnarled old gardener, was a believer. In fact Fred had promised to bury Peter Wilson down by the creek if the operation failed.

Steele squatted near the children, balancing on the balls of his feet. "You're kidding me," he said. Scott's face clouded. "Peter Wilson," added Steele, "can't sleep standing up. He lies down like everybody else."

The Lilliputians regarded him with wary respect. Maybe . . . Scott probed again.

"You think Peter Wilson can feed the panda all by himself?"

Steele weighed the problem. "Yes, but maybe only once a day. After a heart operation a young man should take it easy."

Scott glowed. The stranger knew that Peter Wilson was a young man! Actually he was nineteen years old, he never had to go to school, and he worked as a lifeguard in the summer and a lumberjack in the fall. Scott and Holly traded rapt glances. A believer!

Holly inched forward and leaned against Steele's knee. "Why are you more black than Dora?"

"Dora? You mean the cleaning lady, Mrs. Wilcox?"

"Yeah."

"I was born that way," said Steele.

"That's funny." Holly touched his cheek and smiled at him.

"It's not funny," said Scott with scorn. "Eileen is more black too. And Peter Wilson's best friend is blacker'n anybody."

It had the ring of a pronouncement. Holly looked at her brother in surprise. Perplexed, she knit her brow over this unexpected revelation. She had never given a thought to the color of Peter Wilson's friends. All she knew was that Peter was big and noble. Still she was aware that

Scott, in his superior wisdom, knew many things that were as yet mysteries to her. She accepted Scott's decree and promptly envisioned a silver chain draped around the neck of Peter Wilson's black friend.

"Time for bed," said Liz.

"Not yet," protested Scott. "We haven't met the other people."

"In the morning," said Steele, rising. "You go with your mother now."

"Okay." Scott rubbed an eye, grateful for this neutral reprieve from further wakefulness.

Holly wrestled the panda from the floor, staggered under its bulk, and yielded the animal to her mother. A chorus of good nights choked the children's exit as they scrambled into the hall. Liz faced Steele and asked in a low voice: "What about the others? Is there somebody upstairs—with a gun?"

Steele made a negative gesture, palms down. "They're all outside. You'll see them later."

"I'm going to move the children into our room," said Liz.

"Never," said Steele. "Everything goes routine. . . . There's no danger. And that's a promise."

Liz left, her face tight. Steele sank into the vacant armchair, confronting Tim. They could hear the thud of feet on the stairway, small, muffled cries, and Liz's voice giving a command.

"Good kids," said Steele. "Smart too. How much does that private Head Start stuff cost you?"

"If you mean the Montessori school, I'm not sure. Maybe eight, nine hundred a year for both of them."

"Do you know how much anything costs you?"

"Of course."

"Who were those girls in the car just now?" asked Steele. Tim looked blank. "Your wife called them Bunny and Eileen."

"Oh, they teach a swimming class the kids attend. Nice girls. Eileen's Negro, in case you care."

"Integrated swimming, huh?"

"Sure. Does that surprise you?"

"Naw. It's irrelevant." Steele smiled, crossed his legs,

and fixed Tim with a cool stare. Tim decided to wait this one out.

"You drink a lot, Crawford," said Steele after a time.

"That's my business." Tim was brusque, yet he felt a need to defend himself. "Saturday night. I'm surprised you haven't poured yourself one. The lack of an invitation doesn't seem to bother you."

"We don't drink."

"The Puritan bag traps strange characters." Now that the first alarms had worn off and Steele's rapport with the children had dissolved his initial sinister aspect, Tim found that he wanted to spar with this intruder.

Steele laughed, a single, dry, humorless sound. "The irony bit, huh? . . . No, your ancestors can't take credit for everything. We've got work to do, that's all. When we're on top where you are, there'll be plenty of time for booze."

"It looks like you're in the driver's seat right now."

"Yeah. Well, we'll see."

Steele took a penknife from his dungaree pocket, opened the small blade, and began cleaning his fingernails. He ignored Tim.

Tim looked toward the bar, considered, decided against a drink. He wished he had a sandwich or scrambled eggs. His stomach felt empty and his head throbbed.

"Listen, Steele. What's this all about?"

Steele did not look up from his nails. "That's the third time you've asked that. I told you you'd find out from Perly and me. In the meantime I ask the questions." He tilted his head and looked at Tim. "Do you always fight that way with your wife? The very correct gentleman?"

Tim did not reply and Steele said: "Why don't you tell her off—but good? Slap her down once?"

Tim retreated into himself. He and Liz had never exchanged a blow. The mere thought was both repugnant and enticing. He assumed that Steele sensed this, and the cloaked trespass on the privacy of Fairhill galled him anew. Steele completed his nail cleaning in silence, closed the knife, and slid it back into his pocket.

"I've been around—not to say under—whites all my life," he said, "but damn if I really understand 'em."

"I'm beginning to understand blacks," Tim said.

Steele snorted. "Come off it, man. You haven't got as much feel for black people as your five-year-old son has. How many blacks you think you know good, Crawford?"

Tim, intrigued, thought for a moment. "Well, only three, I guess." He lied. There was Ginny, and the mere flash of her name evoked memories.

"Three, huh? And who are they? One, I suppose, is Hank Everett, your trash man. You kid around with him, give him maybe twenty bucks at Christmas, and after ten years of it you couldn't even tell me where Hank lives."

Tim listened closely, intent on discovering just how much Steele knew about him. As for Hank Everett, Steele was correct.

"Then there's Mr. Joseph Pilcher," continued Steele, "the token nigger executive at the bank in New York that handles your law firm's account. They got him out of Columbia graduate school, Brooks Brothers clothes, leather briefcase, the works. You think you know him pretty good after seeing him maybe once a month and talking to him on the phone. You think the bank's bought him off, bribed him with that upward-mobility crap. You any idea what Joe Pilcher really thinks? . . . Suppose I told you he gives thirty bucks a month to the Blacks of February Twenty-first. Would you believe it?"

Steele paused, eyes locked on Tim's. A picture of Joe Pilcher formed in Tim's mind, the brown, handsome face, the slow smile, the inside financial jokes, the always discreet references to the firm's accounts. Joe Pilcher supporting armed blacks? No. He did not believe it.

"See, you really don't know," said Steele. "Maybe he does. Maybe he doesn't. . . . Then there's Bess Hicks on the Princteon—what's that big mouthful?—Princeton Association for Human Rights. Mrs. Bretherton had her to a couple of dinner parties you attended. I'll bet you liked Bess Hicks. Pliable, courteous, and she don't talk back. Nice, warm, soft voice. South Carolina-bred. No problem."

Tim felt the sag of relief. There had been no mention of Ginny. Steele's intelligence network apparently was not perfect. And curiously Steele's brief outburst calmed Tim for another reason. Despite the rough tone, it was, after all, rational talk, the kind Tim understood and enjoyed. Steele sounded like a man who could be reasoned with.

"No," said Tim. "I suppose I don't know them so well. But what's that got to do with color? You could say the same for a hundred of my white acquaintances, even some of my old friends. How many blacks do you really know? I mean really?"

"All of them, man. I know every member in this country, man and woman, deep down to their soul. Right from my gut I know them. And I know Charley too. When you've got an enemy, Crawford, you've got to study him, figure his moves, his weaknesses."

"I'm the enemy?" Tim knew the answer.

"You ain't nothin' else but, baby. You think I don't know you, Timothy Rush Crawford, Jr.? Listen. For one thing, where did you go in 1963?"

Nineteen sixty-three? That was the year . . . Tim tensed. Did Steele know?

"I traveled some. I'm not sure." Tim fenced for time. "Just what do you mean?"

"You know what I mean." Steele's voice lowered, toughened. "I mean Acapulco. You went to Acapulco in Mexico."

"So what?" Make him say it, thought Tim. Tim wouldn't.

"You met a woman there."

"What's that supposed to mean? Who doesn't?"

Steele smiled. "Yeah, who doesn't, he asks."

Tim felt badgered. "What is this, some kind of blackmail? If that's your idea, Steele, it won't work. That was ten years ago. Who cares now? Liz, for one, would probably laugh." But, he thought, not at all heartily.

"Maybe." Steele pondered. "Yeah, maybe she would. And maybe we'll see. . . . Like you say, ten years ago. Right now we're interested in duller stuff—finances, status, social position, politics, ownership, all that honky crap."

"For instance?" The incongruity of the scene struck Tim as Steele talked. Outside, the night held Fairhill in its serene palm, but also somewhere outside were unknown men, armed men, black skins blending with the night. Upstairs was Liz with Scott and Holly. The kids would be drifting to sleep now after their usual filibuster, ready to caper in their dreams with Peter Wilson and his newly appointed black pal. And here, in the study where colonial rebels reputedly once gathered to plot insurrection against George III, an enigmatic black man now sat in judgment on him, a commander at a court-martial. And he, the accused, was more piqued than alarmed.

"For instance, Fairhill," Steele replied. "The old estate called Oak Farm, part of the house more than two hundred years old. You were born here, and then you moved back with your wife after your father died and left the place to you. Right?"

Tim nodded. Steele certainly did his homework. He felt a lawyer's grudging respect for a rival's competence.

"And how did your old man get the property in the first place? You know the story. At the bottom of the depression he mortgaged his home in Princeton and his office building in Philadelphia—oh, he could always raise money—and he used the cash to buy up Trenton properties at tax foreclosure sales for about two-bits on the dollar. Most were beat-up, old frame houses and stores in the black area. Crawford rented them for what he could get, meanwhile leasing Fairhill for ten years with an option to buy at a fixed price. Then, in the real estate boom during World War II, he sold off the Trenton stuff at big profits—and bought Fairhill for half the value. Man, the old pirate was rich all over again."

Tim was no longer startled by Steele's information. The story was basically true. Every merchant and old family in Princeton knew how tough, taciturn, closefisted Tim, Sr., had dealt himself into Oak Farm at a time when much of Mercer County's old money was being driven to the wall. "Pirate" might be a trifle strong, but Big Tim was frugal and crafty with a dollar. Tim had never felt close to his father, and he was vaguely pleased that Steele had gauged Big Tim's guile so aptly.

"So the old man buys Fairhill out of the bread he takes from the black poor," continued Steele. "That's white justice, man. That's how the honkies do it. And everybody along Great Road says what a smart man, and his son and his grand-kids live happily ever after."

"Now wait a minute." Tim bridled. "It's not that simple."

"Naw, it ain't simple. Black cat's got to smarten up, learn how it's done, start usin' his ol' woolly nigger head. Right, Crawford?"

Tim did not respond.

"The old man gets his eleven-room house and sixty-five acres for a cool eighty grand," said Steele. "He gets him a colonial mansion and later he adds a new furnace, tennis court, some landscaping, and then a swimming pool. The whole deal don't stand him more than, say, a hundred and thirty grand. . . . And today you and the Mrs. could ask three quarters of a million dollars for it—and get it."

"I doubt it," said Tim. Then he conceded: "But you're close."

"Give or take fifty thousand. And you know something, Crawford?"

Tim started. He had been looking toward the casement windows, and suddenly a black face, a round, fat face with a curious, mocking grin, appeared. It was framed like a picture in one of the panes.

"Who's that?" Tim's question was a half cry.

Steele waved at the face. "Couple of minutes yet," he called. Then in a normal tone to Tim: "That's Harve Marsh. I guess he's anxious to meet you."

The face withdrew. Tim turned toward Steele, who was toying with the whiskers of his goatee.

"As I was saying, Crawford, about Fairhill. You could sell it for seven or eight hundred grand, but you're not going to."

"Of course I'm not."

"Right." Steele leaned quickly forward. The medallion, with the embossed bust of Frantz Fanon, swung back and forth. "I'll tell you what you're going to do with this place, Crawford. You're going to give it away—to the Blacks of February Twenty-first."

The sharp sounds of heels descending the stairway could be heard. Liz had put on shoes upstairs. Tim understood. Fully clothed, she would feel less vulnerable—for the moment.

Chapter Three

Liz twisted in the bed, turning again on her side. Her nightgown, so sheer it weighed no more than a feather, felt like binding rope as it wound about her legs. She and Tim always slept in the nude, but tonight she had put on her nightgown, and when Tim came from his dressing room, he wore pajamas. They had lain close together, speculating in taut whispers. Sleep would not come. The sleeping pill only made her head fuzzy. She felt dry and itchy, and she continuously sipped at the water on the night table. She held her right arm aloft and looked at the luminous dial of the tiny gold watch: 2:40 A.M. She had been here two hours without sleep.

Events of the night rolled through her mind like sequences of an old movie, the plot obscure but the characters stalking her as from ambush. Ben Steele: cool, commanding, pliant in voice but as unyielding as his name, his medallion winking in the light from the library desk lamp, the deep brown eyes flooding from some hidden reservoir of strength. Harve Marsh: the shaped African dome of kinky hair, the round, not unfriendly face with a candidly amoral grin, the bulk of a revolver in his hip pocket. Perly Wiggins: yellowish skin like old parchment, the crooked, stained teeth, the high voice that squeaked away like a flock of grackles, the absurd, verbose interpretations of what he called the law. Chili Ambrose: the man who terrified her, somber, the pitted face as black as midnight ebony, peculiar green eyes, one gold tooth, a blue automatic pistol jammed behind his belt. Ambrose was the only one who had not gentled his voice when the children were mentioned. From several remarks she assumed that Ambrose had joined the Blacks of February Twenty-first from the Black Panthers, and Liz was certain he would kill any Crawford in the house, large or small, without compunction. And that incredible demand

31

for Fairhill that the derisively obsequious Perly Wiggins expounded!

She wriggled against Tim, molding her body to his. He stirred.

"Asleep?" she whispered.

"No. I can't." Faint light from the beclouded quarter moon touched his face, exposing the scraggle of blond hairs. Tim's beard grew like weeds in the night.

"Should I get you a pill?"

"No," he said. "I've got to be alert in the morning."

"Tim, what are we going to do?"

"I don't know yet." He turned to her, whispering as though they were conspirators in their own house. "They know everything about us. And we know next to nothing about them. I need time to figure Steele out. He's different from the others—almost, well, as though he intends to force me to give in by sheer willpower. He's shrewd, Puss. And maybe that's our chance. I think he can be reasoned with."

"But it's fantastic," she protested, aware that she had used the word a half-dozen times since they slipped into bed. "Give them Fairhill? Just like that? Just because they marched in here with guns? Why, that's insane. In the United States of America? They must be awfully naïve."

"Naïve Steele isn't," he said. "No, the deal is so simple he thinks it will work. He demands we deed Fairhill to the Blacks of February Twenty-first for one dollar. He thinks he can pressure it out of me on the basis of what Big Tim did. Steele doesn't believe in force. I'm convinced of that. But, by God, the others do. If we don't give them Fairhill, somebody is going to get hurt—you, Scott, or Holly. They know we'll give in at the first sign of, well, strong-arm stuff."

"And I say it's naïve, ridiculously naïve," she countered. "All you have to do is sign the deed, record it at the courthouse in Trenton, and then walk into the township police and say the property was taken from us by force. We'd have it back in no time."

"And a week later somebody would be dead—you, me, Scott, or Holly."

"That just couldn't happen here!"

"Oh no? I grant you it wouldn't if Steele were the only

one. But did you take a good look at that Chili Ambrose?
He'd put a knife or a bullet in you—any white—as quick
as he'd kill a rabbit."

Yes, she remembered. Ambrose had been standing by
the fireplace, an ebony sentinel. Those green eyes, brilliant against the black skin, had bored into her while
Wiggins dripped his multisyllabic legalisms.

"But we could get police protection, Tim."

"For a week or a month," he said. "But year after
year? Chili Ambrose, or somebody like him, might be
shadowing us the rest of our lives. That was implied in
everything they said—except for Steele. This may be the
start of revolution, Liz. If so, all the old rules are off."

"I can't believe it," she said. "Take Fairhill away from
us?"

"You don't buy Steele's moral argument, huh?"

"I think it's absurd." Liz snuggled closer. "What your
father did forty years ago has nothing to do with us now.
Why, if Steele got away with this, nobody could own a
thing in this country."

"But from his viewpoint?" insisted Tim. The challenge
of the encounter with Steele and Wiggins, the legal duel-
ing, forced him perversely into the role of devil's advocate.

"That's just a lame excuse for taking over Fairhill."

Tim wondered in the dark. In a few, short hours Liz
had undergone a swift transformation, from the lady of
causes, afloat on an emotional sea of abstractions, to the
armored defender of Fairhill, her territory.

"Excuse?" he echoed. "Maybe. But damn clever."

He recalled how his initial outrage had been diluted
with grudging admiration for Steele's rationale. Tim always gave points to the man who could marshal a sem-
blance of logic and justice for what he wanted to do.
Steele, lounging against the stone mantel with officious
Perly Wiggins on one side and the lethal enforcer, Chili
Ambrose, on the other, had spelled out for Liz what he
had sketched for Tim earlier: How Tim's father had
bought up depressed black properties in Trenton at foreclosure sales, how he grew rich, and how he exercised the
option to buy Oak Farm, using some of the profits he'd
piled up in Trenton. The renamed Fairhill, argued Steele,

represented the fruits of a white buccaneer raid on the homes of poor blacks. Now it was only simple justice that the estate should be handed over to the offspring of those old Tim had fleeced by guile, craft, and a flinty obsession with the dollar. Many of the sons and daughters of those whose homes had been foreclosed belonged to the Blacks of February Twenty-first, and Fairhill would become the revolutionary movement's "recreation and rehabilitation center." Black kids of members would splash in the swimming pool. The tennis court would be converted to basketball. The three-car garage would be remodeled into a dormitory. Steele was full of ambitious plans.

Perly Wiggins, nodding vigorous agreement, had opened his dispatch case and flourished a sheaf of papers which, he said, contained the addresses of properties old Tim Crawford had acquired at tax sales. Wiggins waved another batch of papers. These were affidavits of February Twenty-first members, certifying that their parents or grandparents had been cheated out of their homes. And when Tim protested: "That's not law, and you know it," it was Steele who replied coolly: "That's justice, man. That's black law."

"How can you say clever?" Liz cut into his thoughts. She gripped Tim's shoulder. "If Steele was so shrewd, he wouldn't need men with guns around him. It's just plain robbery, that's what it is."

"Well," said Tim dryly, "we could always appeal to your World Federalists or Equality Now."

"That's a spiteful thing to say." She tensed, pulling away from him.

"I didn't mean it that way, Puss." But he couldn't resist the temptation to revert to their earlier quarrel. "It's just that you're always in the forefront of these racial crusades. Now that you've got black men in your own home, you've changed your tune."

"I'd feel exactly the same if a gang of white men barged in here," she protested. "Race has nothing to do with it."

"It says here."

"I admit the black skins scared me at first, but it's not race. It's the principle," she said heatedly.

"You sure? The lady doth protest too much, me-thinks."

"Tim, what a perfectly terrible time for a quote like that. Whose side are you on, anyway? You act like you'd *like* to give the place away."

No, thought Tim, not quite. There was that feeling of heaviness, of smothering boredom, when he drove into Fairhill at twilight. He had wanted to break away—for a month, two months—from Fairhill, from endless, dry stratagems of corporate law, from the Brook Club, the Harvard Overseers, the pedestrian federal commission, the works. He wanted to secede for awhile, a double teen-ager drop-out, and think about life and its purpose. He smiled in the dark. Yes, a Wall Street flower child, why not? And then the swift, blunt challenge that Ben Steele had raised. How could he tell Liz that Steele, Wiggins, Marsh, and even the deadly Ambrose were like blasts of chill air, invigorating, fresh? The baldness of their threats sharpened him. He wanted to pit his brains against theirs. After all, it was a game for high stakes, and any game deserved honed contestants to be worth the playing. But all that would sound like occult male nonsense to Liz.

Steele not clever? Liz didn't know how astute he was. First, in the library, had come that allusion to 1963 and Tim's trip to Acapulco. Of course, Steele had not mentioned Ginny, but when he said, "You met a woman there," Tim realized that they both knew. And later, when Liz left the room to go to the john during the long confrontation with the blacks, Steele had said: "By the way, Crawford, we know all about you and Jackson Dill. Do you suppose your friend from Acapulco does?"

So there was no doubt that Steele knew a great deal about Ginny Jones and Tim Crawford. More to the point, Steele understood Tim himself. Steele sensed, for instance, that while Tim might ignore any threat to tell Liz about Ginny Jones, the real pressure point was Jackson Dill. It came down to a matter of honor, of trust, of pledging his word—and Tim pled guilty to all three. Steele had touched him where he lived. The man was either amazingly lucky or shrewd to the point of genius. The trap, Tim knew, had been set.

Perhaps the trap really had been set ten years ago when, in the first savage fight of their marriage, Liz had swept off to Switzerland for a month. They had been married only three years then, and they both had yet to learn that too tight a cocoon could suffocate the man and woman who entwined there. They were young then, more self-willed and stubborn. Now they could survive their rasping quarrels. Then it was torment, a crumbling of dreams. So Liz had gone to Switzerland, and after a few days he had flown to Acapulco. When they were reunited at Fairhill a month later, Liz had wept in chagrin and joy and that night they decided to conceive a child. But it took time, and Scott was not born until much later.

Tim thought of all this and he thought of Acapulco. In those flashes the mind is capable of, those quick, erupting scenes which evoke whole moods and memories in time spans no more measurable than puffs of smoke, he thought of Ginny Jones as he sensed Liz's long, warm body near his and even as he was acutely aware of the children, unknowing hostages, sleeping down the hall.

He could see the scene at Acapulco, Teddy Stauffer's Villa Vera, high above the bay, clasped to the sun like a shimmering ornament. A light breeze scuffed the blue bowl of the Pacific harbor, bellying the tiny sails and streaking the water with curling white ribbons. He was sitting on one of the sybaritic underwater bar stools, his legs dangling in the tepid pool. The sunlight was so pervasive and blinding that he squinted behind his dark glasses. Around the circular bar, shielded by a gazebo roof, sat the Hollywood crowd. The prattle was low, muffled by the heat, and only an occasional gay shriek pierced the somnolence. Toasted flesh, a dark ring of it, banded the bar, the women wearing the thinnest of strips over breasts and hips, the men bare and hairy to their trunks. Half of the patrons sat on the dry patio side. The others hunched on seats which lined the shallow end of the pool like watery toadstools. Tim felt in tune with the languid afternoon, his chest cooled by the shade, his brain sleepy, his legs pleasantly wet.

The water near him churned, he felt spray on his arms and back, and a woman rose from the pool to the seat beside him. She ripped off her white bathing cap. She had a wide nose, a full mouth, and she was quite dark. She was also very small. Tim guessed she weighed not more than a hundred pounds, including the narrow strips of her white bikini and the clustered beads of water on her black skin.

"Hi," he said. He was in a holiday mood.

She looked him over.

"Hi," she replied. The tone was tentative.

"You popped up like a water nymph."

She wiped her forehead and face, propped her elbows on the bar, and inspected him slowly.

"Your first day here?" The accent was American, vaguely Negro.

He nodded. "How did you know?"

She gathered thin, plucked eyebrows in mock concentration. "Haven't seen you here before. Besides, you're not the Villa Vera type. Too city-white, for one thing. Man, you're like a fish belly." She flipped her short, wavy hair.

"I figure I ought to take it easy the first couple of days." Tim liked her but sensed she was in no hurry to narrow the distance between strangers. "This joint is a regular Babylon on the hill."

"Yeah. They live it up."

"Are you staying here?"

She smiled. "Do I look like I should? No, I'm down at the Costero. I come up here to watch the characters."

"I'm at the Americana," Tim said. Then, fearing the conversation might falter: "Where are you from?" It was the stock question of Americans, and he wished he had said something less banal.

"Oh, around. New York mostly. But I'm not on vacation. I work here."

"What do you do?"

"Sing," she said. "At the Aku-Tiki."

"I haven't been there. But now I think I'll make it."

"I alternate with a Polynesian broad and a white dyke from Chicago."

"I'm Tim Crawford."

"How-do. I'm Ginny."

"Ginny what?"

"Oh, gawd. I'm that unknown?" She simulated a pout, then grinned at him. He sensed that he was being accepted. Her face was mobile, as fresh as spring. He guessed she was twenty-four or twenty-five. "Jones," she said. "Ginny Jones."

"Can I buy you a drink, Ginny?"

She considered for a moment, studying him again. "Well, okay. Thanks. Banana daiquiri. It's all calories, so I guess you can build up while you're tearing down."

And so it began, hesitantly at first, then in a growing mood of easy friendship. It was, after all, the Acapulco way.

He ordered two banana daiquiris. She said she came here almost every afternoon, put on a mild jag, soaked in the pool, then napped before she went on at the Aku-Tiki at ten. She knew many of the people who lounged in baking torpor at the Villa Vera and she identified some of them for Tim. . . . The obtrusively virile disk jockey from Philadelphia who was sleeping with the pink, fleshy blonde with the carnation in her hair, a distant first wife of a Hollywood star. . . . The agent, a heavy-lidded man who spoke in gutturals and dripped cigar ashes over his graying chest hair. . . . The Swedish starlet of the year, wide-eyed and deceptively virginal, her shoulder being nuzzled by a lean, mahogany Mexican whose manta-cloth shirt was slit to the navel and who formerly dove for two hundred pesos a night into the boiling gulf at El Mirador. . . . The famous panel-show moderator with the doughy smile who turned the most trivial of human concerns into profound moral dilemmas. They sat there, drudges of hedonism, steeped in their sun, chlorine, and malice.

Ginny Jones, Tim soon learned, took her pleasures on the wing. She was impish, skittering, a girl who clung to the surface of things like a child to a merry-go-round. But she was perceptive and, in flashes, wise. Her voting residence was New York, but she was seldom there, traveling the nightclub circuit with most of the stands outside the United States in spots Tim had never heard of. Her father was a garage mechanic in Winston-Salem, where she grew up. She quit Howard University after one year for a career on the stage. When Tim asked if she was married, she laughed and said she'd had "two cats, no kittens." Tim, of course, was married, she observed. "Yes, but no kids yet," he said.

The time was mid-December 1963, four weeks after the assassination of John F. Kennedy, whom Ginny said she adored. After the days of numbness people were plunging into life as though it were a new discovery. An impetuous recommitment to living, clutching for the youth of which the elegant president had been robbed, made avengers of them all. Death could be parried, wounded, even routed until the day of ashes when the final surrender became irrevocable.

Tim and Ginny drank four daiquiris that first afternoon, swimming, splashing, and gurgling after each round, then hoisting themselves lazily like seals back to the sunken bar stools. The sun dropped toward the cloudless rim of the Pacific, the softness of coming twilight wrapped the bay in gauze unrolling from the lavender hills, and the bar crowd drifted off to postponed siestas and lovemaking. Ginny needed her preshow sleep. He taxied her to the Hotel Costero, promised to listen to her that night, then returned to his room at the Americana and slept soundly for three hours.

She was singing when he strolled down the stairs to the Aku-Tiki that night, and he knew at once that she was mediocre. The nightclub was a thatched-roof effusion with open sides, hung on two levels and nudged by tiny gardens and pools, one of which was spanned by an ornamental bridge. A crush of patrons surrounded the two bars where attendants in flowered shirts rattled bottles and mixed long concoctions in electric blenders.

Ginny wore a low-cut white gown with sequins, spike-heeled white shoes, and no stockings. She tilted the stand-up mike at an angle and sang her bittersweet ballad of love. She saw him arrive at one of the few empty tables and she saluted his presence with a smile and a thrust of her shoulders. Ginny sang three more tunes and one encore to moderate applause. Something was lacking, and Tim wondered just what it was. She sang softly, a catch in her voice, a fetching look in her round, brown eyes, and with small gasps of rapture which broke through the brooding shell in a pleasing, always unexpected way. But nothing grabbed Tim. He heard no passion, no depth, no yearning. She could have been a female Johnny Mathis.

She questioned him with her eyes when she approached the table, saw his answer, and shrugged. "Better than a lot, not as good as some, huh?"

He protested quickly, trailing unmeant words. She frowned, petulantly withdrawn for a moment.

"Listen, Tim," she said. "You're an honest guy. Let's not start saying what we don't mean. Who needs it?"

"Well, I liked your act. And that's honest."

"You liked it. Okay. Liking isn't enough in this racket. But it's a living. So what else is new?"

He knew she was hurt. He offered her a drink, but she declined. "Not until after my last bit—at two." A buxom redhead, the Lesbian from Chicago, was singing in a throaty growl. He compared the woman's style unfavorably with Ginny's, and then, in his judicious, somewhat plodding way, he tried to comfort her. Take lawyers, he said. We work years before we divide the brilliant ones from the merely good or the adequate. There is always some crevice an attorney can burrow into, where he can shine like a mole in moonlight for a time. Any competent man can find that one tiny gap in the forest of opinions through which his client can walk unscathed. Only occasionally are the competent attorneys pitted against the masterminds in the full glare of publicity and the ruthless assessment of their fellows. . . . But she, like every entertainer, must leap instantly into the pit of competition. Every listener is a critic. The fight in Ginny's world is open, unprotected, no place to hide. One woman makes a million her first year. Another works a lifetime for board and keep. To talent must be added that key ingredient, luck. So, he asked, see what three years of graduate school is worth? After a law degree from a top school, a man may never have to face the mirror of his own professional inadequacies in a way that Ginny had to face it her first week at the mike.

She listened with her elbows on the table, her chin cupped in her hands. "I guess that's true," she said seriously. She looked half persuaded. "Anyway the words sound nice. You're a nice guy, Tim. I guess nobody's tried to comfort me since my old man died when I was a kid."

"That wasn't the point, Ginny. I was talking about myself and why I've got it a lot easier than you."

"Yeah." She borrowed his cigarette, inhaled once, and watched the smoke curl away. "You're staying a week?" He was glad she had remembered. "Well, a week can be a good time here. But it's just as well I have to haul it a couple of days later. I open in Taxco a week from Wednesday."

The week slid by in a peculiar jumble of the hazy and the vivid. Tim had trouble later recalling where they ate, danced, drank, and swam. In memory the crescent of Acapulco blurred, a montage of hot skies, mongrel hounds sleeping in gutters at noon, sails, indolent water with a tang of salt, open restaurants, *ceviche* and *tacos,* sidewalk *mariachis,* piano bars, sweating tourists in outlandish shirts and shorts, the purple hills at dusk, freighters unloading Datsuns from Japan, boys' marching bands, the religious processions in which the banners of saints mingled with those of sponsoring soft-drink companies, and, always, the moist languor of nights under a blaze of stars.

The vivid memories were those of Ginny, the soft little face, the toylike body with the proud breasts, the rushes of gaiety, the occasional search for candor in their ripples of conversation about nothing, the slumber of longing in her brown eyes. Ginny resolutely banned any talk of race. The nearest she came to it—on the second afternoon?—was when she asked him, "How we doin', Tim?" Her grin was knowing, and he replied with pretended ostentation that they were making progress "with all deliberate speed." She flared, instantly catching the phrase from the Supreme Court's school decision, and said: "If we went like at that speed, you wouldn't have bought me the first drink yet." She stared at him, swiftly girded, silently condemning his whiteness. He said, hastily, that he agreed, and he began to explain. She gradually relaxed and waved away his words. "That's a long, long road, cousin," she said, "and you and I ain't goin' down it. Not this week. You're white. I'm black and—"

"Ever the twain shall meet," he finished. They laughed.

She regarded him with renewed affection and put her hand on his arm.

But Tim knew that they were both but temporary fugitives, not only from the prisons of their private lives, but from the racial wars at home. Here they sought succor in hybrid, raceless Mexico. They were combatants suddenly immobilized in a neutral field hospital, groping toward their common humanity, yet knowing that out there— back there—the struggle would go on. Tim was fascinated by Ginny, perhaps no more by the black woman than by the black person, the first he had ever really known. An eager, frantic feeling possessed him, as though he had only a small nest of hours in which to discover, to learn a shapeless something that might be torn from him by the roar of a departing airplane unless he hurried into the essence of Ginny Jones. Ginny was more leisurely, and he sensed that she knew him far better than he knew her, a web of knowing spun from a thousand contacts with the white world. She tried to tell him obliquely at times. Once at the Aku-Tiki between her stints, she found him staring at her wonderingly. "Cool it," she said. "You'll learn faster if you don't try so hard. Come back up here with the rest of us kids." Yes, climb back to the surface with Ginny. Don't dig deep or we're both lost in the well that nobody knows.

And so, slowly, without probing, he learned why Ginny was a second-rate singer. She had the tone, the timing, the grace, even the uniqueness that meant there was only one Ginny Jones. But she lacked mystery. She had none of the defiance and longing which flings the soul to lost winds and cries the torment of the self. Ginny was a voice in a black skin singing to a white world. She recoiled from the penned rage within her and thus she hid from her color. What came out was cute, pretty, chic. No one could fault her if she lacked the majesty of Marian Anderson, but where, at least, was the earth of Pearl Bailey? In the humid days and nights of Acapulco, Tim sensed this only dimly. It was later, years later, that the knowledge settled on him with the fastness of certainty.

And so she fascinated. The imp in her abounded. The impatient mind, slipping from place to person like a bug on ice, delighted him. When he thought occasionally of

Liz, somewhere in Switzerland, it was with more defiance than guilt. It had been Liz who tore free from Fairhill after their stormy wrangle, and if Tim now played at romance, who was to blame? He knew that such reasoning amounted to little more than game playing, but he was enjoying himself too much to brood over it.

There was a carnival atmosphere to the Acapulco week. Ginny taunted him for being a stuffy lawyer, asked if he would remember her when he labored at night over a brief about who could steal what legally from whom. She tried to shock him, pretended dismay when he merely grinned. They laughed when she found a paragraph about her in the Acapulco notes section of *The News,* the English-language daily of Mexico City. She was described as the "dusky songbird from North Carolina, the playful Ginny Jones."

They made love twice, once in his room and once in hers. It left them vaguely dissatisfied, as though they were children reluctantly exchanging gifts at a surprise party. They were quite drunk the first time. Ginny lost a glass off the balcony, and Tim upset a rum and soda that dampened half the bed. Their love was a heedless romp which ended with both of them mashed against the headboard and the pillows on the floor. They laughed wildly and drank some more. It was dawn before Tim escorted Ginny back to her own hotel. The next night they were quieter. They searched and quested as new lovers will. They made love to the rhythm of the softly pounding surf, and afterward they held each other, unspeaking, until Ginny fell asleep on his shoulder. But they both knew that a void had not been bridged. They were still strangers in their skins. Ginny's melted into the night while Tim's seemed bizarrely misplaced in the shadows of their passion. Tim felt depleted, but unsuccored, and he could tell by Ginny's lonely smile that she felt as he did. Their good-night kiss at her door was almost one of apology. And curiously, as he rode back to his hotel, Tim thought not of Ginny, but of the murdered Jack Kennedy and of the new desolation that was upon them all.

One scene that stood out sharply through the years was all but platonic. It was their last evening. He would take the 7 A.M. Sunday plane to Mexico City and thence on to

New York. By common consent they would say good-by early, for both were exhausted. Ginny intended to nap between her acts, and Tim knew he would sleep until the desk called him at the ungodly hour of 5:30 A.M.

They taxied out to Pie de la Cuesta to watch the sunset from hammocks slung under shelters. Heavy surf rolled in from the open Pacific, but the coarse, brown beach bore the debris of the day, a litter of discarded coconut shells, torn newspapers, and paper cups. Through the sand plodded an unending parade of souvenir vendors, serape merchants, and scraggly burros for hire by the ride. Tim finally paid a boy in tattered jeans five pesos to keep the horde at bay. In the lull Ginny reached over from her hammock and took Tim's hand. She gripped tightly and he returned the pressure. Hands locked, they pulled their hammocks in slow rhythm. They swayed in silence for perhaps half an hour until the crest of the huge orange sun sank out of the sky into the Pacific and the beach was plunged into quick darkness. The breaking waves took on a new sound, a dull, threatening boom. "Friends?" she asked. "Friends," said Tim. Then they picked their way, arm in arm, across the junk-strewn sand to the waiting taxi. They said good-by at the office of the Hotel Costero.

Tim assumed that someone who knew both himself and Liz had seen him with Ginny during the week at Acapulco, but if so, he was unaware of it. He had met only one person he knew by name, a New York broker he encountered in the hotel lobby just as the man was checking out. As a protective disclaimer, Tim told Liz some weeks later that he had bought drinks in Acapulco for a Negro singer named Ginny Jones. Liz bestowed an honorary smile on him as though he were to be rewarded for good works to the socially deprived. "What a nice thing to do, dear," she said. "Was she pretty?" Tim felt intuitively that if Liz ever discovered by chance that her husband had had a brief affair with a black girl, she would be less concerned than if the woman were white. Liz's liberal creed was like ground ivy, rootless if decorative. But the issue never arose. Nobody who knew Liz had seen Tim and Ginny together.

He kept in touch with Ginny over the years. Early that January he received a belated Christmas card at the office with a scrawl in red ink at the bottom: "How we doin'? Ginny." It was postmarked Taxco, Mexico. He bought her first album when it came out a year later. It was lively ballad stuff, punctuated with Ginny's frolicsome timing. He found out who her agent was and sent her a note to be forwarded from the agent's office. A year later they met for drinks and dinner when she was in New York for three days between engagements. She said she loved his note about the album. They laughed a good deal and re-called scenes and persons from Acapulco in that overly determined and somewhat sad manner of people trying to recapture what has fled. New York was not Acapulco, and they parted without making love, although the kiss in the cab at Ginny's hotel was fond enough. Later he caught fragments of her career in an occasional gossip column, small notes usually tucked near the bottom of the page as payment by the columnist to a helpful flack. It seemed she sang outside the country, in Portugal, Sweden, Mexico, Brazil, France, only occasionally in the States and then in smaller cities. The Christmas cards continued. They met once again for hurried cocktails at a bar on East 54th. She had seen her agent and had to catch a plane for San Antonio. She was her old merry, skittering self, yet with the same soft longing, and Tim had an urge to fly away with her. Ginny mocked him with her eyes, and he realized that they both knew the gulf between their worlds could be spanned only by an immense effort that neither Tim nor Ginny was prepared to make. So, as on the darkening beach at Acapulco, they parted as friends. It was their last meeting in person, but she lingered affec-tionately in a recess of Tim's mind.

One wet, cold fall morning she called Tim at his office. "This is Ginny," she said. She spoke softly, with a touch of the old intimacy, but purposefully. Were they still friends, she asked. Of course, always, Tim replied. Real friends? Sure. Then she wanted to ask a favor of him. A young black man, a graduate student at New York Uni-versity and a member of a militant group, was out on bail on a charge of assault with a deadly weapon. She did not know the boy, but from what a trusted mutual friend told her, he was framed. The boy, Jackson Dill, was not guilty, Ginny contended. She wanted him to have the best attorneys in the city, and she had heard that those were the firm of Brainerd, Fullerton & Crawford. Was that right? Well, replied Tim, they tried and they did have a reputation.

He winced as he said it because he knew the case Ginny referred to. It had been all over the newspapers. The young man was a vocal black revolutionary who said everything calculated to enrage whites. There had been some kind of altercation at a student mobilization and Dill had led his group of angry blacks from the hall. Later, in a skirmish with police on a fashionable block of Park Avenue, Jackson Dill was arrested. Police said a loaded .38 Colt revolver had been knocked from his hand while he brandished it. The weapon was confiscated. Dill claimed the pistol belonged to an unknown black youth who escaped, that he had never carried or owned a gun. Bail was set at $10,000, part of which Ginny supplied. Dill was indicted and the trial was set for next month. Dill's counsel for preliminary maneuvers was a Negro lawyer known in the legal profession to be a man of indifferent skills.

"Will you defend him, Tim?" Ginny asked.

The moment she put the question Tim knew the case was impossible for Brainerd, Fullerton & Crawford. They were a top Wall Street firm with choice corporate clients. Their only criminal case of violence that Tim could remember was one involving the son of an insurance-company executive and that never went to trial. Street crime and antitrust violations, whether civil or criminal, did not mix. Also their clients were for the most part executives who disdained the black revolution and everything it connoted. No need to consult Phil Brainerd or Jamie Fullerton. If Tim took the case, it would split the firm. To know Phil and Jamie was to know that a Jackson Dill case was unthinkable.

"Criminal work isn't our line," he said.

"Yeah, I figured you'd say that—or did I?" Her tone was dead.

"Not so fast, Ginny. I'm just warning you that isn't our field. But the law's the law. Listen, give me Dill's number, let me talk to him. If I decide he's clean, I'll go to bat for him. Where can I call you?"

That was the trouble, said Ginny. She was flying to Morocco that afternoon for an all-winter engagement in a hotel at Agadir. She wanted Jackson Dill to be in good hands before she left. She gave him Dill's address and phone number in the Bedford-Stuyvesant area and the name of the hotel in Agadir where she could be reached. Leave it to him, Tim assured.

"You're a doll, Tim," she said. "I know where Jackson's going if that white judge don't see a white lawyer in front of him."

"That's what he'll see. Don't worry, Ginny."

"I should have been worrying about some things long ago." The old lilt was gone from her voice.

She offered to be responsible for his fee, but he told her to forget the money. He would cable her soonest. When they said their good-bys, it was with some of the warmth of the days in Acapulco.

After a few minutes of thought Tim telephoned the law office of Francis A. Healy on Fifth Avenue. Fran Healy had been a close friend at Harvard Law, a near-brilliant student, a swinger, an Irishman who faced every statute as a personal challenge to his wits. Fran was blunt, pugnacious, ambitious, and ready to undertake almost any case if the fee was right. Also Fran owed Tim one. Tim had put Fran up for the Brook Club. The membership committee balked at Healy's background. "He's one of those pushy Catholics who like publicity," said one member, an Episcopalian whose daughter's debut had consumed two columns of pictures and text in the *Times*. So Tim had failed, but Fran, whose sources in the city were infinite, knew all about Tim's efforts.

"I need help," said Tim.

"We handle anything except old whores and the Mafia," said Fran, "but for you, we'll make an exception. What you got in mind?"

Tim explained. He had to do what he could. Of course Jackson Dill's case was not exactly the line of Brainerd, Fullerton.

"Why, Christ, Tim," Fran cut in, "you nest of WASPs down there wouldn't even know how to talk to the kid. And if you took Dill, half of those Pittsburgh clients of yours would fall over in a faint at the Duquesne Club. Not exactly your line! You take Dill and you're dead."

"Well, let's just say I haven't been in criminal court in ten years."

"Not that you shouldn't have been," said Healy, "what with that bunch of price-fixing bandits you got on the string. What you want me to do? Defend Dill?"

"I'd like you to consider it."

"Get the kid over here and we'll see."

Arrangements were soon made. Jackson Dill agreed to meet Tim and Fran in Healy's office the next afternoon. Tim arrived early. Healy insisted on the full background. When Tim explained his friendship with Ginny, Fran grinned at Tim with affectionate new respect. "For God's sake," he said. "Tim Crawford playing with blackbirds. Who'd believe it?" Tim would pay Healy $5,000 plus expenses.

Jackson Dill was a big-boned, loose, light brown young man whose goatee spread out to his cheeks like a smear of tar. He wore a sweat shirt, unpressed khaki pants, and loafers, and he entered Healy's office as though he had just commandeered the building. His replies to the introductions were curt. Tim explained that, at the request of a friend, he had interested himself in Dill's case and that he proposed Francis Healy, the best trial lawyer in New York, as Dill's counsel. This ignited a five-minute fulmination by Dill on the evils of white-assed judges, the mockery that was called justice in the United States, and the necessity to tear down whitey's world. Tim bridled. Every truth voiced by Dill was draped with a pair of half-truths and festooned with rumors.

Healy listened patiently, then asked: "You want to beat this rap or you want to go to jail for a stretch?"

Dill glowered at him. "Who wants jail?"

"Then knock off that Rap Brown oration," said Healy, "and tell us what happened. If you're clean, I'll defend you right up through appeals, if we have to. If you're not, maybe I will and maybe I won't."

Dill flashed a rancorous look but began relating what happened. He said he could not have brandished a gun because he had never carried one and didn't know one firearm from another. He inveighed against police bru-

tality until Healy turned the diatribe off with a pointed
question. The whole recital took an hour. When Dill finished, Healy leaned over, twirled a dial on a small desk
safe. He pulled out a blue, flat-handled pistol and shoved
it across the desk.

"What kind of gun is that, Mr. Dill? Don't move any
closer. Just tell me what kind it is."

Dill's chair was about five feet away. He squinted at
the weapon. "It looks like the kind the cops brought to
the precinct. They claim I had it on me."

Healy frowned, studying him, then placed another blue,
flat-handled gun on the desk. "How about that one?"

"It looks the same to me."

"What's the make of the first one?"

"Hell," said Dill, twisting in the chair. "I don't know
what you call either of them. Like I said, I only had a gun
in my hand once in my life—for about a minute when I
was maybe twelve years old."

Healy pointed to a wall hanging, a woven yellow fabric
with a prowling black leopard in the center. "Take the
Browning and pretend you're going to shoot the animal."

"Which is the Browning?"

Healy shrugged, watching Dill closely. "The name's on
the grip. Go ahead, please."

Dill leaned over, inspected the names on both guns, selected one with the slightly slimmer handle. He stood up
awkwardly, raised the pistol to eye level in front of him.
"Isn't it supposed to have a sight?" he asked. He aimed
nevertheless and pulled the trigger, then lowered the gun
and looked at it.

"Okay." Healy held out his hand for the weapon and
placed both of them back in the safe. "That was a
Browning .380 auto pistol. The other was a Colt .38 special semiautomatic. A couple of souvenirs from old cases.
. . . Okay, Dill, if you can stand me, I'm yours."

"Thanks for nothin'," Dill growled.

"Well, is it a deal?"

"How much do you cost me?"

"Nothing," said Healy. "I'm doing this as a favor to
Tim Crawford. He's going to back me up, but I'll be your
lawyer of record. With luck we'll win."

"Okay."

Healy questioned for another hour, making notes on a large yellow pad as Dill talked. They agreed to meet again in three days. When Dill left, only slightly less surly than when he arrived, Healy poured two Scotches at the corner liquor cabinet.

"I believe the kid," he said. "If he knows guns, he's a good faker, and if he's lying about the rest, he's such a pro at it I'll never find out anyway. He may be a menace to you and me someday, but on this charge I think he's innocent." He raised his glass to Tim's. "This one ought to be easy."

It was. Healy waived a jury trial, and the session in Judge Prokauer's court lasted only a day. It developed that the officer who arrested Dill was not the same policeman who picked the Colt .38 special off the sidewalk at Dill's feet. The melee involved four officers and a dozen black youths, half of whom ran off. The gun had been stolen from a Harlem storekeeper and fingerprint identification efforts proved futile. On cross-examination the arresting officer was less than positive about seeing the gun in Dill's hand. Under direct examination by Healy, Dill disclaimed all knowledge of guns. Cross-examination only reinforced the impression of innocence. Tim, sitting as a spectator, was convinced that Dill was guiltless. So was the judge. In dismissing the case he lectured the prosecution for faulty preparation of evidence. Because of Dill's fiery denunciation of the "white power structure" over the months, the verdict was big news. The story was the highlight of TV news shows and led most newspapers the next morning.

The next day a cable from Agadir arrived at Tim's office: "You were great. Thanks, Ginny." A week later, via air mail, came a blue envelope with white borders. Tim's secretary, respecting the "Personal" inscription, placed the letter on Tim's desk without opening it.

Dear Tim: I can't thank you enough for all you did. The news reports here were skimpy, of course, but it was apparent that Jackson Dill's lawyer pulled it off by using his head. That's the you I remember. I suspect this may lose you some of your big clients, so I admire your courage. What makes me feel so good is that you did it for a young man you never met before—and for an old friend.

Agadir is not Acapulco, but it has glorious sunshine and nice nights. As for the Americans here, you can have them.

Once again thanks. Hope we can have a drink when I get back so I can say it in person. As ever, Ginny.

Tim pulled a paper from a drawer, wrote the date, and began: "Dear Ginny, I appreciate your applause, but unfortunately I was not Jackson Dill's attorney. As I told you, criminal law is out of my line, so I retained Francis A. . . ." He paused with his pen hovering over Healy's name, then chewed reflectively on the pen. Why go into all that now? Maybe he hadn't handled Dill personally, but he had retained the right lawyer and spent $5,000 of his own, nondeductible money. If it were not for him, Dill might be in jail now. All in all, he would rather explain to Ginny in person. A letter just wasn't the right format.

It was three months later when she called. She was in the city for only a day, then on to Honolulu for a week's stand.

"I had to call you, Tim," she said, "and thank you personally for what you did for Jackson Dill."

"Look, Ginny, you have this all wrong. I guess you didn't get the news in Agadir. I wasn't Dill's attorney. A friend of mine, Fran Healy, had the case."

"Oh, I thought . . ."

"No, the guy you want to thank is Francis A. Healy." He gave the phone number. "I wish I could take credit, but I can't."

"Oh." Her voice was small, remote. They traded a few pleasantries, perplexed on her part, and then she was gone.

She called back an hour later. "Tim, you wonderful liar. No wonder you're such a good lawyer—anybody who can lie like you. I told you you were great."

"What are you talking about?"

"I just talked to Healy," she said, "and he told me everything. How you prepared the case, and worked at night, and interviewed witnesses—and then let Healy handle the case in court only because he was a friend of the judge. And you paid all the costs. You're a love, Tim."

"Now, just a minute," he protested. "I did pay Healy's fee, but that's all—except bring Dill and Healy together."

"See! You lie beautifully. Oh no. I got the whole story from Healy."

"He's kidding you. If you want the straight word, ask Jackson Dill."

"I told you I don't know the man, and if I did, I couldn't find him. They say he's gone underground somewhere. Thanks, Tim. It was a big favor, and maybe someday I can repay it—some day when whitey needs some help from us black chicks on top." She laughed.

He protested again, but she would not listen. She rang off, promising to keep in touch.

Tim reached Healy later in the day. "What the hell was the idea of spinning that fake yarn about me to Ginny Jones?"

"Tim," said Healy, "that dame wants to think of you as a hero. So why not? I don't know how well you two know each other, but she thinks you're Mr. Honorable. So I decided to keep you that way."

"But all that jazz, Fran, working on the case, the witnesses. Jesus. You know I didn't do a thing."

"Five grand is nothing? Come off it, Tim. The little thrush needs her dreams. Also, to be frank with you, you bastard, I figured this was no time to be telling a black girl that her white friend copped out on her. Now when they start telling her no white man can be trusted, she knows different. Am I right? We may need all the help we can get from that side of the fence."

"But when she finds out, she'll be bitter."

"How's she going to find out? Forget it, hero."

And so the hero did nothing. Two weeks later he received a note from her, saying she had a new agent and was developing a new style. It ended with another thank-you note. A second note from her a month later was enigmatic. It said simply: "Dear Tim, I thought you ought to know. I buried the little songbird. What's left is all Virginia Jones. Hope you like her. Your friend, Ginny."

Then suddenly, in her thirtieth year, Virginia Jones became a celebrity. It began in the late spring of 1968 on the "Ed Sullivan Show," where she was introduced as "the black Piaf." Tim and Liz were watching idly at Fairhill when tiny Ginny appeared on the screen against a stark white background. She had redone her hair and the change transformed her whole appearance. Instead of the straightened, waved hair that Tim had seen in Acapulco, she now wore it African style, a natural, severe, close-cropped mound. When she began to sing, Tim listened in amazement. Her song was of love, but there was none of the cute breath-catching or coy timing. Instead she wrenched from deep within her and sang of despair, of solitude, of sorrow. A fierce wind, haughty and savage, rode the lyrics, and when Ginny finished her eyes blazed. Take it or leave it, she seemed to say as she turned away and walked proudly out of the funnel of light.

"Why, I've never heard of her," said Liz, forgetting Tim's casual reference years before. "She's terrific."

Should he remind Liz? No. He passed. "She's great" was all he said.

And soon he discovered what propelled the new Virginia Jones. She had joined the movement. She marched in the demonstrations, sang amid the reeking, shanty tents of the poor people's Resurrection City on Washington's Mall, became a cosponsor of angry advertisements in the newspapers. Earl Wilson interviewed her, reported that she joined the militants early in the year, switched to a Negro agent, and, after the killing of Martin Luther King, was seen with fewer and fewer white entertainers. The new Virginia Jones became as famous in the ghettos as the emperor of soul, James Brown. She sang of love, but of a proud, defiant, and shielded love, a love for blacks only, a love which banished whites from the knowing. Yet many young whites understood. The college set bought her records by the tens of thousands. Their parents listened, half in awe and half in dread. It was soul music with a wild and racking lament, and soon Ginny had a dozen imitators. She grew quickly rich, commanded $15,000 for a single appearance. She bought an apartment in Harlem which became a salon for black culture. She played the lead in an all-black Broadway musical on protest, and she showered money and time on the cause.

Tim watched all this with an ambivalent feeling. He

told himself he was happy for Ginny in her new fame and affluence, yet he knew he resented her rifling of his memories. The girl who had lingered in his dreams was a soft, merry, yielding thing. Now she had been snatched rudely away without so much as a word of apology. And there were no more notes to Tim. He called Ginny's apartment several times, left his name and number with the answering service, but he never heard from her. It was true. The old Ginny was gone.

"Daddy!" A sharp, pleading cry from Holly. Instantly his reverie ended and the floating images were wiped from his mind like a blackboard swept by an eraser. Had the old scenes been unfolding for an hour, minutes, or only seconds?

Liz sat upright. "Something's wrong."

He pushed off the sheet and hurried from the room, down the hall to Holly's door. She had occupied her own room only a month now, since the night Liz decided that Scott and Holly were becoming sexually aware of each other and should have separate quarters. A patch of moonlight fell on the wall where Holly's crayon drawings were tacked, lighting an orange church with a high steeple straddled by a gawky boy. Tim recalled his thought when he first saw it: She's so small and already Freud's at work.

"What's the matter, Holly?"

"Nothing." She sat up in bed, instantly prepared to contend against authority for her rights. The black and white panda with the pink ribbon lay beside her. "I heard a noise and I woke up."

"What kind of noise?"

She tried the tactics of deception. "Peter Wilson's noise. I heard him trampin' around the hall. Did you see him?"

"Yes, but he's fast asleep." The vagaries of Peter Wilson's behavior were unlimited, and Tim was never certain when Holly manipulated the myth for her own purposes.

"I know," she said gravely. She pulled the animal close to her. "Scott let me have it. . . . Did you know Peter Wilson's best friend is a black boy?"

Tim shook his head. "Not until Scott told us tonight."

Holly frowned as she deliberated. "Scott knows, doesn't he, Daddy?"

"Yes, Scott knows a great deal. Now, why don't you go to sleep again? It's almost morning."

"I know." Holly's knowledge was vast, retroactively encompassing anything she had just learned.

Tim leaned down and kissed her. Holly's eyelids closed. Within a minute she was asleep again.

"It was nothing," said Tim when he returned. "She claimed she heard Peter Wilson prowling about. I think she wanted attention."

But Liz was not in bed. She was standing beside one of the windows, her hand holding the heavy folds of the draw drapes. "Look down there," she said.

Through the window Tim saw a black figure, silhouetted by the quarter moon, standing beside the great oak. A rifle leaned against the tree. Chili Ambrose's head was turned toward the long, sloping lawn. His stance was one of vigilance.

"That man frightens me," said Liz. "He's a killer."

They climbed back in bed, cautiously, with apprehension, as though it were an untested bed in a strange house. Liz moved close to Tim and put her head on his shoulder.

"Tim, I can't stand this. What are we going to do?"

"First, we're going to sleep." He kissed her cheek. "Or neither of us will be able to think."

They fell asleep finally, just as the first touch of rose tinted the eastern sky. It was only three hours later when Scott and Holly came tumbling in, their traditional salute to Sunday morning.

Chapter Four

The customary Sunday morning game began. Holly fumbled at the light summer blanket, found and squeezed one of Tim's big toes, and then retreated hurriedly from the bed. Scott was at once noisier and more circumspect. He stood two feet from Liz's pillow and badgered her with a series of domestic bulletins.

"Scott. Please!" Liz bent the pillow about her head, trying to shut out the sound and sight of morning.

Tim, mumbling protests, yanked his foot toward the center of the bed. Mother and father lay inert for a few moments, then slowly came awake. Tim raised himself by an elbow. Liz sat up, looked from Scott to Holly.

"Are you all right?" A series of scenes—black faces, guns, legal papers—crowded Liz's mind. She tensed, sensing a passage foreign to Fairhill, the revisit of fear.

"Sure," said Scott. "Everybody's up. We met them all."

"Mr. Wiggins is hungry," added Holly. Her tone implied that her mother must bear the onus of Perly Wiggins's hunger pangs.

"Ben Steele says we don't have to go to Sunday school," said Scott. He aimed the decree at his father, the weekend emperor, daring him to cancel this boon granted by a stranger.

"That's right. You can stay home today," said Tim. He sat fully upright, yawned, knuckled his eyes.

"Where is that Chili Ambrose?" asked Liz. The memory came like the rush of a train.

"He's outside cleaning his gun." Holly chirped it as though Ambrose might be tending a flower bed. Holly gloried in her role as early morning newscaster. "Scott's going to take a walk with Mr. Steele."

Liz turned to Scott. "You are not to leave this house. Do you understand?"

The severity of her tone confused the boy. He stood glumly, on the edge of protest, but soon remembered his own nuggets of news. "They brought their own food," he said, "enough for days, rations and everything. And they've got a big electric horn you can talk through."

"Mr. Steele says for you to come down and cook breakfast," said Holly.

"Oh, he does, does he?" Liz swung out of bed. "You both wait in the hall while we dress."

The children filed out, exchanging covert glances over their mother's prickly mood. It was apparent that the coming of the strangers heralded some decisive ruptures,

as yet unknown, in family discipline. Scott's look told
Holly that they must be vigilant, ready to exploit any
opening. Holly's smile bound them in eager complicity.
Already Sunday school had been scratched. Perhaps other
conquests loomed. A promising day.

Liz walked to her dressing alcove. "I will not cook for
that bunch of hoodlums," she said. "The gall!"

"Well, let's case the situation first," said Tim. Awareness of the men below had disrupted his small morning
habits. In the bathroom he was still wearing his pajamas
as he squeezed paste on his toothbrush. Usually he
dressed first, then scrubbed his teeth.

"They can cook for themselves," said Liz. She felt the
twin tugs of outrage and anxiety, and she knew she must
tidy her emotions before going downstairs. She stood before the long rack of clothes, trying to concentrate. It
seemed vital this morning to wear just the right thing. She
considered slacks and blouse, discarded the idea after
picturing the outline of her hips in slacks. Often on Sunday mornings she wore denim work pants, but today they
would somehow rob her of authority. She finally selected
a loose cotton shift that hung shapelessly from her
shoulders. She studied herself in the mirror while Tim
shaved. He preferred her in clothes that hugged her body,
but that would never do today. The shift was simple,
proper, unsuggestive. Today she would be Mrs. Sexless.
In her thoughts was the image of Ben Steele, aloof, bizarrely handsome, dominant, black.

Tim's Sunday attire was predictable. Except on the rare
mornings when he attended services at Trinity Church in
Princeton, he wore faded chinos and an old sport shirt
that looked like long-bleached burlap.

The children tagged behind Liz and Tim as they descended the half-spiral stairway with its polished oak
banister. Sunlight slanted in balanced oblongs from the
narrow windows on either side of the front door. To their
right, the familiar shapes of the living room, slipcovered
in yellow for the summer, wore the drowsy look of morning. To the left, high-backed dining chairs stood at attention, eight soldiers awaiting command. Outside, a wood-
pecker drilled at a dead pine with ordered fury. Fairhill

was welcoming the day as usual. And then they heard the kitchen sounds, the husky voices of the intruders.

Ben Steele was standing by the electric stove, pouring steaming water from a kettle into a row of blue china mugs. He looked unconcernedly at the four Crawfords, said, "Good morning," and resumed pouring. His indifference robbed their entry of drama, and Liz felt a twinge of resentment.

At the end of the old hickory breakfast table sat Chili Ambrose. He stared through them, unsmiling. His face, blacker than his high-neck sweater, was stapled in hostility, and Liz noted again the tiny pockmarks which last night had deepened his aura of ferocity. Unlike Steele, Ambrose wore no medallion or chain. The blackness was unrelieved from his hillock of natural hair to the wide, leather belt. He pushed back his chair, and Liz and Tim saw that the flat-handled pistol was still banded by the belt.

"Looks like eight for breakfast," said Steele. He held out one of the mugs to Liz. "That's instant. Me and the electric pot couldn't make it."

Liz made no move to accept the coffee. "Are you implying that I'm supposed to cook for everybody?" When Steele nodded, she said: "Thank you, no. I don't cook for uninvited guests."

"Okay." Steele was unruffled. "Then Harve can burn. Harve used to cook when he wasn't cleaning up toilets. Suit yourself, Mrs. Crawford."

"Mommy!" In Holly's face, quickly brooding, justice vied with puzzlement. "Why can't they eat too?"

"They can, dear," said Liz. "But I am not the cook in this house."

"You are too," objected Scott. "And it's Sunday, so we get pancakes."

"You're always telling us we're supposed to be polite to people," said Holly. She beamed proudly, as much at her trim syntax as at her agility in fetching up a rule of etiquette.

"Mr. Marsh doesn't even know where stuff is," added Scott. What a morning! Never before had he and Holly scored so often so early.

Tim stepped into the vacuum of authority. He rumpled

Scott's mop of curly hair and said to Liz, "Come on. Let's eat. I'll help you."

Liz shot a furious glance at Steele but strode to the refrigerator. "You do the oranges, Tim," she said.

Steele accepted Liz's surrender with equanimity. He strolled to the table and pulled out a chair. "We'll eat with them," he told Ambrose, "and then we'll cover outside while Perly and Harve have some chow."

Ambrose glared at his superior, got up, and stalked to the door. "I don't eat with no damn honkies," he said. The screen door banged behind him.

By the time orange juice, dry cereal, hot cakes, milk, and coffee had been put on the table, Harve Marsh had taken Ambrose's place. Marsh attacked his food like a hungry soldier, chewing loudly and banging his coffee mug down on the table. His round, moon face glowed with mocking humor. Holly, seated next to him, was enchanted by his hearty, noisy behavior, so heretical amid the table manners in order at Fairhill. Several times her fork halted in midair, syrup dripping from a scrap of pancake, while she watched him. Marsh grinned at her and beat out a melody with his knife on a glass of milk. Holly stopped eating and began rapping her glass.

"Holly," reprimanded Liz, "we do not make music at the table."

Holly glanced at Marsh, a sharing of guilt. He winked at her, became quite severe, and gravely inspected the next forkful of pancake before gulping it down. Steele regarded Liz with a faintly amused look. Tim had an urge to laugh, but the furrow on Liz's brow deterred him. He managed to look appropriately stern.

"Hot day," said Steele. "Muggy."

"Gonna hit ninety easy," said Marsh. "Let's take turns at the pool, Ben."

"Business first," said Steele. "Perly and I got a date with Crawford in his library."

"No," said Holly. "We wanta swim."

"Water tag," said Scott. He was pleased at the prospect of so many players.

"You are not to leave this house unless I'm with you," commanded Liz.

"Why?" Holly was alertly suspicious. Newly imposed

rules had to be contested every inch of the way lest they
become inviolable edicts by default.

"Because I said so," said Liz.

"Take it easy, Mrs. Crawford," said Steele. "Everything's okay."

Scott and Holly eyed each other, two scouts on unfamiliar terrain. Ben Steele, the big black man with the im-
posing whiskers, was an obvious ally, but something
warned them that indiscriminate acceptance of his aid
might provoke retaliation from Mother. And where did
Father stand in this new alignment of power?

The breakfast proceeded warily. Marsh bolted his last
mouthful and was replaced at the table by Perly Wiggins.
The lawyer, who spoke in a high, improbable voice,
turned out to be a monologuist who chattered away about
the weather, the house, politics, and bodily complaints
with little regard to whether anyone was listening. With
his fussy language, he seemed an anachronism, as if Steele
had imported him, complete with yellowish skin and tarnished teeth, from some bygone era. Tim, watching and
listening closely, surmised that Wiggins had learned to
deal obsequiously with whites in moldering police courts
and in the shabby, fetid offices of bail bondsmen. He was
once probably what Steele would call an "Uncle Tom,"
and he did not yet know how to wear the armor of the
younger militancy. And yet, beneath the filibuster, Tim
thought he could detect contempt for whites and a sullen-
ness born of frustration.

If Holly and Scott were not sure of the terrain, Tim
was uncertain about two of the opposing players, Marsh
and Wiggins. He thought he understood Steele and Ambrose. Steele was the man of the mind, Ambrose the gut-
ter fighter. All four men, Tim knew, were out to win
Fairhill—but how? He experienced again the quickened
spirits he felt last night. There had been that lift ever
since he first saw the commanding and forbidding figure
of Ben Steele slouching in the doorway of the study. And
yet, with the excitement, Tim felt a streak of guilt, as
though he were abandoning Liz in her time of embattlement and need.

When they finished eating, both Tim and Steele lit
cigarettes—Tim's cigarettes. Steele smoked quietly, tilting

his head back and studying the rings that looped lazily from his pursed lips.

Holly watched, intrigued by the exhibition. "Look, Daddy," she said. "Mr. Steele blows doughnuts." Tim caught the chiding note, an appeal to her father to match Steele's feat.

"Tim," said Liz, "please turn on the air conditioning." She sought to wrench the subject—and Holly's attention —away from Steele. "The humidity's stifling." Beads of perspiration shone on her forehead.

"No," said Steele. "The house stays open. I want to hear what's going on outside."

"Tim, I . . ." Liz checked herself, aware that she was about to enter a foredoomed struggle for command in front of the children. Scott and Holly eyed her narrowly. Tim had a flash impression of two young wolves stalking the flanks of a bruised cow moose, ready to spring at the first hint of flagging steps. He turned brusquely on Steele.

"I want to talk to you," he said.

"Right," said Steele. "You and Perly bring your coffee to the back room." He addressed the children as he stood up. "Tell Peter Wilson I'll see you all later."

In the library the three men arranged themselves with exaggerated formality. Steele took the desk top while Tim and Wiggins seated themselves in the easy chairs. Wiggins opened his dispatch case and began fretting over a nest of papers. The moist heat of a New Jersey morning pressed through the open casement windows, swathing them like a great, damp towel.

"I'm not sure what you're up to, Steele," said Tim, "but whatever it is, leave the children out of it."

"What do you mean?"

"You know, that air-conditioning business."

"Don't cross Mama's orders in front of the kids?"

Tim nodded. Steele's occupation of the desk top was complete if casual. He leaned back, supporting himself on his hands, while his legs swung against the side. He still wore the green dungarees and black moccasins. The feet and hands, Tim noted again, were huge.

"Let's get something straight, Crawford," said Steele. There was the easy, unhurried drawl. "I gave you my word that nobody's going to hurt the kids. But using them

is something else. We're here to get a job done, and I
don't care how we do it. If your old lady don't want to
see the kids siding with me, then tell her not to give
orders unless she clears them with me first. Un'stand?"

Tim did not bother to answer. It was no contest. Scott
and Holly would take the path where the least discipline
lay, unless, of course, they were taught to fear, to share
Liz's concern over the ominous new presence at Fairhill.
And that, Tim would not do. He shrugged.

"I see we dig each other," said Steele. "All right, let's
get down to business. Perly, show him the deed."

The stiff paper rattled as Wiggins plucked it from a
compartment of the dispatch case. He leaned from his
chair, handing the paper to Tim.

"A simple transfer of title," said Wiggins. "I think
you'll find everything in order . . ." His high, rasping
voice connoted the officiousness of courthouses, file
boxes, worn, numbered volumes. "The standard form,
subject, of course to the trust agreement of the Blacks of
February Twenty-first which, however, wouldn't concern
you, Mr. Crawford. As you know, you and Mrs. Crawford sign at the bottom of the second page where I witness as an attorney at law of the state of New Jersey . . ."

Wiggins rambled on as Tim took the document, put on
his reading glasses, and glanced at the opening: "THIS
INDENTURE, made the fourth day of July in the year of
our Lord . . ."

"Of course," said Steele, "this is July eighth, but we
want it dated back to July fourth. Independence Day. Dig
it?"

"No problem, no problem," said Wiggins. "The Fourth
was a holiday, but Mr. Crawford knows that the courts
have held that a duly executed instrument . . ."

Tim tuned out Wiggins and concentrated on the paper:

Between Timothy Rush Crawford, Jr., presently residing at Fairhill, the Great Road, in the township of
Princeton, county of Mercer and state of New Jersey,
party of the first part, and Benjamin Steele, trustee of
Blacks of February Twenty-first, presently residing in
sundry and diverse places, party of the second part;
Witnesseth, That the said party of the first part, for and

in consideration of one dollar ($1.00) lawful money of
the United States of America, to him in hand well and
truly paid by the said party of the second part . . .

Tim skipped through the familiar, stilted language of
conveyance, the zoning restrictions and the boundaries of
the property which had been typed in. The ancient, musty
words, marching like old soldiers on parade, reminded
Tim again of the law's stubborn heritage. The venerable
phrases sought precision in an imprecise, cluttered, and
always shifting world. They creaked along, striving to
walk as erect, proud guardians of a stable order, even as
their front ranks dwindled into distant haze.

Tim traced down to the bottom of the second page:
"In witness whereof, the party of the first part has set his
hand and seal." Below were three empty lines. Tim's
name had been typed under the first line and under the
second, "Elizabeth Faircloth Crawford." To the left,
under the heading, "Signed, Sealed, and Delivered in the
Presence of," Perly Wiggins's name was typed below the
witness line.

"Naturally," said Wiggins, "we'll want Mrs. Crawford's
signature on that second line. While you're the owner, we
both realize that under New Jersey's statute on dower
rights, Mrs. Crawford retains the wife's legal interest in
the property until she waives it by signing the deed. No
problem, really. Just a formality."

"Some formality," said Tim dryly. He could see the
resolute set of Liz's jaw when her dower rights were explained to her.

"Give him the other paper, Perly," ordered Steele.

"Oh yes." Wiggins produced another single sheet of
stiff legal paper. "Of course I assume that should there be
any question over the exact phrasing, there is, so to
speak, room for discussion, since as I say—"

"Let him read it," broke in Steele.

Tim's fingers were moist on the paper, and he noted
that Wiggins had left faint print marks. The cloying humidity was turning the study into a steam room. Tim's
shirt was damp against the leather chair. He adjusted his
reading glasses again.

The Declaration of Independence held certain truths to be self-evident, among them that all men are created equal and are endowed with such unalienable rights as life, liberty, and the pursuit of happiness. Rephrasing another section of that declaration, it is evident that "whenever any body of law becomes destructive of these ends, it is the right of the people to alter or abolish it, and to institute a new system of justice."

Accordingly, I, Timothy Rush Crawford, Jr., intend to do justice as far as the property known as Fairhill, located in the township of Princeton, New Jersey, is concerned.

My father, the late T. R. Crawford, first rented the property known as Oak Farm—now named Fairhill—in 1933 with an option to purchase at a fixed price. He made this the family home and I was born here. My father exercised the purchase option in 1942, using profits he made on the sale of homes in Trenton which he had acquired at depression tax foreclosure sales.

My father's purchase of Fairhill was free and clear, without liens or encumbrances, and was legal in all respects. My father believed this to be a perfectly just and ethical method of procedure.

I think otherwise. While the Fairhill transaction was legal, it was neither ethical nor just, for Fairhill, in essence, represented the life savings of many poor, black families who were forced to surrender their homes in lieu of back taxes during depression days.

To rectify these wrongs, I am now deeding Fairhill to the Blacks of February Twenty-first, many of whose members are sons and grandsons of people who were forced to yield properties which my father bought in at a third to a quarter of their normal valuation.

I am doing this of my own free will, without pressure or coercion, in hopes that Fairhill will become the symbol of a new white justice for the black man. And I would urge my fellow whites whose wealth was obtained, in whole or in part, from similar exploitation of blacks, to make appropriate restitution in order that this country might erase the last vestiges of a system that has shackled this nation since the days of slavery.

I sincerely hope that my action, however small a

token, will help to usher in a new era of racial justice and tranquillity in which equal opportunity for all, regardless of color, will not be thwarted by privileges obtained by one race at the expense of another.

Timothy Rush Crawford, Jr.

As he finished, Tim felt Steele's eyes searching him. He wondered at the reaction if he should grab a pen, scrawl his signature, and toss the paper on the desk. He had a wild impulse to do just that, to sign and walk out—on Fairhill, the law firm, the works, for a month, two months. What was the time a man needed to reshuffle his life and come to terms with himself? But the urge evaporated as quickly as it formed. He moved restlessly in the big chair. Mirages were distorting the real world.

"Very clever," said Tim to Steele. "I suppose you wrote it."

"Yeah. I worked it up with Perly. We tried to use your words. Me, I'd just say it plain like it ought to be. You say clever. I call it justice."

"And obviously untrue," retorted Tim. He was about to spar and he felt the desire to outpoint the foe. "What do you mean, 'of my own free will, without pressure or coercion'? You bust into my house, lugging guns. You hold me and my family prisoner and you threaten us with violence. No pressure?"

"What violence? Anybody lay a finger on any of you?"

"Chili Ambrose wears a gun at his belt," said Tim. "I saw Marsh with a rifle. You listed the firearms yourself."

"Those guns are for our own protection, Crawford." Steele's voice was low, cool. "They're not to harm you."

"The whole climate is one of armed threat and you know it."

" 'Climate' is one of those fuzzy white terms that don't mean a thing. Not a thing."

"Then why not let us do as we please?" asked Tim. "And go where we want to go—starting with sending the kids to Sunday school?"

"Because that would endanger every black man here,"

said Steele. "We came to do a job and we're going to do it. Now, Crawford, we checked you out pretty good."

"You sure did."

Steele ignored the interruption. "And I know you a pretty hip dude." He slid off the desk and paced about for a few moments with his hands in his pockets. "Perly, how about leaving us alone? I'd like some private rappin' with my man—make him see the light."

"Okay, Ben." Wiggins burrowed into his dispatch case, fingering papers, peering unnecessarily into compartments. He snapped the catch and stood up. He glanced toward the two papers on the arm of Tim's chair.

"Leave 'em," ordered Steele.

Wiggins bustled out, closing the door behind him. The air hung still, torpid. God, thought Tim, what a swamp New Jersey weather could be. Steele settled in the vacated chair.

"Like I say, you're a reasonable man," he said, "and this is a reasonable proposition. Your old man squeezed this house out of black Trenton sweat. What the hell did you ever do to deserve this except be born here? You got no more right to it than me. I don't have to tell you that, Crawford. I know you. You're a guy who thinks about morality. You know what justice is. You learned it in school and you dig it now. If it was the other way around, and we blacks had been stompin' on you honkies for centuries, you'd do the same thing to me."

"What I'd do, I don't know," said Tim. "But if the situation were reversed, you'd never sign either one of those papers. . . . Okay, let's talk about being reasonable. If the law took into account all the inequities of the past, we couldn't function. Suppose, for instance, I smash into your car with my car. You sue for damages. I go into court and contend that it wasn't my fault because black people scared me when I was a kid, and when I saw your face behind the wheel, I panicked. So you really ought to be suing your own race for causing the accident. You think that makes sense? No, but that's about what you're asking now. . . . And take property like Fairhill. If you lumped all the property wrongs together and tried to rectify them, why we'd have to give the whole country back to the Indians. . . ."

"Beautiful!" Steele cut in. "You wanta deed this land to some Indians? Go ahead."

"If I took you up on that, you'd collapse." Tim paused to survey his opponent. Steele was slumped in the big chair, his hands clasped over his sweater, partially obscuring the silver medallion of Frantz Fanon. The face was very dark, not the midnight black of Chili Ambrose, but a rich, ruddy black that reminded Tim of the bark of a gumbo-limbo tree once seen in fading twilight. The face behind the mustache and goatee had a soft contour, and yet there was power in the thrust of the jaw, in the tilt of the head, and in the brown, resolute eyes. Black might not be beautiful to many white eyes, but in Steele it had a rugged dignity. Tim had an uneasy feeling that in Steele he was seeing a dark dominion of the future.

"How about evening things up?" asked Tim. "You know all about me. I know nothing about you. How did you happen to pick on Fairhill? Where do you come from? Where do you live? What do you do?"

Steele's slow smile was his first real one of the morning. "I wondered when you'd ask. I don't mind. How much you want to hear?"

"All you care to tell."

"All right. Let's see." He paused as he considered. "I'm thirty-three. I was born in Newark, grew up on welfare. I don't remember my old man. They say he was killed with the engineers somewhere inland of Omaha Beach. My older brother peddled horse for the Mafia. He's still in Atlanta on a narcotics rap. As a kid, I did it all, pimped, stole, played the dozens, cut a guy with a broken bottle, juiced, got high on grass. But I managed to make my grades, just, at Newark South Side High. And I could play football, so they gave me a scholarship to Syracuse, and there, man, I found out that I was bright— not a genius, but bright. So I hit the books and let football take care of itself. I just barely held the athletic scholarship, second-string end for three years. The summer I graduated, top third of the class—not bad, not good—I made the scene with the freedom kids, seminars at Western College in Ohio, then down to Mississippi.

"I was there the day they killed Schwerner and them. Too bad about the kids. They had some fine ones, lots of heart and guts. But I learned something real about myself, especially from your women. I found out I disliked some of the white students almost as much as I hated the sheriff and his deputies. Some of those kids thought they were doing *me* a favor, for Cri-sakes. I gave up on honkies a long time ago. The good ones are so messed up with racism, they can insult me without knowing it. The bad ones are a bunch of nothin'.

"Anyway, when we got our black thing together, I got on board. I met Malcolm X before they shot him. Greatest black man in history. I knew 'em all, King, Stokely, Rap, Farmer—you name 'em. Then I met Danny Smith, a shrewd, rough, gutty man. When Danny formed the B.O.F., I went in as third deputy. Now I'm first deputy. Danny and I don't always agree, like . . . well, anyway . . . Ben Steele is black all the way. Move it over, honky. You ain't got much time left."

"Why do you call us 'honky' so much?" asked Tim.

"It sounds right." Steele grinned.

"Where do you live now?" asked Tim. "How do you make a living?"

"Here and there, this and that, the usual black thing." Steele lost interest. "Why bother? You wouldn't understand."

"And why did you pick Fairhill out of about fifty million homes in this country?"

"The background—and your character." Steele took a green pack from his pants pocket, shook out a cigarette, and lit it. "You see, Crawford, you had everything, bread, the old WASP values, establishment cat. Man, you were perfect. . . . Now, I'm asking a question. What do you really think of that statement you're going to sign?"

Steele leaned forward, his expression one of candid curiosity, and Tim surmised that Steele hankered to know precisely how the white target reacted. Did Tim even detect, perhaps, a desire for approbation? He considered for a moment.

"Well," he said, "I think it's an ingenious idea, as I told you. But it's farfetched and it would hit people wrong, from your standpoint. Invoking the Declaration of Independence to justify the seizure of private property. Why,

any white house owner reading that would hit the ceiling
—and then lay in a supply of guns."

"Yeah." Steele watched smoke float upward. The air in
the room was oppressive. "Whites wrote the Declaration
—and now only blacks believe in it. You see, we really
believe in equality, Crawford, all of us. For instance, you
think you've got the four of us figured out. I'll bet you say
to yourself, 'Now that Steele and that Wiggins, they're
educated and I can maneuver them, but I'd better be
careful with Ambrose and Marsh because they're real
ghetto blacks, tough, primitive fighters.' Am I right?"

"Well, I . . ."

"Sure. But you're wrong. Wiggins and I are closer to
Harve and Chili than we'd ever get to you in a hundred
years. We were all down together. Wiggins had a good law
thing going in Tennessee until he decided to quit Tom-
min' in the courts. Then he went broke. No more crumbs
from the man. Then his wife cut out because he was out
of bread. . . . Marsh's daddy was a tenant farmer in Alabama. Harve came out of the south on a bus. He was a
nothin'. Now he's got status, a private in the B.O.F. . . .
Chili, he schooled on guns and radio in the Army. He's
got battle stars from Vietnam. His buddy was killed over
there, fightin' your honky war on yellow people."

Steele inhaled on his cigarette. "We're all brothers.
We're soul. You understand what that means?"

"I think so."

Steele shook his head. "Thinking's got nothin' to do
with it. Soul is feeling. It's three hundred years of feeling
whitey's foot on our neck, of taking his insolent bullshit,
of scratching for leftovers from the gray man's table in
the richest country on earth. It's you claiming I'm inferior
because I'm black. Soul is being at the bottom, baby, and
when we're there all together, we share and we're equal
and we hate the enemy—all us brothers."

Tim wondered at the dispassionate tone. Steele spoke
of feeling, yet his voice was detached, controlled. Strange
man. How could he hate and never lose his cool?

"That may be," Tim said aloud, "but your method is
something else. What you're trying to do is rob the rich
and give to the poor. I bet you fancy yourself as some
kind of modern Robin Hood."

Steele grinned. "All right," he quickly agreed. "I'll buy that. You know, I used to read about Robin Hood as a kid, and I always knew he was black. He was black and so was Friar Tuck and Little John and the rest of the band in the forest. The ol' sheriff of Nottingham was white like a sheet—and Robin and his men screwed that white bastard every time."

"So you brought your bows and arrows to beat him again at Fairhill?"

"Right," agreed Steele. "But we're not going to use them. You're going to give us Fairhill because you're a man who recognizes fair play and justice when he sees them. What did Goldwater say? . . . 'In your heart you know I'm right.' "

Steele was leaning forward, his elbows on his knees and the cigarette smoking from his hands like a tiny pyre. His jaw was fixed and his eyes centered on Tim's. It was as though he were striving to shift Fairhill from white to black hands by willpower alone. He held the posture for several moments before he relaxed and dropped his gaze.

"Now, Crawford," he said, "I want both the deed and the statement signed today. You and the Mrs. can discuss it all you want, but I need the signatures by 6 P.M.—so we can have a nice, happy, house-transfer party tonight. And you can start counting your tax savings from giving the house and land to charity."

"Charity!" Tim laughed ironically. "You mean I'll have to start adding the gift tax I'd have to pay."

Steele shook his head. "Nope. Perly's got a friend at Internal Revenue. He tells me there's a good chance the B.O.F. will be recognized as educational or something."

Tim thought this prospect totally implausible, and he wondered whether Steele really believed it or was merely advancing another inducement.

"Perly's working on it," continued Steele. "So you sign, we have a big party, and tomorrow at 9 A.M., you and Perly file the deed at the courthouse in Trenton. Simple, man."

"And," rejoined Tim, "at 9:30 A.M. I walk into the prosecutor's office and say you coerced me. We'd have Fairhill back in a week."

Tim had overstated his case. He knew, as Perly Wiggins probably did, that to regain property conveyed by a

valid deed, he would have to go into chancery court and
sue on a charge of being defrauded. That might take
months.

"Now, baby," chided Steele. "You know better than
that."

"Why?"

Steele inhaled deeply and watched the smoke spiral in
the heavy air. "Because you're going to give me your
word that you won't go back on the deed and on the
statement. You're a man of honor, Crawford. Your
word's your bond. You pride yourself on it. Right?"

"But what makes you think I'll make any such promise?"

"Think, man," said Steele. "Tomorrow morning we
give your statement wide publicity through the B.O.F.
We'll give it to the press, the networks. Man, by tomorrow night, you'll be a white hero—a rare guy these days
—to every black in America. Now just suppose this hero
turns around and says he don't mean a word of his beautiful, soul statement, that he's keeping Fairhill for himself
and to hell with justice. Listen, you could set off some
mighty nice little riots." He paused and took another slow
inventory of Tim. "Now naturally the kind of man you
are, you wouldn't want to be the cause of no bloodshed."

"Threats, nothing but threats," said Tim. "This whole
scheme is ridiculous. You talk about morality at the point
of a gun. I'm not signing a thing—nothing."

They stared at each other, measuring the depth of de-
termination. How reliable was Steele's word, Tim wondered. He had promised no harm would come to the children. But how could Tim trust a man of no known address, no known occupation, the deputy commander of a
white-hating guerrilla band? He was seized by forebod-
ing. He had been beguiled by Steele's veneer of rationality. Where were Liz and the kids at this moment?

Steele finished his cigarette in silence, then said firmly:
"If those papers are not signed by 6 P.M., your wife will
be told all about your affair with Virginia Jones in Acapulco." He watched Tim's face for the reaction.

"Oh, come off it," said Tim. "If that's supposed to be
another threat, it won't work. You have no proof, and

besides it was all ten years ago. Liz couldn't care less.
You don't know as much about white women as you
think you do."

"They put property head of their men, huh?"

"No. I mean a woman like Liz values her marriage and
everything connected with it. Anyway, something that
happened ten years ago isn't real anymore."

"Ten years ago!" Steele exclaimed. "Listen, man,
where were you last Monday night?"

Tim blinked. "Why, let's see. . . . I was in Atlantic City
for an electrical-appliance convention. One of our clients
is a manufacturer."

"Yeah," said Steele, "and who visited you Monday
night in Room 1414 at the Blue Heron Lodge?"

"Nobody."

"That's not what Harve Marsh reported." Steele folded
his hands again over the medallion. "Harve says Virginia
Jones spent the night with you."

"He's a liar," Tim shouted. "I haven't seen Ginny
Jones in five years."

"Well, I don't know," said Steele, accentuating his
drawl. "That's what Marsh says. He has a friend, a bell-
hop, who claims he saw her leave in the morning."

"It's a lie."

"And you haven't kept in touch with Virginia Jones
over the years?"

Tim bridled. "In touch? Well, yes, but only a couple of
meetings and some letters and phone calls. And for the
last few years, nothing—except seeing her on TV."

"Your wife know all that?"

"You know she doesn't."

"Hmm. So it's your word against Harve's, isn't it?" He
leaned to one side in the big chair and pulled a paper
from his pants pocket. He unfolded it slowly and
smoothed it on his leg. "What Harve Marsh reports is interesting because I just happen to have something here
that might interest your wife." He bent forward and held
out the paper to Tim.

It was the carbon copy of a typed letter, slightly
smudged. Again Tim put on his glasses and read:

To: Commander B.O.F.

1. I wish to protest the decision last night of the strategy council to invade the property of Mr. and Mrs. Timothy R. Crawford, Jr., and to negotiate the deeding of the estate to the B.O.F.

2. I have no quarrel with the plan as conceived by Deputy Commander Steele and endorsed by you and the council. The concept is brilliant and the operation could become a rallying symbol of the whole cause for which the B.O.F. is fighting.

3. But the selection of Timothy Crawford's property is a grave error. Tim Crawford, who is an old friend, is one of the few whites in my experience who have helped any of us without selfish motives. In one case I know of, Mr. Crawford could not have done more if he were black. He did it out of his sense of justice—and because I was his friend and asked him to do so.

4. I do not believe we will further our aims by destroying decent white people and trampling upon those who give us love and trust. It is one thing to deal fearlessly with our enemies, and another to strike down our friends.

Signed: Virginia Jones
       Staff Sergeant

Tim recognized the looping signature, the "i's" dotted distantly and the "n's" opened wide as doors. Ginny was long gone, but her mark lingered. A wave of affection for her washed over him. Ginny, plighted to friendship, would not desert in time of need. She was repaying him for Jackson Dill and he felt a stab of guilt over that untidy business.

"So Ginny is a sergeant in your outfit?" Tim mused aloud. He was not surprised. His capacity for surprise, in any event, had contracted sharply in the last twelve hours.

"Right. Now I ask you. Does that 'give us love and trust' sound like somebody you haven't seen in five years? You suppose that's the way your wife will look at it?"

"Ginny's referring to an old legal case I helped her with," said Tim. "That's her way."

"Helped her? Jackson Dill, right? I told you last night we know all about you and Dill. It so happens Jackson Dill belongs to our elite guerrilla outfit and he told me Friday just what went on. You didn't plan his defense. You just got your pal Healy, the Irish lawyer, to lie to Miss Jones about your part in the case."

"That's not the way it was," said Tim stubbornly. He felt the need to justify himself even as he recognized the futility of protest. He was the caged mouse responding to a black Pavlov.

"You're in trouble, Crawford." Steele showed his pleasure over the fact. "If you don't sign, your wife is going to know you've had an affair with a black girl that may still be going on. Long time, man. And then we get Jackson Dill to tell Miss Jones what really happened, how you wouldn't take Dill's case for fear of losing a few lousy bucks from your country-club customers. So you lose a wife's trust and a lovin' lady friend—all in one day. It's something to think about."

"And so we go from pressure to blackmail," said Tim. He felt cornered, flayed. "Tell me something, Steele. Why did you waste so much time talking about justice and morality and principles? You don't give a damn about them."

Steele flashed an angry glance at Tim, hoisted himself from the easy chair, and walked slowly toward the casement windows. He stood looking over the back lawn, to the left where mirrorlike blue water reflected the tiles of the swimming pool, to the right where the carpet of grass rolled off to the tangled woods. He spoke without turning.

"No, you're wrong. Dead wrong." There was a long pause and when he resumed, his voice had a sad, bitter tone. "You see, I wanted you to do the right thing because of your own conscience, because I judged you to be, at base, a moral man who knew right from wrong. I wanted us to agree that this house and these beautiful grounds"—Steele swept an arm toward the back lawn—"that somehow they rightfully belonged to the black people your father took advantage of. They lost their humble little cribs. And you, you have all this, and money to burn besides. You have everything—position, security, wealth. And you've got those bright kids too. They can dream of anything and likely get it. . . . God, what a gap! How about the black kids? I got two of my own and I know. How about their dreams? What can they look forward to with whitey tripping them up every step of the way? We all think of the kids and their hopes. . . . I wanted you to see the whole picture."

He hesitated, then exploded: "Goddam it, is that too much to ask of a honky?"

Steele wheeled sharply on Tim. His face was tight, his cool, easy demeanor suddenly charged with rage. "Is that too much, Crawford?" He glared at Tim. "Why can't just one white man, just one, understand our desperation? Do I have to give you the three-hundred-years-of-slavery speech? Do I have to list every sneer, every curse, every honky look of loathing, every goddam, lousy, stinking scene of humiliation? Do I have to tell you the name of every black woman who's been called a slut and treated like a whore by you honkies? Do I have to name every black man, the millions of us, who've been mentally castrated, whipped, and perverted by the monster, Mr. Charley?"

He answered his rhetorical questions with raging particulars from his own life and that of his wife, his mother, and his kinfolk. He told of insults in New York, brute cops in Mississippi, the groveling of his grandfather before a white banker in Virginia. He stormed on for five minutes, a cascade of ignomy, a catalogue of racial wounds that knew no mending. His eyes dilated, his breath quickened. He became a man possessed, and Tim feared he might explode in scattered violence. Steele paused at last, breathing deeply.

Then he took a step nearer Tim, leaned over him with his big fists clenched and his brown eyes boring down. Tim's grip tightened on the chair arms. "When, goddam it, are you people going to learn the meaning of humanity? I wanted one decent act from just one white man, one small little deed signed that might help work a tender miracle in this stinkin' country. I wanted to take that statement to every ghetto from Newark to Watts, and I wanted to shout, glory, hallelujah: There *is* a honky with heart. His name is Tim Crawford and he knows what justice is. He's a white man with soul. Soul, baby! Big, beautiful, lovin' soul. He says to hell with the corrupt old honky law. He stands for black justice."

Steele stopped as suddenly as he began. He seemed baffled by the volume of his own outburst. He straightened slowly, struggling for control, and Tim saw that the large eyes were damp. A single tear formed, glistening in the corner of an eye, then rolled slowly down the dark cheek. Steele turned, as though in a daze, and walked to his chair. He dropped to the cushion, buried his head in his hands—and sobbed.

Tim realized that his own muscles were rigid. He watched for a moment in bewildered fascination, then lowered his eyes. He fumbled in his shirt pocket, found the pack, took out a cigarette, and lighted it without looking up again. From the other chair came racking sounds. Tim felt a surge of exasperation. It was as though a capricious judge had singled him out for punishment for the crimes of others. Why the hell must he be the witness to this private grief and rage? Why not the President, or George Wallace, or the mayor of Chicago, anybody? Why him, Tim Crawford?

The sounds were penetrating, repellent—and brief. There was a cough and some snuffling, and Tim could see a flash of white as Steele dried his eyes with a handkerchief. The incident seemed to have lasted interminably, although Tim knew the span was considerably less than a minute. The tall, dark man stood up, pulled his shoulders back, and faced the windows again. In sudden understanding Tim realized that if Steele had not wept, he might have smashed Tim's face in.

"Now, honky, you've seen it all," said Steele in a low, muffled voice. "You've seen a black man cry." He paused, a bitter interlude. "Yes, we cry, the weak and the strong. The tears of black power." Again a hesitation. "You won't believe it—but we cry for yo' ass too."

Steele jerked his head toward Tim. "I have only two things more to say to you, Crawford." Now the tone was harsh. "The first is, I want those papers signed by six. The second is—goddam you, yo' mama, and every other honky."

He strode to the door, yanked it open, and walked out. The lock rattled with the force of closing.

Tim sat unmoving for several minutes until he felt the heat of the burning cigarette nearing his fingers. Mechanically he mashed out the fire in the copper ashtray on the armrest.

From the hallway he heard Holly's piping voice raised in a question: "Is something wrong, Mr. Steele?" And then a reply in a low, gentled voice. "Yes, Holly—for a long, long time. . . . Let's go find your brother."

Chapter Five

A specialist in military topography would judge Fairhill to be ideal for defense by a small unit. The same contours and surface cover which masked a surprise, furtive occupation also provided a shield for vigilant defenders determined to hold their ground. The estate's sixty-five acres were laid out as a rough rectangle. The terrain rose gradually from all four boundaries to the crest where the eleven-room, brick colonial house and other structures stood. One of the rectangle's long sides lay against Drakes Corner Road, and a short side abutted the Great Road, which ran northwest from the outskirts of the city of Princeton. Motorists leaving the university town via the Great Road passed the Crawford estate on their left several miles out.

A thick stand of hardwoods, firs, and underbrush completely screened the house and lawn from the main highway, and the same woods curved in a horseshoe shape around three sides of the rectangle. Only to the west did the house command a partially open view. Here the green and tended turf sloped downward the length of a football field and merged into a meadow of timothy grass that stretched for perhaps a hundred and fifty yards to the property line. Here stood a boundary fence consisting of loose stone piled several feet high by unknown field hands in the Revolutionary War era. Atop the stone foamed a tangled burden of honeysuckle, ivy, and brambles. Considerably beyond the fence to the west stood the comparatively new home of a childless couple, the Peckinpaughs.

The front of the Crawford house—Ben Steele called it a mansion—was shielded by the huge old oak tree and a scatter of red maples and hickory on the crown of the hill. A number of dogwoods nestled close to the house. The driveway, curving from the lower corner of the property at the intersection of Drakes Corner and the Great Road, was lined on both sides by clumps of white birch and an occasional copper beech. In the rear the lawn reached only about fifty yards before meeting the heavy grove covering the hill. A path led down through the woods to a creek that puttered over stones and fallen branches and eventually flowed into Stony Brook near the western border of Princeton Township.

Steele and his men, who had brought sleeping bags with them, bivouacked on the floor of the living room. Watches were stood in turn. By posting one man in front of the house and another in the rear, Steele could maintain an effective vigil over all approaches. Furthermore, his sentries were in scant danger of being observed, for they could conceal themselves behind any number of trees and bushes. Deputy Commander Steele had honored the oldest of military precepts: seize the high ground. He was unprotected from only one direction—overhead.

And it was the air above that attracted Liz Crawford on this sultry Sunday morning. Perhaps her attention was drawn by the lowering jets that streaked in from the west and wheeled over Fairhill on the wide arc of approach to the Newark Airport, thirty-five miles to the north. Higher in the haze jets eastbound for John F. Kennedy International Airport swam like flashing mackerel in milky, tropical waters. Whatever the stimulus, Liz became conscious of upper levels as she slapped about Holly's room in thong sandals. She was on her detested round of bedmaking and straightening forced upon her by Vivika's vacation. Ordinarily Vivika made the beds on Saturdays and Sundays while Dora performed the task on weekdays. Much as Liz admired neat beds and tidy rooms, she deplored the circumstances that put the work on her back. Still, anything was to be preferred to idleness on this particular Sunday. Vivika would return early next week, for the calendar showed only nine days to go as of yesterday —yesterday, that far-gone and distant day before black men invaded Liz's home and made her prisoner.

She had left Holly and Scott in the kitchen with Perly Wiggins who, upon emerging from the library after only a few minutes, had offered unaccountably to do the breakfast dishes. He attacked the sink after a brief trial of the portable TV set which rested on the counter. A white gospel soprano, reaching for unattainable octaves, was not to Wiggins's taste and he switched off the set.

Strangely, despite the apprehension that made Liz's every step within the house a venture into the unknown, she had no fear of either Marsh or Wiggins. Marsh was disarming, a posturing comic with the children, while she felt that no man who fussed and rattled on like Wiggins could be a threat to anyone. And Wiggins alone among the four blacks did not wear his hair like an African bushman. The reason was simple. He had but little hair left, merely a grayish fringe that gave him the appearance of an aging, tonsured monk. When Liz left the kitchen, Scott was telling Wiggins and Holly of his latest dream, a lurid and preposterous episode in which a herd of purple giraffes wandered into a house and ate the ceiling. Every time Scott paused for breath, Holly nodded sagely and said: "I know."

Looking through the back window as she straightened Holly's room, Liz could see Chili Ambrose. He was standing in the shade of the garage with his arms folded. Liz could see the pistol at his belt. It was while she fingered the sheet on Holly's bed and looked below that the idea struck her. Of course. It was natural. Why hadn't she thought of it before? She walked swiftly to the large bedroom at the front of the house and looked out the window. Harve Marsh was standing against the trunk of the oak tree with only his left arm and shoulder visible. His back was to the house.

Liz thought briefly of Tim in the library, talking, talking, talking while the invaders' grip on Fairhill tightened. What the hour called for was action. Quickened by new resolve, Liz hurried to the hall linen closet and pulled a sheet off the shelf. She ripped off a corner piece, about three feet square, then refolded the mutilated sheet and replaced it on the shelf. Using her teeth, she tore two small holes at either side of the cloth. In a jumble of cleaning fluids, jars and bottles on the floor of the closet, she found a ball of string. She broke off a long piece and tied it to one of the holes.

A door at the end of the hallway opened on the stairs to the upper storage space. Liz climbed to the attic and was at once enveloped in ovenlike heat. She threaded her way in the baking gloom, past ancient trunks, discarded drapes, file cabinets, and dusty boxes, to a stepladder fixed beside the main chimney. Trembling slightly from both eagerness and fright, she mounted the ladder and pulled the chain on a sliding panel which opened on the roof. A wash of fresh air entered. She climbed to the top step and looked out. It was a slate roofing of gentle slope. At the peak was a flat metal strip less than a foot wide, which connected the house's three chimneys and the television aerial. A narrow board walkway lay atop the metal.

Liz stood for a moment, facing the Peckinpaugh house which, at this height, could be clearly seen to the west beyond the meadow and stone fence. She planted her feet wide apart, and, although experiencing a mild sensation of vertigo, she began to flap the torn section of bed sheet. Chances of being seen at this hour were slight, she knew, since the Peckinpaughs were a swinging couple who usually did not arise on Sundays until well past noon. Still, she had to try. She waved and flapped the cloth a few times. Too much activity, she realized, would attract attention from Marsh and Ambrose below. Also she began to feel dizzy. The combination of height and humid heat was too much for her. She eased herself down to her knees and crawled along the runway to the chimney nearest the Peckinpaugh home. Here, because of the peculiar pitch of the roof, a cloth tied to the chimney could be seen only from the west side of the house and only then by an observer who stood thirty or forty yards out from the house. With good luck the white cloth might remain there all day without being detected from the ground immediately below. And, if seen by the Peckinpaughs, it would be sure to arouse them sufficiently so that they would either drive personally to Fairhill or tele-

phone the police. This chimney was not a large one, and
Liz felt she would have no trouble encircling it with the
string so that the white cloth faced west toward the Peckinpaughs'.

The walkway ended on the east side of the chimney.
To accomplish her chore Liz had to brace one foot on the
slope of slate. As she did so, a slate gave way and slid
down the roof with a noise like that of a fingernail being
drawn across a blackboard. The long, scratchy sound—to
Liz it seemed of infinite duration—ended when the slate
plopped to the ground.

"Hey! You!" The shout came from below and in front
of the house. She looked down to see Harve Marsh glar-
ing up at her. There was not a trace of easy humor in the
round face this time. A shotgun leaned against the oak
tree.

She felt ridiculously exposed. She stood under the
fierce morning sun, one hand holding the top of the chimney and the other trailing her limp rag of hope.

"What the hell are you doin' up there?" demanded
Marsh. "You take that sheet and git back in the house—
quick!"

She hesitated. "I'm afraid to crawl back," she said. She
was thoroughly frightened now.

"You better," shouted Marsh, "or I'm comin' up there
and get you and that flag too."

Liz rallied her courage and sank awkwardly down to
all fours again. She cast a last, hopeful look toward the
Peckinpaugh house but saw no one. Clutching the cloth,
she began to crawl back toward the opening. The unpainted wooden walkway was a crude one, and a splinter
pierced the heel of her right palm. Otherwise her crawl
back was fairly free of hazard, although she could see
Marsh staring up belligerently as he monitored her progress.

Liz turned as she prepared to lower herself through the
opening. Facing the rear now, she saw Chili Ambrose.
He was standing on the lawn near the garage. One arm was half raised and the hand gripped the revolver
which had been drawn from his belt. He stared up at her,
his face a black cloud of anger.

She felt suddenly faint at the thought of Ambrose, his

attention undoubtedly drawn by Marsh's shot, covering
her retreat along the narrow walkway. She groped with
one foot for the top step of the attic ladder and found that
her arms and legs were trembling. She closed the sliding
panel, descended the ladder, and sat down heavily on a
wooden crate crammed with old magazines. Her heart
beat faster, and she shivered despite the sweltering heat.
She thought, oddly, of the day in her childhood when she
defied her father's orders and climbed into the old Buick
and played at driving before he discovered her. There was
the same sense of purloined privilege and guilt, the same
cowering before authority when apprehended.

She sat, quaking, for several minutes in the stuffy attic
before descending to the second-floor hallway. There,
with his arms folded over his black sweater and his automatic at his belt, stood Chili Ambrose. His face was set in
fury.

"You a damn fool," he said. The single gold tooth
flashed. "One more like that and somebody's goin' get
messed up."

He snatched the torn sheet from her hand. "Now you
git in that bedroom and stay there until we tell you to
come out." He pointed to the door of the master bedroom. "And don't go near the windows—hear?"

She did as ordered. Ambrose closed the door behind
her, and she heard footsteps retreating in the hallway and
then pounding down the stairs. She sank into a small
wooden rocker. Her breathing was so labored it frightened her. The trembling continued, and she began to rock
in an effort to restore calm. Outside she could hear Ambrose and Marsh talking—near the oak tree, she guessed.
Then there was silence. She rocked for another ten minutes until her pulse slowed and she felt almost normal
again.

Like a new prisoner who never before had seen the inside of a cell, she looked about her as she took stock of
her dilemma. This whole thing was becoming monstrous:
Fairhill occupied and its residents held as secret captives
in an area that teemed with people only a few miles away.
Churches were holding services. Earlier she had heard the
bells. All around her the leisurely life of a July Sunday
morning apparently was sauntering along as usual. In the

distance she could hear the mooing of a cow and the faint
bark of a dog and, nearer, the drone of tires on the Great
Road. This was all absurd, idiotic. Certainly, by this time,
Peggy Abingdon would have called and found the phone
out of order. By tonight, in the normal course, a half
dozen people would call. How soon before the telephone
company came to investigate and repair? Tomorrow? . . .
Tomorrow, ah. Dora always arrived promptly at nine on
Monday. Liz wondered. Could she possibly slip through
the woods and intercept Dora at the main entrance, asking her to go to the police for help? Perhaps. She must
think and plan carefully.

Her foray to the roof had been an impulsive mistake.
Tim's more relaxed, if pedestrian, behavior was the correct posture to take. The thing to do was to obey the invaders, humor them, make sure that she and Tim gave
Steele's men no cause to frighten Scott and Holly. She
would stall—politely but firmly—until Dora came tomorrow. And if she failed to head off Dora, someone else was
bound to show up Monday, if not in the morning, certainly by afternoon. The trash men came Monday after-
noons, didn't they? The ordinary day brought two or
three people to the house—store delivery, pool-mainte-
nance men, meter readers, solicitors, God knew what all.

Yes, it would be stupid to offend or challenge the intruders in any manner. Let them have their way. It would
be short-lived in any event. She felt annoyed with Tim.
He should have had the foresight to discuss this in full
with her last night so that they could have adopted a
common strategy that both would adhere to. What good
was Tim's heralded logic and level head if he did not
apply them in a crisis?

She rocked on for nearly an hour, comforted now and
then to hear the untroubled voices of Holly and Scott
below. This moist heat was deadening. Her whole body,
she realized, was damp and she could feel sweat trickling
from her scalp. She thought yearningly of a cool bath
but promptly rejected the idea. The vision of being
naked in the tub while four black men patrolled the house
and grounds was somehow one she did not care for. What
if one of them should come suddenly into the bedroom?
She could, of course, lock the bathroom door. My God,

she had to bathe sometime! She mulled over the idea,
disturbed at her own timidity in the face of so routine an
act.

There was a knock at the door.

"Yes?" Her fear returned. It had to be one of them.
Tim would never bother to knock.

"It's Ben Steele. I want to talk to you."

She hesitated. If he was coming to punish her for her
escapade, the bedroom was no place for confrontation.
He did not have the right. And a silly thing—the bed was
still unmade. She hadn't gotten that far on her dreary
chores before the venture on the roof. The bed, rumpled
from the bodies of herself and Tim, lay open, suggestively
so.

"All right." She had no alternative. "Come in." She
stood up.

Steele entered as casually as though he were a member
of the family. His goatee and mustache gave his counte-
nance the usual forbidding appearance, but he showed no
irritation. His glance swept the room, centered on her. He
closed the door behind him. This simple act alarmed her.
Steele put an arm on the large chest of drawers near the
door and leaned against the chest. He always seemed to
be slouching or leaning against something, a stance of
nonchalant command.

"That was a stupid thing you did, Liz," he said.

This time his use of the familiar "Liz" terrified her. A
show of authority by the invading chief downstairs was
one thing. Up here, in the bedroom, quite another.

"I took it for granted you were a woman who knew the
score without being told," he said. "It looks like I have to
lay down the law for you."

When she did not reply, he continued: "We have to
figure that nobody at your neighbors' saw you flapping
that damn sheet. But if someone did, we're in for trouble." He paused, looked slowly around the room. "I've
had a long talk with your husband."

"Oh."

"Yeah. You two are going to sign a deed for us at 6
P.M. Plenty of time for ya'll to talk things over."

Liz placed her hands in the pockets of her shift and

straightened her shoulders. "If you're talking about the house and land, they belong to Tim."

"A wife has interests," he said. "We need your signature."

"I don't know what you mean, but I won't sign a thing."

"I think you will." He stared at her, and Liz had the impression again of power flooding from a hidden reservoir. She looked away and took an unconscious step backward.

"What's the matter?" he asked. "You afraid of me?"

"No," she retorted. "But I'm not accustomed to having strangers give me orders in my house—to say nothing of my bedroom."

"Oh, that's it." He smiled knowingly. "The bedroom. Right? The big hang-up of the white beauty. Attracted and repelled by that old black magic. Right?"

"I have no idea what you're talking about." But she could feel the tremors.

"Oh yes, you do. I know you, Elizabeth Crawford." He paused, took a pack from his trousers pocket, lit a cigarette, and blew out a stream of smoke. The man, thought Liz, laid down smoke screens like a fleet entering battle. He was not so confident, after all.

"I checked you out pretty good, as much as I did your husband," he continued. "And last night and this morning I watched you. I've met a dozen like you—the rich, white bitch, talks the liberal line, sure of her looks and her status, all full of causes and good works for the downtrodden. Until you get to the clutch. Until the first black man gets near you. Then you jump back like a filly. You're sure he's going to rape you, and you're half afraid he will and half afraid he won't. . . . Right?"

Liz said nothing. She found it difficult to breathe evenly. Returning Steele's stare, she attempted to put scorn into the look.

"Yeah," said Steele, drawling it. "Well, Liz Crawford, you got it wrong. You got it all wrong. . . . Sure, maybe some black men would like a go at you. We gotta line for that kind. We say, 'They talk black and sleep white.'" He inhaled and this time blew several smoke rings that disintegrated slowly in the heavy air. "Me, I'm black all the

way. Black is beautiful, baby, and you better believe it.
Also I got the prettiest black woman at home you ever
saw—and two black kids as bright as your two. . . . So,
let's put all those sweet little nightmares away, huh, so we
can talk sense."

Liz tightened, drawing up her small reserve of courage.
"You're imagining things, Mr. Steele. As a psychologist,
you'd make a . . . well, good shoe clerk. Or else you take
some perverted pleasure in trying to degrade me."

"Degrade you, huh?" His single laugh was harsh. "See?
Scratch that liberal, ivory skin—and out pours the prejudice. You think you'd be degraded by contact with a
black man." He shook his head. "You're all the same," he
said bitterly. "Well, sister, it's a two-way street. I
wouldn't soil my hands on a honky body. I think black
and I sleep black. And another thing. I'm here to do a
job. Whether you wear a skirt or pants don't mean a
damn thing to me."

"I think—"

"I don't care what you think you think," Steele cut in.
"Right now we're going to talk about rules. For that crazy
act of yours on the roof I ought to lock you in the tool
shed, and maybe I'll have to. . . . But I'd rather have
things go along normal-like. So from now on you're not
to leave this house without permission from me. And
you'll make no attempt whatsoever to signal to people on
the outside. Is that clear?"

"Are you asking me for my word?"

"No. I'm telling you. I'll take a promise from your
husband." He smiled. "He's the type. But your word ain't
worth nothin'. Now you do exactly what I say—or the
tool shed will be the least of what you'll get."

"Now that you've had your say," said Liz, "I'd appreciate it if you leave."

He inclined his head in mock respect. "As madam
wishes." The cigarette drooped from a corner of his
mouth as he opened the door. Halfway out, he turned.
"Oh, by the way, if you want a bath, take one. There ain't
a Peeping Tom on the place. Besides there ain't a damn
thing worth peepin'. So go ahead."

The door closed on her smothered rage. She felt
stripped, humiliated. Then she wondered. Had Tim said

something that provoked Steele? Why the sudden detour into sex? It seemed uncharacteristic of Steele, who had been infuriatingly cool and detached ever since appearing at the library door fourteen hours ago. She pondered for a few moments, then marched to the bathroom. She was dripping with perspiration and she needed that bath. Her defiance buoyed her.

The invaders' advance planning had not foreseen everything. Scott Crawford provoked a strategy huddle of the blacks by his simple reminder that the Sunday *New York Times* rested in its metal tube at the front of the driveway on the Great Road. Ordinarily Tim and Scott walked down and brought the paper back before breakfast, but this morning both had forgotten. When Scott remembered shortly before noon, Steele conferred with Marsh and Wiggins before deciding. It was ruled that Scott would go alone, dragging his wagon to carry the heavy paper. Steele made a game of it. Scott was to go as though on a secret mission. If he saw someone he knew, or if he was questioned by anyone, he was to say nothing of the visitors. Scott, delighted with the trust, carried out his assignment without a hitch—although Marsh slipped into the woods along the highway to maintain surveillance over the boy.

Tim skimmed the headlines as though reading bulletins from another planet. . . . President Randall declares . . . Mayor Ferretti opposes . . . New Jersey's Governor Danzig asserts . . . Britain defends . . . Peking decries . . . consumer prices rise . . . New York Mets lose. Ordinarily Tim and Liz spent several hours reading the Sunday *Times*. Today neither could concentrate. Only Ben Steele went through the entire news section.

With the temperature reaching ninety-four, Scott and Holly clamored to go swimming. The pool party consisted of Tim, Scott, Holly, and Ben Steele. At the children's insistence Tim lent a pair of trunks to the black leader. Harve Marsh stood watch near the pool while Liz, with Steele's permission, sat under the beach umbrella and sipped a lemonade. She still smoldered over the exchange with Steele, and yet, at the same time, she wondered where Ambrose and Wiggins were. It had become habit to keep track of each of the invaders as though knowledge of their whereabouts could somehow help her to chart her own course. She saw Wiggins saunter from the back door near the library with a large book in his hands. He sat down in the shade of a red maple and began leafing through the pages.

When Liz saw the red leather cover, she realized that Wiggins had the family photograph album. At once she was seized by new outrage. What right did this stranger have to inspect these intimate glimpses of life at Fairhill? Neither she nor Tim were snapshot fans. They seldom carried a camera on vacation trips, and they never, never inflicted family pictures on friends. Instead they used the camera sparingly at home, collecting shots that Holly or Scott might enjoy when they were grown. In a sense the album was a sentimental gift to the children. And some of the pictures now open to Wiggins had a private meaning for Liz alone. There was, for instance, a picture of her at the period when she wore her hair so long it brushed her shoulder blades. The picture had been taken by Tim after some forgotten spat. She had cried and the camera caught a lingering residue of her hurt and the new sweetness she felt when they compromised with kisses—or had she surrendered? Now this private, interior moment belonged to a stranger. The thought infuriated her.

Liz walked across the lawn and stood over Wiggins as he sat cross-legged in the shade.

"Who gave you that album?" she demanded.

"Nobody." Her intensity startled him. "I found it in the library."

She knew where . . . on the bottom shelf above the annual from Bryn Mawr and the earlier year book from Chatham Hall, *The Chathamite*. And inside these were the old, scrawled inscriptions that now could only remind her of outworn hopes, of small mountains left unclimbed, of the young girl she was no more. And nearby rested the album of wedding pictures, bound in that ridiculous white satin, now yellowing. Her mother had assembled the photographs, centered one carefully on each page and presented the volume to her on her first wedding anniversary. Had Wiggins pawed through all these too? Had he examined the faded hours and moments like a man fingering old gems on a hidden jewel tray?

"Those are our pictures," said Liz. In her anger she could not find the right words. "They are not for exhibit."

Wiggins's smile was confused. "Oh . . . they're just pictures."

"May I have the book, please?" She held out her hand.

Wiggins, embarrassed, arose and handed over the album. "Nothing to get mad about," he said.

"I'll thank you to leave our personal belongings alone," Liz said.

She stalked off, fearful that if she stayed a moment longer, she would explode and thus sabotage her new resolve to humor the invaders until help arrived. She went to the library, found the two year books and the wedding album on the lower shelf, then crammed all four volumes in a drawer of Tim's desk. She remained in the study for several minutes, trying to analyze her feelings. If only the black men had entered the house for robbery. If they had swept up the television sets, money, her rings and bracelets, yes, even the silver, and vanished in the night, the affront could be tolerated. But to stay here, hour after hour, plucking at her memories, poking into the private corners of herself, exposing all of Fairhill to a kind of dispassionate scrutiny as though they were agents of some nameless inquisitorial power. If that was Ben Steele's method, he would find a tougher foe than he bargained for.

A half hour later, as she was returning to a calmer mood, another incident retouched her fury. The children raised their midday demands for food, exaggerating their hunger as always. Liz broiled frankfurters for four, then yielded the kitchen to Marsh, who warmed some canned vegetable soup and made ham sandwiches for the B.O.F. contingent. Marsh helped himself inside the bronze refrigerator, inspected the contents of cupboards and freezer, and came outside to announce that they could eat for a week before touching the field rations. This breezy occupation of her kitchen, the forays into the stacked foodstuffs, was of a piece with the picture album. The next thing she knew, Marsh would be leafing through her personal recipe book, the one she annotated with waspish comments about some of her friends who provided culinary suggestions. Her life was being slowly dissected like

that of an insect pinned to a laboratory table. Why didn't
Tim understand? Why couldn't he put a stop to this methodical autopsy of their lives?

But Tim's mind throughout most of that clammy afternoon was on other facets of their problem. He was trying
to fathom the motives of the No. 1 invader. Steele's attitude since his outburst and his tears in the library disconcerted Tim. The black commander made no further mention of the deed nor did he once refer to the passing time
or the approaching deadline. Instead he played and joked
with the children and later, in the shade of the oak tree,
he told them a long story. The tale charmed Scott and
Holly. By midafternoon the children were afloat on a
bright sea of affection, and once Scott called Steele
"Uncle Ben" in the hearing of Harve Marsh.

"Uncle Ben!" echoed Marsh. "You better not let Chili
hear you calling any of us 'Uncle,' or he'll tan your bottom."

"Why?" asked Scott.

"Never mind." Marsh grinned. "You got to call him
something, call him 'Cousin Ben.'"

"But he's older," protested Scott. "Uncles are older."

"I know," said Holly.

"I told you, boy," said Marsh. "Don't say I didn't warn
you."

"I tell you what," suggested Steele. "You just call me
Ben. That's what Peter Wilson calls me."

As the sultry afternoon wore on, Tim found the scene
becoming as illusory as Peter Wilson. If Fairhill stood in
peril, there was no outward sign of it. The countryside
drowsed, the dogwood leaves drooped without stirring,
the pool's filter machinery purred with only an occasional
metallic cough, cumulous clouds towered in the west, and
Holly fell asleep beneath a tree after refusing petulantly
to go upstairs for her regular nap. Except for the color of
his skin, Steele could have been any of a dozen weekend
visitors who came to Fairhill from New York or Philadelphia in the warm months. He was as courteous, unobtrusive, and tactful as a guest should be. As for the other
blacks, they were largely invisible at their sheltered guard
stations, and Tim did not see the menacing Chili Ambrose
for several hours.

Yet beneath the placidity lay the tension. Its pervasive-
ness exhilarated Tim. Not once did he think of a drink,
an uncommon occurrence for Sunday afternoon. Nor did
he sink into the potholes of boredom which now marked
so many of his days. He had the feeling that something
untoward might happen at any moment. And so he was
alert in later afternoon when he saw Ambrose and Steele
meet at the edge of the rear lawn. They conversed for a
moment, and then Ambrose took the path that led down
through the woods to the creek. The scene made Tim realize that his own deadline was nearing and that he had
not yet talked seriously to Liz. He had been waiting for
some sign or order from Steele, but there had been none.
He experienced again that curious feeling—that Steele
was determined to change the ownership of Fairhill by an
act of volition alone.

Holly was awake now, and the children were chattering
with Perly Wiggins near the oak tree. Liz was somewhere
inside the house. Tim left his lounge by the pool and went
to find her. He was still in his trunks.

He found her in the living room. She was seated in a
slipcovered armchair, facing a window that afforded her a
view of the children. She looked miserable. Her face,
sticky with perspiration, was bare of cosmetics, her long
hair needed combing, and her posture was so slack she
might have been dumped in the chair. Tim sat down on
an upholstered footstool covered with faded needlepoint.

"Don't, Tim," she said reflectively. "Your trunks are
wet." She handed him a magazine from her lap. "At least
put this under you."

He slid the magazine beneath his rump. "We've got
other things to worry about. Steele is demanding I sign
over the house by six o'clock. It's after five now."

"You mean you haven't told him 'no' yet?"

Tim shook his head. They eyed each other for a moment.

"Tim, are you actually considering the idea of giving
them Fairhill?"

"No." He hesitated. "But if I were, I couldn't without
your consent."

"Why? I don't understand. Steele said something about
my interests. What are they? It's your property, isn't it?"

"Yes, but under New Jersey law a wife must agree before a husband sells or gives away the place where she lives. It's called her dower interest. It was explained to you years ago, but you've forgotten."

"How considerate. Very interesting." She paused, reflecting. "Tim, as I said last night, it's really quite simple. We just go ahead and sign whatever they want us to, and later in the week we tell the police and the prosecutor that we signed under duress."

"No," he said slowly, "I won't do that."

"Why not, for God's sake?"

"Because if I sign, that's it. I won't go back on it."

"Do you think *they* are standing on any such ethical niceties?"

"Probably not. I'm talking about me."

"A lovely time for honor," she said bitterly. "Well, it doesn't make any difference. I wouldn't sign anything for that Steele if he were the last man on earth."

"I don't blame you, but why so rough on Steele? The way he sees it, he's acting on . . . well, principle. He's not a bad guy, Puss."

"That's what you think!" She glared at him. "He's crude. He's impudent. And he has an overpowering ego."

"That's quite an indictment," he observed. "I must say those are three traits I haven't seen."

"Well, I keep my eyes open, which is more than I can say for you."

"Look, Puss." He studied her, trying to understand. "Did something happen? Did he say something that offended you?"

Offended! What an understatement. She wanted to blurt out the scene in the bedroom, but the words would not come. She could see Steele slouching against the chest of drawers with that look of amused, contained contempt. She recalled her accusing words, her sulphurous reaction, the tumble of emotions. Even now, she could not sort out her feelings. It would be impossible to tell Tim precisely —and if she could not be exact, the telling would be more confusing than useful.

"It's just his whole attitude," she said. "That man hates whites—and don't you forget it. He's another Chili Ambrose with a thin veneer of learning."

Hatred? Tim could see Steele in the library, fighting to hold off tears, sobbing in black despair, yet crying "for yo' ass too," as he put it.

Husband and wife looked at each other bleakly, their understanding walled into separate cells. They both felt as uncomfortable, as close, and yet as estranged as they had at the peak of their quarrel last night.

"He lets his men go through every personal thing in this house," she said. "You saw Wiggins with our picture album. And Marsh sticks his nose into every nook and cranny in my kitchen. For all we know they've ransacked my old letters, bills, canceled checks, maybe even my jewelry. I feel I'm being picked over like old chicken bones."

"I know, Puss." He spoke softly, trying to comfort her. "Just don't blame it on me. I'm trying to play it the best I know how."

Liz shifted her gaze to her right palm. The splinter from the roof's walkway was still imbedded. She pressed with her thumb nail and winced at the quick, sharp pain.

"Did you hurt yourself?"

She nodded glumly. "When I was up there on the roof. It's nothing. Just a splinter."

"Roof? What were you doing on the roof?"

"You mean you didn't even hear what happened?" She accused him with her eyes. While he had talked and deliberated, she had acted.

When he shook his head, she rushed into the story of her venture with the torn sheet. The climax, she said, came when Steele threatened to lock her in the tool shed if she tried anything "crazy" again. She made no mention of the sexual talk.

"I'm sorry, Puss," said Tim. He stepped over to her, held her head, and kissed her. She put her arms around him and they embraced tightly for a moment.

"I heard somebody yell at you when I was in the study, but it didn't make much impression." The fact was, Tim knew, that when Steele banged the door of the library, the effect was shattering. Tim had sat there for half an hour, brooding on what he had seen and heard.

"I just had to do something, Tim," said Liz. "Anything. I guess it was foolish."

And Tim thought, by contrast, that he had done nothing except listen to Steele and ponder the implications. Liz, despairing for her home, had hurried to the ramparts with her flag—a kind of modern Barbara Fritchie. While he had merely nagged at the problem like a dog with a bone. As for action, he had done nothing. Well . . .

"What time is it?" he asked.

She glanced at her tiny wristwatch. "Ten of six."

"I'll go find Steele."

First Tim went upstairs and dressed. When he came down, he found Steele waiting for him in the library. The deed and the typed statement lay on the desk, a ballpoint pen between them.

"I'm not signing," said Tim. "It would be useless anyway. Liz is determined not to."

They had not confronted each other since morning. Steele looked at him for a moment, shrugged, and turned to the door. "Wait here," he ordered.

Steele returned with Liz. He held the door open for her, then closed it, and motioned her to a chair. Liz took the seat without speaking.

"Now, Mrs. Crawford," said Steele. "I want you to sign that deed on the line indicated." He pointed to the desk. "Time has run out. We need your signature now."

"No." Liz gripped the arms of the chair. She looked straight ahead, refusing to acknowledge Steele's presence. Delay, delay, she thought. Help will come tomorrow.

Steele leaned against the desk. The medallion settled on his chest. He spoke quietly.

"Then there is something I have to tell both of you," he said. "I don't want to do this, Mrs. Crawford. You'll spare yourself a lot of grief if you'll sign." Her eyes were on the windows. She refused to face him. "When I'm finished telling both of you things you don't know about each other, you'll wish—"

"Ben!" It was a sharp call from the casement windows. Harve Marsh's full, round face was pressed against the screen. "There's a car coming up the drive with a white guy."

"Duck to the other side of the house," Steele ordered. Then quickly to Tim: "You get out there and turn the man away. Whoever he is. Same rules. Speak up loud, man."

Tim hesitated. Why not end it right now? Why not let Steele extricate himself from his own maze? Then he caught a flash of Marsh's gun as Marsh hurried off.

"Step on it!" There was command urgency in Steele's tone. Tim left his chair and walked rapidly to the back door.

The car, a blue Chevrolet sedan, had halted in front of the garage near the Jaguar. A young white man, hatless with a crew cut and wearing a tan gabardine suit, was twisting out of the front seat. Tim walked over to him.

"Hate to bother you," said the man, "but I'm looking for a party named Tumulty. He lives around here some-where."

"I'm sorry," said Tim. "I don't know the name."

"I got an address on the Great Road." The man's sweeping glance took in Tim, the house, the garage, the pool.

"I know almost everyone along the road," said Tim. "I don't think you'll find a Tumulty."

"Mind if I use your phone book?"

Tim managed a smile. "There isn't one. The kids tore it up. We're getting another one from the phone company."

"Oh." The man did not seem surprised. "Your name Crawford? I think that's what it said on the mailbox."

Tim nodded. "I wish I could help you."

"Well . . ." The man made a move toward his car, then checked himself. "God, it's hot. Could I trouble you for a glass of water?"

Tim was confused. "Sorry . . . that is, you see my wife's ill. I'd rather . . . well, I think it best if you leave."

The man frowned but got back into the car and buck-led his seat belt.

"I hope you understand," said Tim.

"Sure. Sure." The stranger started the engine, backed around on the asphalt apron, and drove off.

As soon as the car was swallowed by the woods flank-ing the highway, Chili Ambrose emerged from the bushes beside the garage and Steele ran from the house.

"That bastard wasn't looking for no Tumulty," said

Ambrose to Steele. He stood with his thumbs hooked behind his wide belt. "He was either a fed or some local plainclothes."

"Could be," said Steele. "But there's nothing to worry about. We're going to get this buttoned up tonight."

"Somebody's on to us," said Ambrose. "I can smell the law a mile away."

Steele patted Ambrose's arm. "Never mind, Chili. We got it made, brother."

Ambrose shook off Steele's hand with a wrench of his shoulder. "That guy means trouble. I want us to talk to Lion again."

Steele considered for a moment, then said: "Okay." He turned to Tim. "You wait inside, Crawford. I'll be back in a few minutes."

The two black men walked to the edge of the lawn and disappeared into the woods along the meandering path that led to the creek. The trespass at Fairhill was in its twenty-second hour.

Chapter Six

Twelve hours earlier on that Sunday a young police trainee in New York City neared the end of his shift. He stretched, yawned, and glanced at the wall clock. Six forty-seven. Forty-three minutes yet to go before he could drag it home. Most of Manhattan slept—at last—but for Trainee Norton Levy these were the gritty hours. Before he could slide into bed, he faced the last grind of duty, the check-out and change of clothes, the rattling ride uptown in a near-empty subway car, and a walk of three blocks past littered gutters in the spongy, sweet-sour air of a city convalescing after another strangled night.

Grief always courted the city at night. Since 11:30 P.M. Levy had answered 197 emergency calls—one almost every two minutes—under summons of the silent computer that harkened to the city's collective, suffering wail, sorted it into single cries for help, and beckoned a waiting ear from the long rows of uniformed patrolmen and trainees who manned the headsets.

It was the muffled isolation of the communications division, occupying a whole floor of the spanking-new police building at Park Row and Pearl Street, that frequently bothered Norton Levy. He was twenty years old, a man still pondering the squalor and sublimity that streaked every human life like a freakish layer cake, and he could not yet accustom himself to the contrasts. Here he sat in cool, conditioned comfort, soundproofed, muted. Here the computer reacted, selected, reigned. Here there was not even a hum of voices at the long tables, for each man spoke quietly to complete strangers through the mouthpiece of his headset. The faces of Levy's colleagues mirrored no distress, no agony, no shock, for the city's long lament was too great for any single man to bear. Outside, beyond these soundproofed walls, the city slashed, ran, fought, shot, cut, screamed, bawled, wept, and bled. It had done so through forgotten generations, and it would do so through many more until at last, drained and bloodless, with no more rivers of red to offer its sidewalks, it would die.

Here, inside, Trainee Levy was just another potential cop doing his job. Four months from now he would take the oath as a patrolman, change from his gray to blue uniform, place a .38 revolver in his new belt holster, and hit the streets, half in pride and half in fear.

Now, a few minutes before seven in the morning, the streets' ballad of disaster had slowed under rays of the climbing sun. The battered city tossed in its restless sleep. The communications room, a bright fluorescent tomb, had passed from night to dawn to morning without interior recognition, save for the thinning calls. Levy had not answered his phone for nine minutes. On the big board no lights glowed at any of the categories of special stress: IRT Sub Tie-Up, BMT Sub Tie-Up, Snow Emergency, Alt. Prk. Suspended, Power Failure, Traffic Plan. The board had but one decree—"Oon Mo-Men-Toe Pohr Fah-vohr"—the constant, phonetic reminder to operators of what to say to a Puerto Rican caller while he was being shifted to a Spanish-speaking patrolman. SPRINT's computer was not yet a linguist.

A green light flashed on Levy's console and simultaneously a recorded voice poured into his ear: "Manhattan south, Manhattan south." Someone in the lower end of the island was calling the city-wide police number, 911. Levy spoke into his mouthpiece: "Police emergency. Operator seventeen. May I help you?"

"Yeah. See . . ." It was a young, breathless, male voice. "There's this guy, see—"

"Easy," said Levy. "Talk slowly. Don't panic."

"Okay, but there's a guy shot on the sidewalk."

"Give me the address, please."

"On Orchard. Orchard right near Broome. He's got blood under him. I think he's dead."

"Orchard near Broome?"

"Yeah. By a parkin' meter. In front of Hymie's store."

"May I have your name and number, please?"

The phone clicked off. It figured, thought Levy. In cases of violence that question broke half of the emergency phone connections.

Levy punched keys on his console and instantly a message showed on the small screen above the keyboard: "Possible D.O.A., Manhattan, Division One, Precinct Seven, Orchard at Broome. Opr. Seventeen." The time was 6:51 A.M.

The unseen computer, its millions of circuits pulsing with electric current, digested the message, selected available patrol cars in the seventh precinct, filed the information in its memory, and alerted the next link in the communications chain.

Three seconds later a green light glowed on the console of a radio dispatcher in an adjoining room. Below his lighted and colored map of lower Manhattan, this message appeared on his screen: "Possible D.O.A., Manhattan, Division One, Precinct Seven, Orchard at Broome. RMPS A, D, G."

The dispatcher noted by his lighted map that Radio Motor Patrol Car D was closer to the scene than Cars A and G. He pressed the panel broadcast button and spoke into the mouthpiece of his headset: "Seven David. Seven

David. Investigate D.O.A. on Orchard near Broome. Investigate D.O.A. on Orchard near Broome. K."

Patrol Car David was cruising north on Allen Street, western boundary of the seventh precinct. A divided artery, Allen flowed past a forlorn isthmus of iron railings, park benches, and soot-laden plane trees. Later in the day old men would sit on the benches and vie with the foliage for whatever scraps of fresh air eluded the clouds of exhaust fumes. Car David, a green and white sedan with a row of roof lights like popping eyes of a hydra-headed bug, sped north, wheeled right into Broome Street and braked to a crawl at Orchard, one block to the east.

Ancient brick apartment buildings, five and six stories high, walled the intersection. Accumulated grime of the years caked the structures into anonymous and dreary uniformity. A green fire escape, featuring the intricate ironwork of other decades, clung to one apartment like petrified ivy. The corner of another building held a ten-foot-high brassiere advertisement. The faded female model could have been the figurehead on a battered scow. Store windows at the street level offered cluttered displays of shirts, towels, underpants, and tablecloths, for this was near the heart of the lower east side's wholesale soft-goods market. Orchard and Broome slumbered now, but by 9 A.M. the narrow sidewalks would overflow the curbs with customers. Closed on Saturdays for the Jewish Sabbath, the district teemed with buyers and sellers on Sundays.

The officers in Car David looked up and down Orchard. At once their eyes were drawn by a knot of people, a half-dozen men and one woman, standing about fifteen yards south of Broome Street. Patrolman Pete DeGrazia maneuvered the car south and against the curb. He marked the time when he saw the body. It was 6:53 A.M., exactly two minutes after Trainee Levy punched out data from the anonymous phone call.

The body was that of a Negro man. The torso lay upright on the sidewalk, the left arm wedged against the base of a parking meter. The legs fell over the curb into the street like those of a discarded dummy. There was no sign of a wound on the front of the body, but a splotch of red showed beneath the left shoulder. The man wore a green sport shirt—frayed, soiled, and open at the neck—

black pants, and dark socks, and scuffed brown loafers. DeGrazia leaned over the body. The head lay rigidly to one side and the eyes stared straight ahead. DeGrazia surmised that the man had been dead for some time.

DeGrazia stepped to the patrol car's radio and called his dispatcher: "Seven David reporting. D.O.A. confirmed on Orchard just south of Broome. Body of male Negro; about thirty; on the sidewalk. Probably shot or stabbed in the back. K." Less than a minute later Patrol Cars A and G pulled up to the curb.

Within a few minutes two dozen police officers, alerted by the notifications desk in the communications room at headquarters, were gathered about the body. A throng of spectators materialized from nowhere, and three patrolmen took up guard duty to keep the crowd back. The windows above were alive with people now, many of the men barechested and the women wearing nightgowns or house coats. Down the street a flowerpot fell off a ledge and crashed on the pavement. Small boys yelled from window to window.

Despite seeming disorder police movements about the body were briskly routine. Patrolman DeGrazia searched the clothing under supervision of a sergeant. Detectives from Precinct Seven fanned out to question onlookers and people living in the neighborhood. Cameramen from the police photographic unit snapped pictures of the sprawled body. An assistant from the medical examiner's office inspected the corpse, made a tentative finding of death by bullet wound. He surmised the victim had been felled by a gun fired from a fair distance. The hands were undamaged, and a specialist from the police laboratory's mobile unit inked the finger tips and took ten prints, one from each finger and thumb. A member of the homicide squad scrutinized the clothing, found a laundry mark on the inside collar of the sport shirt. Detectives from the ballistics squad searched the area for spent bullets and empty cartridge casings despite the belief that the killing probably had occurred elsewhere with the body dumped on Orchard. A paper sheet was drawn over the corpse. Fifty-seven minutes after Trainee Levy answered the emergency call, the lifeless remains of the unknown black man were carried to the morgue wagon, a panel truck, and driven to Bellevue Hospital's morgue. Another item would be added to the twice-daily police "unusual" list, although murder was less than unusual. New York City's homicides were averaging almost three a day this year.

Fingerprints of this new statistic were promptly searched in city police files, and photographic blowups were placed on the facsimile circuit to the New York State Identification Intelligence System in Albany. Another circuit carried the print pictures from Albany to the Federal Bureau of Investigation in Washington. Reports from the city files and from the NYSIIS in Albany soon came back to Park Row headquarters: negative. But an hour passed with no word from the FBI in Washington.

It was 9:10 A.M. when the phone rang in the East 72nd Street apartment of James P. Carnahan, New York City's police commissioner. Carnahan, whose pink jowls shone from his recent shave, was settled comfortably at a table in the breakfast alcove. The bulky Sunday editions of the *Times* and the *Daily News* rested near his orange juice. A fragrant mist hovered above his coffee cup. Carnahan savored the aroma. It reminded him that he could eat at leisure this morning and browse through the Sunday papers. He still wore his pajamas. His wife, an imperturbable, brown-haired woman, answered the unlisted phone at an extension niche in the kitchen.

"It's for you, Jim."

"Take the number," he countered. He had just drained his orange juice and reached for his spectacles.

"It's Brenner of the FBI," she said. "He's sorry, but says it can't wait."

"Oh, Jesus." Carnahan pushed himself up from the table. These occasional Sunday morning calls were hard on his stomach. The commissioner's bulk sheltered a digestive system as fragile as butterfly wings. Scowling, he walked to the kitchen and took the receiver from his wife.

"Hello. I won't say good morning. . . . What's up, Carl?" he asked. Carl Brenner was the special agent in charge of the New York FBI office.

"I hate to do this to you on Sunday morning," said Brenner, "but we need your help. I just got a call from the director."

"Okay. Fire."

"You've got a body at Bellevue," said Brenner. "Male, Negro, thirty-two. It looks like he was shot early this morning somewhere and his body dumped off at Orchard and Broome on the lower east side."

"All right."

"Here's our problem. His prints check him out to be one of our men. The name is Sprague, Delmar Sprague. I'd like to ask a couple of favors. First, I'd like you to order a copy of the autopsy report and then let me drop by your place and pick it up when it's ready. For reasons I'll explain I don't want to show myself at the morgue or send anybody from this office."

"Easy enough to handle. What else?"

"I want you to let us hold back the print report to your department for a few hours, maybe a day. His prints weren't found at your shop or in Albany, but we've got a positive ident on him in Washington. Sprague was on a special assignment. Deep cover. If the press got hold of the data right now, we'd be in trouble."

"But the loo in communications probably already has called the press," said Carnahan.

"I realize," said Brenner, "but the way it is, they've just got a dead Negro in old clothes. He could be anybody."

"I see. How important is this to the bureau?"

"Plenty."

"Okay. I'll play along."

"Then with your permission we'll put an answer on the teletype, saying we're having trouble with the print identification. That will hold things for a few hours. . . . Jim, thanks. That's one more we owe you."

"Forget it. Just don't call back until I finish breakfast."

But the phone rang again while Carnahan was forking up the first portion of scrambled eggs. It was Jesse Pedersen, the director of the FBI, calling from Washington.

"Good morning, Mr. Director," said Carnahan. "God, you guys are at it early today. Doesn't anybody go to Mass in your shop?"

"Can that 'Mr. Director' stuff, Jim," said Pedersen. "Hoover's long gone. The name is Jesse—as in James."

"Okay. I just had Brenner on the horn."

"I know," said Pedersen. "We appreciate the cooperation. Not that we haven't always had it. . . . Look, Jim, this one is extremely sensitive. We just can't let it get out that Sprague is—was—a bureau agent. What has to be done up there to keep the press off of it for a while? Say, until tonight or tomorrow morning?"

"Nothing," Carnahan replied. "As long as you hold back the print identification, I don't see what could develop. Laundry, dry-cleaning marks, that kind of thing, they all take time to check out, as you know. How well known around here was this agent?"

"Not very. He's out of our L.A. office. Never worked the East Coast until three, four months ago. I doubt if more than two or three of your officers know his face."

"Well, then, you're safe for a day anyway," said Carnahan. "I might add, though, that I'm not very happy about deceiving my own command. You know how *that* goes."

"I understand. That's why I wanted to add my personal thanks. Maybe we'll be able to let it go by tonight. I'll get back to you as soon as I can, Jim. I'll clue you in as fully as the attorney general allows."

"Okay, Jesse." But, thought Carnahan as he hung up, Pederson might clue him in and he might not. Working with the bureau was a two-way street, but the side leading to Washington always carried a lot heavier traffic than the return trip to the new fifteen-story police headquarters at Park Row.

A half hour later Director Jesse Pedersen pushed back from his desk in the large office of the new FBI Building on Washington's Pennsylvania Avenue. He was a small man, nervous and driven, who lived forever with the knowledge that he was no J. Edgar Hoover. Not that he wanted to be. He had tried to retain the bureau's reputation for efficiency and perseverance and at the same time shed the halo of righteous omniscience that shimmered over the director's office during Hoover's long tenancy. Pedersen liked to think that the caprices of the martinet were gone but that his agents still labored as diligently as ever under the stern code of the bureau. He hoped he struck the right note between Calvinistic discipline on the one hand and slovenly methods on the other. But he wasn't sure. . . . A murmuring breeze from the air-conditioning outlet rippled the folds of the American flag beside his desk. The layers of his in-out box were bare, but a half-dozen scribbled notes lay on the large green desk blotter. He tapped his teeth with a pencil as he concentrated.

This last call from Brenner was the fourth from the New York SAC that morning. Each had added a few more pieces to the puzzle. Brenner's own police informant at the morgue reported that Sprague's pockets held nothing of significance—thirty-seven cents in coins and a wallet with two twenties, a ten, and three ones in a hip pocket. The wallet held not a single card or identifying paper. The pants had no dry-cleaning mark. All the New York detectives had to work on were the laundry mark at the shirt collar and the brand names of the clothes, shoes, belt, and wallet. They'd be lucky to make any progress before tomorrow.

The autopsy was now in progress, but it would probably confirm the medical examiner's tentative opinion relayed to Brenner by his police informant—that Sprague had been shot twice in the back, one bullet entering the heart and proving instantly fatal. The condition of the body indicated Sprague had been killed around 4 A.M. Since there had been but little blood on the sidewalk, it was assumed the murder had occurred elsewhere than at Orchard and Broome.

Sprague's last call to the bureau duty agent in New York had been made at 3:03 A.M. Sunday from a pay phone in Harlem, a station about six miles from the spot where the body was found. And it was this call which had yielded the most intriguing information: Sprague's relay of six numbers which he had found. Each had ten digits. Sprague also added his own opinion: "They're probably phone numbers, assuming the first three digits in each series are area codes." Sprague ended his check-in abruptly. He thought he was being tailed and should leave the phone booth at once. He was scheduled to call in again at 5 A.M., but by that hour—according to the medical examiner's experienced guess—Special Agent Sprague was dead.

Pedersen referred again to his notes and nodded approvingly over the procedure that had been followed. New York turned over the series of numbers to the bureau in Washington. Don Gunckel, his top telephone specialist, had been roused from bed in suburban Virginia and was at his desk in the Pennsylvania Avenue building by 4:30 A.M. Gunckel, agreeing with Sprague's surmise, researched the numbers and prepared a list of names and addresses of phone subscribers whose telephone numbers matched those called in by Sprague. This took several hours, chiefly because it turned out that two of the numbers were unlisted. Locations were obtained only after Bell System officials gave sleepy permission to release names of the unlisted subscribers to the bureau. The six telephones were located in different area codes in widely scattered sections of the country. Interesting item: Each of the six subscribers was listed in *Who's Who in America.*

No effort had been made to call any of the numbers because of the early hour. Pedersen had reached his office at eight fifty-five, fifteen minutes after the news from the fingerprint division on Sprague's identity had been relayed to Pedersen's home. When Pedersen arrived, the numbers and Don Gunckel's explanatory report were among the papers on his desk.

Immediately after his talk with Commissioner Carnahan, Pedersen had ordered calls placed to each of the six telephone numbers. Now he awaited results.

His desk squawk box sounded its metallic drone. He pushed a button. "Yes, Bill."

"Gunckel's on the line, sir."

Pedersen picked up his intrabureau phone. "Okay, Don."

"We called all six numbers. Every one is out of order."

"All six?"

"Yes, sir."

Very odd, thought Pedersen. A few minutes before he's murdered by unknown assailants, Sprague relays six phone numbers. All belong to prominent persons. All are out of order. Considering Sprague's assignment and the whole background, this was an ominous development. The mathematical chances against pure coincidence were enormous. Now what? Pedersen pondered for a few moments.

"Okay, Don," he said. "Let's start a full rundown on each location, exactly where and what it is, everything we can find out about the places and their residents or owners. I'd like a preliminary progress report in an hour. Put as many men on it as you have to."

"Right."

Pedersen hung up and returned to the squawk box. "Bill, get Williams, Kaplan, and McCabe in here as soon as they can make it. . . . Alert the SACs of all offices in those six area codes. Have them stand by. . . . But first send for a pot of coffee."

"Yes, sir."

Pedersen shucked his suit coat, loosened his tie, and rolled his shirt sleeves to the elbows in neat folds. Sprague was the first special agent to be murdered during Pedersen's regime. He detested the very thought. Murder was so pervasive in its taint, spreading its canopy of guilt not alone to the murderer, but to the victim and his friends as well. A thin finger of censure pointed to the victim's family, his house, his friends, his business superiors, as though unexpected death were a shadow of infinite length and culpability.

Sprague had been a bachelor, but his unsought death was a rebuke to the bureau and especially to Pedersen, who had made his own arrangement with the agent. Pedersen's mind went back to the lengthy conference with Special Agent Delmar Sprague, the anguished black man. The session lasted four hours, the most intense, grueling, and thoroughly unsettling exchange with any bureau employee since Pedersen became director. In the end he had accepted Sprague's word. He had gambled—a better than even-money bet, he calculated. Now Sprague lay on a morgue slab. Had the gamble paid off for the bureau?

He pushed his squawk-box button again. "Oh, Bill. One more thing. Find out if the Attorney General's back from Martha's Vineyard. He was due in late last night. But wherever he is, have the number ready for me."

Director Pedersen sighed. It would be a long, thorny day. Where was that coffee?

Chapter Seven

At last he was calming himself. He slowly buttoned the top of his blue pajamas which had that fresh, slightly stiff feel of newly laundered fabric. He kicked off his leather slippers and pulled back the sheet and light summer blanket from the precise triangular fold. Sarah, the maid, always turned down the covers as though measuring with a huge pair of calipers. He arranged the two pillows lengthwise for his nightly reading nest, then turned on the bedside reading lamp. Ten minutes of T. H. White's *The Once and Future King* and then to sleep. He considered turning off the air conditioning. No. Much as he disliked the filtered, sapless air, the sodden weather outside the White House was worse.

With luck he should be asleep by midnight, if only he could corral that galloping herd in his mind. He knew all the symptoms: the exhilaration of new ideas thundering along, the quickened pulse, the goad of adventure, the impatience to act, the need to tell his friends, the horde of civil servants, the nation—everybody. This desire to move in a hurry was a failing, he knew, but he usually curbed himself and let prudence take its leavening course. In the meantime he enjoyed the ferment. In this stage he always thought in vivid pictures, like an always-panning camera, and emotion was the power behind the lens. Phil Randall was an emotional man.

Joe had warned him again, in that bantering tone, in the last phone call just a few minutes ago. "Sure, I agree," Joe had said. "But be careful, Phil. Why not put it on ice for a couple of weeks? Already you're going too fast for the boondocks. Don't get out ahead of the cities. A little throttle right now, please."

Of course he would apply throttle. He had to. He was the President, and a president had to balance every innovation against a hundred considerations. Yet, he knew

Joe was as caught up in this new idea as he was. Together they had undergone the most convulsive, yet invigorating, experience of their middle years. And their wives as well had been shaken like poplars in a storm. Helen Randall, the cautious one always reluctant to try the new, had been shattered at first. But this morning, just before she left with Kathy for the West Coast, she admitted she felt refreshed, like a young woman again. It was a kind of rebirth, she said.

Well, sure, he would put the idea on ice for a while. Still, he knew it made sense: personal ambassadors from the President, spreading the word and the feeling in small, electric groups, communicating to the whole nation his own grasp of this new emotional weapon, nothing less than a revolution in attitudes that could make America over.

All right, Philip Garland Randall, with your three-tier name like a doctor of divinity and your bubbling enthusiasms like those of a college boy, let's cool it. Fasten your mind on the book. Turn off the galloping herd. He fixed his eyes on the earmarked page and tried to lose himself in the clouded adventures of the Wart, Merlyn, and the Questing Beast. The Arthurian fantasy would soothe him. It was just right for the final minutes before midnight of this Sunday, July 8, the last of a long week-end he would never forget.

One telephone in the cluster of five instruments on his bedside table purred a discreet summons, so low that if he were asleep, he would not hear it. He ignored the sound for a few moments, but it persisted. He picked up the phone with a feeling of being put upon.

"Gertrude, Mr. President." His favorite night switchboard operator spoke as gently as the lap of small waves. "It's the Attorney General. I told him you had retired, but he insists on speaking to you."

"Please, Gertrude." He tried to smother his irritation. After 11 P.M., when the last of the appointment staff went off duty, Gertrude was his buffer. She always protected him at these hours, sensing the unseen line between the critical and the merely important. "Ask him to wait until morning. I'll take his call promptly at eight."

"Yes, sir."

But almost at once the purring renewed. This time he grabbed the phone. "Gertrude! I said no."

"I'm sorry, Mr. President," she said, "but he refuses to leave the line. He says it's the kind of emergency you'd fire him for if he failed to alert you at once."

Ah, Gertrude. The world is commanded by its lovely, skirted battalions of operators, secretaries, and receptionists. Still, he trusted her. Only twice before had she insisted on putting through such unwanted calls at midnight, and both times her intuition was justified.

"All right. Put him on."

"My apologies, Mr. President." Attorney General Frank Garrity was stubbornly brisk despite the disclaimer. "I'm sorry, sir, but this won't wait. It's imperative that Jesse Pedersen and I see you at once."

"See me? Why can't we talk it over right now and then meet in the morning if we have to?"

"There's something you must see for yourself," said Garrity. "And I know you'll want the kind of give-and-take we can't have without a face-to-face meeting. Frankly, sir, this involves a direct threat to the national security. Even an hour or two may make a difference."

President Randall considered. Frank Garrity seldom ran ahead of his ticket. He might be a bit wearying, but he was a solid, painstaking young man, slow to alarm and actually more hesitant than most cabinet members about intruding on the President's time. If Garrity said a threat to security, he meant it. And Randall's curiosity was piqued. What was so vital as to demand a meeting at midnight?

"All right, Frank. Come up to the Treaty Room."

President Randall replaced the book on the night table, threw back the covers, put on his slippers again, and took his light bathrobe from a hook in the clothes closet. What the hell was bugging the Justice Department and the FBI in the middle of the night? Neither Frank Garrity nor Jesse Pedersen was exactly his dish of tea. Both men were thorough and meticulous—and unimaginative and humorless. Of the last two traits the lack of humor annoyed him the most. He had yet to recall a problem that owed its solution to a long face. Try as he might to lighten this ponderous federal bureaucracy by continual needling, its

visage remained as gray and as uninspired as ever. Oh,
well. . . . His mental picture of the visitors made him re-
consider his clothing. He reluctantly took off his bathrobe
and pajamas and changed into his lounging attire, a beige
terry-cloth sport shirt and dark blue slacks. But he wore
his loafers without socks, a peep of protest.

He walked to the thick, paneled mahogany door and
spoke to the Secret Service agent on duty in the great
corridor which, at this west end of the White House second floor, served as the family sitting room.

"Attorney General Garrity and Director Pedersen are
coming up," he said. "Knowing Pedersen, I guess that
calls for coffee. We'll be in the Treaty Room."

The three men assembled nine minutes later beneath
the grossly ornate chandelier in the green papered and
carpeted room that had been the scene of presidential
conferences since Andrew Johnson met his Cabinet here
more than a century before. Randall, by now a strategist
in these matters, ignored the lion-footed cabinet table and
its primly placed chairs. Instead he seated his callers on
the ancient sofa, a forbidding piece of Victorian furniture
whose designer had neglected the needs of the human
backbone. Visitors relegated to the sofa seldom extended
their stays longer than necessary. Randall himself took a
venerable cane-backed swivel chair, a relic fancied by the
White House curator as representative of nineteenth-cen-
tury *décor*. Randall faced the two high windows. In the
distance, beyond the fountain of the President's Park and
the Ellipse, he could see the lighted dome of the Jefferson
Memorial.

At once the invisible links among the three men began
vibrating with the attitudes of each man toward his fellows. For his part, Randall regarded his two chief law
men as rather drab obstacles in a course yet to be run.
They epitomized his bonds with the old politics which he
tried so desperately to break. It was less a question of
substance than of style. Their presence was vaguely oppressive, so different from the ebullience he felt after the
profoundly revealing encounter session which his daughter Kathy had brought to the White House.

Pedersen, sitting self-consciously and uncomfortably
erect on the sofa, felt himself unfairly imprisoned between

two symbols of authority, both superior to him by statute and by custom, yet oddly inferior in fact. He was a professional bracketed by a couple of amateurs.

As for Frank Garrity, who sat holding a manila folder, he felt aggrieved that Pedersen had allowed the bureau to be stained by murder, a most unfortunate homicide that now somehow had contaminated the entire Justice Department, Garrity's domain. . . . And Garrity's attitude toward his President was distinctly ambivalent. In theory he might admire Randall's unorthodox interests, his zest for a new candor with the people, and his enthusiasms, yet Garrity instinctively recoiled from the excesses these very traits implied. This sunny, swinging, forty-seven-year-old President was going much too swiftly for the country, whatever the national mood might have been a few months ago. This new politics might be fine in principle, but in practice it was beginning to make many Americans uneasy. In a word Attorney General Garrity distrusted his President.

The night-duty butler placed the silver coffee service unobtrusively on the long cabinet table and faded from the room.

"That's for you, Jesse," said Randall. "I won't need any. I assume you two bloodhounds have picked up some scent that'll keep me awake most of the night anyway."

Garrity bridled. The President had a way of minimizing a problem before it was stated. Garrity shook his head at Pedersen's offer of coffee. The FBI director stepped to the table and poured a single cup for himself, then returned to the sofa and balanced cup and saucer on his knee.

"Okay," said Randall. "Let's have the bad news."

"We're damned worried," said Frank Garrity, dropping the words like heavy weights. He was the youngest of the Cabinet but the oldest in demeanor, a lean, intense man with a Boston Irish accent and a pink face. "I think Jesse ought to tell the story right from the beginning."

Pedersen put his coffee cup down on the carpet with an awkward clatter. He leaned forward with his elbows on his knees. He was never at ease in these rare meetings with the highest authority.

"Why don't you loosen your tie, Jessie?" invited Randall. "You look like you're choking."

Pedersen undid his top shirt button but failed to loosen the tie, the gingerly gesture of the guest whose hostess has invited him to pick up the chicken leg with his fingers.

"Mr. President," he said, "early this morning one of our best Negro special agents was murdered in New York City. He was shot twice in the back and apparently he died at once. This agent—his name was Delmar Sprague —was on a classified assignment. He had infiltrated the guerrilla organization known as Blacks of February Twenty-first, the outfit named to commemorate the day Malcolm X was assassinated."

"I know the background of the B.O.F.," said Randall impatiently. "But what do you mean, 'infiltrated'? You mean he was spying on the B.O.F.?"

"He was reporting on B.O.F. plans and moves, yes, sir."

"But that's against my orders." Randall, flaring, looked from Pedersen to Garrity. "You know of my meeting with black leaders in March. I gave my word there would be no federal surveillance of black organizations. The only exception was when and if we had a clear suspicion of subversive activity—and then only under direct authorization by me. I didn't give any such orders."

"I know that," said Pedersen. Color rose in his thin, gray cheeks. "We withdrew our agents in March, Mr. President, but this was a highly unusual case. . . ."

"But I gave my word," insisted Randall.

"I'll take the blame," cut in Garrity, "but I wish you'd hear Jesse out. I think you'll see we had no alternative."

"All right. Go ahead." The President folded his arms, a barricade to his dissatisfaction, and faced Pedersen.

"Unknown to us," said Pedersen, "Agent Sprague secretly joined the Blacks of February Twenty-first early this spring—in clear violation of bureau regulations. He agreed to supply B.O.F. leaders with information from inside the bureau. In effect he became an informer against the government, breaking his oath of office." Pedersen nervously rubbed his palms. This whole seamy business was a reflection on his bureau. Betrayal, double-dealing, murder. He felt like a man being prodded into the confessional against his will. "Then, last Tuesday, he came in to see me—sent by Carl Brenner, our SAC in New York. Sprague was very agitated. He confessed his secret membership in the B.O.F., saying frankly that his allegiance to his race had won out over his oath of office. He admitted giving the B.O.F. information about the bureau. . . . Fortunately the material wasn't too significant, mostly procedural stuff. . . . Anyway he'd now had a change of heart. One reason was that the previous week he learned that a shipment of arms was put ashore secretly on the North Carolina coast. Handguns, machine guns, rifles, a few small rocket launchers, all in all a fair-sized consignment. The arms were rowed ashore from a small African tramp steamer— Guinea registry, we believe—by B.O.F. men. Then private autos distributed the arms around the country to units of the Blacks of February Twenty-first. Sprague also learned there had been two prior shipments, both, of course, in violation of the import laws and federal gun-control and registration statutes."

Pedersen eyed the President, fearful of another interruption, then hurried on. "Sprague picked up reliable word that these three arms shipments were in preparation for some major move for the July fourth period when a lot of people would be on the long five-day week-end. I gather Sprague had a tussle with his conscience. On the one side there were the loyalties to his people. On the other, I assume, there was his feeling for the bureau and his agent friends, as well as concern for the country. I'm just not sure what went on in his mind." Pedersen gestured with open palms, a confession of helplessness before the mysteries of the human brain. "In the end it was the guns that decided him. He feared an outbreak of civil war, and he knew that might mean a massacre of his fellow blacks. So he went to Brenner and told all about his B.O.F. membership. Of course Sprague fully expected to be fired, at the least, or tried under some statute or other."

Pedersen hesitated, fingering his knuckles. "My meeting with Sprague was a long one, Mr. President. I questioned him thoroughly, trying to evaluate his state of mind. . . . Well, to cut it short, I decided to gamble on him. I proposed that he continue inside the B.O.F., only now he would report everything he heard to Brenner. Sprague finally agreed—reluctantly, I'm sure—but nevertheless without qualification. I have no reason to doubt his subsequent loyalty to the bureau. His reports proved his good faith, to say nothing of his sudden death. Now, just before—"

"But why wasn't this cleared with me?" broke in Randall. "This means I've broken my word to the black leaders. Whether I would have okayed the assignment—and I assume I would have—is beside the point."

"If there's a fault, it's mine," said Frank Garrity. "You see, Mr. President, Jesse took this up with me at once. I immediately phoned for an appointment with you, but your staff said it wouldn't be possible until Monday."

"I did tell them to keep me free over the Fourth," said Randall. He thought fleetingly of Kathy, of the promising new project. Now he had a premonition that Pedersen's story would torpedo the venture. This B.O.F. business had an ugly look. "But you could have insisted. After all, you did tonight."

"That's true," said Garrity, "but then we had nothing solid to go on. And frankly, unlike Jesse, I was skeptical of Sprague and his arms story. I thought we might test him a bit before making a major case with you. At any rate, I acted on my own authority in approving Jesse's course. If you said 'no' when I did get through to you, the deal could have been ended at once. . . . But now, I'm afraid, we're in real trouble." He looked at Pedersen. "Tell him, Jesse."

"Well," said Pedersen, "Sprague called Brenner at home about midnight last night. He told him the big move he'd heard about was under way. He wasn't sure what it was, but he was convinced it involved some widespread guerrilla action with plenty of arms of all types. Sprague said he was trying to find out. An hour later, at 1 A.M. Sunday, Sprague reported in that top leaders of the B.O.F. apparently had vanished from Harlem. The organization's most recent headquarters—the B.O.F. changed locations from time to time—was in a third-story apartment in an old building on East 127th Street.

Sprague found that it had been abandoned. The head-quarters watchman was an elderly Negro who lived across the hall. The old man knew Sprague by sight and thought him to be one of the B.O.F. officers. So Sprague got the key from him and made a search.

"Sprague's last call was made from a phone booth some distance away, near 108th Street. It was logged at 3:03 A.M. Sprague at that time reported on his search. He said he found the B.O.F. quarters pretty well stripped except for an old, battered typewriter, a few pencils, some posters, that kind of thing. But he did find a few notes on scraps of paper in a couple of desk drawers. Rather than disturb anything, in case any of the B.O.F. leaders returned, Sprague made copies of the notes. There were some scribbled names of B.O.F. members and a couple of addresses of B.O.F. units outside New York, all of which we already had. But one piece of paper did contain information that proved to be interesting. Written down was a list of six numbers, each of ten digits. In his call at 3:03 A.M. Sprague read off the list and said it looked to him like it might be telephone numbers. So did we. We—"

"Just a minute," cut in Randall. "When was Sprague killed?"

"We're not sure," said Pedersen. "Probably an hour or so after that last call at 3:03. Sprague cut that report short, telling the duty agent that he believed he was being tailed. The body was found just before 7 A.M. at Orchard and Broome in lower Manhattan. We think he was killed elsewhere, probably uptown, and his body taken down there by car."

"Were those notes he made found on his body?" asked Randall.

"No, sir," replied Pedersen. "We assumed Sprague destroyed his notes immediately after the call. Very little was found in the body's clothing. A wallet and some money, that was about all. No cards, identification, or writing of any kind. Sprague's identity was established through his fingerprints."

Pedersen described his conversation with Commissioner Carnahan. "So New York police are still unaware that they have an FBI agent's body in their morgue. . . . Of course, Mr. President, we think Sprague was killed by

B.O.F. members who discovered, or suspected, his double-agent role."

"The main thing right now," interposed Garrity, "is the bureau's rundown on those numbers Sprague turned in."

The Attorney General removed a sheet of paper from his manila folder and handed it to the President.

"The bureau, agreeing with Sprague, went on the assumption that the list was one of telephone numbers," said Garrity. "That has proved to be correct, as you'll see."

Randall glanced through the single-spaced, typewritten memorandum, then returned to the first line and read slowly:

(602) 844 3538. Out of order. Cattle ranch forty-seven miles from Flagstaff, Arizona. Owner, State Senator Arthur P. Broderick. Former state chairman, Randall-for-President Committee. Married. Three children. Family maid in Flagstaff residence reports whole family, plus two domestics, at ranch since July third.

(315) 975 2437. Out of order. Summer lodge on small Angell Island in St. Lawrence River near Alexandria Bay, New York. Owner, William O. Dittmar, president, Empire Motors, Detroit. Member President's Commission on Black Capital Investments. Married. Two children, aged seven and twelve, by second wife. Family reported weekending at lodge from Grosse Pointe, Michigan, residence.

(904) 959 5632. Out of order. Residence about fifty miles southeast of Tallahassee, near Shady Grove, Florida. Owner, Charles T. Delaney, retired. Consultant on industrial development to governor of Florida. Father of Michael Delaney of White House staff. Married. Divorced daughter with two children, aged three and eight, also living on premises. Two domestics.

(609) 936 8660. Out of order. Large estate, Fairhill, just north of Princeton, New Jersey. Owner, Timothy R. Crawford, Jr., New York lawyer, Brainerd, Fullerton & Crawford. Member President's Commission on Corporate Law Revision. Married. Two children, four and five. Family in residence.

(209) 555 3577. Out of order. Mountain lodge near

Silver Lake, California, about twenty-five miles south of the southern end of Lake Tahoe. Owner, Fritz D. Tiegert, president Brotherhood of Truckers & Haulers. Headed Truckers' drive supporting Randall for President. Tiegert and family, including two daughters and six grandchildren, aged six through twelve, spending month of July at lodge. Two domestics.

(802) 711 4623. Out of order. Lake Champlain summer home seventeen miles north of Burlington, Vermont. Owner, Jacob A. Shapiro, playwright. Speech writer for President Randall. Married. Four young children. Family on premises. One domestic.

"Now, the thing is, Mr. President," said Pedersen when Randall finished reading, "there is a clear pattern to these six locations. Each is a private residence. Five of the six are located in fairly isolated areas. The owner in each case is an influential man who is in some way connected with your administration. All of the homes are being used by the owners at this moment—and all have children on the premises."

Randall's expression was a puzzled one, and Pedersen continued: "The bureau called each of these numbers. All phones were reported out of order and—"

"You're making what point exactly?" Randall broke in. He looked at Pedersen and Garrity in turn.

"May I, Jesse?" asked Garrity. The FBI director nodded.

"Mr. President," said Garrity, "we are convinced that each of these homes has been seized by the Blacks of February Twenty-first, the telephone lines severed, and the resident families held captive."

The thought did not sink in at once. Randall frowned. He looked at the two men in bewilderment. "But that's fantastic." His bright new visions were scattering like birds before a gale. "How can you be sure? What's the evidence?"

"I'm coming to that," said Pedersen. In the apology of his tone could be detected the thin alloy of self-vindication. "I was taking it step by step so you could get a feel of the bureau's procedure."

When the President did not reply, Pedersen continued

at a swifter pace: "First, we at once faced the possibility that this might be a coordinated, planned, nationwide move by the B.O.F. We had Sprague's reports of the arms shipments, the plans for July fourth, the disappearance of B.O.F. leaders from Harlem, the numbers. But in addition Sprague provided us with a key tip. Yesterday Sprague reported to Brenner that B.O.F. leaders he was in contact with talked as though Daniel Smith, the exiled national commander, was back on American soil somewhere. Although Sprague did not see Smith, or definitely confirm that he had returned, he did think Smith was in this country. Then from other sources early this afternoon we heard that Smith and a band of men had gone to an isolated region of the Great Smoky Mountains and were heading up operations via a clandestine radio. Smith was born and brought up in Raleigh, and our file shows he made a good many trips to the western mountains as a youth.

"So we alerted the monitoring system of the Federal Communications Commission, and in midafternoon the FCC monitors picked up an unlicensed broadcaster sending from the vicinity of Mt. Mitchell in North Carolina. This station is using the code name 'Lion,' and it has had exchanges with four unlicensed rigs operating somewhere near four of the seized homes. The FCC people have run two voice prints on this so-called Lion and they're convinced, beyond reasonable doubt, that 'Lion' is Daniel Smith. As you know, before his self-exile Smith did considerable talking on radio and TV. Right at this moment the monitors are making progress toward exact pinpointing of 'Lion's' station and also those he'd had short conversations with. In brief we have no doubt that the B.O.F. campaign, whatever its ultimate intent, is being personally directed by Smith."

Pedersen paused for a moment, and Randall asked: "What about the homes? What have you found out about them?"

"Yes." Pedersen took a sheaf of notes from his jacket pocket. "Starting with the property nearest to Washington, the Crawford home in New Jersey, a bureau agent from our Trenton office drove into the property. Mr. Timothy Crawford, obviously distracted, met the agent in the driveway—"

"I know Tim Crawford," interjected Randall. "I named him to the group studying revision of corporate law."

"Yes." Pedersen nodded. Amateurs had to be indulged. A professional would have remembered the corporate-law reference in the bureau memorandum. "Well, our agent tried a number of devices to gain access to the house, but Crawford wouldn't even give him a glass of water. He seemed determined to get our man out of there in a hurry. . . . About two hours ago our Trenton office reported in again. The agent returned to the far side of the Crawford property, a wooded area, with an infrared telescope for night vision. He saw two Negroes in turtle-neck sweaters behind the house. One carried a rifle. They appeared to be standing guard duty."

Randall was all attention now. He had slid down in the old swivel chair, but his face had tightened in concentration.

Garrity watched the President as Pedersen talked. The ruddy, unlined face, usually alive with some new idea, was serious now, and Garrity realized, with a start, that he could not recall a conference with Randall which had been unrelievedly somber. Randall seemed to regard solemnity as the refuge of small minds. The President relished the quip, the tart remark, the urbane view of human failings. And, thought Garrity with a twinge of envy, Randall had been lucky, very, very lucky. Not a single major crisis had cracked the spangled facade of this President's regime since the inauguration almost six months ago.

These had been months of euphoria for Randall as he sailed blithely ahead under the fluttering pennants of "the new politics." Teen-agers adored him. Young women, with long hair falling over their guitars, sang ballads in his honor. The college crowd, captivated from the start by Randall's bantering, slightly patronizing attitude toward the commercial and social establishments, cheered when their President returned from a spring fishing trip off Florida with long, handsome sideburns. The strips of fa-cial hair stretched clear to the jawbones, and in hair-con-scious America they became immediate symbols of the political change in Washington. Cartoonists, photographers, commentators, and editorial writers played with the theme for days. Randall joked about hair at his news conference. Comedians squeezed the satire dry. It was all very jolly and lighthearted, but Garrity, who had been reared in the highly personal nuances of Boston politics, began to detect a subtle change in national mood. Older voters were puzzled by the long sideburns. Conservatives, leery of Randall from the beginning, now began to make mordant remarks. The jokes among the great white middle class in suburbia took on a sharp, querulous edge. After all, hair on the male face was a vogue of the blacks, the young, the disaffected, the artistic and entertainment worlds. Of course it was not just the sideburns. It was the fact that Randall seemed as eager to challenge his older countrymen's ingrained political and social attitudes as their styles in hair. He seemed to be saying to the majority of white adult Americans: "Look, I'm not really one of you. I'm for change. You aren't. Get with it, squares."

Garrity sensed that for all their kidding, many Americans subconsciously felt betrayed. They had gone to the polls, as always, to elect a national father. True, they had picked the younger and the more carefree of the two major candidates, but they assumed his insouciance cloaked the usual solid, reliable qualities of the father tradition. Now Randall was being revealed as less the parental figure than the young swinger next door. Suburbia might not be fully aware of it yet, but its faith in Randall was being shaken. Something, Garrity had surmised, was due to explode—something that would blow Randall right off his glory perch atop the public-opinion polls. Perhaps here, in the staid old Treaty Room, Garrity was feeling the first quivers of that upheaval.

Pedersen had digressed into an explanation of FBI methods, but a look of impatience on Randall's face fetched him back to his narrative.

"In the case of the Arizona ranch near Flagstaff," said Pedersen, "we had a flyover in a chartered plane at dusk, or about an hour ago our time. Our men observed a handkerchief being waved out an upper window. Two Negroes were clearly seen near the stable. They also wore black turtleneck sweaters, the standard garb of the B.O.F.

As the plane passed to the north, one agent aboard reports that he saw one of the Negroes run toward the ranch house."

Pedersen paused to study his notes for a moment. "Yes, that's right. With respect to the St. Lawrence River island where Dittmar of Empire Motors has his summer place: Two agents out of our Rochester office flew to Watertown this noon. While no contact has been made with the Dittmar family yet—our men are awaiting orders from Washington—the agents report that a party of black men, unknown in that area, was seen to put two outboards in the river yesterday. This was at a point several miles downstream from Alexandria Bay and not far from Angell Island where Mr. Dittmar has his place. Thought to be five Negro men, all young. The two Dittmar children, who cross in an outboard each morning for the daily papers, did not show up on the mainland today. Nor did the Dittmar family attend church in Alexandria Bay. The Dittmars are regular churchgoers."

"Bill called me two weeks ago," mused Randall. "Crusty old guy, but honest. He levels."

Pedersen gratefully took advantage of the interruption to pour himself a new cup of coffee. The others declined his offer. "Well, as for the Delaney home in north Florida, our agents out of Jacksonville found two heavy logs thrown across the narrow macadam drive which leads from the country road to the house. When they tried to walk to the house, about a half mile away through thick pines, they were stopped by a young Negro who called himself the caretaker. He said the family was not there and he had orders not to let any strangers in. . . . Of course, Mr. President, in this preliminary investigation all our agents were instructed not to identify themselves or to make forced entries. And none of them had search warrants. . . . So the Jacksonville agents returned to their car. However, inquiry made among neighbors disclosed that Delaney, his daughter, and two grandchildren were definitely on the premises as of yesterday. Furthermore, the actual Delaney caretaker is not a Negro. He's an elderly white man."

Pedersen shuffled his notes, sipped at his coffee. "We have no information in yet on the Tiegert mountain lodge near Lake Tahoe. Agents out of San Francisco are expected to report soon. . . . But as for the summer home of Jacob Shapiro, the playwright, on Lake Champlain, there is no doubt in our mind that the residence is being held by black invaders. A bureau agent rented an outboard and tied up at the Shapiro dock in midafternoon. A young black man, again in a black turtleneck sweater and wearing some kind of silver medallion, was seated on the dock. He said he was a house guest of the Shapiros and that the family, including the four young children, had driven in to Burlington and would not return until after dark. The Negro was pleasant enough, but when the agent said he was a friend of Shapiro too and that he would wait, the Negro said he was sorry but he'd have to move on. No reason given. As the agent left in the outboard, and just before he rounded a point which shields the house, two small children came out on the porch in the company of a black man."

Pedersen made a neat little pack of his notes. "There are some other corroborating details, Mr. President," he said with a touch of professional pride. "On the basis of the preliminary inquiry we think the evidence strongly indicates that at least five of these six homes have been seized by armed members of the B.O.F. and the families held prisoner under orders of Commander Dan Smith."

"I'll go further, Mr. President," said Garrity. "I'm certain of it."

"Of course," observed Pedersen, "we owe an enormous debt to Special Agent Sprague. If it hadn't been for his list of numbers, I don't know how many hours, or even days, might have passed before we got a handle on the situation."

"But the motive?" asked Randall. "What could the motive be? Are these families being held as hostages against some national demands? Ransom? After all, mere seizure of property accomplishes nothing by itself, since the B.O.F. couldn't possibly expect to hold on indefinitely by force."

"We have no clues at all," said Garrity. "Of course Jesse and I have speculated. There are a number of possibilities."

"In totals," said Pedersen, referring to his notes, "we

believe these seizures involve about 40 captives or hostages, including a number of domestics and, we think, nineteen children."

"And the owners are all well heeled and well known," added Garrity. The political implication did not have to be stressed. "Two of them, Dittmar of Empire Motors and Tiegert of the Truckers, are household names to millions."

Randall nodded. He could envision the tumult on Wall Street and in the great corporate canyons when it became known that an industrialist and a labor boss were held prisoner in their own homes by blacks. "I know all six men," he said. "As you pointed out, each of them has some link with my administration. Now what do you suppose that means?"

Garrity shook his head. "My guess is that the B.O.F. will show its hand soon, undoubtedly through Dan Smith. The prophet will speak from the mountains."

"But what exactly does it all mean? I wonder." Randall arose and walked toward the long windows. The glow of the Jefferson Memorial could be seen in the distance. Nearer, the driveway globes on the back lawn glimmered dully in the night haze. What a sorry ending for his project. He had promised his daughter Kathy. Right now, out in Palo Alto, she was probably chatting along with her mother, speculating on when her father would act. But what could he tell the country now of his own profound experience? How could he dare challenge national racial attitudes now—when homes had been seized by armed blacks?

One thing he knew. Whatever steps needed to be taken to counter this B.O.F. venture, he must discuss the matter first with Joe Voorhees. With Joe he could think aloud, bat his ideas against the wall of Joe's candid judgment, plan in an atmosphere of relaxed confidence.

He walked to the end table near the sofa and picked up the phone. He carried the instrument, trailing its long extension cord, outside of earshot of Pedersen and Garrity.

"Gertrude," he said softly, "get Joe Voorhees out of bed and have him come upstairs as soon as he can make it. Tell him to wait for me in the Oval Room."

"Yes, sir," she said. "And there's a call here just now

from Mr. Pedersen's office with an urgent for him." She spoke in a voice of rustling waters. Randall assumed that if New York suddenly were vaporized by a hydrogen warhead, Gertrude would relay the news in a tone of solicitude for his peace of mind.

Randall carried the phone to Pedersen. The director listened for a full minute before hanging up.

"We've just heard from the Tiegert property in California," he said. He appeared to flinch as he eyed the President. The courier of bad news must always fear for his skin. "This is a new wrinkle. The gate to the property is closed and locked. In some bushes along the fence agents found the body of Tiegert's black Labrador watchdog—knifed in the throat and chest. It appears certain that the B.O.F. holds the property at gunpoint. The Tiegerts have only one Negro domestic, but the agents saw three black men in the distance near the lodge."

Randall paced the room as Pedersen talked. Garrity wondered at the scene: a sockless President in terry-cloth sport shirt and blue slacks, hardly an appropriate costume for decisions of state. Again Garrity had that curious feeling of disgust. What was passing through that handsome head, that mercurial mind, this time? The President paced about with his hands in his pants pockets, glanced at a portrait of President Ulysses S. Grant without really seeing it.

"I must say the bureau put in a long day's work today," Randall remarked tartly. His listeners caught the implied rebuke: hours of investigative spadework on a critical matter without notifying the President.

"We didn't think we should come to you unless we had really hard evidence," said Garrity. It was impossible to break even with the White House: A man spoke either too soon or too late. "The whole thing seemed incredible at the start—to both of us. I didn't want to bother you on the basis of rumor and half-clues, and then have our theory evaporate when some perfectly logical explanation came up."

"You mean you didn't want to chance looking the fool." Randall's smile was a thin one.

"That's partially it, of course. But also I felt it would

be irresponsible to burden you until we were sure of our ground."

"And now, Frank?" Randall halted in front of the Attorney General. "What's your recommendation?"

"We have a number of courses open." Garrity patently was prepared for this moment. "One is to place sizable squads of bureau agents on each property with search warrants and, of course, the necessary arms for protection. We can go ahead under the statutes that give us wide powers to investigate the killing of a federal agent—also those involving broadcasting without a federal license. . . . Another plan is to inform the governors of the six states involved and let them take over via state and local police."

"I wonder," said Randall. "I'll grant that your theory seems to be a good one, but actually, when you analyze it, we have nothing but a chain of circumstantial evidence."

"True, but it's a damn strong chain. Looking at the whole background, I can't regard this as anything but critical." Garrity studied the President's face for reactions. "You know our reports on the Blacks of February Twenty-first. There was a struggle for leadership between those who wanted to fight for black dominance of the country and those who wanted to overthrow the whole system. With the solidifying of Dan Smith's control, the revolutionaries got the upper hand. Smith believes, as he has said publicly, that this society is rotten, corrupt, and doomed. You know his creed: Not until American 'colonial' institutions are destroyed will black power have any meaning. He's for revolution now. What comes after, he'll worry about later—although some experts think that Smith secretly favors a separate black nation."

"But we're not dead sure that Smith is running this show," said Randall.

"I am," replied Garrity. "There is hard evidence of Smith giving radioed orders to four of the six seized properties. My hunch is he'll surface somewhere tomorrow with a statement that will enflame the black population."

Randall turned to Pedersen. "What's your estimate, Jesse?"

"There's no doubt about Smith's leadership. Those voice prints prove it. Voice prints today are as reliable as

fingerprints. And I'm convinced Smith's real aim is revolution." Pedersen hesitated. "On the other hand, from
what Sprague told me in our long talk, I'm inclined to
think there are still some leaders around Smith who are
not committed to an all-out uprising. What the precise
situation is at this moment, I can only guess."

The three men were silent for a moment as Randall
continued to walk about the room.

"Look, Mr. President," said Garrity. "I think it's pretty
obvious we're sitting on dynamite. At the least, we've got
a guerrilla outfit, nationally organized, seizing the homes
of six prominent citizens. At the most, we've got the stage
set for black revolution. I think what we ought to do right
now is prepare ourselves—be ready to move in any of
several directions as early as, well, daylight."

"You mean with force?" asked Randall.

"Yes, sir. Or the threat of it certainly."

"Do you agree, Jesse?" asked Randall.

"I do. Whatever the B.O.F.'s objective, these seizures
obviously were planned with great care. I think we'd better do some quick, detailed planning of our own."

Randall walked slowly to the windows again, stood for
a moment gazing into the night and toward the distant
glow of the Jefferson Memorial. When he turned, he
spoke in a quiet, matter-of-fact tone.

"I agree it looks bad," he said. "Let me kick this
around for a while. I'll let you know in an hour or so. . . .
In the meantime you can keep tabs on developments over
at your place. Don't hesitate to call, especially if there's
some new word on Smith. Okay?"

The two law men nodded. They exchanged a few words
of leave-taking before Randall opened the door and
beckoned to a Secret Service agent on station in the hall.
The agent escorted the late callers across the wide, silent
hall to the private elevator.

When the elevator door closed, Randall spoke to the
agent: "When Joe Voorhees arrives, Steve, bring him to
the Oval Room."

The Oval Room was the most cheerful on the second
floor, a medley of yellows as bright as sunlight, a reminder of the Camelot days of Jack Kennedy. For some
reason, thought Randall, the Oval Room and Kennedy

belonged to the living. The tomblike Treaty Room belonged to the dead. Besides there wasn't a comfortable chair in the place.

Joe Voorhees entered five minutes later. He was made for the sunny *décor* of the Oval Room, thought Randall as he greeted his friend. Joseph W. Voorhees was an immense, brash, jaunty man whose girth indicated his disdain for exercise and his fondness for the good life. Voorhees was the Postmaster General. He held the cabinet post not because of expertise in the complexities of the creaking postal service, but because he was the President's best friend and Randall did not quite know where else to put him. Thus far Voorhees had spent more time in the White House swimming pool than he had slaving over the mail sacks.

Right now he looked like an unmade bed, and it was apparent that he had heeded Gertrude's orders to come to the White House without delay. He wore an open sport shirt, unshaven whiskers darkened his jowls, and sweat glistened in the folds of his neck. Voorhees was usually damp with the exertion of carrying two hundred and fifty pounds of flesh.

"What's our problem, Phil?" asked Voorhees after the opening pleasantries had been dispensed with. Voorhees always first-named his friend in private, never in public— and "public" meant the addition of any third person, even if that person was Helen or Kathy Randall.

"This is a weird one," said Randall. "It'll take time. Make yourself comfortable."

They each occupied an end of the sofa, slipcovered in yellow, which rested at right angles to the marble fireplace and the surmounting portrait of George Washington. They faced toward the three high windows, framed by rich, golden drapes, overlooking the back lawn and the dimpled night beyond.

Randall talked for more than twenty minutes with only an occasional interruption by Voorhees. When he concluded, Voorhees spent another five minutes studying the list of homes which Pedersen had left with the President.

"So the question is, what do you do now?" asked Voorhees.

"Right."

"Let me ask something, Phil." Voorhees had been bur-rowed in a corner of the sofa, facing the high windows. Now he turned to his friend. "What's your instinct? What would you have been inclined to do if you hadn't called me?"

"My instinct?" Randall tilted his head as he thought. "Why, sleep on it, I guess. Get five or six hours' good sleep and then look at it again in the morning."

"Sound enough." Voorhees made a triangle of his fingers on his great belly and studied the pattern for a moment. "Except in this case. I think delay might be dangerous."

"Dangerous?"

"Yes," said Voorhees, "not dangerous in fact maybe, but dangerous politically—the way it might look after-ward."

"Do you mind explaining, Joe? I don't follow."

"Look at it this way," said Voorhees slowly. "We real-ly have no idea what's on this Dan Smith's mind. But from what we know of the guy, he's unpredictable, a man of visions, liable to do anything. And his following is enormous. A lot of blacks believe in his horoscope. He's got a good sign, as they put it. . . . Hell, Smith could call for revolution right this minute while we're sitting here."

"I don't think that's likely."

"Neither do I," agreed Voorhees. "But it's possible. Now suppose he does move before dawn? You're asleep and so are all your top advisers. You've been tipped off, but you haven't done a thing. . . . Now, I ask you. How's that going to look to the public?"

"But who would know until somebody gets around to writing history years from now?" countered Randall. "And then it wouldn't matter."

Voorhees laughed, a single, dry, sardonic grunt. "You think so? Then you don't know Pedersen and Garrity. Hell, they'd have the word out on the press grapevine in no time. Pedersen especially. Don't forget, you're a tem-porary officeholder, but Pedersen figures to be running the bureau for a long, long time. And you won't catch Pedersen being saddled with a bad public image. No, sir. He'd let it be known that the bureau urged immediate action, but the President dawdled around, sleeping on it, et cetera."

"So you think I ought to do something right now?"

"Not 'do' necessarily," said Voorhees, "but at least act like you're acting. Call a conference at once. Get it on the record that you didn't delay a single hour after being alerted. Then nobody can claim that Randall and his Hessians slept while ol' George crossed the Delaware in the middle of the night." He looked up at the portrait.

"I'd hardly call Dan Smith another George Washington," said Randall.

"He is to a lot of blacks. Anyway you know what I mean. You've got two problems. One, what to do, and two, how it looks politically. You may stub your toe on number one, but there's no damn reason to fail on number two."

"You're a cynical bastard, Joe."

"Sure, I am, but that's part of the reason you hauled me up here in the middle of the night, isn't it? You want it straight, not a lot of craperoo."

Randall considered for a few moments. "And who should we have at this"—he glanced at his wristwatch— "at this 2 A.M. session?"

"You've got to have Garrity and Pedersen, naturally," said Voorhees. "Then you and me. That makes four. And since this is a black deal, you have to have Hal Osborne." Harold Osborne was Secretary of Transportation, one of the two Negroes in the Cabinet. Osborne also functioned as Randall's chief adviser on race problems. "Not that you shouldn't have him. You should. Hal knows the score. He's got antennae out in every ghetto."

"Ed Lee?" asked Randall. Edward J. Lee was the scholarly but curt, and somewhat discomforting, Secretary of the Treasury.

"Yes, Lee. If something big breaks, it's bound to affect the money markets abroad. And Lee keeps insisting the dollar is sicker than we think." He shrugged. Lee reminded him of sandpaper on tender skin. "You've got to include Lee."

"Who else?"

"Hildebrand and Edelstein." General Walter Hilde-

brand was Chairman of the Joint Chiefs of Staff and Paul
Edelstein was the Secretary of Defense.

"Hildebrand and Edelstein!" The names startled the
President. "Are you thinking about federal troops?"

"Of course," said Voorhees. "I don't mean you'll have
to use them, but you ought to be ready."

"That's overkill," objected Randall. "Look, Joe. We've
got six private homes seized and a black prophet somewhere up in the hills. That's all. Why does this justify
mustering the Department of Defense? Jesus, we'd scare
the country to death."

"Wait a minute," said Voorhees. "Who's going to know
we even had a meeting? As long as they're in on it, Pedersen and Garrity won't talk. Who else? . . . No, I'm
talking about how you'll look in hindsight. You hold a big
nighttime conference. Everybody there from the FBI to
the Army, Navy, and Marines. Who can fault that?
You're taking every precaution, dotting every *i* and crossing every *t*. You're ready on all fronts, no matter what
happens."

He paused and the two friends studied each other
across the sofa.

"Another thing, Phil," said Voorhees. "I think you really ought to be prepared—and not just for the looks of
the thing. Let's just suppose this B.O.F. is poised for real
revolution, ready for guerrilla warfare in a hundred cities
upon some word from Danny Smith. It could happen, you
know. And if it does, brother, you'll need every soldier in
the country."

They were silent again.

"Phil?"

"Yes?"

"Look at it this way. What have you got to lose by
calling a skull session?"

"Nothing," said Randall, "except a couple of hours'
sleep."

"So? What's our next problem?"

Randall rose and walked about the room a minute. The
thing about Joe, he thought, is that he often articulates
precisely what goes through my mind, yet frequently in
simpler terms than I could express it myself. Randall returned and picked up the phone on the ornate, gilded

table near the fireplace. "Gertrude, please." He waited a moment.

"Gertrude," he said, "I want you to call the following men for me. They are to come to the second-floor Oval Room at once. Tell them to throw on whatever is handy. First, the Secretary of Defense, Paul . . ."

Randall reeled off the names, replaced the phone, and turned to Voorhees.

"Let's hope it *is* overkill," he said.

Then he walked to the door and asked the Secret Service agent in the hall to order coffee for eight.

Chapter Eight

The trouble with advice, thought Phil Randall, was that nobody had discovered how to tax the commodity at the source. The adviser, like the preacher, tended to flood the landscape with his wares, leaving the consumer to hunt about for the crafted article amid a glut of largely shoddy goods.

The time was 3 A.M. Monday, the conference had been under way for an hour, and tobacco smoke settled like a haze over the bright jonquil fabrics of the oval sitting room. Eight men were present, and President Randall sensed that perhaps six of them looked upon his dilemma with less than total regret. Only Joe Voorhees and himself, thought Randall, shared the depths of his quandary. Of the others, several relished his plight, anticipating the sure wounding of the leader who had ridden so high and so gallantly in the days without storm. Other men evidenced their simple relief that the final decision would be Randall's, not theirs.

Their talk was of the nation, duty, policy, constitutional rights—the grand rhetoric of statecraft—but personal motives moved below the surface like moles in buried runways. When Attorney General Garrity spoke so intensely of law and order, he really meant to rebuke his

President for encouraging a climate in which dissent prospered to the detriment of order.

When General Walter Hildebrand, the elegant, poised Chairman of the Joint Chiefs of Staff, made oblique reference to "the area of political decision outside my competence," he really meant to stress his belief that President Randall was encumbered by his election debts to the blacks. Randall, after all, came to power with 86 per cent of the Negro vote while he, the general, rose to eminence on pristine merit in the profession of arms.

When Edward J. Lee, the brusque and somewhat overbearing Secretary of the Treasury, used the word "stability," he evoked pictures of a fiscal mastiff guarding the vaults while an ebullient President wasted himself in ephemeral romances with the voter.

And the mere presence of eight men brought a complicating human factor. Their number meant that fifty-six personal reactions—count 'em, thought Randall—raced at lightning speed along the invisible emotional lanes that linked the conferees. Paul Edelstein, the Secretary of Defense, had varying feelings toward each of his seven colleagues, and the seven in turn had their individual thoughts—and suspicions—about him. Harold Osborne, the Secretary of Transportation, was the lone black man in the room. His blackness meant a mingling of fourteen attitudes on the seven strands that tied Osborne to his white associates.

Ah, consensus, thought Randall, what a frail monarch you are, your crown the flashing jewel of inconsistency, your throne a muddle of emotion, self-justification, half-knowledge, and sometimes faultless logic never to be sorted out for history, let alone for the memory of any single man tomorrow. History, for instance, might conclude that Paul Edelstein favored the use of massive federal power, but did he do so solely to preserve the nation or partially because he wished to show his non-Jewish colleagues that he could move as swiftly as Moshe Dayan did against the Arabs? Or because he inwardly seethed— as Osborne intimated—at evidences of anti-Semitism among the militant blacks? For his part Harold Osborne counseled a policy of vigilant restraint. But did he do so because he was wise, because he was black or primarily because he detested General Hildebrand's smug assumption of superiority and therefore would oppose anything the general advocated? Who would ever know?

Yet, thought Randall, whatever the motives of men, there beside them crouched the dilemma. The unwanted shape of quandary had become clear to all shortly after 2 A.M. when they assembled.

By that time Director Pedersen, in addition to giving a synopsis of the B.O.F.'s armed occupation of six white homes, had been able to provide further details about the North Carolina command post of Daniel Smith, the black Gideon of revolution. Monitors of the Federal Communications Commission, using triangulation methods, had spotted Smith's powerful transmitter on a hilltop between Mt. Mitchell and Bakersville to the north. Smith had now conversed with all six of the seized properties, confirming that each occupying guerrilla band was supplied with radio transceiver equipment. Some of the traffic was in encrypted Morse code on which bureau cryptologists, aided by experts from the National Security Agency, were now working. But there had been several voice conversations in plain language, sprinkled with a few code words such as "Lion" and "Gamal," which had definitely established Smith's command and the home sieges as a coordinated venture of the Blacks of February Twenty-first. While the B.O.F.'s objectives remained obscure, the radio exchanges strongly hinted that the occupation of six homes was but the first stage of a broader plan for insurrection.

Pedersen also provided an estimate on numbers. Splicing information from a variety of sources, the FBI believed the hard-core membership of the B.O.F. totaled about 10,000 black men organized into well-knit and disciplined bands operating in some 100 cities. It was believed, said Pedersen, that all members of these central units were either armed or had ready access to weapons caches. In the event of an armed uprising the FBI estimated that as many as 100,000 young blacks might rally to fight under the banner of the black fist raised in a field of crimson. Beyond that, it was felt, were literally hundreds of thousands of sympathetic blacks who might join a revolt in the event of initial successes.

Garrity added another development. The Tiegert property at Silver Lake, California, was in the Eldorado National Forest on land leased from the Forest Service. This raised the question of whether the B.O.F. had seized federal land.

Now, after an hour of grappling with the shape of crisis, the eight men in the oval sitting room were trying to break it down into identifiable pieces much as the puzzle solver returns to finite problems after failing to discover the master clue through intuition.

"I think it would be helpful," said Joe Voorhees, "if Jesse went through the whole list of suspected B.O.F. members for us."

Postmaster General Voorhees was regarded as an interloper at the meeting. After all, the Post Office was not a kiln in which the clay of major policy was fired. Voorhees, they all knew, was here solely because he was President Randall's best friend.

Pedersen responded only after a permissive nod from the President. "Of course," said Pedersen, "we're checking all these names, but we've had some of them for only a day or two. I've put most of my manpower on the homes. A simple question of priorities."

The FBI director read aloud the names of men publicly identified with the B.O.F., beginning with Commander Smith and his first deputy, Benjamin Steele. Then, more slowly, he read off the names of men thought to be secret members of the organization. "We're just beginning our check of these," he said. The list was alphabetical, and names rolled by like anonymous boxcars in the night.

"Now here's an unusual one that bothers me," he said. "The name is Alfred Nicolet. I assume that he is the economist. If so, as you gentlemen probably know, Nicolet ranks as one of the leading financial experts in the country. He's an immigrant from Jamaica and for some years has been on the faculty of the Harvard Business School."

"Nicolet!" As he echoed the name, Treasury Secretary Lee shot a troubled glance at President Randall. "You remember, Mr. President, we hired Nicolet to do a confidential study of tax-exempt foundations."

Randall nodded. "It was sometime in May."

"That's right," said Lee. "Well, something a bit unusual happened last Tuesday. Now it begins to make sense." Lee peered over his spectacles at the circle of men. Fatigue etched their faces. "Nicolet called me Tuesday and said he regretfully would have to resign from the study group which he was chairing. He said that his summer load at the university was heavier than expected and that a number of personal family problems had arisen. Shuttling from Boston to Washington twice a week was too much for him. I tried to argue with him, but he was adamant and I finally had to let him off the hook. I was surprised. It seemed strange that he would break off a prestige government study at a very respectable fee because of 'family problems,' as he put it. Nicolet has no children, and his faculty friends assure me that he and his wife get along beautifully. It wasn't at all like him."

"Are we certain Nicolet's tied up with the B.O.F.?" asked Edelstein.

"No," Pedersen replied. "We just got the name Saturday afternoon from Sprague. But all of Sprague's other leads have checked out—and I should add that Nicolet's wife told an agent who phoned that her husband had gone off on a vacation by himself, place unknown, or so she contended."

"That's totally out of character for Nicolet," said Lee. He made a business of shaking out a cigarette and lighting it. "I must say that if Nicolet is advising the B.O.F., we've got a new dimension. It raises the question of possible financial objectives. There's nothing unsophisticated about Nicolet's knowledge of the monetary system. Nothing whatsoever. If that word gets out, you're going to hear a loud reaction in the banking community."

"If it's any louder," said Voorhees, "than the one we'll hear when business and Wall Street learn that the boss of the Truckers and the president of Empire Motors are prisoners in their own summer homes, I'd rather not hear it, thanks."

Lee did not deign to look at Voorhees, the interloper. "Nicolet intrigues me," he said. "Just what advice of his could tie into the seizure of the homes of six wealthy and influential men, I'd love to know."

There was a brief, moody silence. Randall suddenly realized that Edelstein was staring at his sideburns. Caught in the act, the Defense Secretary abruptly shifted his gaze. My God, thought Randall, is he worrying about sideburns at a time like this?

Pedersen renewed the reading of his alphabetical list. The names passed unremarked until he came to that of a Howard R. Underwood.

"Wait a minute," said General Hildebrand. "Is that Howard *R.* Underwood?"

Pedersen glanced at his sheet. "Yes. An 'R.'"

"Is there any title or identification?"

"No." Pedersen shook his head.

"One of my aides is named Howard Ralph Underwood," said the general. He hesitated as he reflected. "No, that couldn't be possible. I've known my Major Underwood since Vietnam. He was decorated for bravery."

"Is he the new Negro in your office?" asked Edelstein with a frown.

"Yes," replied Hildebrand. "You know him, Mr. Secretary. He's been in on a couple of your recent briefings. He's my link with the Joint Staff's internal security protection unit—" The general halted, a puzzled look on his face.

"Internal security protection?" asked Osborne.

"Yes." Hildebrand turned to the big-framed Negro. "That's our unit that has its finger on the sensitive spots in case of major civil disorder—computerized power centers, telephone relay stations, railroad yards, master controls for the TV networks." He hesitated again. "The unit works from quite detailed maps. . . . Major Underwood knows cartography. He's also an engineer."

"What do we know about him?" asked Edelstein.

"He's up from the ranks," said Hildebrand. "Sharp as hell. Better than most of my West Point officers. . . . Underwood! I can't believe it. Must be somebody else."

"I was shocked when I found out about Sprague," said Pedersen. "Since the B.O.F. managed to infiltrate the bureau, it wouldn't surprise me to find recruits at the Pentagon." The prospect that the FBI was not the only agency tarnished by secret defection seemed less than displeasing to him.

"We'd better check Underwood out in a hurry," said Edelstein.

"Right," said Hildebrand. "First thing in the morning."

No one spoke for a moment. The scope of the B.O.F. was swiftly widening like ripples from a tossed rock.

"It begins to look like the B.O.F. is no amateur lash-up," said Voorhees. "At least it seems to know its way around the federal government. Agent Sprague, Alfred Nicolet, maybe Major Underwood. So how many others?"

"It would take two years to investigate every Negro government worker," said Secretary Lee. "There's no place to begin."

Several pairs of eyes drifted involuntarily to the face of Harold Osborne, the Negro among seven white men. The Transportation Secretary was a heavyset man who carried more weight than was good for him. He wore his hair naturally, but clipped short, as though to strike a neutral balance between the bush style of the black militants and the straight, limp hair of his white colleagues.

"What do you think, Hal?" asked Edelstein. "Could the B.O.F. possibly have won many converts among Negroes in the middle and upper layers of the Administration?"

The question seemed to surprise Osborne. He raised his right hand. "Gentlemen," he said unsmilingly, "I am not now, nor have I ever been, a member of the Blacks of February Twenty-first."

"No pledges of allegiance, please," said President Randall with a hesitant laugh. "Nobody was hinting at anything."

"Are you sure?" Osborne flicked his eyes toward Edelstein.

The Defense Secretary would recall later Osborne's expression as he asked the question. Edelstein thought he detected veiled pride, as though Osborne's own status in the room had been bolstered by the raid of armed black men which seemed to have brought a case of jitters to the world's most powerful white government.

"I know that everyone here has only one overriding commitment," said General Hildebrand, "and that is to the security of the country."

"I have a number of commitments, General," said Osborne quietly. He paused. "The security of the United States is one of them—but security has many faces."

"Right now the face seems to be armed rebellion." Hildebrand's tone hardened and color rose in his cheeks. "And right now the question before us is what to do about it."

"I thought the issue was rather one of finding out exactly what confronts us," replied Osborne, "and then deciding what to do about it."

"The facts are clear beyond any reasonable doubt." Hildebrand addressed Osborne directly.

"I don't think so," countered Osborne. The black cabinet member was as firm as the nation's top military officer. "I'll grant the seizure of six homes by the B.O.F., but we haven't a clue as to the purpose—and until we have, we can't be certain how to proceed."

"I consider the B.O.F.'s objective to be secondary at this point," said Hildebrand heatedly. "The fact is that private property has been seized by a nationally organized band of armed men."

"Armed *black* men, General," corrected Osborne.

Hildebrand shifted in his chair and glared at Osborne. "I'm perfectly aware of that, Mr. Secretary—as I suppose Major Underwood may also be."

The implication was plain. If Major Underwood was found to have betrayed his Army oath, then his general assumed that every black American must share the major's perfidy.

"Now, gentlemen." President Randall raised his palms in a pacifying gesture. Distrust had quickly expanded in the room. To the group's displeasure with the presence of Joe Voorhees had been added a new factor—a question as to the loyalties of Secretary Osborne. Randall could sense that at least two men, Edelstein and Hildebrand, believed that the face of this conference should have been all white.

"Let's get back on the track," said Randall. "We've been here almost two hours, and I don't think further personal exchanges will be helpful at this stage. I think that both Walter Hildebrand and Hal Osborne are right. The B.O.F.'s objective is a secondary concern, but it is also important. I'd like to handle both questions. First, what is our best guess as to the purpose of these seizures?"

After some hesitancy Attorney General Garrity ventured the first opinion. "I think it's fairly clear that Commander Dan Smith is holding the families of six prominent Americans as hostages. My hunch is that some spectacular demand will follow, probably tomorrow and probably addressed to the President."

Paul Edelstein nodded, the movement of a massive head that might have been sculpted for a national monument. "It has the stamp of a direct challenge to the power of the federal government." The Defense Secretary always spoke with the weight of stone. "We've had seizures before—university offices, welfare centers, even city council chambers. But now the B.O.F. strikes at the American home."

"Yes, homes," said Joe Voorhees. "Frankly I don't get it. If Dan Smith wanted to challenge Washington to a showdown, why not grab Capitol Hill—or, better yet, the Pentagon?"

"In this country," replied Edelstein, "the home is more than a man's castle. It's a sacred American symbol. The Constitution protects it against unreasonable search and seizure. We let Americans keep guns in the home, making it a kind of personal fortress. The home, as a man's territory, is regarded as inviolate. How many juries will convict a man who kills an unarmed burglar or rapist in the defendant's own home?"

"And," added President Randall, "no civil-rights effort aroused such an unholy storm as the fair-housing laws. The home owner believes he's a monarch who can do as he pleases with his property, and no government official is going to tell him otherwise. . . . But, Paul, how does this fit into the B.O.F.'s strategy?"

"I look at it this way, Mr. President," said Edelstein. "Take Joe Voorhees's point. The Blacks of February Twenty-first couldn't seize Congress or the Pentagon without a bloody battle they'd be sure to lose. But seizing six homes is something else. In the first place, there's not much problem about the initial occupation. Armed men can always occupy unguarded properties. Second, the B.O.F. attacks a symbol more sacrosanct than the flag or the church steeple. The leaders make an instant, fiery statement of revolution, a visceral wrench to every home owner. This move strikes at almost every family, whether home owners or apartment renters. And if the B.O.F. can seize six homes today, why not a hundred tomorrow and a thousand next week?"

"I agree," said Treasury Secretary Lee. "All revolutionary movements, like theologies, need their demons." Ed Lee fancied himself a leisure-hour social anthropologist. "A number of Negro leaders have been damning private property for some time. Now the B.O.F. tells the country that the worst demon of all is the private home."

"Of course," said Edelstein, "there's the very practical point that Frank Garrity touched on. Holding some three dozen people as captives in fairly isolated areas gives the B.O.F. room for maneuver and bargaining. But also there's a kind of contempt for government and social values in this move. The B.O.F. is saying to hell with private property."

"I'd amend that slightly," said Osborne. "They're saying to hell with white private property. Don't forget that a lot of these B.O.F. men came from the slums where a home is a couple of sleazy rooms rented from some white landlord. I'm not condoning the move, mind, just trying to analyze it. Also let's not overlook the fact that all of these seized homes are fairly substantial and they all belong to men of means."

"Exactly," said Edelstein. "Each home represents wealth, but each one also belongs to a man who is connected with this administration. That can't be by accident. The B.O.F., in addition to alarming every property owner, is thumbing its nose at President Randall. And that brings me to my central point. I think these seizures are a symbolic gesture intended to rally the B.O.F. nationwide to armed rebellion. To me it's not conceivable that the B.O.F. would stop with the taking of a few homes. That accomplishes nothing unless they spread out from there. In short we're dealing with fire, and we better damn well put it out in a hurry."

"I don't quarrel with any of that," said Secretary Lee. "However, I'd like to add a possibility. If Al Nicolet is an adviser in this operation, he's somehow aiming at our financial structure as well. The dollar just isn't healthy today. We all know that, but I don't think some of you realize just how vulnerable it is. We might see Nicolet surface as an ally of some hostile foreign bankers."

Lee looked about as if inviting comment. No one spoke, and he sighed and shook his head. He was the lone financial expert, his demeanor seemed to say, in a company of economic simpletons.

"Let's face it, gentlemen," said General Hildebrand. "We're up against the possibility of armed rebellion." His stern glance around the ring of faces stirred the reaction that Lee failed to elicit. "With the temper of this country what it is, that could mean protracted guerrilla warfare in city after city. I see eye to eye with Paul Edelstein. It's as inconceivable to me as it is to him that this armed capture of six homes is anything but a prelude to revolt. If only one or two homes had been seized, we might conclude that we were dealing with some escapade that, however sticky, could be handled by local authorities. But here we have a well-planned operation, backed by shiploads of smuggled arms and including central direction by a radio-equipped commander who's hiding in the mountains. The homes were picked with obvious care, and they're located in widely separated areas of the country. I accept the symbolism stressed by Paul, but I also believe we're dealing with skilled, dangerous revolutionaries who can derail this country if they're not halted at once."

There were other ideas. Director Pedersen believed that some type of ransom was involved, perhaps akin to Fidel Castro's demand for American supplies in exchange for Cuban prisoners after the Bay of Pigs. Joe Voorhees thought that the Administration should be prepared for anything, that trying to read Smith's mind was a wasteful game. Secretary Osborne agreed with Voorhees. Osborne said that while Negroes liked President Randall personally, black rage smoldered everywhere against whites and no one could be certain how and where Daniel Smith intended to ignite the fire. The clock ticked on as they talked until it marked 4:10 A.M.

"Now the question is: What should we do?" asked Randall. He arose and flexed his muscles under the terry-cloth sport shirt. "If you don't mind, I'm going to make some notes on this one. I want constructive advice from each man, and I want to get it down accurately."

There was a new tension in the room as Randall walked to a slim-legged Louis XVI desk and took a ballpoint pen and note pad from one of the small drawers. The men looked apprehensively at one another while the President's back was turned. This time advice would be taxed at the source. They were to be pinned down for history. The buck might stop with the President—Harry Truman's aphorism had become a political cliché—but it accumulated many ineradicable thumbprints as it passed from hand to hand on its way to the man.

Randall noted the dismay as he returned to his chair. "Blame it on my poor memory," he said with a smile. But the faces turned toward him were those of men who felt their superior was taking unfair advantage of them. History could be cruel to those who served it carelessly or unwisely.

"Let's just go around the room," said Randall. "You lead off, will you, Jesse?"

This time each adviser gave his views without interruption. Except for the lone, strained voice, the only sound in the room was the hum of the central air-conditioning system. Philip Randall's note pad told the story:

Jesse Pedersen, FBI. Send units armed FBI agents to each home. Search warrants. Investigate killing federal agent. If resistance, pull back, await President's orders. Alert federal troops now in case necessary later. FBI agents to locate Dan Smith in Smokies. Apprehend on charge broadcasting without federal license.

Frank Garrity, A.G. Ditto Pedersen except each FBI unit equipped with bull horn. Ultimatum to B.O.F. from President: Come out peaceably. If B.O.F. refuses, await President's orders.

Joe Voorhees, P.G. President to go on TV to nation, explain situation. Promise amnesty to B.O.F. if surrender promptly. If no surrender, be prepared to move any direction—FBI, troops, National Guard, state police. Remember: Children involved.

Paul Edelstein, Sec. Def. Move at once massive federal troop force. Do not wait. Move first, then explain.

If not crushed at once, possible *the* black revolution might convulse major cities. Any temporizing might threaten health of nation.

Walter Hildebrand, Ch. J.C.S. Ditto Edelstein. Specifics. Alert 82nd Airborne, Fort Bragg, N.C., at once. This division specially trained for civil disorders. Split division six ways and fly men to air bases nearest seized homes. Logistics simple, but take some time. Troops could be all in place by nightfall. Troops to use antiriot procedures, CS gas, etc. Arms only last resort. FBI agents and federal troops seize Dan Smith in mountains. Bring him to trial sedition laws.

Edward Lee, Sec. Treas. Respectfully, emphatically disagree Joe Voorhees. Operation must be massive, per Gen. Hildebrand, but quick, secret. Don't think group realizes how shaky dollar is right now. Antidollar pressures strong. If U.S. can't halt private property raids immediately, confidence in U.S. Government will diminish. European central bankers might flee from dollar. Even possibility Alfred Nicole, in league financiers abroad to put U.S. in money squeeze. Could be big drop on Wall Street if Pres. not firm. Sure to be sell-off anyway. Main job stave off panic. So don't rely measures like FBI. Move at once with airborne troops.

Harold Osborne, Sec. Trans. Not aware finances as Lee is, but is aware black mood. Big troop movement could *provoke* riots at least, rebellion at most. Impossible keep fed. move secret, so agree Voorhees. President should go on TV, perhaps with black leaders who oppose B.O.F. Then whole deal should be turned over to governors of six states. Seizure private property is state violation, not federal. Investigating killing federal agent, as Pedersen suggests, is subterfuge. Must act strictly within law. President must let blacks know he stands for them and asks *their* help against B.O.F. extremists. Certainly must be amnesty for B.O.F. if surrender. Main thing: No federal force until all else exhausted. Otherwise may alienate all blacks.

The word "blacks" hung in the air. Randall tucked the note pad and pen beside his chair cushion. The room became very quiet, so that the sound of the air conditioning swelled unnaturally. The advisers had spoken, a shifting of burdens to the shoulders of one man. Joe Voorhees would remember the scene in the image of a vise slowly closing on his friend the President. Frank Garrity would recall the look on the President's face, the puzzled look of a host whose guests suddenly depart en masse. And Randall himself would always recall the moment as one of quick loneliness.

Randall's movements were not at all theatrical. He arose and rubbed his palms together in the manner of a man ready for business. But as he looked about the room in a show of confidence, he could see a glint of doubt in some eyes. This President, they were thinking, is untried in crisis. Well, of course, they were right. But he was determined to do his best and he had no inner qualms.

"Thanks, gentlemen," he said. He glanced at his wristwatch. "I'll have the word for you by 7 A.M. I think we might as well resolve our course as soon as possible. So let's say by seven. In the meantime . . . now, let's see. . . . We want to be ready to move in several directions. General, you'd better alert the 82nd Airborne at once. . . . Jesse, the same with your agents. If you need Air Force transport, arrange it with Paul Edelstein. And of course you'll let me know any new developments from those homes." He turned to Treasury Secretary Lee. "Ed, let's start tracking down Alfred Nicolet right away. Jesse will give you what help you need."

Randall thrust his hands in the pockets of his slacks, lowered his head, and thought for a moment. Then to Osborne: "I'm not sure about TV, Hal. But just in case get me some names of black leaders who would sympathize with us and whom we could contact in a hurry." He walked to the marble fireplace and spoke to the whole group. "It goes without saying that this is to be kept under wraps until we decide. One final thing. I'll set up Joe Voorhees down in the situation room as a kind of White House coordinator. Let's all funnel through him." He grinned. "And I must say this is a great time for the Vice-President to be larking around South America on a goodwill tour. Smart timing."

Secretary of Defense Edelstein stepped forward and shook Randall's hand. That set a precedent. Each man in turn gave his President a firm grip, and Randall thought ruefully that he could be the bereaved receiving the condolences of friends. If they just weren't so damn solemn. The last man, Joe Voorhees, was less severe. He smiled as he shook Randall's hand, a private smile that said he thought that this was all a bit pompous. Randall held Voorhees back as the others filed from the room.

"Park it here awhile, Joe." Randall eased down on the long yellow sofa which angled from the fireplace and the surmounting portrait of Washington. He crossed his legs. "Our friends acted like pallbearers. It's serious, sure, but I don't need the funereal bit."

Voorhees dropped into a corner of the sofa, and his belt promptly lost itself in the folds of his belly. Lengthening whiskers smudged his jowls.

"The fact is that some of them don't trust you, Phil," he said. "Maybe it's those damned sideburns of yours. When Edelstein looks at them, he thinks he sees the enemy."

"The hell with hair," said Randall. "If they'd known the project I had in mind before this broke, they'd have really seen the enemy."

"You mean Kathy's encounter stuff?"

Randall nodded, then leaned back, clasped his hands behind his head, and stared up at the ceiling. "Joe, seldom in my life have I felt anything as moving as that."

"I felt the same."

Voorhees waited patiently in silence. Since he knew this President so well, he could sense the tack Randall's mind was taking. He had witnessed similar scenes in the past. Faced with a decision, whether large or small, Randall liked to set it aside to simmer while he engaged his thoughts on other matters. It was, after all, good psychology. After ten, twenty, thirty minutes on another subject, Randall could return to the central problem with a fresh viewpoint.

"Imagine the reaction of Garrity or Hildebrand," said Randall, "if they knew the President of the United States had been lying flat on his back on the floor, touching the fingertips of a strange Negro on one side and a Negro woman on the other?"

So the detour from the armed expedition of the Blacks

of February Twenty-first would wander back through the strange paths of Kathy's encounter group? Voorhees understood.

"Or if they had seen the President's wife," Voorhees added, "embracing a black dame and both of them crying like schoolgirls."

"If only millions of people could go through the same thing," said Randall quietly. He was still gazing up at the ceiling. "It's an experience you don't forget."

Randall said no more, and Voorhees knew that his mind was slipping back to the eventful Friday, only a little more than two days ago. Phil and Helen Randall and their close friends, Joe and Susan Voorhees, had agreed to submit to a "marathon encounter" with five young Negroes whom Kathy Randall had met at Stanford University.

Kathy, just twenty-one, with long chestnut hair that fell to her shoulders like a roadside shrine, was a sweet clutter of roses and thorns. She loathed the old, rejoiced in the new, and sighed for the passing brevity of her own youth. She worshiped at the altar of mankind but would cheerfully sign any petition to banish some of its priests—and most of its communicants. She had the truculent impatience of the young, and yet in a moment she could become as affectionate as a kitten. Voorhees knew that Phil Randall loved his daughter with the sadness of a man who sees his own cracked dreams knit together again for a few fleeting hours.

Kathy had volunteered for the Peace Corps after graduation from Smith, had done her training on the Stanford campus. There she had participated in a twenty-four-hour group encounter of white and black recruits. The next day she was on the phone to her father, describing the experiment. "It's hell, Dad," she said. "It's great. It's awful, but beautiful too. It's where it's all at." Phil Randall mumbled the appropriate sympathetic, if meaningless, phrases that fathers do when confronted by a daughter's unknown transports. He dismissed the incident from mind.

But several days later a six-page air-mail letter arrived from Kathy. She painted the scene in breathless prose, liberally strewn with dots and exclamation points, and added a postscript: "This would be great for you two to try at the White House, no?" Phil and Helen Randall discussed the letter. Phil, always the innovator, was intrigued, but Helen said it all sounded rather repellent, the kind of impulsive thing young people did these days. The next day came a packet of clippings and a psychology paper about encounter sessions. Phil skimmed the material with interest.

That night Kathy telephoned with a direct proposal for her parents. Please let her try the encounter group at the White House. She would bring a group of black students from Stanford plus a "trainer." Take her word for it, the session would work dramatic changes in their outlooks and attitudes. It would be another Randall first at the White House. Phil Randall felt himself being pushed too far. "For God's sake, Kathy, when are you going to realize I'm President of the United States? That just wouldn't be, well, dignified, damn it." To which she retorted: "That's the whole point, Dad. You think of yourself as with it, but maybe you're afraid to look at the truth about yourself and other people."

This time President Randall telephoned Joe Voorhees and asked him what he knew about encounter groups. Not much, said Joe, except reading about them. And he did have a sister who had tried it once and claimed it was an experience everyone should have. When Kathy phoned once again two nights later, Phil Randall was ready for surrender. "Come ahead with your friends, Kathy," he said, "but please, for my sake, keep quiet about it." His schedule was light for the long Fourth of July weekend, and he would keep Friday open for Kathy's somewhat alarming project.

There were further precautions. At the insistence of the head of the White House Secret Service detail, agents guarding Kathy at Stanford made a swift but exhaustive check of the five young Negroes and the group trainer. Then, on a sober second thought, Randall phoned Kathy and asked her to exact a pledge from each of her friends that they would not reveal the purpose of the White House visit. All agreed. They were merely friends spending a holiday with the President's daughter.

And so Kathy arrived at the White House Thursday

night with five young Negroes and an owlish white "encounter trainer" after the flight from San Francisco in one of the jets of the Air Force's presidential fleet. It was agreed that Joe and Susan Voorhees would join the encounter, which took place in this same yellow Oval Room which had been so tastefully decorated a decade ago by Jacqueline Kennedy. It had been an unusual scene to unfold before the two flags, the American and the presidential, which flanked the doorway to the President's bedroom. The session began at eight o'clock Friday morning and ran nonstop until midnight.

Under orders from the trainer, a serenely nagging psychologist named Mort Yahn, the four middle-aged whites joined Kathy and the five young blacks, three men and two women, in a tight circle, arms touching. All titles and status symbols, said Mort, were to be jettisoned. All were to call one another by first names. They were to ignore, if they could, the image of the presidency in this room. They were to live and interact only in the immediate present. And, in this first stage, they were merely to look silently around the circle.

"Look at each person the way you really feel," ordered Mort. "If you have a negative reaction, don't try to mask it. If you like someone, express it the best you can. Whatever you feel, let it come out front."

Within a minute the tension pulled tight as a drumhead. Some eyes riveted on a face. Others faltered. President Randall found it difficult, for instance, to look at his wife on the beam of truth. What did he really feel about her now after twenty-three years of marriage? A welter of memories—sentimental, melancholy, and merely irksome —engulfed him.

In the second stage they were instructed to tour the circle and touch each person in turn. "Touch like you feel," said Mort. "Be honest." A young black girl stood for a full minute before Joe Voorhees, studying his face. Then she coolly shook his hand. Helen Randall kissed her husband lightly on the cheek. One black man clasped a black woman to his chest and held her head against his shoulder. Susan Voorhees, embarrassed, looked away. "No," said Mort. "Watch. You must try to feel what others feel."

The third stage was another round robin, this time with words. "Tell the lady frankly what you think of her," said Mort. "No copping out with wisecracks. Be front with your feelings." The tension lessened with the first spoken thoughts, then built rapidly again. One Negro told Voorhees that his friendliness was a facade that hid an indifferent white heart. Helen Randall asked a black woman if her hostility toward whites was as rabid as it appeared.

As the encounter progressed, the words became sharper, the mood more captious. The three black men cursed increasingly. Randall felt himself beleaguered, isolated, regretting that he had agreed to cast aside his shield of authority. No one had upbraided him to his face in months. Joe Voorhees began to feel like an open wound. This effort to sweep away conventions, hypocrisy, the whole fabric of small social lies accumulated over a lifetime was almost more than he could bear. He sweated at the armpits and at the belly. To his amazement he found himself telling Helen Randall that her serenity had always bugged him. Why did she fake a role of cool composure in the White House when she was a woman of earthy emotions? A young black man blurted out to Kathy Randall that he didn't like her white smell. Phil Randall told a black girl that her shrublike growth of natural, kinky hair frightened him. She looked savage, he said. The same black girl placed her forehead smack against Joe Voorhees's and stared into his eyes as though to drown them. Finally she shrugged. "What I see, I don't like," she said.

They paired off for intimate, forthright talks of race, of sex and race, of the whole hierarchy of smells, myths, rumors, dialects, truths, and customs that divided blacks from whites. They lay on the floor in a long line, completely silent, finger tips touching those of the persons on either side. They performed a psychodrama, blacks acting white roles and vice versa. One black man, assigned to portray a "good white cop," tried but failed. Acting the part of a good white policeman was impossible, he said. There weren't any. When sandwiches arrived in later afternoon, the group was ordered by Mort to feed one another. Then they told the stories of their lives, as intimately as they dared, to hushed audiences. Later they each gave an answer before nine critics to the question: "If your daughter slept with a black man (or white) what would you tell her—and what would you really think?"

Susan Voorhees confessed in this phase that she had always feared rape by a black man. She was at once startled and abashed by her revelation. Mort tossed her a yellow pillow from one of the long sofas. "All right," said the trainer, "take it out on this. Shout at it. Beat it. Let it all hang out." Before an almost hypnotized audience Susan Voorhees fell upon the pillow and hammered it with her fists. Earlier, embarrassment would have inhibited her. Now, in some deep, primeval torment, she was oblivious of the others. She struck, cursed, and stamped. At last she collapsed like a bundle on the floor and stared forlornly at the yellow object in her hands.

Mort kept at them like a scourge. They went from one experiment in raw emotion to another without a breather. He flailed them with the phrase "Check reality." He reprimanded them for disdainful remarks. Anyone could laugh or cry in this room, he said, but no one was allowed to purchase immunity with a quip. Forget the past and ignore the future. Speak and feel only in the present. Reach down, he ordered, down into your guts and pull out every scrap of malice and prejudice you can find. Say it out loud. Purge yourself.

Night fell like a blanket over the back lawn, the ellipse, and the monuments to dead statesmen, and still the tortured probing of the self went on. They groped for identity, speaking five minutes each on the subject "Who am I?" At times Joe Voorhees felt as though an iron claw had dragged down his backbone, tearing away the flesh and leaving the spinal nerve exposed and quivering. The starch slowly drained from everyone. They became human sponges, pliant, humble, frightened of their open selves. Old attitudes crumpled like wrapping paper. And as the night hours wore on, a new mood fastened on the room. The group began to feel a new compassion for one another. Tones gentled and the fits of anger and irritation vaporized. The sad, yearning smile replaced the hawk's eye. Once a hush fell on the room as sounds of sobbing came from the fireplace. There, leaning against the mantel, were Helen Randall and Ethel Morrison, a twenty-year-old black woman. They were locked in an embrace and both were crying.

The climax came at midnight. As the final act Mort ordered them to form once more in the same tight circle where they began sixteen hours before. "Now join hands," he said, "and remain silent for one minute."

No one knew how it happened. It began slowly, tentatively. It was as though some giant magnet hung above them, attracting with a power that could not be denied. The ring of clasped hands inched upward, then moved faster. Suddenly all twenty hands were flung upward in unison in one magnificent explosion. They reached, not for the ceiling, but for the vast, arching heavens beyond. They gripped one another's hands tightly, straining to hold this new crown of truth lest it be lost forever. It was, they knew, the sunburst of their humanity, their misery and their rapture, their supplication. Theirs was the power and the glory. As he glanced around the circle, Joe Voorhees saw a glow on every face.

"Now you know," said Mort softly. The professional trainer looked at his charges with a tender smile. "We are all just human."

The next hour was a noisy, frothy aftermath. They compared their feelings, chattered away with a great sense of relief, wondered whether the presence of a president had impeded or stimulated the flow of their emotions. Consensus: It lent an added dimension of intensity. They gulped down ice cream, cake, and coffee. They rippled with the delighted recall of shared feelings. They must keep in touch, they said, and they should become missionaries for the encounter experience. They laughed constantly. And finally one black man, Hank Ulam, capped their mood when he said to Randall: "Mr. President Phil, you're a great, lovin,' crazy cat, and when I'm President, I'm going to make you king—for a day."

And now, it was fifty-three hours later, the coming dawn of a Monday that seemed decades away from that scene of catharsis, exuberance, and the common awareness of humanity.

"It might have worked, Joe," said Randall. "I was hoping that millions of Americans could go through the same experience. We had a chance to influence racial attitudes all over the country. . . . A boost from the White House, encounter ambassadors spreading the word. I even thought of a slogan, 'Know Thy Neighbor'. . . ."

"I know, Phil." Voorhees brushed at the air as though to order the memory from mind. "But the Blacks of February Twenty-first have ended that possibility. We might as well forget it."

"Hard to forget," said Randall. "It was the most profound sixteen hours for me in a long while. . . . Of course I can't see it as the panacea that Kathy does. Poor kid. She thinks it can mean a new world."

"There are no new worlds," said Voorhees. His natural cynicism returned and he welcomed it like an old coat.

"No, there aren't." Randall tugged at his thoughts. They were momentarily a continent away, with Kathy and Helen at Stanford. Helen would watch Kathy graduate from the Peace Corps training class, then Kathy would fly to Ghana where she would teach English for two years. Dear Kathy, his roses and thorns. Soon her dreams would waste away too.

"Well, back to the B.O.F.," said Randall.

The detour, Voorhees knew, had ended. They were back on the highway and ready to press ahead.

"Joe," said Randall, "what I need from you are some definite lines of thought. I've got to decide soon."

"I gave my ideas at the meeting." Voorhees scratched at the folds of his neck. He was sweating profusely despite the cooled air.

"That was for the record."

"It sure as hell was. We all saw ourselves skewered in your little doomsday book."

Randall ignored the complaint. "We're alone now. I want you to level with me."

"Okay." Voorhees leaned his head back and closed his eyes. "I did level, but you missed the point."

"You advised me to go on TV, ask the B.O.F. to give up the homes, and promise amnesty if they did. Then be prepared to move in any of several directions if they refused."

"Right." Voorhees's eyes were still closed. "But you didn't get the message, Phil."

"What message? For God's sake sit up and look at me."

Voorhees did as ordered. If he had crossed his legs under him, he could have been a fat Buddha. "The children, Phil. The children. Do you realize that I was the only one of eight men who mentioned the kids?"

"Suppose you were. What are you driving at?"

"Look, Phil," said Voorhees. "The kids in those six homes are your greatest asset. There are kids in each place, more than a dozen altogether. Now I ask you: What's every mother in this country going to be thinking about when she gets the word? The invaded homes? Yeah, some, I guess. The adults who are held captive? The sanctity of private property? Hell no, Phil, her mind is going to be on those kids."

When Randall said nothing, Voorhees leaned forward and gestured with a forefinger. "Who does every cereal manufacturer aim his ads at? The kids. Who do the rock bands play for? The kids. Why does every father sweat his life away in some boring job? The kids. Who have you thought about and loved most in the last twenty-one years? Kathy, your kid."

"That's enough. I'm no idiot. What's your point?"

"Phil," said Voorhees, "I think you ought to play those kids for everything they're worth. Wrap the flag around 'em. Make people cry over them. Forget the private-property bit. Who cares about some rich guy's acres and bricks and plumbing fixtures? Make every mother and father in the country, white or black, think about those poor little kids held at gunpoint."

Randall twisted on the sofa and shook his head slowly. "As I said before, Joe, you're really a cynical bastard."

"But I make sense. Right? Phil, you can't fool me. I know you're not going to call out the troops and crush the B.O.F. without a word to the country in advance. You can't afford to. General Hildebrand may be a stone-ager by our standards, but the guy put his finger on the bind you're in. Negroes helped elect you big, and maybe they will again—if there is an again. So you're not going in with a big shoot-'em-up and mass sedition trials and all that."

Voorhees paused and looked his friend in the eyes.

"No, you're going on television and you're going to make the greatest appeal of your life. And when you do, all I'm saying is: Hang it on the kids. Jerk every damn tear you can in the country."

Randall was quiet for a moment. He shook his head. "Exploit a lot of captive children?"

"Aha!" Voorhees shot a forefinger at Randall. "You said it. Captive. Those children are prisoners. Now what the hell is dishonest about emphasizing that fact? I'm not advising you to lie. I'm just telling you to act like a good newspaperman. Make the children the lead of your story. Make the country see and feel the plight of those innocent little kids. Why, Christ, some of them aren't much more than babies."

"I don't recall that the world exactly cut its throat over those children in Biafra," said Randall. "And there were thousands of them starving to death."

"But," insisted Voorhees, "it was the shrunken faces of those Biafran kids that finally brought the relief mission. We *were* concerned. The whole world was. And those kids were thousands of miles away from us. They were a mass, not individuals. And, let's face it, they were black. Now you've got white American kids held by gunmen in the kids' own homes. Each one of these kids will be a distinct individual, probably with his name and picture in the papers. My hunch is this will be a lot more emotional than Biafra was."

Randall reflected as he studied his friend. "You've got a point, Joe. You usually have."

"But you don't like the way I say it, huh? Well, dress up my words any way you want. Just don't forget the kids, period."

"Anything else?" Randall's voice was growing husky. He was a man who needed his sleep.

"No, except I'm worried about those five young Negroes who went through the encounter with us. Suppose one of them tips what happened here? That could be murder right now."

"Kathy got a pledge from each one of them before they came," said Randall. "She's satisfied they won't talk."

"Well, if this story gets out, you can kiss good-by to any influence you may have with conservatives. When you appeal to the country for calm and restraint, a hell of a lot of people would yell 'nigger lover' and grab their guns. . . . How about me calling Kathy and get her to talk to her friends again?"

"Good idea," said Randall. "I think you better. She'll pay more attention to you than she would to me. . . . Is that all?"

"That's all, Phil." Voorhees stood up and put his hand on Randall's shoulder. "Except, good luck. Pardon the way I talked. I was just trying to get my idea across. . . . This is a rough one, Phil. I'm glad you're the man and not me."

"Thanks, Joe. I appreciate your help. . . . Say, use the guest room down the hall."

"No, I'll have them fix me a cot down in the situation room. If I'm going to coordinate there, I might as well be where I'm supposed to be."

The two friends parted at the door.

President Randall returned to the sofa. Dilemma was his only companion now. Not even Joe Voorhees had been able to reason it away. Randall reached for his note pad. He glanced through the jottings, found that the words blurred. A kind of torpor settled momentarily on his brain, then was replaced by a welcome clarity. Thoughts began to assemble from all directions, slipped into formation, and marched ahead. He sat for a full five minutes concentrating.

Then he rose and walked to the phone resting on the slim, gilded table near the fireplace. Gertrude answered in her voice of gauze. Randall asked to be connected with Jesse Pedersen's office.

In a moment he heard Pedersen's "Yes, Mr. President," a faint echo in a well of fatigue.

"Anything new?" asked Randall.

"We've got seven task forces of agents ready to move."

"Good. . . . Jesse, how many children are held in those homes? Is it fourteen?"

"No, sir. The total of the minors, all of them white, is nineteen."

"Nineteen. That's all, Jesse. Thanks."

He left his wake-up call with Gertrude for 6:30 A.M., only ninety minutes away. Outside the ash and slate hues of early morning flowed across the immense lawn like a silent, rising river. He walked slowly through the flag-flanked doorway to his adjoining bedroom. Five hours ago, when Attorney General Garrity called on that bed-side phone, Phil Randall had been a happy man, abrim with his new idea, as buoyant as youth. Now he felt the dry flaking of age. He was utterly beat. Poor Kathy. Poor Dad. Poor everybody.

Chapter Nine

It was a few minutes before seven o'clock Monday morn-ing at Fairhill when Scott Crawford opened the door of his sister's room and tiptoed toward her bed. He was dressed in a pair of rumpled jeans and a T-shirt which shouted "ZAP" in large crimson letters.

Delicate sunlight slipped across the room, melting the shadows and brightening Holly's crayon drawings on the wall. The laughing, pumpkin-headed boy teetered on the steeple of the orange church. Holly lay beneath a sheet, her head tucked between the forelegs of the panda which Scott had surrendered for a second night. Holly's own legs were drawn up toward her chin, and she smiled du-biously in her womblike sleep.

Scott shook his sister's shoulder. "Wake up, Holly," he said in a stage whisper borrowed from television dramas. She slept on and he shook again. "Holly!" This time he breathed into her ear.

She came awake with a start, sat up, and rubbed her eyes. Scott leaned over the bed, holding a forefinger to his lips.

"Shsh," he whispered. "Come on. Get up. There's a secret meeting and everything."

She edged out of bed and stood uncertainly in her nightgown with the blue ribbon at the neckline. Her straight blond hair tumbled about her head like scattered

straw. She yawned, then gazed at her brother, ready for
the leader's commands.

"You got to get dressed," he said in a low, conspira-
torial tone. "And don't make any noise."

"I know," said Holly. She went to the bureau drawer
and took out a blue cotton blouse and a fresh pair of
jeans. She pulled off her nightgown while Scott solemnly
inspected her bare body. After struggling into the clothes,
she put on yesterday's socks and attacked her shoes. She
had trouble with the laces.

"You're dumb," said Scott. "Let me tie them." But he
found he could not fashion a bow while facing the wrong
way, so he settled for a tight knot in each shoelace.

"What are we going to do?" asked Holly, imitating her
brother's furtive tone.

"Shsh. Shut up and come on."

With Scott in the lead they tiptoed along the hall and
descended the spiral stairway a step at a time, seeking to
muffle the scrape of their shoes.

"Tell me," demanded Holly at the bottom of the stairs.

Scott quieted her with a peremptory wave of his hand
and went to one of the narrow windows flanking the front
door. Peering out, he saw Harve Marsh standing near the
large oak tree.

"Okay," said Scott. He led the way to the rear of the
house, down the corridor which passed the library. At the
back door he said: "Now run as fast as you can across
the yard to the path in the woods. And don't yell or fall or
anything."

"Why?"

Scott ignored the question. He opened the back door,
guided his sister out by the hand, then closed the door
softly behind them.

"Okay. Beat it for the path."

The Lilliputians raced across the lawn to the shelter of
the woods. Scott crouched in the path and pulled Holly
down beside him.

"Perly and Ben and Chili," he whispered, "are all
down by the creek, I think."

"How do you know?" Holly was as breathless over
forthcoming adventure as from her short run.

"You'll see. We got to sneak down the path like Indi-

ans. Don't break any twigs or something. When I hold up
my hand, you stop. But don't talk unless you whisper."

Bent over, Scott and Holly advanced cautiously down
the path. After about fifty yards the cleared area near the
creek came into view. Scott stopped his sister and held a
finger to his lips again. His prediction proved correct.
Standing beside the stream were Ben Steele and Perly
Wiggins. Chili Ambrose squatted on the ground near a
long box with a panel of knobs and dials. He was turning
one of the dials. A metal rod extended high above the
box. The three black men were about sixty feet down the
sloping pathway from Scott and Holly.

"That's a radio Chili's workin'," Scott whispered into
his sister's ear.

"I know," she whispered back.

"And Peter Wilson's with them."

"Where?"

"Standing beside Ben," said Scott.

At once Holly saw the mythical Peter Wilson. He made
a tall, noble figure beside the puttering stream, and he
was looking down at the crouching Chili.

"I saw them all from my window," explained Scott. "I
knew they were going to the creek for a conference or
something. So I woke you up." Scott grandly implied that
generosity dictated inclusion of his young partner, but, in
truth, the prospect of a solitary mission to the woods had
not appealed to him. Scott Crawford was not yet of the
cut of heroes.

"Let's listen to what they're doin'," he ordered. The
children sat down in the path at a spot where a bush
partially masked them from below. The early morning air
was nippy, and Holly hugged her knees.

Chili Ambrose turned several dials. A crackle of static
could be heard. Ambrose took a microphone from a panel
bracket and spoke into it: "This is Position One. Position
One. Come in, Lion. Come in, Lion."

The radio burped and sputtered for a moment. Then a
scratchy voice said: "This is Lion. Come ahead."

Ambrose handed the microphone to Steele who squatted down beside the set.

"They've said 'no' to Plan A here," said Steele, "but I

want to try again today. How about extending the deadline until this noon?"

"No," said the radio voice. "Plan A never had a chance. . . . F.Y.I., Sprague double-crossed us and has been wasted."

"When and where?" asked Steele.

"Yesterday morning. In Harlem."

"Why didn't you tell us?" asked Steele.

"Shorty just arrived here with the word." The voice swelled and faded. "We figure the bureau already knows or will soon. So you go to Plan B at once."

"I'm against Plan B as stated in council," said Steele. "I want to try my alternate."

"No." The radio voice was emphatic. "You're to go ahead with Plan B right now."

"I refuse," said Steele heatedly. "You know Plan B means blastin'. No. I won't do it."

"I'm repeatin' my order to Position One." The far voice rode a high whine of static.

Steele looked from Ambrose to Wiggins but said nothing into the microphone.

"Position One! This is the Lion. I want a receipt for my order. Speak up!"

"I hear yah," said Steele. "I say no. Brothers are gonna get killed. . . . Plan B was never okayed by council."

There was a rustle of static and then: "The Lion has complete authority in the field. I'm askin' you one more time. Will you carry out Plan B?"

"Negative. No."

"Are you there, Chili?" asked the radio voice.

Ambrose snatched the microphone from Steele's hand. "Yes, sir. Chili speakin'," he said.

"Chili," said the voice, "you take over from Ben as my deputy commanding Position One. Then you go ahead with Plan B. You got it? Repeat what I said."

"I take over," said Ambrose. "I carry out Plan B."

"Check. The Lion is signing off. Contact us again in six hours."

"Okay," said Chili. He stooped down, flicked a switch, and replaced the mike on its bracket. Then Ambrose straightened, folded his arms, and faced Steele.

"You heard him, Ben baby," he said. "You out. I'm takin' over."

"No, you not." Steele's low voice barely carried up the slope to Scott and Holly. "I'm deputy commander until the council throws me out. Here, I'm Number One."

"Says who?" barked Ambrose. He took a step toward Steele. "You ain't no blood, Ben. You nothin' but a hanky head."

Up the path Scott leaned against his sister and whispered: "You scared? Let's go." His plea made no impression on Holly. She was staring at the scene below, totally absorbed in the words and actions of the two men.

Steele put out his hand. "Gimme that gun, Chili."

Ambrose stepped back quietly, yanked the blue automatic from his belt, and aimed it at Steele from waist level.

"Come get it, cat," he said.

Steele remained motionless. He stood perhaps five feet from Ambrose. The two men stood in taut silence for a moment, then Steele said evenly: "Use your head, Chili. Anybody gets hurt here, we blow it all."

"I'm the man now and we goin' to B," said Ambrose. "Ben, you ain't nothin' but talk, a talkin' Tom. Now me, you know my motto: Take ten." He flicked his eyes toward Wiggins while keeping the gun aimed at Steele. "Take ten. That right, Perly?"

The question broke the spell for Holly Crawford. She felt her brother's arm trembling against hers and she was suddenly overwhelmed by fright. She scrambled to her feet, yanked at Scott. "Come on," she said. She meant it to be a whisper, but the words came out on a high, squeaky note. The children turned and began to run blindly up the path.

"Get 'em, Perly!" It was a startled command from Ambrose below.

Both Holly and Scott screamed. Scott, running, felt the soles of his shoes slip on the well-worn path. The upward slope was a gradual one, but it seemed steep and interminably long to Scott. He heard heavy, thudding footsteps behind him. In his panic he outdistanced his sister. As he reached the edge of the woods and the open lawn, he heard Holly let out a single shriek behind him. He turned his head as he ran and caught a fleeting glimpse of Holly falling and Wiggins's hand grabbing her blouse.

Scott fled across the sun-bright lawn, fearful that Harve Marsh would round the corner from the front of the house at any moment. He yelled, "Mommy . . . Dad," a strangled cry. He fell against the back door, fumbled with the doorknob, pushed the door open, and ran down the shadowed hall to the stairway. He tried to run up the stairs, gripping the spokes of the banister for support. The spiral stairway seemed as high as a mountain. He cried again for his parents in a spasm of terror. His limbs were watery-weak by the time he reached the upper hall.

Then Scott saw the long, pajama-covered legs of his father striding from the big bedroom, and he fell against them, burrowing into the haven. Almost at once his mother was kneeling beside him, and not until he was safely buried in her bosom could Scott find the strength to cry. When he did, the tears poured forth and spilled down his cheeks.

Liz rocked him gently. Tim kneaded the boy's shoulders. Sharp cries punctuated the sobbing, and fright convulsed his reddened face. Finally Tim slapped Scott's cheek a single time. The boy looked up in surprise, understood, and began to fight for control. The sobs subsided gradually, but some time passed before Scott could utter a word.

"They, they . . ." he began.

"Easy, Scott," said Tim. "You're okay now. Try to tell us what happened."

"They got Holly down by the creek," he said. He wiped his eyes with the back of his hand but promptly burst into another fit of crying.

"Come, come," said Liz. "You're all right now." She held him to her breast.

"Take your time," said Tim. He waited a moment. "But you've got to tell us, so we can help."

"Yeah." Scott struggled anew to calm himself. "Well, see. Chili was talkin' on this radio down at the creek, see, and Holly and me were listening on the path, and then this guy on the radio says to do B or something. . . ."

"What radio?" asked Tim.

"The radio they got down there." Scott's tone became

quickly, if shakily, querulous over this adult stupidity.
"It's got a big antenna and everything. So there's this guy
on the radio. His name is Lion."

"Lion?" asked Liz.

"Yeah." Scott backed off from his mother's arms. The
drama of his narrative, and his central role as witness,
overcame his fears. "So when this Lion tells Ben to do B
or something, Ben says no. Then Chili pulls his gun on
Ben. That's when me and Holly took off. But Chili yelled
at Mr. Wiggins to grab us and he came running up and
got Holly at the top of the path, but he didn't get me."

Scott stood proudly alone now, blinking to ward off a
new freshet of tears. He was a man with "ZAP" on his T-
shirt. He looked eagerly from Liz to Tim. Sometimes his
parents believed and sometimes they did not.

"Do you mean that Wiggins has Holly now?" asked
Liz.

Scott nodded vigorously. "Yeah, him and Chili got
Holly and Peter Wilson and Ben too. I'll bet they're all
prisoners down at the creek."

Tim and Liz exchanged mystified glances.

"Scott, let me get it straight," said Tim. "Do you mean
that Chili Ambrose is the boss now?"

"That's what I told you." Scott frowned. His father
could be very dense at times. "This Lion on the radio told
Chili to take over."

"What were you doing on the path at this hour?" asked
Tim.

"I saw Ben and them go down the creek path from my
window," said Scott. "So I woke up Holly and we followed 'em." He struck a defiant stance, daring authority
to reprimand him for using independent judgment on a
risky mission of espionage.

"I see." Tim decided this was no time to squander
dwindling resources on disciplinary lectures.

Liz looked helplessly at Tim. Scott's burden of fear had
been shifted to her back. "Holly," she said. She bit down
on her lower lip.

"I'll find out what I can as soon as I put on some
clothes," said Tim.

As he turned to the bedroom, they heard a loud slam
of the front door.

"Is that kid up there?" The question was a harsh shout. The voice was Chili Ambrose's.

"Yes," Tim called back.

"Nobody leaves the house," Ambrose said. The words pounded up from the foyer. "You hear? . . . Nobody." The door slammed again. The floor quivered with the shock.

"Oh, dear God," said Liz. "If that man hurts Holly . . ."

"Steady, Liz," said Tim. He took Scott's hand. "You come in the bedroom with us while we get dressed." Liz rose to her feet, and the three people filed into the large bedroom.

Scott, sensing that he was the sole custodian of valuable information, sat on the bed and gabbled in fits and starts while his parents dressed. Under Tim's prodding Scott finally told his story chronologically from the time he looked out his window. He extolled Ben Steele's performance and said he doubted if Chili Ambrose would ever manage to kill Ben with the gun, because Peter Wilson would jump Chili from behind and strangle him. Not for the first time Tim became exceedingly annoyed with Peter Wilson, whose presence at the wooded scene made it difficult to separate fact from fiction.

"And if Peter Wilson grabs Chili," concluded Scott, "then I bet Holly will bite Chili's leg or something."

At the new mention of Holly, Liz stepped quickly to Tim and threw her arms around him. "What can we do?" she whispered. "I'm not sure I can hold up much longer." Tim embraced her and nuzzled her cheek. It was a brief interlude. Liz, uncomforted and struggling to control herself, walked to the bathroom where she splashed water over her face, scrubbed her teeth, and spent several minutes combing her hair. When she returned, she seated herself in the small wooden rocker.

Tim sat beside Scott on the bed and put his arm around the boy. "Good man," he said. "You did fine."

"You're not mad because I left Holly?" asked Scott.

Tim squeezed the small shoulder. "No. If you were a bigger boy, maybe, but you did right to run to us."

"Dad," asked Scott, "what does 'take ten' mean? That Chili, he said it two times."

"Take ten?" Tim's arm tightened involuntarily about

Scott's shoulders. How should he answer? Tim was aware
of the term. In the litany of young black warriors of the
ghettos, it had an ominous meaning: If racial showdown
comes and the guns speak, make sure that if you are to
die, you kill not one white person, but ten. On some lips
the phrase was but a figure of speech in the rhetoric of
black power. But other blacks sounded it as a literal war
cry for white blood. On the lips of Chili Ambrose? . . .
Tim knew intuitively that this was no time to enlighten his
already shattered wife and son.

"I'm not sure," he said casually. Then in a serious
tone: "Scott, we didn't tell you the truth Saturday night
because we didn't want to frighten you. The black men
didn't come here as guests. They came to take the house
away from us. Now that you know, you've got to be brave
and help us figure out what to do."

"Okay." Scott squared his shoulders under his father's
arm. "But are they all bad guys? Ben Steele and Harve
Marsh too?"

"I'm not sure," said Tim. "Steele wants me to give
them the house. The others, including Marsh, I guess,
want to take the house away from us whether we agree or
not."

"Why? Don't they have their own house?" Scott looked
up gravely at his father.

"Well . . ." Tim hesitated. How could he explain without raking through the long years of racial history from
the fetid holds of slave ships to the haunted rage in Ben
Steele's eyes?

"Because they're gangsters," said Liz with sudden sav-
agery. "Because they're cutthroats and killers."

"Now, Liz." Tim feared the impact of the words on
Scott. "I don't think we can call them killers, and that
certainly isn't true of Steele."

"Don't you dare!" Liz shouted her order, glancing at
Tim. "Don't you dare defend Steele or any of the rest of
them. . . . Damn it, Tim, in the name of Christ, what kind
of man are you? Those crazy men have your daughter
prisoner in the woods and you sit there like Emerson or
Plato or somebody, trying to be temperate and judicious.
. . . I don't want to hear another word of that asinine talk,
not one more word."

"Please, Puss." Tim lowered his tone to a soothing level. "Let's both try to be as calm as Scott is. We're not going to solve anything—"

"No, no, no." Liz clapped her hands to her ears. "Stop it. You'll drive me crazy."

"Puss."

"Shut up!" She shrieked it. A wild look glazed her eyes as they darted frantically from Scott to Tim. The contagion of bewildered fear spread to Scott, and the boy dissolved in fresh tears.

Scott ran to his mother and threw himself in her lap. Both sobbed as one. Tim tried to embrace Liz, but she shook off his arm with a furious twist of her shoulders. Tim tried for five minutes to restore calm to his stricken family. Not until her sobs were exhausted did Liz permit Tim to hold her. At last the three Crawfords became a comforting huddle at Liz's rocker. Liz dried her eyes with tissue, then mopped Scott's swollen face. Silence held them as tightly as Tim's arms.

"You misunderstood me, Liz," said Tim at last. "I wasn't defending any of them. I was just afraid we'd frighten Scott all over again."

"I'm sorry, Tim," she said. She seemed relieved that he had spoken. "And I do realize that Steele is different. Take last night. He threatened us with what he was going to tell us about each other, and then he never said a thing. He just sat in the library and tried to, well, hypnotize us into signing the deed."

"Strange guy. He's really complex as hell."

"He mentioned Acapulco, then stopped as if he'd said something he shouldn't." Liz frowned. "Now what could Acapulco have to do with anything?"

Tim shrugged.

"Do you suppose Lion is that Daniel Smith?" asked Liz. "Do you think he's back in the country, Tim? If so, where?"

"I have no idea," said Tim. "They obviously have a shortwave transmitter and receiver down by the stream. If they're talking to Smith, he could be anywhere."

"Tim, I'm sorry I blew up. I couldn't help it." She gripped his hand. "But now, please. Tell us what to do?"

Tim considered, once again beset by frustration. "Chili's

in command now. That means danger. I don't know
how to handle him. . . . But Holly?"

"You've just got to get her back in the house."

He nodded. "If Ambrose will listen. . . . Now I think we
should go downstairs to the kitchen. You fix some breakfast, Liz, while I try to have some kind of parley with
Ambrose."

"I'm not sure I'm up to it," she said. She sagged in defeat. Her face, bare of cosmetics, looked exhausted,
drained.

"Let's try," said Tim. "Okay, Scott? You can help your
mother, can't you?"

Scott nodded silently. A shiver, of the kind that overcame him when he stayed too long in the pool, ran over
the small, thin frame. His new black playmates had
turned into armed bad men who held his sister and Ben
Steele.

They entered the kitchen like the intimidated hostages
they were. Sunlight poured through the windows now,
glinting on the copper pots and pans and throwing bright
patterns on the bronze refrigerator and freezer. An odor
of food and cooking fat hung in the room. Unwashed
dishes littered the sink and counter. The B.O.F. had eaten
early this morning.

Scott stepped to the small portable television set which
rested on the counter next to the electric toaster. He
reached up and turned it on.

"Please, Scott," said Liz. "Not now."

"That's all right, Puss," countered Tim. "It'll give him
something to do." He turned to Scott. "But keep it low,
will you?"

The windows facing the garage and driveway were
open. Yesterday's humidity had vanished. A new dry,
fresh heat rolled into the kitchen with the sunlight. Tim
peered out, searching for Ambrose.

"Hey," he said. "Look!"

He pointed for Liz. About a hundred yards distant,
partially hidden by a clump of birches, a stout Negro
woman was walking slowly up the driveway toward the
house.

"Dora!" Liz exclaimed.

Liz swiftly chided herself. She had remembered yesterday, but this morning the capture of Holly had swept everything else from her mind. She thought for an instant, then shoved Tim aside.

"Dora!" she yelled through the window. "We're prisoners here. Turn around and run for the road. Fast."

Dora Wilcox, startled, stopped in the driveway and looked toward the house as if trying to ascertain where the shout came from.

"Quick," Liz called. "Run. Run. Get the police."

The stout black woman hesitated briefly, then turned and began to run ponderously down the sloping driveway.

Into Liz's vision from the back of the house came Perly Wiggins. He held a rifle against his chest, and he was running as fast as he could with that burden. He swiftly closed the gap between himself and Dora Wilcox. Then he halted and yelled, "Stop or I'll shoot!" When Dora looked over her shoulder, she saw Wiggins standing on the asphalt drive, his feet firmly planted and his hands pointing the rifle at her. She stopped.

Wiggins walked down the drive, grasped her by an arm, and led her up the hill. Chili Ambrose rounded the house from the front at a trot. The two men conferred on the asphalt in front of the garage while Wiggins maintained a tight hold on the woman's arm. Wiggins nodded after a moment and then propelled Dora to the tool shed beside the garage. He shoved her inside. Ambrose walked over, pulled a bunch of keys from his pocket, tried several in the lock until he found one that fitted. It seemed apparent that the escapade of Holly and Scott had upset the blacks as much as the Crawfords, for the invaders must have known that Dora Wilcox would come to work Monday morning.

"That guy even found my keys somewhere," mumbled Tim. He and Liz were standing rigidly at the kitchen window. While they watched, Chili Ambrose strode across the lawn toward the kitchen. His automatic was jammed in the green dungarees, and, Tim noted with surprise, Ben Steele's medallion of Frantz Fanon now dangled from Ambrose's neck. Ambrose came so close to the window that Liz could see the tiny pockmarks in the midnight face.

"You want us to waste you, woman?" he asked. "This is your second warning. That's all you git."

"Where's my daughter?" asked Liz. She refused to flinch before the searing green eyes. "What have you done with Holly?"

Ambrose stared at her. "None of your goddam business."

The silence, a frozen moment, was cracked by Scott.

"Mommy, Dad," he called. "Look! The President or somebody is on TV and he's saying something about us."

Liz and Tim wheeled around and stepped in front of the small television set. There, on the gray, flickering screen, with the seal of the President of the United States and above it, amid a thicket of microphones, was the familiar face of Philip Garland Randall.

Chapter Ten

President Randall stood behind a podium which rested on a long, eight-sided, highly polished table. Over his shoulders could be seen a quite formal mantelpiece and a portrait of Thomas Jefferson. Tim Crawford recognized the backdrop as the Cabinet Room of the White House. Randall, who normally faced television cameras with an insouciant air, appeared drawn and somber. Though he was speaking in a low-key, conversational manner, his voice had a taut, incisive quality.

"It is significant," the President was saying, "that all of these homes, with the exception of Mr. Timothy Crawford's place near Princeton, New Jersey, are in relatively isolated areas. As I say, telephone wires have been severed at all the residences.

"The evidence gathered by the Federal Bureau of Investigation indicates that the Blacks of February Twenty-first are holding forty-one persons captive. Nineteen of these are children who range in age from a girl of ten months to a boy of fourteen. Except for four Negro employees, all the captives are white.

"We don't yet know the motives of the Blacks of February Twenty-first in seizing these six properties. If the homes are being held in ransom, so to speak, the price for their release remains unstated."

Liz turned to Tim, standing beside her. "Five other places. So it isn't only us." Tim's eyes were fixed on the TV screen. "I should have guessed," he said.

Liz glanced down at Scott, huddled against her thigh. She saw that, for the first time in months, he was sucking his thumb. His gaze was riveted on the small picture of the President.

She heard a movement behind her and turned to see Chili Ambrose standing in the kitchen doorway with folded arms. He too was transfixed by the televised image and voice.

"We probably wouldn't yet know what had happened if the FBI had not turned up some puzzling information yesterday morning. This included a series of numerals which proved to be the telephone numbers of the six homes. When called, all phones were out of order. This led the FBI to the discovery of a nationally organized plan to seize property from Vermont to California.

"I'd like to detour for a bit right now. This Administration sympathizes with many of the aims of the Blacks of February Twenty-first. We too believe in a society of total equality of opportunity in every walk of life. The laws designed to achieve this are all on the books. What this country needs now is a wholesome change in attitudes —and I mean the attitudes of white people—so that black men and women will be accorded the same dignity, respect, and opportunity that whites take for granted. This is far more than a matter of law. It is a matter of the heart, of your heart and my heart. We whites have got to change if this country is going to survive, and as long as I'm President, I intend to do my utmost to bring that change about. To the extent that the Blacks of February Twenty-first demand full and equal partnership in our system, in the whole economic and social fabric from

schools to church, from factory to Wall Street, from
sheriff to President, from city apartments to country estates, from unions to professional societies and clubs, to
that extent I'm with the B.O.F. 100 percent.

"On the other hand, the Administration cannot con-
done the views of some B.O.F. leaders, including those of
Mr. Daniel Smith, who is now leading this B.O.F. venture
from the Great Smoky Mountains. These men have
threatened violence, sabotage, and even revolution if certain demands—most of them but vaguely articulated—are
not met. In fact one can't help suspecting that the demands are kept purposefully cloudy because the real goal
of Mr. Smith may be, not the reform of injustices, but the
destruction of the American system."

"That's it, baby!" It was an exclamation from Chili
Ambrose in the doorway. The three Crawfords turned
as one, but Ambrose did not deign to look at them. He
still stood with arms folded, and beside him now was
Harve Marsh, who held a shotgun against his hip.

That, thought Tim with a sinking feeling, settled the
question of Harve Marsh's loyalties. He was Chili's
man.

"Tim, I've got to sit down," said Liz.

Tim dragged two chairs from the side of the hickory
breakfast table. Liz slumped into one and Scott leaned
deep into her lap.

"But for the moment the aims of the B.O.F. are aca-
demic. This morning we Americans are faced with a single, overriding fact—private property has been seized on
a national scale in violation of law. Indeed, public land
has been occupied in one case, for the Tiegert home in
California is on ground under long-term lease from the
Forest Service. Such confiscation cannot be tolerated in
the United States, regardless of motive or provocation.
This administration has always put individual rights above
property rights, but unless both sets of rights are honored,
we can't function as an orderly society. So, with some re-
luctance but with no apology, I have decided to take certain steps under the powers vested in me by the riot and
insurrection acts. These are:

"One. I have ordered units of the 82nd Airborne Division at Fort Bragg, North Carolina, to emplane for airports near the six homes in question. The first of these troops will take off in a few minutes. The men are under orders to surround and cordon off each home site and to await my further orders as commander in chief. Although they are in full combat status, the men are under strict instructions to use no lethal weapons of any kind except in self-defense. They are fully equipped with standard antiriot gear such as CS gas and Mace."

"Good God, Tim," said Liz. "If they try to get in here. . . . Holly?"

Tim shook his head. Never had he felt so impotent to influence any facet of his own behavior. It was as if his brain recognized the futility of sending further messages to a body locked in paralysis. Before him was a remote, flickering President and behind him was the shadowy Chili Ambrose, opposing powers in a struggle for Fairhill.

"Two. I have talked to the governors of the six states involved and asked them to provide such supporting state police forces as may be necessary. They, in turn, are requesting aid and support from local police. All six governors promptly agreed.

"Three. I call upon members of the B.O.F. at each site to lay down their arms and give themselves up to the authorities. All B.O.F. members have my promise, as well as those of the governors, that if they surrender promptly, no further legal action will be taken against them. However, if they do not surrender, they will be brought to trial under pertinent laws—both state and federal."

Scott tugged at his father's arm. "He's coming to help Holly, isn't he? And Ben Steele too?"

The question echoed in the cave of Tim's mind. The cadence of the President's words, the mottled, dancing lines on the TV screen, and the diminutive size of the set itself all combined to produce an aura of fantasy. It was as though Tim were watching the unfolding of some distant fictional drama, presented for the entertainment of a disembodied audience floating somewhere in space. The spectacle demanded no personal reaction, only a fixed, numbed stare.

"Yes, Scott," was all that Tim could say. He wondered at the boy's ability to link the President's electronic voice to the reality of their own claustrophobic dilemma at Fairhill.

"Four. I ask all Americans, white and black, to remain calm during the next four hours. I urge that no one walk, cycle, drive, or fly near these six homes. The roads must be left open for official traffic. And, of course, I expect the media to exercise restraint in handling the news. This is no time to air unchecked rumors and gossip.

"While I'm concerned about the safety of the adults in these homes, my big worry is the children. There are nineteen children held prisoner, and it would be a sorry mark on the record if any harm befell them. Here in Washington we have moved with caution precisely because of the children.

"However, I can't believe that any member of the Blacks of February Twenty-first would intentionally jeopardize the safety of a child. The fact that these particular youngsters are all white boys and girls is immaterial. We understand that some of the invading B.O.F. members are themselves fathers. It would be a travesty on the memory of Malcolm X, for whom the B.O.F. is named, if harm came to any child. I met Malcolm X in the last months of his life, and I can assure you that he was a man of compassion for all races and all peoples. Underneath our white and black skins, we are all just humble human beings. Malcolm X understood that. He would never have risked the lives of small children to achieve any goal. I trust that those now organized in his name will give these youngsters the same protection and the same immunity from harm that Malcolm would have done."

"Man, them honkies is slick with their rap," said Harve Marsh from the kitchen doorway.

"Yeah," said Chili, "but we still takin' ten."

He held out his open palm and Marsh slapped it smartly.

"One final word. Some black citizens may think that I speak solely for the white population. I hope I speak for all Americans, but to satisfy any doubts, I have asked three respected black Americans to talk to you now. I know that all three share my anxiety at this hour, but, aside from giving them the facts, there has been no attempt by me to influence them or to suggest what they should say. They will speak as Americans. First, a surgeon who is president of the National Association for the Advancement of Colored People, Dr. Raymond George Henderson."

"Dig that white nigguh!" said Chili Ambrose. "Take eleven," added Harve Marsh. They laughed.

The TV scene switched from the presidential podium to a table at which sat a thin, bespectacled man of light brown color. He leaned toward the microphones before him.

"Good morning, fellow Americans. I am Ray Henderson, president of the N.A.A.C.P., speaking to you from New York City. I endorse the statement of President Randall. For white citizens, I can add nothing to what he has said. But for my black brothers, let me say this: The President of the United States has acted with restraint, perhaps more than I myself would have exercised. He has offered amnesty to members of the B.O.F., and I accept his word on this. He intends to hold back the paratroops until the answer comes from the B.O.F. leaders. There can be but one answer. They must yield. Otherwise we face an outbreak of fighting that could trigger something very ugly. You know that and I know it. So let every brother and sister remain calm. Go about your business. Provoke no incidents. Place your trust in President Randall. I know that he believes in our cause. Thank you."

Television cameras zoomed back to President Randall. "Are soldiers coming here?" asked Scott. His mother nodded.

"I would now like to introduce a good friend of long standing, Stephen Langford, head of the Congress for Racial Equality. He also speaks from New York City. . . . Mr. Langford."

The scene shifted back to the same studio table from which Dr. Henderson spoke. Langford, a former pro football fullback, was a huge man with an ebony face and natural, Afro-American hair.

"I'm Steve Langford and I want to speak exclusively to my fellow blacks. We all know that historically in this country we've gotten the meanest, the most unjust, and the most cynically oppressive deal of any ethnic minority since the world began. But that's history. Today President Phil Randall speaks our language. We know that he's a man of his word, that he brought black men into the top ranks of his campaign by the dozens, and that since his inauguration he has given us real hope by everything he does and says. So let's talk hard politics. We gave Phil Randall 86 percent of our vote, and he's been repaying it with fair play for black people. Finally we've got a real chance for some progress in this country. And I don't want to see it destroyed by one reckless move by some misguided brothers with guns. . . . So let's keep the faith with the man who's playing straight with us. This is no time for preaching. I've got just two words for my brothers: Cool it!"

Again the camera faded back to Washington and the White House cabinet room. The lens caught President Randall an instant before he realized that he was again on camera, and Tim and Liz caught his perturbed look, the candid look of a man in trouble.

At that moment an arm protruded from the side of the screen, handing a piece of paper to Randall. The President absentmindedly took the note, sensed that he was again facing the country, and held the paper in his

right hand without looking at it. He smiled somewhat
awkwardly.

"Finally, a remarkable woman who has become famous
through the poignancy and majesty of her voice. I never
met her, but she has given me hours of pleasure via her
records and her television appearances. . . . The great vo-
calist of soul, Miss Virginia Jones."

Back to New York went the camera to pick up Virginia Jones in the same studio where Henderson and
Langford had appeared.

The sight of Ginny became a swift magnet for Tim,
tugging at his memories of the mauve dusk at Acapulco, of the ephemeral dark girl of yesterdays, of Jackson
Dill, of so many things past and lost. He dropped into
a mood of relentless melancholy.

Ginny was a tiny knot of tension. She sat with her
hands clasped tightly in her lap, her eyes boring into
the camera. She wore a simple cotton dress and two
gold loop earrings. She was unsmiling.

"Good morning. I'm talking to you from New York.
President Randall called me about an hour ago and explained what you now know. He asked me if I would appear on this program and speak to you about the situation
—including the nineteen children he has mentioned. I am
grateful for the opportunity. It is unthinkable that harm
of any kind would come to any of these innocent children.
I am sure that no member of the Blacks of February
Twenty-first—and I know many of them—has any intent
to hurt a single girl or boy. But in case the thought of sac-
rificing the security of a child to the aims of the organization has entered the head of any B.O.F. member, well, I
now urge him as the soul sister that I am to think again
about what he's doing."

Liz looked at Tim with a bemused expression, the
slow dawning of recognition.

"Isn't she the girl you knew in Acapulco, Tim?"

He nodded abstractedly, from the fastness of his
memories.

"Acapulco," said Liz slowly. "So that was what
Steel intended to tell me, but never did." Her eyes
dwelled on Tim, curious, questioning. Then Ginny's
voice drew her attention back to the screen.

"However, having said that, I must respectfully disagree with President Randall's request that people stay
away from these six places he has named. I would like to
tell you something that your President is either ignorant
of, or if he is aware of it, he intentionally withheld from
you. Whichever is the case, it is a fact that the President
knows each of these property owners quite well. They all
have some political connection with him. Also I happen
to know what he didn't tell you—that the owners of every
one of these properties has been guilty of profiteering, directly or otherwise, from the sweat and toil of us—the
oppressed."

Tim pondered. Oppressed? It was difficult to picture
a woman making $15,000 an engagement in the ranks
of the downtrodden. And did President Randall know
that Ginny was a secret member of the B.O.F.? Why
was she on this show? He recalled her signature at the
bottom of the memo to Commander Smith protesting
the seizure of Fairhill.

"Let me tell you briefly about these six homes. In the
case of Bar Triple X ranch in Arizona, owned by State
Senator Arthur Broderick, more than 14,000 acres of this
vast holding were claimed by Broderick's grandfather
under titles stemming from old land grants of the Spanish
crown some four centuries ago. Broderick's grandfather
reactivated these shaky claims at a cost to him of about
one dollar an acre. This kind of white man's cunning dis-
possessed several hundred Mexican-American families who
had been grinding out a hard, but adequate, living on the
land. These poor people who were called squatters—a
white man's term—were evicted from their shacks and
forced to go elsewhere.

"And let's talk about the island lodge in the St.
Lawrence River. The owner, Mr. Dittmar of Empire Motors, has a wife whose chief income comes from shares in

a savings and loan institution. This company holds mortgages in Detroit's black neighborhoods and charges outrageous 'points,' as they are lightly called by white profiteers, to any black person who needs a mortgage. Moreover, Mr. Dittmar has steadily refused requests of black economists that black men be placed on Empire's board of directors to represent the hundreds of thousands of blacks who drive Empire cars. Mr. Dittmar contends that the directors represent shareholders, not car owners. But I ask—where do a lot of Empire's profits come from?"

"I'm beginning to get the pitch," said Tim to Liz. "This has all been stitched together for the B.O.F. by some very clever people. I wonder if Ben Steele is one of the masterminds."

"Do you suppose he's alive?" whispered Liz. "And is Holly with him?" Her voice faltered. Liz realized that her feelings about Steele had suddenly shifted. Now he was no longer the focus of her fears but of her hopes for Holly. In her mind Steele had assumed the role of guardian, and somehow she trusted her intuition.

Tim turned toward the doorway. Chili Ambrose was seated on a chair now just inside the kitchen. His arms were folded over the Frantz Fanon medallion, and he was staring at the screen, totally engrossed.

"As for the Florida residence the President talked about, the owner is Charles Delaney, who is consultant to the governor of Florida on industrial development. Mr. Delaney made his millions in a New York civil-engineering firm which, during all his years of control, deliberately denied jobs to blacks and Puerto Ricans despite the fact that many of these applicants were graduates of top engineering schools.

"Fritz Tiegert owns the mountain lodge at Silver Lake, California. He is also a very powerful man in this country, president of the Brotherhood of Truckers and Haulers, which has a giant pension and welfare fund. Although many union members are black, Mr. Tiegert admits no blacks to top union leadership and he refuses to name even one black man to the board of the vast pension fund. Is this simple racism by Mr. Tiegert, or does he fear an honest black voice on the board of Tiegert puppets? For remember, the fund is a tremendous social and political weapon which Mr. Tiegert runs as he sees fit—and he has not seen fit to invest in or aid the black communities of the nation. And another count. Mr. Tiegert's pension fund has some millions of dollars invested in South African mines. Did you know that? No, because he has kept it a secret from the public and from the rank and file of the union. He's an investor in a country where blacks are held in economic and social slavery. And naturally, for all his red-white-and-blue equality talk here at home, Fritz Tiegert never once has raised his voice against the despicable antiblack practices of the government of South Africa."

"How you like your lovin' black doll now, Crawford?" asked Chili from the kitchen doorway.

"Oh, the words!" said Harve Marsh admiringly. "That woman sure can rap."

"The Fairhill estate near Princeton, New Jersey, was bought by the present owner's father from money he piled up in Trenton. He picked up tax-foreclosed black properties at twenty-five cents on the dollar during the depression. The blacks, of course, lost their homes. The son and present owner of Fairhill, Timothy Crawford, Jr., knows about this but has never made a move to make restitution to the defrauded blacks, nor even taken an interest in their problems."

Liz glanced at Tim, a shy, covert look. If there were ever anything between Tim and Virginia Jones, she thought, the singer had cut the ties as cleanly as any woman could. She wondered. Virginia Jones seemed so small, so austere, so alien, so frightening in her self-discipline.

"Lastly, there's the Lake Champlain home of Jacob Shapiro, the playwright. Jake Shapiro's father grew rich through ownership of a chain of ghetto pawnshops that regularly cheated blacks by charging exorbitant interest on pawn loans. Mr. Shapiro's private fortune, apart from his modest earnings as a playwright, is based on this ghetto loot amassed by his father. Oh, of course, Mr. Shapiro's plays always carry a deep social message. But not deep enough, I submit, to ever touch his own conscience.

"So you see, fellow Americans, there are two sides to this story. The President speaks of property rights in the same breath with human rights. Sure, we blacks believe in property rights, but blacks do not believe that white fortunes pirated from the sweat and exploitation of black people have any moral quote 'right' unquote to exist. Blacks believe in justice for all, not justice for the majority race only. To the white mind, used to acquiring wealth by any means, ownership is a holy virtue in itself. As a black I don't see it that way—not at all. I do not believe that whites should profit outrageously from the sweat of blacks, any more than I believe the Mafia fortunes, based on trafficking in drugs, prostitution, loan sharking, and murder-for-hire, should be allowed to control large business enterprises.

"Now a word about President Randall. I agree with Mr. Henderson and Mr. Langford that the President has made an honest attempt to change the climate for blacks in America. I agree that he has talked our language. But can any white man be thoroughly trusted by us? I ask this because I think President Randall broke his word to black leaders. He promised them in March that no black organization would be infiltrated by federal agents. How then does he explain the information about the phone numbers that the FBI obtained? Could the FBI get that without infiltrating the B.O.F.? It's rumored that a black FBI agent was killed in New York yesterday. Was he perhaps caught spying on the B.O.F.? Where did those phone numbers come from?

"Finally, I urge every black person to ignore the plea of President Randall to keep away from the homes we've heard about. Instead I urge you to drive, fly, walk, or crawl to those luxurious white estates as fast as you can get there—and I urge you to gather at the fences and the barriers so that you form a living wall of black flesh. The mercenaries of the white man, be they soldiers, state troopers, or policemen, will have to dig their way through ramparts of black people to regain the six mansions. Do not carry arms. I repeat. Do not carry firearms, knives, or other weapons. But hurry to those homes and show the white man that we can build a great, black wall of resistance.

"Brothers and sisters, let's go to the barricades singing that rich and powerful song of soul."

Tim, Liz, and Scott watched hypnotically as Ginny Jones stood up from the table. She stood rigidly, clenching her fists at her sides, as she swung into her deep, haunting theme song, "Black Is Soul, Soul Is Love."

She sang one verse and the chorus, flinging her voice at the eye of the camera and letting the proud lament well up from within. She stood straight and defiant to the last, high, throbbing note.

In the momentary blackout after she finished, the kitchen of Fairhill was hushed. Even Scott held himself quietly without speaking.

The announcer reappeared on the screen. President Randall, he said, would make a few closing remarks. Back to the White House went the camera.

"Friends, I must add a few words. First, I did not break my word to Negro leaders, as Miss Jones implied. It is true that a federal agent worked with the B.O.F. All I can say at this time is that the fault lies with a misunderstanding inside the government. It was not intentional on my part. I keep my word. Second, I did not know the background of the properties which Miss Jones so adroitly described. Neither, to my knowledge, did any of the advisers I consulted on this matter. Had I been aware of the circumstances, I would have told you so. I was not.

"There are many wrongs to be righted in this country, but none of them can be helped by a mass confrontation of blacks and whites on isolated roads near the six homes in question. While I can understand Miss Jones's outrage, I must warn you in all candor that her prescription could lead to senseless violence.

"Therefore, I request black citizens to ignore Miss

Jones's appeal to move toward the properties involved. I make the same request of white citizens. Please stay away and let the authorities handle the situation. If we act wisely, coolly, and prudently today, there is no reason why this business can't be solved peaceably and in short order. I have been frank with you this morning, giving you all the important information that I have. In return I trust that you'll respond with restraint, composure, and common sense. Thank you."

The podium scene faded out and the camera switched again to the New York announcer, a man whose monk-like visage brooded over a daily quota of human folly. Just as he was about to speak, a stocky black man rushed from the side and grabbed the hand microphone from the table.

"What you don't know," said the black man in a tumble of words, "is that an FBI agent in the studio tried to keep Miss Jones from appearing. He would have used force if some of us hadn't held him off just as Miss Jones went on camera. That's so-called white justice. A white president could speak, but a black woman wasn't going to be permitted to expose the hidden lies of what the President said."

He banged the mike down on the table and vanished from the screen as abruptly as he had appeared.

The announcer, flustered for once, managed a bleak smile as he retrieved the microphone. "Well," he said, "now you *certainly* know both sides." He struggled to regain his usual composure. "The man you just heard, Bill Walker, is an assistant producer in the news department. I'm afraid he misjudged my commitment to the news, for I was about to tell you a number of background developments in addition to the, er, business with the FBI agent here.

"The note you saw handed some time ago to President Randall, which he had no chance to read, was—according to our White House reporter—a note from the FBI director, Mr. Jesse Pedersen. It informed the President that Miss Virginia Jones was herself a secret member of the Blacks of February Twenty-first.

"So . . . oh, yes." He glanced at a note on the table. "We are further informed that after President Randall's

TV appearance, he had an argument with his Secretary of Transportation, Mr. Harold Osborne, who is one of two Negroes in the Randall Cabinet. Mr. Osborne was in the cabinet room during the broadcast along with some other presidential advisers. Our White House reporter says that it was Secretary Osborne who recommended the names of the three Negroes who shared today's program with the President. We assume the exchange between the President and Secretary Osborne involved the connection of Miss Jones with the B.O.F., but we aren't sure yet. In deference to President Randall's request we'll refrain from further speculation until we learn the facts—if we can. Meanwhile stay tuned to this station. We will bring you developments in the home-seizure crisis as they occur."

The scene faded into a beer commercial in which a sympathetic white bartender poured a glass of foaming liquid for a black customer. The customer leaned on an elbow and began telling the barkeep of his latest domestic woes.

"Another one of them funky white nigguhs," said Chili Ambrose from the doorway.

The three Crawfords turned. Ambrose stood up and shoved his chair away. Harve Marsh, holding the shotgun, stood beside him. Ambrose spoke to Marsh, ignoring the Crawfords.

"All right," he said, "let's you and me start stacking furniture at the doors and windows. Them jump-boys start comin' up that hill, and we'll kill ten mothers for every one of us they get. . . . Harve, we gonna fight."

Marsh gazed at his new commander, a hesitant, quizzical expression on his face.

Liz arose from her chair and stood with a hand on Scott's shoulder.

"Where is Holly?" she asked.

"That's my business," said Ambrose.

"If you do a thing to my child," said Liz slowly, "I'll kill you in your sleep with my bare hands."

Ambrose stared at her for a moment. "Woman," he said with equal force, "you get within five feet of me, anytime, you're dead. . . . Come on, Harve."

The two invaders left the kitchen.

Chapter Eleven

An Army major tore a sheet of paper from the clacking teleprinter, walked across the brightly lighted room, and handed the strip to General Walter Hildebrand.

"The last flight's in the approach pattern at McGuire," said Hildebrand. His diction was as correct as his tailored Army uniform. "We'll be able to go to the closed circuit in a few minutes."

He handed the paper to President Randall. Three C-141 Starlifters and two of the giant C-5 Galaxy cargo planes, carrying 1,500 troops of the 82nd Airborne Division, were about to land at McGuire Air Force Base, New Jersey, after the flight from North Carolina.

"That buttons up the airlift," said Hildebrand with relief. The delay of this last of the six jet flights still irked him. He was not accustomed to such baring of military snags before a civilian, much less a civilian who was his commander in chief.

Tension sparred with fatigue in the paneled room with its false, soundproofed ceiling. A clanging of bells drew Joe Voorhees to another of the teleprinters that chattered along the wall like a picket line of furious housewives.

"It could have been worse," said Voorhees over his shoulder. "The Dow fell thirty-one points. The exchange composite of all stocks was down $1.37 at closing."

A telephone rang and a red light winked in the cluster of phones resting at the end of a long table. Voorhees stepped over and lifted the receiver. He fingered his sagging paunch as he listened. "Yeah . . . okay . . . right."

Voorhees turned to Randall. "Ed Lee says the market was bad, but no smell of panic—yet." His double chin bulged at his open shirt collar. "Worst hit were motors and trucking stocks. Empire was off four and an eighth at the close."

"What about Alfred Nicolet?" asked Randall.

Voorhees shook his head. "Ed can't locate him anywhere around Boston. But he's got all his lines out."

Randall nodded glumly. He was slouched in a chair
with his legs extended and his feet resting on the rim of a
metal wastebasket. Like Voorhees, but in contrast to the
impeccably elegant General Hildebrand, President Randall had long ago discarded his jacket and loosened his
tie. He held a half-empty cup of coffee. The long day had
marched inexorably toward an uncertain pit of night.
Sweet Kathy was a continent and an eon away. Huge
transport jets smoked across the skies, dragging their
contrails to an unwanted rendezvous. Randall's skin
itched and his eyelids had a grainy feel. He had managed
but two brief snatches of sleep in the last thirty-two
hours. The time was 3:40 P.M.

The situation room in the basement of the White
House west executive wing had been converted into a
command post. Ordinarily this room, which adjoined the
smaller area where the National Security Council met,
held little beside the long table and chairs, a direct telephone line to the Pentagon war room, and a tie-in to the
"hot line" to Moscow. Today the fluorescent ceiling panels shone down on a cluttered domain.

A map of the United States covered one whole wall.
Green plastic ribbons marked the airlift of six detachments of the 82nd Airborne from Pope Air Force Base,
adjacent to Fort Bragg, North Carolina. Thin red tapes
showed the progress via ground transport of paratroops
who had now landed at Air Force bases in five of the six
states. Enlarged highway maps highlighted roads, bridges,
hills, towns, rail lines, and rivers in the vicinity of the six
occupied homes. A topographical map covered the terrain
near Mt. Mitchell, North Carolina, and a yellow tape
marked the route of a posse of FBI agents tracking toward Dan Smith's clandestine command radio. Two Army
majors, carrying handfuls of colored pins, hovered near
the maps. A neatly made cot, where Joe Voorhees had
napped, stood in one corner, a portable liquor cabinet in
another.

A number of teleprinters had been moved in from the
nearby basement communications room and placed
against one wall. Near the machines stood several televi-

sion sets and radios. A Marine sergeant at a typewriter table kept a minute-by-minute log of developments in this White House command post. President Randall seldom snubbed history. A Navy yoeman manned a teleprinter reserved for outgoing orders of President Randall and General Hildebrand. A Marine orderly, ready for errands, chatted with a Secret Service agent at the doorway.

The government's council for its confrontation with the Blacks of February Twenty-first had narrowed now to five men: President Randall, General Hildebrand, Secretary of Defense Paul Edelstein, Transportation Secretary Harold Osborne, and the ubiquitous fat man, Postmaster General Joe Voorhees. Each had his duties in "HICOM," as Voorhees had dubbed the group. As Chairman of the Joint Chiefs of Staff, General Hildebrand directed the military operation. Joe Voorhees handled a nest of phones linking the command post to the Justice Department, the FBI, Treasury Secretary Lee's office, and the outside world. Osborne handled three more phones which kept him in touch with Negro leaders around the country. Paul Edelstein, in addition to military consultations with General Hildebrand, served as liaison with the six governors and state police forces. President Randall commanded.

They had been here now for more than six hours, and, as men will, they were learning to walk with crisis as on a treadmill. Randall sensed a spirit of camaraderie as the unfamiliar became the routine in this air-conditioned room, connected by wire and tube to the entire world, yet insulated in time and space. He had often wondered how he would behave in a time of national stress when his single word could send a parade of men, machines, and events clanking off toward obscure horizons. Who dared utter such a word when the tide might engulf unknown valleys and rush through new passes from which retreat was impossible? Now he knew. He had made his prime decision and, having made it, each new choice dwindled in magnitude. Decision, emergency, peril—such mighty abstractions for small deeds. Actually what a man did differed but little from what he did every day. He looked, he listened, he weighed, he guessed, he acted—or, more frequently, reacted. It was as though, in a more mundane context, he crossed the street, canceled the flight, made the speech, kissed the woman, held his temper, patted the dog. Not once since he entered this room had Phil Randall felt the flutter of indecision. Rather he flowed with events. And he rather liked the sensation. He realized why. He had savored, finally, the rich wine of personal power in a time of national hazard.

One nagging problem was that of keeping in mind an orderly sequence of what had happened. It was easy to forget when one event tumbled at the heels of another like a pack of crosscountry runners. Now he had a few minutes before the last convoy formed at McGuire and rolled out of the air base under the eye of the mobile closed-circuit television. Swiftly he reviewed events of the hectic day in the HICOM post.

First had come his emotionally charged apology to Harold Osborne. Randall had erupted immediately after that television speech, accusing Osborne of knowing that Ginny Jones was a member of the B.O.F. Osborne angrily denied any knowledge of Ginny's complicity. Later, in this situation room, after both men had simmered down, Randall regretted his accusation and reaffirmed his full confidence in the Transportation Secretary. Osborne accepted the apology calmly. The two men shook hands. Still the incident grated in memory, a bit of grime in the delicate engine of their relationship.

The long watch in the situation room, Randall reflected, had been a curious blend of military schedules and civilian alarms. By 10:15 A.M. three flights were airborne from Pope Air Force Base without incident. Each group of planes carried two battalions, antiriot gear, and some motor transport. The third flight headed cross-country for Mather AFB, California, there to form a road convoy for the drive to the Tiegert home at Silver Lake.

Randall's first of many decisions came a few minutes later when Joe Voorhees reported that bus lines were being inundated with Negro customers. Apparently the ticket buyers intended to travel to the seized properties in response to Ginny Jones's appeal. Randall passed instructions to the bus lines not to interfere with commercial road traffic. If Negroes later gathered at the home sites, troops and state police would handle the situation.

Next Governor Elton Danzig of New Jersey telephoned, informing the President that he was ready to call
out the National Guard. Randall, sensing that Danzig was
anxious to burnish his image for his own reelection campaign that fall, patiently dissuaded him. The 82nd had
special skills, said Randall, and the only help needed at
this moment from the governor was his state police.

Soon after, bells rang on the news ticker, announcing a
sharp stock-market drop in the first hour of trading. The
market was especially upset by a mimeographed statement, signed merely "B.O.F.," which was delivered to the
offices of news media and New York brokerage houses.
The manifesto said the B.O.F. was demanding two seats
on the Empire Motors board of directors and one black
man on the board of the Truckers & Haulers' pension
fund. If these demands were met, said the statement, the
Tiegert and Dittmar homes might be released. No mention was made of the other homes.

Shortly after eleven came the first sour note in the
military movement. The Pope AFB commanding officer
notified General Hildebrand that the sixth and last flight,
destined for McGuire AFB, New Jersey, would be de-
layed because of C-5 engine trouble. Some smaller C-
141s were being ferried in. General Hildebrand, obviously
annoyed, demanded all speed possible.

Treasury Secretary Lee phoned in an hour later to report a sell-off of American securities in European markets. Because of the time-zone difference, European
traders did not have time to digest the meaning of the
U.S. crisis before the closing of markets. Lee told Randall
that the major test would come tomorrow if the B.O.F.
was not ousted from the homes tonight. Randall caught
the implication: Lee shed responsibility for what might
ensue if the President procrastinated.

Also at the noon hour came word from New York police of heavy Negro traffic through the Lincoln Tunnel.
Carloads of blacks were thought to be heading for the
Crawford property near Princeton, New Jersey. Similar
reports came from Boston and Syracuse where blacks
were believed driving north toward the Lake Champlain
and St. Lawrence River summer homes.

General Hildebrand was disturbed by information

phoned from the joint staff's security office at the Pentagon. Major Howard R. Underwood, who had gone on emergency leave Friday, ostensibly to visit his ailing mother, could not be located at her home in Indianapolis. Furthermore, he had not been there. Still further, the mother was in excellent health. The general ordered a prompt security search for the missing Major Underwood, then conferred with the President. Because of the major's specialty they decided, as a precaution, to invoke the first stage of War Plan Y-51. This would place military guards at designated power stations, phone-relay points, rail yards, and some communications centers. Randall noted that Hildebrand appeared relieved to take some positive action. The game of watchful waiting until the 82nd troops were on station was proving a test of nerves in the situation room.

A little after two the teleprinter carried news that the last flight was off smoothly from Pope AFB, two C-5s and three smaller C-141s heading for the McGuire base in New Jersey. An added wrinkle: A small detail of paratroops landed on Lake Champlain in a Coast Guard amphibian Albatross. The plane taxied to a point a half mile off the Shapiro home while the main body of troops took up station on the land side of the property.

In midafternoon the news ticker carried three items giving a clue to the temper of the country. The chairman of the National White Rights Party assailed President Randall for offering amnesty to the B.O.F. He contended the 82nd Airborne should march in and disarm "the black anarchists," and he castigated General Hildebrand as "the pawn of a president who prostrates the national interest before the black vote which elected him." The Associated Press, in a country-wide survey, reported that the day's business was slowing down. Office workers huddled about TV sets, and absenteeism was recorded in factories, mines, and mills. Bars were crowded, but most suburban streets were empty. Children, it appeared, were at home watching television with their mothers. The third item came from Chicago. A local of the Truckers & Haulers union threatened to organize a national strike of protest if Fritz Tiegert was not released by dawn.

Following these reports Randall was informed of news

originating from the New Jersey state police. Virginia Jones had been spotted in the first car of a twelve-vehicle motorcade with New York plates as the caravan turned off the New Jersey Turnpike at the New Brunswick exit. The cars headed south on Route 1 toward Princeton.

Randall's thoughts were interrupted. An Army major, tuning a dial on one of the TV sets, said: "The convoy's forming at McGuire." General Hildebrand pulled a small armchair from the table and sat down next to the President. The others arranged themselves for a view of the screen.

The closed-circuit picture focused on two huge cargo planes, tails as high as six-story buildings, and three smaller C-141s, parked on a cement apron. Near them stood a long line of motor vehicles of varying dun-colored shapes. Helmeted and booted paratroops climbed into the waiting trucks. As the President watched, the last man disappeared into the vans and the motorcade moved forward.

General Hildebrand looked at the large wall clock. "Very good," he said. "The convoy's off just eleven minutes after they killed the last engine." His note of pride was a bit truculent, as though these eleven minutes could somehow retrieve the schedule's three missing hours, lost to faulty maintenance somewhere on the Pope AFB flight line.

"How's the audio with McGuire?" Hildebrand asked an Army major, who was now wearing a headset and trailing a twisting length of wire cord.

"Clear and steady, General."

Hildebrand turned to President Randall. "The convoy's command and control van keeps in touch with McGuire and we're on another band to McGuire," he explained. "Once on station, the detachment commander will be able to communicate directly with us."

Randall nodded. The general's preoccupation with electronic gadgetry irked him. The world had become a wondrous fabric of instant communication, linking millions of people in the same old abundance of problems and poverty of solutions.

The red light winked on the phone cradled in Edelstein's lap. "Absolutely not," said the Defense Secretary

after listening. "At this stage the President wants that
kind of case handled by state authorities."

Edelstein turned to Randall as he hung up. "The Florida highway patrol picked up four Negroes in a car near
the Delaney home," he said. "Found a revolver and two
shotguns under the back seat. The governor's people
wanted to turn them over to the Army."

Randall sighed. "We made that quite clear at the start.
Some of our friends are great states' righters, including
the right to dump their troubles on Washington."

The head of the long column cleared the entrance of
the McGuire base. Two New Jersey state police patrol
cars took the lead followed by an Army jeep with machine gun mount and three military policemen. State police cars blocked the intersection on either side. The convoy rolled ahead on a four-lane divided highway through
undulating farm land and wooded clumps. The landscape
had a dry, wilted look under the glare of the western sun.

The motorized line stretched for more than a mile.
Covered trucks, troop transports, command cars, jeeps,
vans—all had headlights turned on. In the transports rows
of helemeted paratroops faced one another from opposing
benches. They wore pistol belts crammed with ammunition pouches, bayonets, canteens, gas masks, and first-aid
kits. Rifles were held upright between knees. Padded, double chin straps under the steel pots gave the faces
a grimly cramped appearance, as if eyes and noses had
been squeezed in as an afterthought.

The scene on the closed-circuit screen proved strangely
unsettling to Randall. Here, for the first time today, he
was seeing with his own eyes some of the forces he had
unpenned. He thought of the immediate provocation, the
invasion of white homes by blacks, and his mind swung
back to the old wounds and the old outrages. Here before
him, in a sense, rode the barbed and bitter harvest of
hundreds of yesteryears. In the mists of memory a legion
of forgotten politicians had walked the white side, sowing
the seeds of neglect and despair. His countrymen harkened when Walt Whitman sang of the land and its peo-
pled majesty, but who had heeded the fierce lament of

Frederick Douglass for the land's dark toilers, for the calluses of their bleeding palms and the sweat of their black backs? And now had James Baldwin's fire-next-time come at last to consume the hillside guns of the Blacks of February Twenty-first and the glinting bayonets of the paratroops? President Randall found it an effort to concentrate on the flickering screen. In his boyhood he had hated guns. He still did. Yet now he commanded a fantastic arsenal of guns, bombs, and missiles that pitted the plains and mountains from ocean to ocean.

The convoy rolled on, a long, brown, lethal ribbon. The road narrowed to two lanes of black top and began to twist through drowsing farm lands. A sign to the right read "LAMBS FOR SALE." A man and a dog sat atop a tractor, watching the troops go by.

After a few miles the lead police cars turned sharp left and then as quickly right, and the convoy snaked west into Route 68, a four-lane concrete divided highway. Knots of people gathered along the road. Ahead the escorting state police cars shunted traffic to the shoulders. It was an area of truck farms and stubby rows of corn, slightly more than knee-high. The sun, veiled in a bowl of haze, rode high in the west.

In the situation room General Hildebrand spoke approvingly: "Very smooth. They're maintaining a steady fifty an hour." But he looked less than satisfied, and it was apparent that those three lost hours still nagged like the memory of an overlooked appointment.

Harold Osborne spoke from his end of the long table. "Trouble in San Francisco," he said. His wide, black face was impassive. "Four Negro players of the San Francisco Giants were on local television to appeal to the black community. Three of them backed you, Mr. President, asking everybody to stay put. But the last one pulled a Ginny Jones. He urged blacks to head for Silver Lake at once. There was some kind of scuffle in the studio."

"The B.O.F. recruits baseball players?" asked General Hildebrand. The question bore the sting of accusation, as though he held Osborne responsible for every black act of disloyalty.

"I have no idea, General," said Osborne.

Their eyes met briefly, a hostile encounter with no flags of truce. From the start Hildebrand's attitude had etched his conviction that the two civilians, Voorhees and Osborne, had no business tainting the purity of a military command post. And clearly he felt that the President's decision to include Osborne, a black man of dubious allegiance, bordered on the foolhardy. For his part Osborne regarded the general's bemedaled uniform as he would the banner of the enemy.

President Randall shrugged. "We got the best of the break in San Francisco."

The convoy moved past dairy farms where cattle raised their heads to contemplate the spectacle. The line of trucks forged ahead, a hurrying brown caterpillar, and curved to the right as the highway merged with Route 206. The police cars in the van approached a bridge, an overhead crossing of the New Jersey Turnpike. A canvas banner, about thirty feet long and perhaps ten feet high, hung from the railing of the overpass, and as the column neared, three men ran off the bridge. The lettering on the canvas sign was crude but legible:

> BLACKS OF FEBRUARY 21ST IN
> THE 82ND. TURN BACK. THE HELL WITH THE
> MAN. TURN BACK NOW.
> COMDR. DAN SMITH

M.P.s in the lead jeep looked up in surprise at the banner. The convoy rolled forward at undiminished speed. Twenty, thirty, forty vehicles passed beneath the turnpike crossing. Suddenly a large truck filled with soldiers swerved out of the line and ground to a halt, effectively blocking both right lanes of the divided highway. The driver was black. The transports directly behind stopped with a screeching of brakes and tires. The entire convoy hesitated, slowed, and gradually came to a halt.

A company commander, wearing a helmet with captain's bars, ran toward the rebel truck from a mid-convoy jeep. Another officer, holding walkie-talkie gear, stood up in the jeep and began speaking rapidly into his set. Two noncoms ran after the captain. Up and down the long column helmeted heads protruded from the rear of the transports.

The white captain stood beside the cab of the isolated truck, shouting orders. The black driver stared straight ahead, ignoring the presence of the officer. The captain pulled a pistol from his holster, aimed it at the driver, and barked a single command. A helicopter began circling over the scene.

Three black paratroopers, rifles in hand, jumped from the truck and circled the white captain. He ordered them to remount the vehicle. They refused. Angry words shot back and forth. A jeep scuttled up. A white officer, whose helmet bore the silver-eagle insignia of a colonel, stood up in the jeep. He too ordered the black soldiers back to their truck. As they stood motionless, noncoms rushed from behind to wrest the rifles from their hands. One black paratrooper swung at a sergeant, clipping him on the chin. Two more black soldiers, unarmed, leaped from the truck. Soon there was a melee of flailing arms.

President Randall, who had been able to see most of the action on the screen, sat upright in his chair, gripping the armrests. He kicked away the metal wastebasket and it clattered across the floor.

"Arrest those men!" shouted General Hildebrand.

"Is that an order for Colonel Gilmour?" asked the major.

Hildebrand seemed startled by his own outburst. "No, no," he said. "He's handling it."

A second transport truck, which had stopped some forty yards to the rear of the scene of the fighting, suddenly whipped out of line, turned sharply, accelerated, and sped to the rear. The driver was black. The colonel in the jeep gave another order which his aide relayed via walkie-talkie. Two more trucks swung out of line and headed back.

The end of the convoy rested on Route 68 where two state police cars were parked. Two jeeps and a bulky van, responding to the colonel's radioed orders, swung length-wise, barricading the road. The three fleeing trucks head-

ed for the roadblock. Several fist fights, whites against
blacks, erupted in the transports. A shot was fired and a
puff of smoke drifted over the highway. The first escaping
truck veered away from the barricade, careened out of
control, smashed into a tree, and slowly toppled over. It
lay there like a giant helpless bug. Several soldiers
crawled out and soon others were dragged free. An ambulance, red-cross pennant flying, raced to the spot.
Three men were carried to it. The two other fleeing trucks
braked to a halt at the barrier. Up and down the long
column troops swarmed to the ground.

The colonel in the jeep shouted an order, and gradually, as though a tangled string were being straightened,
men fell into line along the highway. They squared off in
squads beside their transports. Soon soldiers with black
faces took several paces forward.

In the situation room the major with the headset said:
"McGuire advises that all Negro personnel are being removed from the detachment." He spoke to General Hildebrand, but his eyes questioned the President.

"Who gave that order?" snapped Randall.

"Colonel Gilmour, commanding the two battalions,"
replied the major.

"General," said Randall, "I want that order counter-
manded. That's a hell of a mistake."

"Now, Mr. President . . ." began Hildebrand.

"Hold it," broke in Randall. "If we go into a showdown with the B.O.F. with an all-white army, we could
really blow it. Let's get Colonel Gilmour on the Mc-
Guire relay before this goes any further."

"With all due respect, sir," said Hildebrand, "that
would be very unwise right now." He spoke rapidly, obviously attempting to throttle his anger at this civilian intrusion. "A basic rule is: The commander on the spot
must have leeway to use his own judgment."

"But he's committing me to a policy, goddam it," protested Randall. "This might have tragic results."

"Walter's right, Mr. President," said Secretary Edelstein. "I don't like it any more than you do. But Colonel
Gilmour has no idea how many B.O.F. members and
sympathizers he has among his men. If he doesn't act

now, he could have mutiny up the road. He has no alternative."

"The hell he doesn't," retorted Randall. "We saw the situation ourselves. There weren't more than a couple of dozen black troops ready to follow the B.O.F. The rest were obeying commands."

"Two dozen now," said Hildebrand. "A hundred or two hundred five minutes from now. Colonel Gilmour's right. He can't take the chance."

Harold Osborne had swung around from his phones to listen to the dispute.

"Hal?" asked Randall hurriedly. "What do you think?"

"I can see the box the colonel's in," said Osborne. "It's the old story. He's white, so he sees B.O.F. written on every black face."

"My God, man," exploded Hildebrand. "That officer must act. He can't wait around for a psychological survey." He vented all the wrath and frustration that he could not aim at the President.

"I know that, General," said Osborne. There was a look of something akin to sympathy in his brown eyes. "I'm not blaming the colonel. . . ."

"It would be lunacy to let the convoy go ahead all-white," said Joe Voorhees. "When the ghettos get that word—look out, brother."

Randall rose to his feet. A melange of roads, guns, soldiers, and bloody pavements swept past the camera of his mind. He walked over to the major who wore the headset.

"Tell McGuire to have Colonel Gilmour stand by for orders from me," he said.

The major spoke quickly into his small, silvery bulb of a microphone. There was a moment of hushed immobility in the room. On the screen they could see Colonel Gilmour standing in his jeep, conversing with an aide who held a walkie-talkie set.

"Colonel Gilmour is standing by, sir," said the major.

"Here are my instructions," said Randall. "Colonel Gilmour is to have the platoon sergeants find out which Negroes wish to return to McGuire and which are ready to proceed under orders. Those who want to go back are to surrender their arms and walk to the rear. The rest are to move ahead with the column."

"I protest those orders, Mr. President," said General Hildebrand.

"Give the order, Major," said Randall calmly. He turned to the Marine. "And Sergeant, note the general's objection in the log."

The Army major, his face expressionless, repeated Randall's instructions into the set which framed one side of his head in a glimmering arc. The Marine sergeant beat at his typewriter. The wall teleprinters clattered in symmetrical fury. General Hildebrand's jaw set and a flush slowly spread over his face.

"Colonel Gilmour receipts, sir," said the major tonelessly. "Your orders are being carried out."

A flurry of motion could be seen on the screen. Colonel Gilmour summoned two lieutenant colonels, commanders of the two battalions, to his jeep and conferred briefly with them. Then officers and noncoms began jogging up and down the highway, relaying orders to company and platoon commanders. Slowly the troops moved into line, leaving isolated knots of two and three black soldiers standing together. Platoon sergeants collected arms from these dissidents. There appeared to be but one incident. A Negro trooper who refused to give up his rifle was pinioned by two white soldiers while another tore the weapon away from him. The disarmed blacks, perhaps a hundred of them, began walking toward the rear.

The President stared fixedly at the tableau. It was the moment of truth. If all or most black troops joined the exodus, he had lost his gamble. But the file of retreating men was not long, and Randall could spot quite a few black faces among those remaining in the column. Occasionally, as the disarmed blacks passed a truck, a Negro soldier stepped out of line, handed his rifle to a noncom, and joined the rearward march. But these added defections were few. Randall could feel the tight band at his chest begin to loosen. A full ten minutes elapsed during this strange military minuet and hardly a word was spoken in the HICOM post. The teleprinters jabbered their metallic chorus.

"Ask Colonel Gilmour to estimate the number of black troops standing by him," said Randall.

The major, morosely unflappable, communed with his

microphone. "About three hundred, sir," he replied
shortly. "The six rifle companies were about one-fourth
Negro leaving Fort Bragg, he says, and about a hundred
Negro personnel have opted out of the operation. . . . The
column is ready to move, sir. Any further instructions?"

"No," said Randall. "Just thank the colonel for me and
tell him well done."

Black troops could be seen climbing into seven or eight
large troop trucks at the rear of the convoy. Along the
highway soldiers clambered back into their transports.
Colonel Gilmour's jeep moved back in line. He waved a
signal and the column rolled forward.

Randall leaned over General Hildebrand. "I didn't like
that any more than you did, Walter," he said in a low,
strained voice. "But we were about to embark on something that could have torn the country apart."

"Yes, sir." The general sat stiff and straight. His face
was still flushed. His judgment had been superseded by
higher authority. It happened to every soldier a score of
times down the years of a long career. The tightness in his
face relaxed somewhat. "You made your decision, Mr.
President. I support it."

Randall smiled thinly. "Thanks, Walter. I know it's a
gamble, but it's one I had to take."

The tension in the room eased. "Seventy-five percent
of the black troops stayed with us," said Voorhees. "If we
can score three for one right on through, we'll be okay."

"I agree," said Osborne. The black cabinet officer
crossed his legs as he leaned back in his chair. "Frankly,
Mr. President, I'm surprised. I thought a lot more would
take a walk. Maybe it's a sign. Many blacks do trust you.
We may ride this one out—I hope." He held up crossed
fingers.

"Let's have some more coffee in here," Randall called
to the Marine orderly. There was a lilt to his voice.

But no sooner had the fresh coffee arrived and the
President had taken his first swallow than he turned on
Hildebrand.

"Damn it," he said, "how did that banner get on the
overpass? Isn't there any kind of security around that
convoy?"

"Just the state police for traffic and a few jeeploads of

M.P.s. An army is supposed to protect itself," said the general. Though he sounded slightly patronizing, he was not unsympathetic. Now the President could appreciate the ordeal of military command, he seemed to be saying. Welcome to the club. "It would be physically impossible to sweep the entire thirty-five miles from McGuire to the Crawford place."

As seen on the closed-circuit TV, the convoy, somewhat shortened in length, cruised along at normal speed. With headlights glowing like yellow cat's eyes in the flood of the afternoon sun, the motorcade curved into Route 130. This four-lane highway flowed to the north past gas stations, unpainted frame buildings, truck farms, and the unkempt fringes of small towns.

Hildebrand passed Randall a yellow strip torn from the command teleprinter. All 82nd detachments, save the one now moving through New Jersey, were in position. Troops had surrounded the five homes at distances varying from a half mile to a mile. All commanders awaited the President's orders. Randall's reply: Stand by as is until the detachment in New Jersey arrives on station.

The rolling convoy attracted more onlookers now. People lined the highway and others peered from the windows of cars flagged to the shoulders by state police. The column turned left and headed west on Mercer County Road 571. The vehicles swept past the publishing complex of McGraw-Hill, crossed above railroad tracks at Princeton Junction, rolled by the RCA laboratories, traversed U.S. 1, and headed for the leafy ridges of Princeton with the square tower of the university's graduate school looming on the left.

Crowds thickened as the trucks lumbered along Washington Road which divided the Princeton University campus. Summer-school students milled about a cascading fountain in front of the gleaming, pillared Woodrow Wilson School. Bearded young men and pallid, long-haired girls jiggled a thicket of homemade signs: "SDS BACKS BOF"—"GINNY JONES, SI, RANDALL, NO"—"82ND, GO HOME"—"SEX MYSTERY: WHY DOES GENERAL HILDEBRAND LOVE PRIVATE PROPERTY?"—"WELCOME, DOLLAR MERCENARIES." To one side stood a small band of black

youths wearing dashiki blouses and purple berets. Word of
the fracas at the turnpike overpass apparently had not yet
reached Princeton, for the young blacks unfurled a banner
of wrapping paper which read: "BLACKS OF THE 82ND: TURN
BACK. DON'T FINK FOR HONKY." The Negroes searched for
black faces in the convoy and flapped the banner each time
they saw some. Across the road on the lawn of the Fire-
stone Library a dozen middle-aged white women held a
sign which read: "HURRY, 82ND. THE CHILDREN NEED
YOU."

The column wheeled left into Nassau Street. Spectators
massed on both sides of the thoroughfare, extending from
curb to store fronts on the right and back to the university's high iron fence on the left. The convoy slowed to
twenty miles an hour as it moved through the heart of
Princeton, then accelerated as it veered into Stockton
Street and rolled past Morven, the pre-Revolutionary
mansion where New Jersey's governor, Elton Danzig,
lived. At Elm Road, Princeton police cars barred the intersection as the convoy turned sharp right.

The motorcade rolled beneath a leafy bower of syca-
more, oak, and maple branches, the roofs of some trucks
brushing low-hanging limbs. Graceful homes, half hidden
by trees and shrubs, slumbered in the oppressive July
heat. Hundreds of children and adults watched the motorcade as it left Princeton and began climbing the Great
Road. The convoy passed the Princeton Day School,
rolled by the Tenacre Foundation, and moved into a cut
that had been blasted out of rock. There it halted, a half
mile short of the Crawford property.

The scene was chaotic. Four state police cars formed a
barrier at the intersection of two tree-lined roads, Great
and Drakes Corner. The convoy jammed in a solid line,
bumper to bumper, behind the barricade. The shoulders
of the Great Road teemed with several thousand people
of all colors, sizes, ages, and dress. Some of the whites
cheered. Many blacks booed the soldiers who had now
dismounted and were standing at parade rest beside their
vehicles. Officers and noncoms hurried back and forth.

A cluster of blacks encircled a slight woman dressed in
a dark skirt and blouse. She planted her legs apart in a
combative stance and spoke with some vehemence. Other

blacks along the road recognized her. "Hey, Ginny!" they called.

Drakes Corner Road, which bordered the Crawford estate, was a tangled mass of abandoned cars for a mile. Sweating policemen told one another it would be hours before they could tow enough vehicles away to cut a new channel for traffic. Apparently many black motorists who had been frustrated in their efforts to leave cars on the Great Road had circled around to the north and jammed Drakes Corner Road before police were aware of the maneuver.

While police had denied Ginny Jones her goal of a wall of living, black flesh, they had also failed to clear a wide path for the paratroops. The soldiers, after several minutes of confused waiting, assembled in compact squads and marched forward along the column of parked trucks. A number of black onlookers shouted provocative remarks at the black troops, but the soldiers plodded on with eyes straight ahead. Scores of state and local policemen circulated warily through the crowds along the road. Someone lobbed a missile. It arched through the air and struck a soldier on his helmet. The object split upon impact. It was a banana. Some bystanders laughed. Others jeered. The soldier ignored the hit.

In the White House situation room a major was explaining the troop movement with the aid of a pointer. He tapped a large blown-up map of the Crawford estate and vicinity.

"The detachment is being placed in position around the perimeter of Fairhill," he reported. "Except for this open western slope, bounded by a stone fence, the estate is heavily wooded, so the camera will never have the house itself in view. . . . Governor Danzig is in the communications van now, Mr. President, and wishes to speak to you. Perhaps you'd better put on the headset."

Randall adjusted the metal semicircle to his head and spoke into the microphone. "This is Phil Randall, Governor. What's the situation there?"

"Good evening, Mr. President," said Danzig. "I'm sure glad to see these troops arrive. I'm not sure how long we could have contained this mob. We've had several racial brawls and one stabbing, not fatal. . . . But things should settle down. The police can devote full attention to the crowd now that they don't have to maintain guard duty around the property. The police have disarmed most of those with guns. We've had five or six arrests for carrying concealed weapons. . . . Incidentally it's possible that one young black fellow, wearing the turtleneck and green dungarees of the B.O.F., slipped through the woods, and reached the house."

"What about conditions in the Crawford house?" asked Randall.

"We're not sure. We think the B.O.F. is holding, in addition to the four Crawfords, a Negro cleaning woman who went up the drive this morning. That was before your speech. But the silence up there on the hill is troubling. I haven't tried to communicate with the house. Our understanding was that your word to the B.O.F. was to come first."

"Thanks, Elton," said Randall. "That's right. I wanted to wait until all detachments were in place. . . . What's your estimate of the temper of the Negro spectators?"

"I'd say we've got a touch-and-go problem," said Danzig. "Perhaps four or five thousand blacks came to this area after Miss Jones's appeal, but most of them are milling around in downtown Princeton. Out here the mood seems to be one of curiosity as much as belligerence. I'd judge that not more than several hundred are of the militant stripe of Miss Jones. Of course what they're thinking and planning, we just don't know. . . . Mr. President, I'd like to discuss the exact command setup here with you."

"Sure, Elton. Go ahead. Personally I'm for complete federal-state cooperation."

"Of course. But I think I should have the overall decision here. I am the governor and I'm responsible if something goes wrong. I'd just like to get that straight, in case Colonel Gilmour and I have a difference of opinion."

"No problem, Elton," said Randall. He knew that Danzig, a good party man, could use an aura of triumph for his reelection race in New Jersey that fall. And, if things fell apart, there was always the President to blame. The political nuances, thought Randall, were not very subtle. "I agree with you. All I ask is that you check back with me on a major problem. This is a national operation by the B.O.F., you know." He laughed softly. "Also, of course, those troops of the 82nd do answer to me."

Danzig's answering laugh sounded a trifle strained. The point was clear. Paraphrasing Stalin's remark to Churchill about the Pope, how many divisions did Governor Danzig of New Jersey have?

"Okay, Elton," continued Randall. "We understand each other. Now the major here will dictate my statement which will be read at each of the seized homes. Put someone on the bull horn with it as soon as you're ready."

"Right," said Danzig. "I'll be in touch, Mr. President."

The statement soon moved through the air to the command van near Fairhill and via teleprinter to the five other troop stations:

To: Blacks of February Twenty-first.

From: The President of the United States.

I hereby request you to lay down your arms and walk out of the grounds you are now occupying.

This property is now surrounded by 1,500 troops, both black and white, of the 82nd Airborne Division. This is also true of the five other homes seized by the B.O.F. In addition, agents of the FBI are closing in on your commander, Daniel Smith, in the North Carolina mountains. Time is running out on your endeavor.

It is now 6:20 P.M. eastern daylight time. Any and all members of the B.O.F. who comply with my request within the next three hours, that is, prior to 9:30 P.M. eastern daylight time, will be granted full amnesty.

You will be held by federal troops only long enough for authorities to make sure that no person in the occupied home has been harmed. If there has been no injury, you will be released immediately to go as you please. You will not be followed, nor will you be required to identify yourself. You may, if you wish, say nothing at all. For all this, you have my promise as President.

If you have not evacuated the grounds by 9:30 P.M., E.D.T., you will be held fully accountable for your actions under federal, state, and local laws.

I urge you in the name of common sense to surrender at once. For you to do otherwise is to risk your life in a venture which has no possibility of succeeding.

Philip G. Randall

The President returned to his chair and slid to the base of his spine. "Nothing to do now but wait," he said. He sat for several minutes, staring at the blowup maps of the six homes. He glanced at the wall clock.

"It's that time," he said. "Who else for a drink? . . . Make mine a martini on the rocks, Sergeant."

Other HICOM members called out their orders to the Marine, who busied himself at the walnut cabinet in a corner of the room. Drinks in hand, the men gathered again at the long table. Randall took a sip of his martini and jiggled the ice about.

"What happens to the black troops who went back, Walter?" he asked.

"Those who mutinied will be held in the stockade at Fort Dix," replied Hildebrand. "In the ordinary course they would face court-martial charges. Of course the others were offered the chance to return, so they're not guilty of anything."

Randall savored his drink and shook his head slowly. "Well, so far, gentlemen, we're in luck. I was afraid we'd have some killings by this time."

"Not a fatality, as far as we know," said Edelstein. "Plenty of arrests for concealed weapons, but not much violence aside from the fight and the smashed truck near the New Jersey Turnpike. . . . One rock hit a soldier in Arizona. Somebody set an abandoned car on fire along the convoy route to Silver Lake, California. And one banana thrown at the New Jersey detachment. That's about it."

"How about it, Hal?" asked Randall. "Is our luck going to hold?"

The Negro cabinet officer studied his drink. "I honestly don't know, Mr. President," he said. "Thus far there's been no stampede to follow Ginny Jones. On the other hand there are rumbles of impending trouble in the black communities. Kids mostly. The men are just coming home from work now on the east coast. Ask me again at midnight."

"Midnight." Randall glanced at the clock. "Jesus, I'm tired."

The Army major spoke to the President. "Governor Danzig says your message has been repeated twice on the bull horn. There's no answer, sir, from the Crawford home."

A few minutes later the major handed a sheet of teleprinter copy to Randall. "All stations have reported in now, sir."

The President read rapidly, sighed, and handed the strip on to General Hildebrand. "Nothing," said Randall. "Not a word of reply from any of the six homes. And no B.O.F. men making any move to surrender."

"It figured," said Voorhees. They all looked at the President. Randall drained his drink and stood up.

"We'll hold as is until nine-thirty," he said. "I'm going over to the house and catch a couple of hours' sleep. Walter, you take over in my absence. Joe, call me in an emergency—or if there's any big break."

He left the room, trailed by the Secret Service agent. Edelstein stretched. The machines stuttered on. Joe Voorhees looked longingly at the cot.

Governor Elton Danzig, a singularly neat and jaunty figure in the sticky heat of the July night, walked several feet beyond the paratroops who guarded the foot of the Fairhill driveway. Mobile searchlights illumined the roads with a brilliance of noonday and wrestled with shadows of the arching trees. The crowds had been pushed back, and no one was permitted to come within two hundred yards of the paratroopers. Bayonets were fixed to rifles now as the soldiers stood in relaxed posture at intervals of five yards. The night held the heavy fragrances of summer, insects swarmed in the searchlight bands, and cicadas sang their pulsing chant.

Danzig's lightweight blue suit had an immaculate press, and a handkerchief peeped from his breast pocket. He was a short, wiry, dapper man, a former professional boxer. Ordinarily his complexion was swarthy, but now, under the lights, it resembled a mask of chalk. The governor, carrying a battery-operated megaphone, stood on the asphalt driveway perhaps four hundred yards from the Crawford house, which was masked by the night and the thick belt of trees.

"This is Governor Danzig," he said into the bull horn. "The time is now nine-forty. Under the emergency powers vested in me by the constitution of this state, I order those persons who have illegally seized this property to drop whatever arms they may have and come out at once."

A searchlight threw a stark, white band along the birch-lined drive. The light blazed for perhaps fifty yards. Then the woods blotted it out.

"I am extending the President's offer of amnesty for a few more minutes," said Danzig. The words boomed up the slope like the croaking of a giant bullfrog, an enormous sound from so small and compact a man. "I promise that no legal action will be taken against any person who surrenders now."

The words echoed like erratic thunder along the ridge of Fairhill. Then the estate was a vault of silence. The only sounds were the rhythmic racket of the cicadas and the hum of machinery in the communications van. The paratroopers stood at ease, rifles held by the barrels and the stocks resting on the pavement. Governor Danzig stood like a puppet on a brilliant stage. He lowered the megaphone and waited. As the minutes ticked on, Danzig began to sweat in the heat of the lights and the sullen night. Nothing moved on the roadway leading from the Crawford house.

Danzig spoke again into the void. "I wish to speak to the leader of the Blacks of February Twenty-first on this property." The sentence lumbered up the hill. A minute passed.

"You got him," came a scratchy, metallic reply. "What do yuh want?"

"Did you hear my offer?"

"Yeah." The unseen bull horn had less power than Danzig's.

"Do you accept it?"

There was a moment of silence. "No," came the reply. "This place belongs to the Blacks of February Twenty-first and we ain't movin'. Anybody comes up to the house is gonna be shot."

Danzig lowered the megaphone and mopped his forehead with a handkerchief. Then he tried again.

"May I speak to Mr. Timothy Crawford?"

A minute went by. Then came a new voice. "This is Tim Crawford. Go ahead, Governor."

"Are you all right?"

"Yes, we are. May I make a request, Governor? Mrs. Crawford and I ask that no move be made toward this house by troops, police, or anyone. The situation here is very delicate. We are trying to work it out."

The night swallowed the words.

"I'm now speaking again to the B.O.F. leader," said Danzig. "Do you hear me?"

"Yeah. You rattlin' the house."

"May I come up the driveway halfway to talk with you? I will come alone and unarmed."

The distant bull horn held only the sound of heavy breathing, bizarrely amplified.

"Governor," came the reply after a moment, "you can go to hell. We got this place and we gonna keep it."

Chapter Twelve

Two voices fused outside like the drone of bees. Tim recognized the husky timbre of one. It belonged to Chili Ambrose. The second voice was new to Fairhill, but something about it, a low insistence, a certitude, tugged at distant memory. Subconsciously Tim matched a youthful brown face to the voice.

Sweat oozed beneath Tim's pajamas as he sat in the deep leather armchair. The night was thoroughly uncomfortable, sluggish, warm, moist. Tim had seen two flashlights wink in the dark and heard the tread of feet on the lawn. Then, through the bay windows, had come muffled voices.

"You not making sense, Chili," said the new, yet faintly familiar voice. "What good is Ben to us, kept down in the woods with no gun?"

"Ben ain't for Gamal," said Chili. "I know that."

"Who said Gamal? Danny tell you that?"

"Naw. But he said Plan B," Ambrose said doggedly. "That means Gamal." The accent was on the second syllable of the curious word. "And Dan told me to take over. He don' trust Ben no more."

"You wrong, Chili. Plan B is the alert. On account Delmar Sprague double-crossed us and they had to waste him. That blew the cover."

"You for Gamal?" Ambrose's question had a suspicious ring.

"I follow Danny's orders. So far he hasn't said."

"I dunno," said Ambrose skeptically. "You been with Nicolet, and Nicolet, so they tell me, ain't for Gamal. How about that stuff on the TV that supposed to come from him? Blacks on honky boards, Empire and the Truckers. That's all bull, man. You want another hundred years of ass kissin'? Not me."

"You just guessing. Nobody knows until Danny gives the word. And up to now, he's said nuthin'. . . . You reckon they got him?"

"Ain't nobody gonna trap Danny," said Ambrose with abrupt ferocity.

"How long since you raised Lion?"

"Five, six hours. He's changing hideouts. Don't worry. We'll hear soon."

"In the meantime, Chili, you not playing smart."

"What do yuh mean, Jackson?"

Jackson? Jackson? Tim fumbled with the name in the dark cell of the study. Of course. Now he recognized that voice. How long ago? Five years? In Fran Healy's office. Jackson Dill, the angry, contemptuous young black for whom Ginny Jones had interceded on the assault charge. Tim recalled the cocoa face with the spreading goatee, the big, loose frame, the fulmination against "white-assed" justice. And Ben Steele had said that Jackson Dill was a B.O.F. member. When had Dill come to Fairhill?

"I mean like this, Chili," said Dill. "You keeping that girl, Holly, down by the creek. That's not smart, man."

Tim, so tensely silent he could hear his own pent breathing, leaned toward the window at the mention of Holly, straining to catch each word.

"Why not?" asked Ambrose heatedly. "The white bitch upstairs don't dare pull any more crazy stuff now."

"You're wrong, Chili." The rebuke was not unkind. "If she's got both kids with her, where she can see 'em, she'll more likely do what we tell her. But with the girl down in the woods, where she don't even know if the kid's alive, that Crawford woman's liable to do anything."

"I'm Number One here." Ambrose growled it defensively.

"Sure. Nobody says you're not." Dill's tone was patiently conciliatory. "I'm just suggesting, man."

"I dunno," said Ambrose. "I'll think about the girl in the morning. She's okay where she is now. She's got Harve's sleeping bag and she's got Ben to talk to."

Tim relaxed slightly. This news of Holly was his first solid information since her capture many hours ago. He wished he could tell Liz at once, but his wife was a drugged bundle of exhaustion upstairs after two sleepless nights. Scott dozed beside her in their bedroom now, his small bed pulled close to the large one. Tim, keyed to a high pitch ever since the bull-horn exchange with Governor Danzig, had come alone to the library, hoping that a drink of Scotch would calm him. In the dark, he had just drained the last of the drink when he saw flashlights and heard the voices.

"And how about Ben?" asked Dill now. "Chili, you gonna need him. That Steele, he got brains."

"And I don't, huh?"

"Sure you have. But there's fifteen hundred jump boys out there and maybe a couple of hundred cops. We're only four. At least, with Ben, we'd be five."

"No!" Ambrose snapped. "Ben stays where he is. That mother tried to make me give up my gun."

There was a pause in the conversation. "You're in charge, Chili," said Dill slowly, "but you got a lot to watch. Ben and the girl, the Crawfords inside the house, that fat broad, Dora, locked in the tool shed. And all them troops. We ain't no army, man."

"I know. I know." Ambrose seemed at once stubborn

and uncertain. "Gonna be different when Danny gives the signal for Gamal."

"Yeah. Gamal."

Tim wondered. There was that strange word, curiously accented, again. And had he detected a note of skepticism in Dill's abbreviated assent?

"You got lots of work, Chili," continued Dill. "How about me taking on Crawford? You want me to talk to him?"

"No. We through messin' with that white nothin'. We got the house and we gonna keep it and maybe a thousand more until they git down on their knees and beg us. Then it'll be Gamal, man."

"You sure keep the faith, baby. . . . Meantime why can't I rap with Crawford? I know him from way back and I know how to put the squeeze on him."

"I said no. You stay away from that man, Jackson. Danny told me to take over, and now we gonna do it my way."

"Awright. Awright. I'm with you, Chili."

"Okay, then." Ambrose said nothing for a moment, then: "I'm gonna relieve Perly. You take this side until morning."

Tim could hear the sound of retreating footsteps on the turf. In the gloom he could barely make out the figure of a man near the dogwood outside the casement windows. So Jackson Dill wanted to talk to him? Clearly this evidence of a split between Ambrose and Dill needed to be exploited.

He was about to ease himself out of the chair and tiptoe to the window when he saw the figure of Jackson Dill move away. Tim slumped back against the cushion, bathing in his own sweat. A score of questions begged for answers. What did the word "Gamal" mean? Had Dill talked to Steele? Was Holly frightened? Who was Delmar Sprague and why had he been killed? Was he connected with the phone numbers mentioned on television by Randall? How serious was the friction between B.O.F. men, and did it exist only at Fairhill or at other occupied homes as well?

In the medley of noises along the Great Road, Tim could distinguish a whine of tires and a shouted command. The sounds clamored a reminder that two battalions of paratroops ringed Fairhill, an exotic fact difficult to entertain in the prosaic parlors of his mind. It was as though Fairhill were a remote island, hidden in the wastes of unexplored seas and isolated in its destiny. Governor Danzig and his echoing bull horn seemed to belong to a land of dreams. What mattered was not the frail image of a dapper governor, marching troops, and the mutterings of national crisis, but this small, real world, a world of Chili Ambrose, of Liz in drugged sleep, of Holly and Scott, of a cleaning woman locked in a tool shed. All else was fantasy.

The realization beckoned him into a cloistered mood. Here he sat in the big chair, dripping sweat like a pressed sponge, and yet he felt resigned. His fate, whatever it was, was being resolved. To be denied the labors of liberty, those endless selections and choices which tax free men, was to shackle the mind in a kind of serenity. As a prisoner he could almost pity those free men staggering under the burden of adversity. No longer did he have to tax himself with the thousand and one choices offered by his life as a lawyer, as a husband, father, citizen, neighbor, or even as a tippling armchair philosopher. No, all he was required to do in this new existence was to react to danger and to answer whenever someone summoned him.

The thought brought a measure of comfort at this moment—about 2 A.M. Tuesday, wasn't it?—some fifty-three hours after he first saw Ben Steele lounging in the library doorway. A man could live on the raw edge of fright only so long. Then he either sank into a comatose state or he went mad. He became kin to the turtle who, finding himself in the middle of speeding highway traffic, withdraws his head while trucks thunder past his unseeing shell. Panic was not an infinite condition: Rather, the gates of the nerves finally closed against incessant alarms, permitting the body to recuperate in relative calm.

Tim, the prisoner, the withdrawn turtle, also found himself resenting President Randall. He had met the man only twice, had taken a prompt liking to him as a person. But now, in his public role as President, Phil Randall had become an irritant, a pebble in the small oyster of Fairhill. It seemed vastly unjust that the President should have elevated the siege of Fairhill—this private concern of the Crawford family and its B.O.F. captors—to the pinnacle of national crisis. Tim felt vaguely offended that complete strangers such as the mayor of Denver, a school principal in Shreveport, Louisiana, or a feed-grain dealer in Iowa, should be vested with solicitude over the fate of the Crawfords and their home. Indeed, why was the plight of Fairhill any of their business? Or any business of the President of the United States, for that matter? If left alone, Tim Crawford and Ben Steele could settle the affair in their own time and in their own way.

In fact, in the context of this place, this home, and this troubled night, Ben Steele had become more friend than foe, more benefactor than brigand. For one thing Tim and Steele shared a common goal: They both wanted Fairhill. President Randall, the 82nd Airborne Division, and the unknown mayor of Denver cared nothing for Fairhill. They were all meddling intruders, threatening to disrupt the striving of men pitted in a private battle of wills over this house and this land. And another thing, Tim and Steele were now allies against Chili Ambrose. As the infantryman in war finally comes to loathe his own generals more than the enemy soldiers across the gulley, so now Tim thought of President Randall with injured truculence.

Tim reclined in the big chair as thoughts of this new alignment of friendly and hostile forces tumbled through his mind. He became sleepy. His head fell back against the leather cushion. He pictured himself and Ben Steele squatting beside a camp fire, bargaining in low, amiable tones, while far away vast armies clanked into position for slaughter under a bloody moon. One handsome general, with the features and elegant sideburns of President Randall, pointed a revolver toward a misted hill. And upon that crest, in a fog that curled around his feet like smoke, towered the great, dark chieftain, Chili Ambrose. General Ambrose flourished a black ensign that bore a single enigmatic word: GAMAL.

Half in reverie, Tim heard the muffled sound of steps outside the window. He sat up and peered out. Jackson Dill had moved back to the shelter of the dogwood tree.

Rousing himself, Tim walked quietly to the window.

He could see Dill plainly now, standing in profile, his face toward the garage.

"Jackson Dill?" asked Tim in a stage whisper.

Dill turned, then visibly stiffened.

"I'm Tim Crawford. You want to talk to me?"

Dill glanced about him in all directions, then walked slowly over, and slouched against the window frame. In the distance the lance of an Army searchlight pierced the hooded sky. The heat was heavy, and the cicadas chanted in dolorous chorus.

"Crawford?"

"Yes, I'm right here."

"Put your head against the screen, so we can whisper."

Tim placed his face only a few inches from Dill's. He could hear the young man's ordered breathing. The air was as still as an unwrinkled pond.

"I've brought you a message from Ginny Jones. She says to tell you that I can be trusted." Tim noted that Dill, a college man like Ben Steele, switched off the idiom he used when talking to Ambrose. "I'm going to level with you. As long as Chili Ambrose has command here, we're all in danger."

"You too?"

"Yes. All of us."

"Why? . . . What's this 'Gamal'?"

Dill ignored the question. "There's been a foul-up. Chili's committed to a course that means killing." He spoke slowly and distinctly. "You know what Ben Steele wants. I'm with Ben. We've got to get Chili's gun away from him."

"What about Marsh and Wiggins?"

"They're still with Chili, but I'm working on them. Main thing—"

"How and when did you get in here?" cut in Tim.

"I sneaked in through the woods before the troops came. Main thing right now is this: Will you help us when we need you?"

"Why should I?"

"You want a shoot-out up here?" asked Dill. "Maybe your wife and children hit?"

"Of course not."

"Then you'd better be with Ben and me. If I yell for you, you do what I tell you. Okay?"

"All right." There was no other choice.

Jackson Dill moved quickly away, melting into the moonless night.

Chapter Thirteen

Through the long night the occupied homes stood like sphinxes on a trembling plain. The nation, a dubious giant, heaved and tossed as countless voices lashed it with conflicting counsel. Radio stations blared. Pollsters conducted midnight surveys. Patriots unfurled spangled platitudes. Editors hammered typewriters with Olympian gravity. Television talk shows spilled their loose seed of advice as if in frantic, interminable orgasms. Keepers of the pressure boilers—from labor to commerce, from white supremacists to black mutineers, from police benevolent associations to civil libertarians, from militarists to pacifists—all had their say. America, the vocal society, was in night-long disputatious assembly. President Randall's appeal for calm was shredded by a hail of words. For every judicious ear there were a hundred intemperate tongues.

As the night wore on, threads of common interest could be untangled and identified. First was that of the children. The Speaker of the House, an ashen ruin of a man who threatened to outlive his own obituary, informed the country via television that all considerations must yield to that of the safety of the nineteen captive children. He wound up his lugubrious talk with a paean to the sanctity of ownership. The Speaker's ancient eyes watered, but viewers might wonder whether he grieved for the boys and girls, for his own lost youth, or for the threat to private property. An auxiliary note was sounded by the head of the auto workers' union. He pleaded for restraint in the name of little children, but his intonation seemed to say: "Look here, fellow Americans. Custom dictates that we care about children above all, therefore we do care."

Since American tradition enshrined children as objects of compassion, so every speaker paid lip service at the altar before passing on to graver economic matters. In offices of the great corporate conglomerates, lights burned late over the labors of public relations specialists. These gentlemen distilled tonight's private alarms of executives over the seizure of property into tomorrow's public outrage over the predicament of the youngsters. Here and there sincerity rattled the shell of the symbol. On a San Diego radio talk show a mother of six voiced the anguish she would feel were her own brood held captive. And in New York City a band of Negro and white mothers marched to the apartment building of Virginia Jones to plead with the singer to help free the children. They were turned away by the doorman, who said Miss Jones was at the barricades in Princeton. But these demonstrations of sympathy for the small captives were the exception. Whatever many American parents might feel viscerally, the children in the six occupied homes were becoming pawns in a mighty game of social and economic chess.

Another theme, swelling from the political Right, congealed on the nation's air waves: I told you so. It was a vindictive and piously solemn uproar from John Birchers, white citizens' councils, remnants of the George Wallace legions, Klansmen, decaying generals and admirals, rednecks, blue-collar omniscients, and pinch-faced daughters of the little old ladies in tennis shoes. The splenetic medley carried a common message: "We told you so. You whimpered over the plight of the ragged, indolent minorities. You curried favor with the black anarchists of the ghettos. You elected as your President a man who bartered away his proud Anglo-Saxon birthright for a mess of Negro votes. Now you reap the whirlwind." Curiously, although it gloated over Randall's dilemma, the Right did not venture far beyond its indictment for past transgressions. It did not advocate the bombing of the B.O.F., tear-gas barrages, or bayonet charges by the paratroops. Why not? Well, those children, you know.

From the Left rose a chorus of jubilation. Students for a Democratic Society lifted huzzahs of encouragement to the Blacks of February Twenty-first. At Berkeley a thousand youths, white and black, pounded the dark streets, chanting, "Ho! Ho! Ho Chi Minh! Property out. B.O.F. in." Danny Smith became a midnight saint of the New Left, instantly canonized to take his niche beside such disciples of revolution as Che Guevara, Herbert Marcuse, Daniel Cohn-Bendit, Mark Rudd, Mao Tse-tung, Frantz Fanon, and P. Burnham Outerbridge, a recent elevation. Outerbridge was a redhaired, 135-pound sophomore who some months earlier had singlehandedly seized the financial offices of Purdue University. Outerbridge vowed to dynamite the premises unless Purdue football were disbanded and replaced by choral societies composed exclusively of undergraduates who took an oath never to bear arms for their country except in event of invasion. Outerbridge fasted, more or less cross-legged, for twenty days and nights within reach of a cigarette lighter and three sticks of fused dynamite. Purdue and football eked out a funky triumph only because Outerbridge finally fainted, allowing campus guards to carry out the emaciated body and ditch the dynamite. Outerbridge lost 43 pounds but hardly missed them, since he won prompt sainthood and went on to write his life story for *Playboy* for $45,000, or more than $1,000 a pound.

The cries of the New Left this night were strident and discordant, yet they lacked a certain sustained malevolence. Perhaps the young Robespierres of the Left, finding themselves on the brink of revolution, peered over the precipice and blanched at what they saw. If taunted for lack of bellicosity, they had their excuse: those children, you know.

The one crucial voice, that of the ghettos, was an uncertain trumpet. The narrow, fetid alleys of the black slums were as mute as the littered vacant lots and the fettered store fronts. Precinct station houses were stacked to the locker rooms with reserves and extra-duty policemen, all ready to pour forth with gun and club at the first signs of rebellion. But an ominous calm fastened on the streets where chartreuse-trousered young men and mini-skirted black girls usually roamed the night. According to less than dependable gossip inside the police stations, the calm had numerous explanations. Some said Negroes were all home watching the drama of the seized homes on TV, just like white folks. Some said this was the eye of the hurricane. When new winds flung a command from Daniel Smith, the ghettos would erupt and put the white suburbs to the torch. Others said that blacks were rejoicing boisterously at home, delighted that the action had moved out where it should be, to the rich, white communities and the plush honky summer hideaways. Some sensed a prevailing ghetto mood of relief which surfaced in quips. Let the B.O.F. make life miserable for whitey on his own turf while we circulate in carefree leisure. There appeared to be only one common, identifiable phenomenon from Harlem to Watts. Everywhere in the black belts members of the Blacks of February Twenty-first came forth in uniform. Wearing olive-green dungarees and black turtleneck sweaters beneath swinging medallions of Frantz Fanon, they walked the slums on cats' feet and purred advice into the ears of other youths. Just what was being said, no one knew for sure, although occasionally a strange word, "Gamal," was overheard. It was also said that the stars were propitious for black enterprise because "Danny got him a good sign." And Smith was openly lauded for his heedless courage. What impressed police observers most about these young men was their discipline, their icy courtesy, and, above all, their numbers. There were hundreds in the big cities where there had been only fives and tens last week. When questioned by older Negroes, the young militants merely laughed, low and privately. What did they intend to do? For tonight, nothing, man—those kids, you know.

As the long night ground toward dawn, much of America was still awake, huddled about television sets in millions of living rooms, bedrooms, and kitchens. The people waited with a growing sense of being put upon. Like a man who listens to the remorseless ticking of a time bomb, then waits in vain for the explosion that promised to dismember him, the nation pondered the vagaries of catastrophe.

Nothing so disturbs faithful adherents of a reasoned universe as the failure of doom to keep its appointments. It is one thing to reach a sudden, shabby end by seeming accident, but quite another to be cheated out of scheduled, redemptive annihilation by mere luck. The first is understandable, the second unpardonable. If all signs, portents, and logic decree imminent disaster, yet disaster dawdles along the way, a man has the right to doubt the rationality of existence.

The trouble this long night of July ninth was that calamity had set its stage, then unaccountably failed to show up for the performance. Hour after hour went by and nothing happened.

The stage was certainly set. Twelve battalions of the 82nd Airborne Division, nine thousand men in all, surrounded six homes in as many states. Guards changed. Jeeps rattled. Bayonets glinted and insects swarmed in the whitewashed arms of searchlights. Mobile kitchens creaked into place to serve hot food to the patient warriors. Command posts were established—in a post office, a school basement, a boathouse. Bull horns had spoken with no answering rumbles from the besieged houses, save at Fairhill where there had been one exchange, then silence. At the Broderick ranch in Arizona, a searchlight-equipped helicopter clattered over the main house like an awkward Peeping Tom until a rifle bullet punctured the fuselage. The White House sent word by teleprinter that the venture was not to be repeated. Detachment commanders prepared CS gas canisters, selected men for belly-crawling reconnaissance missions, planned surprise assault teams, scanned topographical maps and plotted tactics. Yet Washington said "no" to all suggestions. Only one two-word instruction, monotonous in repetition, came from the White House situation room: Stand by. Colonels and their staffs muttered over the inactivity. They were the proconsuls of paralyzed legions.

Daniel Smith, the elusive commander of the Blacks of February Twenty-first, was sheathed in the hush of mountains. Not a word had been heard from his clandestine North Carolina transmitter since sunset. The last conversation, monitored by experts of the Federal Communications Commission as well as by a growing number of ham-radio operators at their rigs, was an elliptical exchange with the B.O.F. unit occupying the Tiegert home at Silver Lake, California. It was surmised that Smith had shut down his radio and changed locations, but this was conjecture only. When the original posse of fifty FBI agents failed to surround Smith's retreat by midnight, Director Pedersen ordered another hundred agents into the area. By dawn the wooded vales and hills near Mt. Mitchell would be alive with federal men.

The siren fell upon the night, wailing like a ghost in pain. A red light whipped in sweeping circles, gashing the tall pines and wounding the loneliness of the highway. The trailer van slowed to a halt with a hissing of air brakes. An officer of the North Carolina state highway patrol alighted from his squad car and walked back to the cab of the truck. It was shortly before 4 A.M. on the highway south of Greensboro, North Carolina.

The officer's flashlight fingered the side of the long van, picking out the legend, "Higginbotham Bros., Movers, Lynchburg, Virginia." The beam moved to the driver, lingered with accusing brilliance on the face. Arched eyebrows, like a startled gnome, receding chin, bleary eyes, sallow skin. The flashlight snapped off. The driver leaned from the cab.

"What's up?"

"Routine check," said the officer. "Permit and registration, please."

The patrolman torched the tendered documents briefly, then unfolded a paper which accompanied them. "What's this?" he asked.

"Invoice," replied the driver. "Takin' a load of furniture from Asheville up to Lynchburg, Virginia."

"Oh." The officer examined the paper, then handed it back with the testaments of identity.

"This have somethin' to do with them niggers?" asked the driver. "The gang up in the mountains with that Smith bastard?"

"Yeah." The guardian of the highways was being stroked by rotating rays from the red light atop his patrol car. His face dripped crimson, as though bloodied. "You seen any suspicious niggruhs coming up from Asheville?"

"Nope. Not much rollin' tonight. I guess they's all home watching TV. . . . Anything new?"

"No. They haven't found Smith yet. One report says he

might've left the mountains. . . . Okay. Take it easy, Mac."

The officer walked back to his car, his heels snapping at the pavement. The red light ceased its roving to be replaced by headlights shoveling aside the darkness. The car moved off, cut across the prohibited grassy strip dividing the highway, and sped away to the south. The van driver craned his neck, looking to the rear until the taillights became tiny red spots on the sable horizon.

He reached above his head and slid a wooden panel to one side. "Okay," he said. "We got about five more miles before we turn off. . . . You hear that pig, Commander?"

"Yeah," said a voice through the panel. "You done real nice, Shorty. You kin even talk white."

The driver chuckled. "Hell, I been passin' twenty years. . . . All clear. I'm closin' up again." He shut the panel and started the motor. The van moved forward, bruising the night with its clamor of gears and slowly accelerating to fifty miles an hour.

The trailer slackened pace ten minutes later. Shorty waited until the lights of an approaching car had passed him and been swallowed to the south. Then he drove forward a few hundred feet and wheeled right onto a gravel road. Stones crunched under the big tires and shot off to thump the trunks of scrub pines in an erratic fusillade. Shorty doused his lights, crawling through the purple gloom by seeming instinct at ten miles an hour.

About two miles off the main highway the van passed a cleared field, ribbed with young corn, and turned into a dirt road. Two structures brooded on a slight rise. As the truck drew closer, one building took on the shape of a house with sagging porch. A light winked twice. Shorty flicked his dim parking lights twice in response. In a moment a black man appeared beside the cab.

"The barn's open," he said. The voice had the droop of age. "We'll shut 'er as soon's you're in."

Shorty maneuvered the trailer into the long, high barn. The doors promptly closed behind the tailgate. There was a stuffy odor of dust and grain. At one end of the barn a kerosene lantern stood on an upturned pail and shed a clump of feeble light. Several muddy blankets were draped over a sawhorse, and a leather harness hung from a rafter. Farm implements of assorted shapes slumped along the wooden walls like a defeated army.

Shorty went to the rear of the van, unfastened a pad-lock, and opened the doors on a clutter of furniture, a faded mattress, an upended bedstead, several piled wicker chairs, and an unpainted chest of drawers. He pulled the mattress off the van and moved the chest to one side.

Immediately a file of black men, wearing black turtle-neck sweaters and green dungarees, emerged from the dark mouth of the truck and jumped to the dirt floor. Each had a pistol jammed behind a wide leather belt. Shorty, remarkable in this company for his greasy sport shirt, grinned as his charges landed in the safety of the barn. There were eleven men in all, and they moved in a discipline of silence.

The last figure to alight was a tall, spare man who might have been a sprinter or an underfed person. His face was narrow and yellowish with a small, trim, pointed beard. The face bore a stamp of perplexed severity as though the owner might have mislaid something of im-portance. A wrinkle of frown at his forehead hinted that he was not sure he would find it. His frizzled hair grew in a patch without a part. A medallion of Frantz Fanon swung from a silver chain about his neck.

The moment his feet touched the ground, orders rattled from him like rain on a metal roof. . . . Jerry, set up the radio rig over in the house. Let me know as soon as all six stations are standing by. Muggs, turn down that lan-tern. Bill, man the kitchen and turn out some grit. Pete, Bo, Fishbait, Lothar, take up guard posts about five hundred yards down the road, both ways from the house. Jake and Fred, take charge of the guns and ammo. Shorty and Howard, come with me.

Commander Daniel Smith strode to the end of the barn where the lantern flickered on the upturned pail. He squatted on the ground between Shorty, the driver, and Howard, a man whose surprising blue eyes shone like sapphires on black velvet.

"We oughta be safe here for a day," said Smith. His voice was high, hoarse, rasping. "Them G-boys ain't no mountain goats. It'll be tomorrow, anyway, before they figure we hit the road."

"I ain't so sure, Commander," said Shorty. "That state cop said there was a report we'd left the mountains." His dissent was sculpted in respect, and he spoke with almost equal deference to the man Howard. "Did you hear him, Major Underwood?"

Underwood nodded, a dark scarf with twin beads of turquoise. "Yes, but they don't believe it yet. There's no alert out. If there were, there would have been roadblocks and that officer would have searched the van. The eagle has flown to a new nest."

"Right, Howard," said Smith. "We're okay here for maybe twenty-four hours. . . . Now what about the brothers in the 82nd?"

"You know the answer already, Danny," said Underwood. He was seated with his hands clasped about his knees as he gazed at the uncertain glow of the lantern. "There was a report of some kind of brawl at the New Jersey Turnpike where our sign hung. But the radio commentators have been making a big thing about all the black faces among the paratroops around every home."

"Why?" Smith's eyes raked Underwood like claws. "You're the Pentagon man. You said we'd get half."

"I was wrong." There was no bitterness, only jettisoned hopes. The blue eyes sank as though submerging in a shadowed pool. "It takes strong meat to wean grown men from Army discipline." Major Underwood was given to figures of speech far removed from the ghetto idiom of his youth.

"Yeah," agreed Shorty. He was as pale as the lantern rays, more runted Appalachian than Negroid. One skinny arm bore a purplish tattoo of a woman with enormous breasts. "When I was in cans, I'd have jumped overboard if the skipper told me to. You want to beat the services at their game, you got to speak up loud and clear, Commander."

"Gamal?" asked Smith. He swung his head sharply, regarding each man in turn. Major Underwood and Shorty both nodded.

Smith froze like a prophet summoned by sudden tongues. His black eyes glazed and his muscles tensed beneath the yellowish skin. It was a trancelike state that lasted almost a minute. Then he reached into his hip pocket and pulled out an object resembling a wallet. It was a document backed by cloth and soiled plastic. Smith unfolded it in sections and spread it on the soft, manured ground before the lantern. It was a map of the United States.

"Gamal." Smith breathed the word as though in worship. "Down home." The phrase melted in nostalgia, but quickly the tone hardened. "They gonna give us Gamal or we gonna grab a thousand honky homes and then ten thousand and then maybe a hundred thousand." The shrill voice climbed the peaks of oracles.

He paused. The hand pointing toward the map became a fist. "Reacher's Neck and Rabbit Hill. Bidwell's Ferry an' Sligo and Risin' Sun and Apple Creek." His voice rose to a high chant with the rhythm of names long remembered. "They gonna be black lands an' black mills an' black ships an' black senators and black beauties on the balconies, and, yes . . . goddam . . . a black army."

He was nearing frenzy now and his eyes burned like torches. He thumped Shorty on the back. "You gonna pray you had a black skin, man. Gonna wish you could drain ever' drop of that stinkin' white blood outa you. . . . We gonna think black, talk black, work black." He turned to Underwood in a blaze of unfettered joy. "And Howard, we gonna love black—nothin' but them big, smooth black women with them tits like shining midnight. . . . And black doctors and black hospitals an' black scientists in all them beautiful black universities. Man. Man."

He rose from his crouch and stood towering over the map like a dark colossus. The reluctant lantern light played over a visage of wrathful glory and plucked at the harness which dangled from the rafter above like a dripping halo. Smith clenched his fists as though to hold the dream forever in a vise of black flesh.

"Yeah, Danny. We know," said Underwood gently. He straightened and his head barely topped Smith's shoulder. "The question about Gamal isn't 'if.' It's when."

The commander looked down at his subordinate, searching the blue eyes as though for some bottomless truth. Smith slowly relaxed. The fists came unclenched, his shoulders fell, and he scuffed at the map with the toe of his military boot.

"You think we ready, Howard?" he asked.

"Almost," replied Underwood. "But not quite. Look."

He pulled at Smith's sleeve, easing him down again to the damp dirt floor. The three men crouched about the map once more. Underwood pointed to red dots which clustered like measles about the names of major cities.

"Take Detroit," said Underwood, indicating the name on the map. "The unit's set. We got seven hundred men ready when you say 'Gamal.' They got the arms, the plans. Fifty homes spotted in the Grosse Pointes, twelve more in Bloomfield Hills. Every big white name in Detroit."

Underwood moved his finger to the right. "The same goes for Philly. Jimmy Fitt's been ready for a week. The unit has arms for a thousand men who're all trained and eager. Hell, they're as tough as Marines, which is what a lot of them were. And two hundred homes all staked out, right through the Main Line, Wynnewood, Haverford, Bryn Mawr, Radnor, Stafford, Daylesford. And we've got insiders on the Main Line too. Must be a couple of hundred chauffeurs, maids, and yard boys ready to come over the minute the first B.O.F. men walk in."

Underwood's voice, low, methodical, unhurried, moved on around the fashionable white suburbs of the land, from New York City's Greenwich and Westport in Connecticut to Los Angeles's Beverly Hills. Smith had heard all this many times before, but he loved it, so the major once more explained and elucidated. He was the military staff technician naming forces, terrain, arms, logistics, chances. At times Smith listened with brooding intensity, but at times his eyes dwelled far beyond the lantern and he became lost in private ecstasy. A lesser man than Underwood might have felt the gnawing of jealousy to be subordinated to such a man of visions. But the little major was a realist. He knew the power of dreams, the charisma of men who, once having glimpsed the grail, never again bother to count the horses. Only this towering son of the ghettos, this black Jacobin of revolution, Daniel Smith, could fire the hearts of black men and lead them in the cause named for Malcolm X. But Smith did have to listen. One critical error in judgment now could explode Gamal forever.

"You've got to face some facts, Danny," said Underwood. "We're ready, but so is Al Nicolet. In the six homes we hold now, how many where Nicolet and Steele men are in command?"

"Not that Crawford house," said Smith angrily. "Chili Ambrose is my man there. He took Ben's gun off him when Steele refused Plan B."

"But the other five." Underwood was patient. "You know at least four of them are still with the plan of Nicolet and Steele."

"Honky bait!" exploded Smith. He raised a finger as though in prophecy. "Nicolet and Steele talk about justice and gettin' a piece of white power. . . . All crap. . . . They ain't got the guts to fight and die for black independence."

"They won in council and you had to back down," persisted Underwood.

"I never backed down." A look of guile came into Smith's eyes. "I put off."

"I know." Underwood thought for a moment, studying his man. Smith could never be handled carelessly. His moods had a fierce stubbornness. "Look, Danny. Here's the way I figure it. If you give the signal for Gamal now, you're liable to blow it."

"Why?"

"First there's those kids. I can't explain it exactly, but those nineteen children are something like the flag. People salute whether they give a damn or not. You've heard how it goes on the radio. Everyone crying fake tears. As long as we're holding the houses for what Nicolet and Steele want—a piece of the action—those kids are valuable to us. No troops are going to fool around and risk killing a girl or a boy. But once we go for Gamal, that means fighting and shooting and seizing thousands of homes. So we'd have to let the kids go then. Free 'em all and let them walk out of those homes. We can't kill kids."

Smith was listening closely again. Underwood continued: "And you can't give the word for Gamal while Alfred Nicolet's operating. He's got contacts. Hell, he could walk into the White House right now. You call for Gamal now and Nicolet will spoil us good, go on television, maybe even give the feds the location of every one of those first thousand homes. His chart shows them, same as ours. We've got to gag Nicolet."

"Gag him?" repeated Smith. His eyes burned. "Waste the bastard!"

Underwood shook his head. "Black killing black is no way to launch Gamal. Later we're going to need every smart man we've got. We can't spill a drop of black blood. Never. Never." He paused, eyeing Smith shrewdly. "No. There's another way. You could send Shorty up. With his white face, Shorty can go anywhere, no questions asked. Let Shorty go up to Philadelphia where Nicolet's hiding out, get him five good B.O.F. men, then take Nicolet by surprise, hold him prisoner. Then, when Shorty comes back and tells us Nicolet's under guard, then you call for Gamal."

Underwood knew that Smith would not launch any major move without Shorty at his side. Smith considered Shorty his talisman. Also Shorty had great usefulness—the white face, a crafty mind, unlimited courage, mastery of any engine or motor, an intuition about danger. And Shorty knew their immediate objective, Raleigh, as well as Smith himself.

Smith folded his arms and gazed at the pulsing lantern. There was a slow murmur of conversation from the men tending the guns and ammunition. Outside, a hawk's cry broke the night. Smith swung to Shorty.

"How about it? Can you cut it?"

"Sure." Shorty rubbed his greasy arms, wrinkling the purple nude. "All I need is the address in Philly where Nicolet is—and some bread and wheels. I gotta have wheels."

"Take the old man's heap into Greensboro," said Smith. "Then fly from there. Can you make it back by tomorrow morning?"

"Tomorrow morning," said Shorty. "By dawn for sure."

"Give him some bread, Howard," ordered Smith.

Underwood counted off six ten-dollar bills into Shorty's hands. Dawn was brushing the cobwebbed windows of the barn now, and Underwood turned down the lantern wick and blew out the flame. Shorty, shivering in the chill, climbed into the van's cab and found his leather jacket. He opened the side door of the barn on the sweet, crisp smell of morning. Mist hugged the low fields like a lover. Shorty, a packet of bones, turned back to Smith.

"Gamal," he said as though in supplication.

"Gamal!" roared Smith in return. It was a great cry of exultation that boomed through the doorway and rolled off in the billowing mist.

Chapter Fourteen

Many Americans were still awake that dawn of July 10.

Edward Lee, the Secretary of the Treasury, was waiting for a phone call in the living room of his home in Langley, Virginia. The curtains were drawn back on an expanse of glass overlooking the steep wooded bank of the Potomac River. The hesitant light of dawn entered the room like a gray embezzler. The early American furniture had an unkempt, grizzled look as though awakened before its time. Newspapers littered the long sofa, crushed cigarette butts filled several ashtrays, and a pair of cordovan shoes sat like empty rowboats beneath the marble-topped coffee table.

Both the room and its occupant had a leftover appearance. Ed Lee's shirt was limp and stained. Emerging gray and black whiskers made his jaw feel and look like sandpaper. He had slept but two hours on the sofa, and, being a fastidious man, he felt a kind of self-contempt for his soiled exterior and for the sour taste in his mouth. He supposed his breath would be foul.

This whole business, he thought, was insufferable, the nation and the Randall administration as untidy as his second-day shirt. He had heard most of the news through the long night, over the special line from the White House situation room and from the television which seemed determined to prove, by mere exposure, that America was a land of knaves, sentimentalists, and idiots. Lee, himself the father of two sons who were now young bankers, thought if he heard one more word about the plight of those children, he would become nauseated. And to compound his disgust he was Secretary of the Treasury in the Cabinet of a man who must surely have flunked freshman economics. For Lee, Phil Randall was not only a fiscal innocent, but one of those gossamer liberals who somehow felt that money was evil and thus bound to taint any administration that worried about it.

The President had refused all along to become exercised over the ailing dollar. Ed Lee had explained until his jaws ached: balance of payments still adverse; gold drain small but steady; three tourist dollars spent abroad for every one spent here; German, Japanese, and Russian goods underselling a hundred American products in world markets; the dollar suspect. Phil Randall always listened with a pained smile as though all this were the exclusive concern of Secretary Lee and some third party such as the president of Chase Manhattan. If Ed Lee and the economists and financiers couldn't right matters, Randall's attitude seemed to say, what did they expect a mere President of the United States to do about it all?

And now these homes. Lee rubbed his sandpaper cheeks, lit another cigarette, and quickly recoiled at the acrid taste. As he had warned at the White House conference twenty-four hours ago, the dollar was in trouble. If the federal government did not wrest those homes away from the black brigands and turn the properties back to the rightful owners—and do it swiftly, children or no children—then Lee feared a severe financial crisis. A mammoth dumping of American stocks in European markets was a dire probability. Then, in quick succession, could come a flight from the dollar, turmoil in New York's financial district, and perhaps even panic. Hadn't he told Randall time and again that the structure was so flimsy that one good storm could topple it? And now this storm could be a real howler.

A phone sounded, a metallic growl in the gray, disheveled morning. It was the line linked through the White House switchboard. Lee glanced at his wristwatch. This would be Herr Frederick Hochwald, his Swiss banker. Hochwald was punctual, and it was now ten-fifteen in

Geneva, the agreed time. Lee was right. The urbane voice, a trifle syrupy, flowed through the English diphthongs with suave authority.

"It will not be a cheerful day for American shares over here," said Hochwald after the brief opening banalities.

"How bad?"

"I would say you should prepare yourself." Hochwald honored his $50,000-a-year informant fee from the U.S. Government with a certain delicacy of expression. If he were an undertaker, thought Lee, he would stress the elegance of the corpse, the impermanence of mortality, and the beauty of the services. Yet Hochwald's meaning was always clear.

"In the first few minutes of trading," continued the banker, "your shares are off sharply. All motors, of course, and especially Empire."

"Will it get worse?"

"Ah, that depends on President Randall, does it not?"

"What if Randall continues to stand by—the homes surrounded by troops but no effort made to retake the properties for the time being?"

"Is that the plan there, then?" Hochwald was not above soliciting an occasional bonus in the form of useful inside information.

"I didn't say that." Lee immediately regretted his sharper tone. Blame it on the ghastly hour. Ordinarily he and Hochwald sparred with pillowed gloves. "Actually the plans are quite fluid from minute to minute. A question of the children, you understand."

"Ah yes, the children." Hochwald paused as though out of respect. "There has been considerable discussion here of the youngsters. After all, we in Europe have been watching the television in family groups. And bankers have families too. Very interesting, the children. I would say there is an appreciation here for President Randall's, uh, dilemma, shall we call it?"

"Do you mean we might count on some help in defending the dollar, if it came to that?" Lee was bitter. My God, he might as well have called his country a charity case and be done with it. Tawdry business. America on its knees like a beggar.

"No. As we both know, while sentiment often feeds on

money, money seldom breeds on sentiment." Hochwald's tone hinted at his distress over money's soulless habits. "Perhaps if central bankers were mothers . . ." He sighed.

"And the dollar?" pressed Lee.

"Trouble," said Hochwald. "Again it all depends on your President. If he acts swiftly to free the properties, you have bought time again. How much, Edward, you know as well as I. What did he estimate at our last meeting? A year, wasn't it? I would say that would still hold. But if Randall temporizes too long, or finally compromises in some unsound manner, then, my friend, the weeks will shorten into days."

"May I quote you on that to the President? You know his attitude."

"Yes, I know his attitude." There was lament in the voice. "I often think we should require our statesmen to present certificates of clearance from both their psychiatrists and their bankers before taking office. . . . But yes, please do quote me to the President." His voice firmed. "Edward, this is serious."

They traded a few graceful amenities before hanging up. Hochwald promised to call back in two hours. Lee walked to the long sea of glass, now glittering with the full ardor of the rising sun. He squinted, half blinded. His shoulders ached for sleep and his stomach felt queasy. Would Randall heed him this time? Or would he continue to vacillate? That was the precise word for it, vacillation, nothing so honorable as restraint or forebearance. How had Hochwald said it? Money seldom breeds on sentiment. No, but politics often wallowed in the stuff. Nineteen children versus a financial crisis that might sap America's strength as a world power. There was really only one choice.

He shrugged, then walked upstairs to shower, shave, and change his clothes. This would be another gritty day.

She sensed at once that this was one of those rancid hotels where the desk clerk collected two dollars for every girl who walked past him to the rickety iron-cage elevator. She averted her head as she passed his cubicle, but she knew there would be the single unshaded bulb overhead and keys dripping from their boxes like the tongues of panting dogs. There was that mingled odor of cheap perfume and disinfectant, reminiscent of dressing rooms in a hundred nightclubs where she had sung in other years. Down the hall she heard the flush of a toilet bowl and the groaning of old pipes.

The young man at her side was embarrassed for her. He was forlornly young, not more than eighteen, and clearly ill at ease escorting a celebrity. He whistled nervously, and he fretted with his tie as though it might flee his throat if not constantly pampered. He held the elevator door for her, and they vaulted upward convulsively.

"I hate to bring you in here, Miss Jones," he said. "But I'm only doin' what they told me to. . . . He's on the third floor."

She patted his hand, chocolate over midnight blue.

"That's all right, honey. I've seen plenty of these flea bags in my time."

The boy had fetched her from Princeton, driving surely if swiftly, making certain they were not followed, then threading his way through the dark, deserted streets of downtown Philadelphia. They had reached the Gaylord under the last cover of night.

"He's in three-oh-eight," the boy whispered. The hall carpet was worn to threads in spots, and the boards creaked like old regrets. As they passed one door, she heard a gasp and then a long, low moan of anguished rapture. The boy coughed protectively.

He rapped three times at 308. The door opened on a sliver of light, then swung wide for her. The boy retreated down the hall. He would return by appointment in an hour.

The man was short, black, neatly dressed in a blue suit. He wore rimless spectacles, and she noted at once that the brown eyes were friendly, quickly concerned for a visitor's sensibilities in such dingy quarters. He motioned her to a small rocking chair.

"This is an honor, Miss Jones," he said. "I wish I could have greeted you in a better hotel, but you know the situation."

"Forget it," she said. "And call me Ginny."

He fussed at a hot plate on a small table while she settled herself. When he turned, she saw that she was being offered a cup of coffee and a sugar roll.

"How nice of you! I'm starving."

He smiled his contentment at being able to please her. "I've heard you sing so many times," he said. His accent was the melted Oxonian of the educated West Indian, as full and rich as papaya. "I'd always hoped I'd meet you."

"Oh, come on, Dr. Nicolet. You're the famous one. I read your book on gold. . . . Well, no, I didn't read but three chapters. Gawd, my skull caved in."

They laughed together and he said: "Call me Al. . . . You're very pretty."

"And if you weren't married . . ." She slapped at the air. "I know those lines by heart, Doc."

"Al, please." His smile was deep. "And yes, I am married."

They chatted on. By the time she finished her coffee and roll, they knew they could trust each other, or thought they could, which for their purposes amounted to the same thing. It was an understanding soldered by scores of gestures, intonations, smiles, and movements, and if this mutual intuition proved false, then neither of them had yet lived long enough.

"I knew you wouldn't ask me to come here unless it was important," she said.

"Of course, Ginny." He was sitting in an uncomfortable, straight-backed chair, and he maneuvered forward until they were only a few inches apart. "I'm sorry we didn't meet earlier in the B.O.F. so we could have discussed this and both been prepared. Now I'm afraid the B.O.F. is headed straight for disaster unless some people act. There aren't many of us who can help prevent it, but two of them are Alfred Nicolet and Virginia Jones."

She hunched her shoulders. "I'm not very smart. But I try. What's the bad news?"

"Ginny, how do you stand on Gamal?"

She frowned. "Gamal?"

"You mean you don't know the word? Never heard it?"

"Gamal." She savored the sound and combed about in memory. "Gamal. . . . Yeah, once I think. Some cat at a B.O.F. party. I remember asking him what it was. He

mumbled something. I don't know. I forget just what. . . .
How do you spell it?"

"G-A-M-A-L." He looked perplexed. "At least a
hundred people in the Blacks of February Twenty-first
knew the meaning of that word—and by now probably
many more. It seems odd that you don't."

"I don't. So help me."

"I thought you knew everything that went on in council," he observed.

"You know Danny Smith's ideas about women," she
said with a grin. "I love the man, but for him women are
second-class citizens. Being black, that makes me third-
class, doesn't it?"

Nicolet studied her a moment, reknitting his intuition
of trust, then reached to the small table for a magazine
and a sheet of paper. Using the magazine for support, he
sketched rapidly with a pencil. "There. That's a rough
map of the United States. Here's Gamal." He cross-
hatched an oblong in the southeast section. "Gamal
means the states of Georgia, Alabama, Mississippi, and
Louisiana."

"Yeah." Her mouth opened slightly as she watched.
"So what?"

"Gamal is the Republic of Gamal," said Nicolet slowly,
"an independent black nation that Daniel Smith intends
to carve out of the U.S. It would comprise all of those
four states save for a narrow strip along Georgia's Atlantic Coast, running through the cities of Savannah and
Brunswick, so the whites could have an access corridor to
Florida." He paused. "Even Dan Smith isn't so sanguine
as to think whites would surrender Florida without war.
Besides he detests the state."

"Georgia through Louisiana," murmured Ginny.
"Down home! Why, goddam. And Danny thinks we're
going to get that?"

"He does. What's more, he's ready to seize a thousand
homes and then ten thousand more, and then still more,
until the President and Congress agree to cede the four
states for a new black nation."

"Wuu." Her eyes were wide. "Is he going to buy it or
what?"

"A trade," said Nicolet. "He'll trade the broken bodies

of two hundred years of slavery for the soil on which they were brutalized. He'll also throw in the thousands of white homes he hopes to be holding under black guns."

"Gamal," said Ginny softly. She gripped the armrests of the rocker as she stared at Nicolet, not quite seeing him, her eyes on far places beyond the cracked and peeling wallpaper. Beneath the small arc of her Afro coiffure —so symmetrical that Nicolet wondered if it could be a wig—two long gold earrings, fashioned like scimitars, swung as she rocked. Sullen light, the first of day, bickered at the unwashed window.

"You not kidding me, Al?"

"I've never been more serious in my life," he said. From the shelter of his glasses his brown eyes searched hers.

"But why . . ." She fumbled for direction. "How come I never heard about this from somebody on council? . . . Gamal! Four states. All shining black. I think it's beautiful."

"You like the idea?" He was taken aback.

"God, yes. Don't everybody? For years they been talking about a black nation, a black president, and capital. I always loved the talk but thought it was pothead stuff. Now Danny Smith will make it come true. God love that man!"

She rocked slowly, drifting gradually into ecstasy, the flesh of dreams. Nicolet watched her, this goddess of soul whose haunting songs called to the hearts of ten million black men like a train moaning in the night. He wondered, with sudden dismay, whether she was a daily reader of her horoscope. He could cope with practical, bone-sure women. He was not prepared for a seeress.

He cleared his throat impatiently. She rocked on, bathed in the luster of unknown tomorrows.

"Ginny!"

Her eyes came back into focus. "Yeah."

He leaned forward and took her hand. "Ginny, Gamal is Smith's holy vision—and the movement's sure route to hell. Believe me, right now it could destroy us all."

"So?" She withdrew her hand. "We dyin' anyway."

"You're wrong," he said. "We are just beginning to live." The loamy Caribbean voice had a sudden lilt.

"Black power is at our fingertips. We are about to grasp it—if we hold steady and do not falter. . . . Ginny, what am I?"

"You a sweet black man." She smiled with a trace of shyness. She had returned to the cheap, threadbare room now.

"Thanks. I mean my profession. I'n an economist. Right?"

"Yes, dear. You're the gold man, crackin' girls' skulls."

"Then listen carefully to me." He leaned forward again. "Dan Smith is a man of visions, cut from the cloth of prophets. Like all messiahs, he has the gift to foretell the future. His holy grail, his Camelot, if you will, is the Republic of Gamal. And the beauty of his quest is that fifty years from now Gamal will make sense. Smith, perhaps unknowingly, has glimpsed the truth. Those four states, populated by blacks under wise, progressive leadership, could become a magnificent land, a proud and rich country."

Ginny yielded to the metronomic beat of the words. She could have been a tribal girl at the feet of the village teller of ancient stories.

"Georgia," he said. "That rich red soil yields tobacco, peanuts, cotton. The forests give us lumber, pulpwood, turpentine. Fine minerals too, bauxite, mica, zirconium. Move across to Alabama. More cotton and pulpwood and deep in livestock. A great steel industry at Birmingham and large deposits of soft coal. Mississippi has soybeans, sugar cane, pecans, more cotton, and thousands of square miles of timber. But mostly oil and gas, producing at $250,000,000 a year. Lastly Louisiana, billions of dollars in oil and gas reserves, sulphur, sugar cane, rice, and more forests. From the Gulf comes an abundant catch of fish and shrimp."

Ginny listened hypnotically, fascinated by a litany of commerce that ordinarily would have bored her to yawns.

"One of the world's great ports at New Orleans," continued Nicolet. His eyes shone behind the spectacles. "And others at Mobile and Gulfport. Fine cities and towns from Augusta in the east to Lake Charles in the west. A shining capital at Montgomery, the black flag with crimson fist flying where once flew the stars and bars

of the white man's old Confederacy. Gamal, a rich, indus-
trious nation, could trade with the world and send its
ships to the seven seas. Danny Smith has seen the future,
and Gamal someday will be his glory."

Ginny cocked her head and a golden scimitar at one
ear brushed her shoulder. "You ain't poor-mouthin'
Gamal, Al. You talking like an angel."

He shrugged and shook his head. "But, Ginny, all that
is a half century away. Today, we're in no shape to run a
nation. We'd be bankrupt and plunged into our own riots
and bloodshed within a decade. Ginny, we blacks just
don't have enough skills yet. We need managers, merchants, financiers, captains of industry, entrepreneurs and
scientists, machinists and technicians by the carload. Let's
face it. We don't have a thousand blacks in America
today capable of running even one industry, like petrole-
um. We need a million."

Ginny brooded in an accusing cloud. "Now you're
switching sides again. Why can't you stay put?"

"I'm talking facts," he said. "I believe everything you
said on television yesterday morning. Today the B.O.F.
must demand black justice, recompense for past agonies,
and a big piece of the industrial action. We want two men
on the Empire board and a black economist on the
Truckers' pension fund to start. We're going to learn." He
struck a fist in his palm. "We're going to educate. We're
going to become managers, bankers, corporate experts,
scholars, scientists. We're going to learn to play whitey's
game better than he can play it. And then, when we're
ready . . ."

Nicolet rose from his chair, suddenly 140 pounds of
zealot, and brandished a forefinger at her. "When the
blacks are ready, they won't beg or bargain for Gamal.
They'll just march down and take it. They'll have the
arms. They'll have the brains. They'll have the stuff of
nations." He paused, theatrically, and held up his hands
in a gesture of self-sacrifice. "But all this is for our
grandchildren. We must prepare the way wisely for them.
Today we must act within our means—including the
means to frighten whitey half to death as we're doing
right this minute."

Ginny gazed silently at him and he continued. "Right

now Danny Smith's Gamal is suicidal. We couldn't run it if we got it, and we won't get it. Smith's plan involves the seizure of thousands of white suburban homes upon the rallying cry of Gamal. Ginny, that could mean a black massacre. Dan's men say, 'take ten,' but for every ten we'd take, we'd lose a hundred. Black brains and black guts would rot in the gutters of the ghettos. Black men would be murdered by the thousand. And then, for the survivors, the barbed wire of concentration camps. Face it, Ginny. Dan Smith's way is madness. It would take us at least a hundred years to recover."

"You're an economist," said Ginny in soft protest, "not a military man. Sounds like you ought to stick to Wall Street."

"To paraphrase an old saying, the future of black America is too vital to leave to generals," he said. "And generals, by the way, is what the B.O.F. has none of. We have a few knowledgeable officers, including the best, a major, Howard Underwood, who's with Smith now. But Underwood is no genius. Determined and intelligent, yes, but no great strategist. Furthermore, he's mesmerized by Danny. At this crucial stage I wouldn't trust his judgment."

Ginny folded her hands in her lap. Her shoulders fell and there was a far, sad look in her eyes. "Just what do you want from me, Al? Why did you have the boy bring me here?"

"I'm convinced that Smith will sound the call for Gamal," he replied. "I can't prove that. I just feel it in my bones. And when he does, the B.O.F. will follow him like lemmings off a cliff unless some members rise and stop him. For that we need television. There are only a few of us in the B.O.F. with the prestige to be given TV time, and, just as important, to command a black audience that will pay attention. One of these is you. Another is me."

"Are you alone in this?" she asked.

"No. The commanders at five of the six seized homes believe as I do. We won in council."

"Ben Steele at the Crawford place?"

"Yes, and now Jackson Dill too. I'm informed that Dill got in before the troops arrived."

"Yes, he did." She eyed him closely. "Was he on some mission for you, Al?"

"In a way. I thought if Smith called for Gamal, Ben Steele might need help there. The second-in-command, Chili Ambrose, is a fanatic. Tough and honest, but a gunman."

"I suspect Jackson Dill fooled me some," she said. "He asked me if he could tell Tim Crawford that he, Jackson, could be trusted. I thought that was strange, but Jackson said he had an idea to get the house. You see, I knew Crawford years ago."

"Yes, I know." Nicolet threw this affirmation of rumors to the winds of bygone years. "Ginny, will you help me? Take your time in answering. A matter of consequence—involving tens of thousands of lives, maybe."

She began to rock again, the earrings swaying in reverse motion as though refusing to obey orders. She studied his face, so intent, and a glance took in the conflicting purpose of the eyes and the softness of the hands. He was the dean of the black intellectuals she so adored, these men whose learning matched the best of the white world, yet whose souls were as tender and pliant as their uncallused palms. There was that sweetness she used to see in Tim Crawford before he snapped back into his white shell.

"You're a good man, Al," she said.

"I do share Danny's dreams," he said shyly. "But also I look at facts. You trust me, Ginny?"

"Yeah," she said, breathing upon the word. "But revolution is no time for sweet men. It's a time for Dan Smith and Chili Ambrose."

"Half-revolution, Ginny. If we stay with those six homes, we'll win, believe me. Leave Gamal for our grandchildren."

"I'm no thinker, Alfred. I dig the last man who tries to persuade me to his thoughts." It was a candid self-revelation as though she had bared her bosom. "If Danny were here, I'd probably grab a gun and follow him."

"Then I'm fortunate." He took both of her hands in his. "I can only say what I believe, and I believe we must be prudent right now or the vision of Gamal will be lost in rivers of black blood."

"Okay." There was a wisp of sadness in her voice. "What do you want me to do, Al?"

"When you leave here," he said, "I want you to call Harold Osborne. He'll be at the White House, and he'll take any call from you."

"Osborne! He's a nigger shoeshine boy for Randall."

"No. That's not fair. Harold chose the system long ago, and now he has his loyalties. But so do you, Ginny. Once you joined the B.O.F., you accepted a new black-power discipline. It makes demands on you, traps a part of you, twists your conscience. You find you have to compromise with men. Their skins are black, but they act much the same as white politicians."

"They do not," she protested hotly.

"Oh yes. Dan Smith knows how to use you, how to make you play his game, even as President Randall did. Why, honey, Danny would sacrifice your life for his visions without a second's hesitation."

"I promised you, Al." She sounded as though she rued the pledge.

"All right. You call Osborne. He knows now that you're a B.O.F." He retained his gentle grip on her hands. "Tell Harold that we've talked and we both want prompt television time if Commander Smith sounds a call for revolution. Tell him you're speaking for me as well. Tell him we'll plead with the blacks of America not to heed Danny's cry."

"Why don't you call him?"

He shook his head. "I can't use the phone here. I'm registered as Bill Pearson. I can't take a chance on the switchboard. . . . Don't, of course, mention Gamal to Osborne. Don't be too explicit. Just let him know you'll be back in touch the moment Danny speaks."

"Okay. But I feel dirty. Betraying people's not my bag." She withdrew her hands, virtue reconsidered.

"I know." He felt the loss of honor like a vow snatched from his lips by a wind at sea. Betrayal since the charnel days of slavery, a sickening treachery of the spirit, the black curse of centuries.

"After you talk to Osborne, call me here at 308 as Bill Pearson." He jotted the Gaylord's number on a corner of the map sketch, tore it off, and handed it to her. "We have no choice, Ginny. Danny's way means black bodies stacked like pig iron and barbed wire for those left behind."

"We never have a choice," she said dully. The morning light flooded the room now, flowing unbidden through the smeared window and washing like dishwater over the cheap furniture and the wasted carpet.

Nicolet coughed, a renunciation of faith. The slack new day was unwanted and the soul a tattered thing. Ginny rocked slowly, regarding Nicolet with a look very near revulsion. They shared their shame as though they had traded bodies for simultaneous acts of onanism and now saw their self-ravishing mirrored in the other's eyes. Daniel Smith would march into history without his captains.

"It's not a pleasant world," said Nicolet.

"Oh, Christ." In moments such as these the understated resignation of West Indians infuriated her.

They sat for a while and then he left their vacuum, moving to the small table and the hot plate to prepare more instant coffee. Three raps were heard at the door. Nicolet turned toward her, and they stood for a moment in shared, silent despair.

Ginny suddenly uttered a small birdlike cry, threw herself against Nicolet's chest, and kissed him feverishly. She hurried out, to the boy with the nervous whistle and the troublesome tie.

Bunny Jeffers sat up in bed with a start, and her first, involuntary movement was to part her blond hair at the forehead and caress the long strands until they fell to her shoulders like drifting sunbeams. It was the first of her daily devotions in the chapel of her hair.

Had she dreamed it, or had the idea been shaped in those fertile moments before full awakening when the brain waves a hundred ephemeral patterns? No matter. It was a gorgeous idea, and it bloomed full and lush with no little nagging doubts to hint of eventual decay. It was an idea to rejoice over and to communicate at once. But to whom? Then, abruptly and shrewdly, she knew. It had to be Eileen, Eileen Duncan, her black partner for the weekly integrated swimming class at the Pretty Brook Tennis Club. Was it too early to phone Eileen?

Sunlight skipped through the corkscrew willow behind her window and frisked about the room. It would be hot again today, but right now the air on Library Place in Princeton still had a tang of early morning, a freshness that would last until the dew faded from the grass. Bunny guessed it was about seven o'clock. She felt wonderful, and she confronted the new day with her bare, tanned body, offering her confident breasts as gifts to the sun. Bunny was thirteen years old and quite sure of her future. She would win the Olympic backstroke championship three years from now, she would go to Radcliffe, be taken by a half-dozen grateful lovers, and, finally, she would marry a very smooth and witty man who would worship her without corny outward manifestations. She would bear him three beautiful children, and someday, she thought with delicious contrition, she would commit adultery and have to writhe around in sappy guilt. At last, freed from the enslavement of concupiscence, she would return to the familiar, warm, hairy chest of her husband. She could even see that chest. It would have a nice little mattress between the nipples, a kind of animal fur, if you will, very comfortable yet tending to tickle at times. But love and carnal sin weren't all. Bunny would accomplish any number of shimmering good works because she loved people more than anything. Yes, she did. She couldn't imagine work without people. With people you got involved and you could see them admiring you, the girls with envy, the boys timidly, and the men with quick shadows of lust smoking at their eyes.

She pulled on the beige jeans sawed off just below the knees, the tan shirt that fit as snugly as skin at her breasts. She walked barefoot to the bathroom to wash her face and scour her teeth with the electric brush that hummed and shivered like an outboard on a lake. Then off to fix her breakfast while her parents slept. She raced down the carpeted steps in muffled thunder, shaking the wooden railing.

Everyone said the seizure of the Crawford home on the Great Road was the most shocking thing of their whole lives, but while frowning and miming properly, Bunny was privately buoyed by the capture. The invasion ripped the masks off people and showed them for what they really were. She detested Princeton with a passion reserved only for a loved one: the adult custom of affluent dismissiveness, an art sanded to such exquisite fineness that one drove a muddy Mercedes, spoke of Harvard with good-natured condescension, reacted without shock to an unwed daughter's pregnancy, and let the bills from Palmer Square and Nassau Street mount for months without settlement. Bunny truly believed that her town must be the most hypocritically enlightened one in all America. Everyone knew absolutely everything and everybody, but to show off one's knowledge was to risk a yawn or a patronizing smile. People were secretly proud of famous residents such as Stalin's daughter and, in past decades, Einstein, Thomas Mann, and Woodrow Wilson; but they were too mannered to admit it. The adults were really intolerable even if she did love so many of them. They had created a town that every kid she knew couldn't wait to get out of—to some rough, smelly, sloppy, and barbarous reality. Princeton was a lovely stage set that the audience applauded when the curtain went up, not because it represented truth but because the designer had been so clever. The "green phoenix," F. Scott Fitzgerald called it years ago, and little green phoenix it remained.

But now this sudden seizure of Fairhill had stripped people to their raw selves. Last night Bunny's mother, a faculty matron of unruffled graces and a cloying concern for what she called "the disadvantaged," had become almost hysterical. She double-locked every door, demanded that her husband borrow a gun from Stu Frelinghuysen— the only man on Library Place who hunted—and phoned her sister in New York for advice about what to do if a black rapist broke into the house. On Palmer Square last evening a borough cop had ripped a B.O.F. sign from the hands of a black high school student. On ordinary days the patrolman would not have dared touch a black boy. The mayor imposed a 10 P.M. curfew for all residents, so the town's streets were turned over to heavy and ominously aimless traffic from Philadelphia and New York. Every carload of Negroes had been searched for guns, and people said there were a hundred state police cars circulating in Princeton and vicinity.

Rumors ran like frothing greyhounds through the streets, and Bunny believed most of them. Liz Crawford's friend Peggy Abingdon, the plump, bustling little woman, had collected thousands of dollars for Negro causes over the decades. But yesterday she fired off a shotgun in her wooded driveway at the mere sight of a black man. He turned out to be a cousin substituting for the ailing trash collector. No one knew Peggy even owned a gun. Sally Bretherton, who specialized in precious, integrated dinner parties, screamed over the phone to police that she was being robbed by a black man. When the patrol car arrived, Sally grudgingly confessed that she had lied. What she really wanted was a special all-night police guard for which she'd pay the borough $100. When officers demurred, pleading a lack of manpower, Sally slammed the door.

Gil Hughes, who once coached Princeton tennis teams and who prided himself on indoctrinating his pupils with as much gentlemanly tolerance as court technique, headed a band of elderly men who marched on the borough hall and asked the mayor to deputize them as armed watchmen. When the mayor declined, Hughes punched him in the chest, the first recorded blow he had ever struck in his life. He was now out on bail on a charge of assault and battery. At Princeton Hospital it was said Dr. Smallwood refused to treat the torn and bleeding scalp of a black construction worker until he had tended to three white women with summer flu. Dr. Smallwood was a past president of PAHR, Princeton Association for Human Rights. Bunny was so incensed by this rumor, passed on by her mother, that she personally called Dr. Smallwood, the Jeffers family physician. No, he said, the story was false. The only Negro to appear for emergency treatment all day was a boy with a broken arm, and it had been set promptly by the doctor on duty. Despite this disavowal, Bunny heard the story three times Monday—and each time Dr. Smallwood was applauded for ignoring the phantom Negro with the bloody scalp.

What really irritated Bunny, though, was the town's attitude toward Holly and Scott Crawford. "Those poor little children" was a phrase she heard fifty times yesterday. The pitying tones were artificial, squiggly, and soupy. People said not what they thought but what they thought they ought to feel. Personally Bunny imagined that Scott and Holly were having a ball. She could envision Holly, bright as a diamond, skittering about her black captors and daring them to find her invisible friend, Peter Wilson, or Scott, his hair rumpled like tangled yarn, yelling for attention while he turned somersaults or chinned himself on a tree limb. Bunny liked the Crawford children. They had been excessively shy of the water on the first day of swimming class, but she had shamed them into competitive duckings and jumps from the edge of the pool. Now they would stay in the water until shivers convulsed their tiny bodies and the skin on their fingers shriveled into ridges. But people yesterday spoke of Scott and Holly in hushed, distressed tones as though the children were already dead and honorary pallbearers were being named.

It was an idea about Holly and Scott which had so excited Bunny upon awakening. It was neat, workable, she knew, and would prove a grand rebuke to all those phony adults who stood around talking dolorously about those poor little children. Bunny finished the last of the bacon, toast, and milk, put the dishes in the sink, and went to the hall telephone to call Eileen.

She could hear the phone ringing in the small white cottage on Birch Avenue in Princeton's Negro section. At the same time Bunny could almost smell the musky odor in Eileen Duncan's home, an odor pleasant and languorous and yet so alien to the smells of the Jeffers household that Bunny always felt a bit alarmed, even offended, by it. One of those race things, she guessed, something like her feeling for Eileen, at once warm and yet estranged. She and Eileen were going to be champions together. That, she'd bet. She in the backstroke and Eileen in the butterfly. They had great fun as swimming instructors, loose and easy with each other. But later in their dry skins, so different, and in their dried hair, so different, they drew gradually apart. Bunny supposed the veil really fell at sundown. After dark their thoughts turned to boys, and it was very difficult to trade intimacies about boys when Eileen's boys were black and hers were white. It was all very perplexing.

"Hello." Sleep coated Eileen's voice.

"Eileen. It's me, Bunny. You awake yet?"

"Sorta. . . . Oh. You heard anything about Holly and Scott?"

"No. I just got up. But that's why I'm calling. Eileen, how do you feel about all that at Fairhill?"

"I don't know, Bunny. My pop's for the B.O.F. My mother would chase 'em all out of town with a broom if she could. I don't know. I like Mrs. Crawford some, but I guess if I were a man, I'd join the B.O.F."

"Oh." Bunny was shocked. For some reason, it had never crossed her mind that Eileen might favor the B.O.F. Murder, shooting, pillage, Lord knew what all. How wild, really! Bunny thought fast and she knew she must dissemble with her friend. "But you wouldn't want to have Scott or Holly hurt, would you?"

"Oh no, no. Never." The dismay in Eileen's voice was as genuine as sudden rain. "I can't believe any black man would harm them."

"Well, I've got a terrific idea to make sure of it. Can I come over and talk to you about it?"

"Tell me on the phone," said Eileen. "I can't wait." The fact was that Eileen was not sure that she cared to have a white person enter her Birch Avenue home this morning.

"Not on the phone. I've got to see you."

"Is this against the B.O.F.?"

"No, of course not." Bunny spoke swiftly, pushing aside her own doubts. Was it? Well, maybe in a way. But she could never confess such a thing to Eileen. She needed her help badly.

"Then okay. Come on over if you want."

As Bunny hung up, she felt a quick flush of guilt. She was about to attempt to deceive a friend. But the cause was just, a shining temple of good works. So, of course, she was happy. Virtue's talent for corruption knows no generation gap.

Chapter Fifteen

General Hildebrand stood behind the chair, slowly massaging the green leather as though it were a human muscle. On the wall to his rear hung the map of the United States, laced with green, red, and yellow plastic tapes like some huge birthday gift. Fluorescent light from the ceiling panels glinted on the general's eight silver stars, four on each shoulder. Rows of tiny, varicolored ribbons decorated the left breast of his faultlessly pressed blouse. Save for the metallic symphony of the teleprinters, the situation room was quiet. Members of HICOM sat before the general like pupils before the teacher.

"The risk to life is minimal," he was saying in a textbook voice. "The timing has been perfected in innumerable riot games. Tactically the maneuver presents no problems. The CS gas barrage from the choppers is to be coordinated precisely with the advance on the double by elite assault troops at each of the six stations. These men are seasoned veterans who will carry out orders to the letter. Casualties will be zero to light."

Hildebrand looked as untroubled in his predictions as a weather forecaster announcing a passing squall. President Randall shifted uneasily in his chair. Why did generals invariably slip into this emotionless, pedagogical tone whenever they discussed the imminence of bloodshed? From a skirmish with small arms, to napalm dumped on a village outpost, to a hydrogen-bomb holocaust that would consume continents, the tone was the same. Dry, polite, confident, speaking of death as though it were a footnote in a West Point manual written by MacArthur, edited by Patton, and published with a commendatory foreword by LeMay. The voice never sheltered doubts, never hinted at crushed limbs and bloody eye sockets, never descended from the cool heavens where abstractions dwell. All was numbers, guns, forces, levels, terrain, and synchronized timing. Phil Randall felt himself a stranger on this broad plateau of unpeopled certainties.

"Under no circumstances will the assault forces fire on the white hostages," continued Hildebrand. He kneaded the leather chair top. "They will engage black B.O.F. guerrillas only if fired upon and then only in self-defense. Chances of mistaken identity are practically nil. The B.O.F. men all wear black sweaters and green dungarees."

Hildebrand paused, the professor challenging his seminar to question his logic on a problem which patently had but one solution. There were five men facing him now, for Treasury Secretary Lee had recently joined the group to provide instant contact with the esoteric precincts of finance.

"Isn't there danger of the gas falling over the troops as well as the people in the houses?" asked Harold Osborne.

Hildebrand nodded approvingly at the black cabinet officer as though a bright student had raised a very good but long-discounted question. "No," he replied. "The assault forces will wear gas masks. Also, assuming the helicopters are on target—which we have no reason to doubt, due to the surprise element in the attack—then the perimeter of the gas can be calculated quite accurately. The troops will maneuver just outside that line, letting the fleeing occupants of the house come to them."

The general looked about the room with a pleased expression. He was ready for the next question. It came at once from Joe Voorhees.

"Suppose the B.O.F.-ers use the children as shields and come running out of the gas, firing at the troops?"

The general nodded confidently again. This too had been anticipated. "Our men are under orders not to fire in such circumstances. They are to accept their casualties until they can close on the enemy and disarm them."

President Randall had slid slowly down in his chair until his neck nudged the top of the leather upholstery. Another nap of two hours had left him unrefreshed, and now he felt as if he had bivouacked for weeks in this room.

"Isn't that asking a lot of a soldier, Walter?" Randall was mildly exasperated by Hildebrand's pedantic approach. "His buddy next to him has been shot down, he knows his turn may come any second, yet he holds his fire. That's hard to imagine."

Hildebrand frowned. In his Pentagon haven such absurdly small losses as the President's question envisioned would hardly rate the dignity of the word "casualties."

"Remember these men are all elite veterans, Mr. President," he admonished. "They were under fire in Vietnam. They will follow orders despite severe provocation. I have no qualms on that score."

Randall brooded in the depths of his chair, studying Hildebrand as he fielded another question from Osborne.

"You say the assault troops are all volunteers," he observed. "How many of them are black, General? Do you have any figures on that?"

Hildebrand flushed slightly, a defensive coloration. "I didn't ask. Frankly, though, in view of yesterday's incident, I'd be surprised if many black troops are among the two hundred volunteers at each station."

When no one spoke for a moment, the general asked his own question. "May I sum up the military view, Mr. President?"

Randall nodded. Hildebrand gripped the top of the green leather chair before him.

"This is the situation as Secretary Edelstein and I see it," he said. "It is now 10 A.M. The homes have been held since Saturday evening, a matter of more than sixty hours. Save for one defiant challenge at the Crawford property, there has been no word from the occupying forces. They have ignored your offer of amnesty. They have not surrendered. Each hour that goes by increases the risk to lives of the captives. Worse, each hour increases the possibility of armed revolt by blacks in the major cities. We know, since Miss Jones's phone call to Harold Osborne, that even some members of the B.O.F. fear that Daniel Smith may raise some insane call for revolution. It is almost certain now that Smith has fled from the mountains. We are sitting on dynamite with a hundred fuses that can be ignited at any moment."

He paused for effect, scanning the faces before him. "The combined CS gas and assault plan is 95 percent foolproof, far above the odds considered acceptable for risk in a normal military operation. I am confident that all hostages can be freed within a few minutes after you give the order to proceed, Mr. President. And freeing the homes should promptly defuse the whole situation."

Randall moved about in his chair again. "It sounds quite tidy in theory, Walter, but a lot of things could go wrong. The choppers might miss targets with the gas. Several could be shot down. Advancing troops might get rattled and open fire. A child might be killed. Any number of things. And a prolonged firefight at just one of those properties might touch off the very black uprising we're trying to prevent."

"Possible, of course," rejoined Hildebrand, "but I repeat that the risks are minimal."

Randall glanced about the circle. "Paul?"

"I agree completely with Walter," said the Defense Secretary. "The time to move is right now. Further delay could be extremely hazardous."

"I'm against the plan," said Joe Voorhees. He spoke with a candor reflecting the security of his personal ties to the President. "We've managed to contain this thing so far, and I think we should continue as is—for the rest of the day at least."

"I do too," said Osborne. "If B.O.F.-ers are killed by paratroops, the ghettos may erupt. The situation in the black communities is still very touchy."

"I'd put General Hildebrand's plan into action at once," said Treasury Secretary Lee. "American securities are being dumped all over Europe. Traders already are selling dollars for safer marks and francs. Another day could see a massive raid on the dollar. American markets, opening now on the East Coast, are sure to fall hard again today. Further delay would not only be dangerous, as Paul says, I think it would be flirting with chaos."

Randall arose, walked to the long table, and sat down on a corner, one leg dangling. In moments of decision he seemed to have a need for casual movement, as though the brain might refuse to function if confined to one spot. "Three to two for an assault." He thought for a bit, then turned to Osborne. "When is Miss Jones due at my office, Hal?"

"Any minute now," said Osborne. "Her charter was scheduled to land at National at ten. It's ten-seven now."

Randall pondered. "I want to talk to Miss Jones first," he said. "I'll have my answer for you about eleven. I doubt if things will change much in an hour."

"I must respectfully disagree, Mr. President," said Hildebrand. "Postponement now greatly amplifies the risk."

He still stood with his hands gripping the top of the chair. He looked at Randall, ignoring the others in the room. The teleprinters were curiously hushed for the moment as if deliberating between the general and the President.

"Grounds for impeachment, Walter?" Randall managed a small smile.

"No, sir," said Hildebrand. "You're the commander in chief. You know I abide by all your decisions. But I repeat, as emphatically as I can, that delay is unwise."

"I understand your position." Randall turned to the Marine at the typewriter table. "Note the general's views for the record, Sergeant." Military dissent had become a sturdy flower in the log's dry turf. Would history award its prizes to the general? "We'll stand as is for an hour," said Randall. "I'll try to be back by eleven."

The President walked out the door. Escorted by a Secret Service agent, he took an elevator to the first floor and strode briskly down a corridor to his sunlit oval office.

He had only a brief wait before Miss Jones was announced. She entered through the French doors, coming directly from the back driveway and thus avoiding the public lobby where newsmen waited. Randall greeted her in the middle of the room where the seal of the President was tufted into the ivory green carpet. She was a wisp of a woman in a simple black dress and wearing gold earrings shaped like scimitars. Through the French doors, opening on the colonnade and the rose garden beyond, Randall caught a glimpse of the White House limousine which had fetched her, presumably in secret, from a charter-service hangar at National Airport.

"I didn't like that pawin'," she said after their exchange of greetings. Her dark eyes accused him.

"Pawing?" Randall was confused.

"Those agents searched me," she complained. "Even in the White House we're treated like dirt."

"I'm awfully sorry, Miss Jones. I should have told them. But I'm not sure it would have done any good. The Secret Service operates under its own law, and today, well . . ."

"They searched me and my handbag because I'm black," she said flatly.

"No, Miss Jones. Really. Color has nothing to do with it."

"They'd search a white woman you invited here? I don't believe it."

Randall could sense a prickly hour ahead of him. He knew she was right. And he also knew that no Secret Service agent would permit a member of the B.O.F. within yards of the President today without a thorough search. He could see by Miss Jones's indignant expression that no explanation would satisfy her.

He led her to one of the facing sofas occupying the inner end of the room near the marble fireplace. Ginny placed her gold-trimmed handbag on the coffee table and settled into a corner of the sofa.

"I guess I shouldn't blame you," she said, relenting. "This is my first time here, Mr. President. It's a lovely office. Real bright and cheery."

He welcomed her lightened mood. "Sort of a cheerful job too—on most days." He sat down on the other sofa opposite her. "Today I could do without it, thanks. Miss Jones, I don't need to tell you how much I admire your singing. Mrs. Randall and I are great fans of yours."

"Thanks." She waited, he noted, with more composure than most of his first-time callers.

"I'm sorry about our differences on television yesterday," he said. "But I want to tell you personally that I had no idea of the background of those homes as you outlined it. Every issue has two sides—at least—and you gave your side very effectively."

"I told the truth." She said it with an edge of challenge.

"Also I want to apologize on another point," he said. "It's true the FBI infiltrated the Blacks of February Twenty-first. But it did so without my knowledge or consent." He sighed. "It's a big government. A president's orders aren't always carried out. . . . Do you know about Delmar Sprague?"

She nodded. "I know now he's dead. He double-crossed the B.O.F." Her tone left no doubt that Sprague's perfidy justified his murder.

Randall explained Sprague's dual role, his finding of the telephone numbers, and the discovery of his lifeless body on Orchard Street in Manhattan.

"Rotten business all around." He paused. "Miss Jones, I don't want to expend a single additional life in this, well, collision, if you will. That's why Hal Osborne asked you to come here. We deeply appreciate your offer, and that of Alfred Nicolet, to help us if needed, but I must say I'm uncertain about what's in the offing. Do I understand that you fear Daniel Smith may put out some secret code word, a signal for revolution?"

"That's right."

"Well, just how, in what manner? It's hard to plan anything withot knowing more."

"I realize that, Mr. President. Since I agreed to come here, I've checked back with Dr. Nicolet, and he's authorized me to tell you something in confidence. . . . Mr. President, did you ever hear the word 'Gamal'?"

"It's one of Nasser's names," he said.

"No, I mean something else. Have you heard it in connection with the black movement?"

"No." He looked puzzled. "I'm afraid I haven't."

"I didn't know what it meant either until a few hours ago." She folded her hands in her lap. "Gamal is the name of a separate black nation that Commander Smith wants to establish down south in the present states of Georgia, Alabama, Mississippi, and Louisiana."

She pictured the vision and Smith's plan to implement it: the call for Gamal, the seizure of 1,000 more homes in the wealthiest white suburbs, the preparedness of B.O.F. forces in major cities, the eventual capture of 10,000 homes, the ultimatum to the President. Randall listened intently. "And you and Dr. Nicolet don't go along with Gamal?"

"Someday, yes. It's got to come, Mr. President. Integration will never work. For every reasonable white man like you, there's fifty who hate us."

"Fifty! Oh, come now, Miss Jones."

"Fifty, forty, thirty," she said with husky anger. "What difference does it make? I'm up against white hate a dozen times a day. Don't tell me. I know."

He said nothing, sensing that any show of sympathy would be as incendiary as further challenge.

"I'd love to live in Gamal right now," she said, "but we couldn't run it yet, and anyway Danny's plan might mean civil war with thousands of blacks killed."

"Whites too."

She hunched her shoulders. "A million whites die, I couldn't care less. That's your problem. We got our own. I don't want dead black men. . . . Frankly we're split in the B.O.F. Some of us want those six homes for bargaining. Others want to go Danny's way—blasting and dying."

"And your proposal is what exactly? How can you and Nicolet help us?"

She flared. "Help you? Oh no. Help ourselves, save our black men to fight another day when the odds are better."

Randall felt a quick spurt of hostility. Was there anything he could say to which this young woman would not take mordant exception? He wanted to lash back at her, but he recalled the theory of President Kennedy during the 1962 missile crisis with the Russians: Always give your opponent elbow room. Never crowd him to the wall where conflict is inevitable. Then Randall realized that he was thinking of the blacks of America as the enemy and he colored at the thought. Thank God this bristling slip of a woman was no mind reader.

"I am to help you to help yourselves then," he said, trying to suppress any trace of irony. "And just what am I supposed to do?"

"If Commander Smith gives the code message for Gamal," she said, "Nicolet and I want you to get us immediate television time. We would tell our black brothers just what I'm telling you—that to follow Danny now would mean black suicide."

"How do I know you won't use the air time to rally support for Smith?"

She glared at him. "Because you got my word that I won't—and neither will Nicolet." She paused, fiercely intent. "That's a black promise, Mr. President, not to be compared with those slippery white promises that are made to be sneaked around tomorrow."

This is like dealing with a porcupine, he thought. He could imagine General Hildebrand or Secretary Lee sitting in his place. Ginny Jones would have been ushered to the door by now.

"And you think black people will heed you and Nicolet rather than Smith?"

"Yes. They will if we can offer them something solid." She challenged him with her eyes.

"Meaning?"

"Oh, the usual bone from whitey when he's frightened."

She was really thorny, this one. Why didn't she curse her President and be done with it?

"Please, Miss Jones. Could you give me the facts without the, uh, editorializing?"

Her eyes flashed in quick triumph. She had scored. "When y'all hear facts you don't like, you call them editorials. I said a bone from whitey and that's exactly what I mean. If I go to the brothers and sisters on television, I have to tell them we've won something."

"Some concession from me? Is that what you're getting at?"

There was no mirth in her smile. "Now you dig, Mr. President."

He studied her for a moment. "I'm sorry, but I don't understand. Private homes have been seized. They must be returned. What could a public official concede that would be binding on the owners of homes?"

"That's a laugh." She shook her head in dismay. "That really is. You're the most powerful person in the world, Mr. President. I may not be so smart, but I'm smart enough to know that you could make other people do a thousand things if you wanted to."

"What, specifically?"

Ginny thought swiftly. She was here to extract from this man a promise to see that blacks were placed on two boards, Empire and Truckers, but why not try for more? What better opportunity would any B.O.F. member ever get? She had the President of the United States worried now. She could try. She groped hurriedly for ideas. Something that would please and surprise Al Nicolet, perhaps. Ah, that was it.

"First," she said, "something that we desperately need. Suppose you agree to set up an all-black prestige university with federal funds? But I mean all black. Not a white man with a word to say about it. Total control in black hands—trustees, faculty, students, the works. You ask Congress for the funds in a special message."

Randall thought for only a few seconds. The idea was not new. Actually Hal Osborne had discussed a similar project with him several weeks ago. "I think that might be arranged," he said, then quickly: "But only on condition the homes are released first."

"You mean I couldn't announce it?"

"Not publicly. But you could get word to B.O.F. leaders that if the houses were released, they had my promise of full White House support for setting up a first-rate, all-black university, best in the land."

"It's a deal," she said promptly. "Now, I got to have something to tell the brothers out loud on television when Danny makes his move."

"Something else?" Randall felt he had been had. This female bargained like a labor lawyer. A caution light flashed in his mind. "Just what?"

"Look," she said, "you know as well as I do that you could break the back of this thing in ten minutes. So far there have been only two public demands: one, that ol' man Dittmar puts two black men on Empire's board of directors; two, that Fritz Tiegert puts one black man— just one black face—on his pension-fund board. If that happens, two of these homes will be turned loose—and you know that would probably bust the others." She shrugged. "Like I say, just a little ol' bone from the man."

"And you really think that would work, Miss Jones?"

"Yeah." Her face sagged. "Yeah, dammit, it would, or at least I bet it would. We're so used to giving in every time the bone is tossed, it's second nature. Conditioning. You people been conditioning us for three hundred years."

The oval office was garishly bright, flooded by the late morning sun of July. He could imagine the heat outside rising like a newly lighted oven. The long limousine which had fetched Miss Jones waited on the back driveway. The uniformed chauffeur was chatting with two Secret Service men in the shade of the great magnolia tree.

"You understand, don't you, Miss Jones," he asked quietly, "that I have no control over the Empire board or the Truckers' pension managers?"

"Oh no!" Outrage burst, charging attempted deceit. "Why, you could pick up that phone"—she pointed to a nest of instruments on his desk—"and in fifteen minutes you could get the job done. Control, influence, White House threats, call it whatever you want. It's all the same thing. You and I know you can do practically anything, Mr. President."

She was serenely and abidingly confident in her embattlement. King Honky, it was obvious, was clothed in the raiment of unlimited power, a monarch who had but to raise his finger and the outermost lords of the realm would quake.

"Well, not quite anything," he rejoined. "For instance I haven't been able to make the B.O.F. withdraw—even with a pledge of amnesty."

"They got their pride," she retorted bleakly. "They not comin' out until they win something. Win? That's another laugh. Three spots of black in a ring of white faces around a couple of big, expensive tables. Gawd, that's a nothin'." She stared at him bitterly as her speech lapsed further into the idiom, a defensive growl. "You know, I ought to be ashamed of myself, comin' in here and pleadin' with the man. If I had the guts of Danny Smith, I'd say to hell with you and ever' other hon—uh, white man, and walk out of here. Why not? Let the blood flow. It's going to someday anyway. What's the difference? Now or ten years from now."

He watched her in silence, groping for the key to this tiny, fierce woman. She writhed in her loyalties, but which exerted the strongest pull?

"So why did you come here?" he asked quietly.

"Because Alfred Nicolet asked me to," she said. "He's a smart man. Our best."

"I see." He fell silent again, less because he was thinking than because he hesitated to provoke her anew. She was like General Hildebrand's dynamite, trailing a hundred fuses. "And if I could negotiate some arrangement for black members on the Empire and Trucker boards, in addition to the black university, then as I understand it, you and Nicolet would urge black citizens not to follow Daniel Smith?" He selected the words with care.

"Yeah."

They sat watching each other as though estimating hidden resources. Randall knew the stakes were high. If he declined, and if the elusive mystic, Dan Smith, were not captured within a few hours, then a messianic call for Gamal could unleash killings that might convulse the country. If he agreed and if pressure on Empire and the Truckers were successful, then the country would say Phil Randall had caved in at the first threats from the blacks who elected him. And if he wilted once, they would say he would do so again and again. A bone, she called it. A small and juiceless bone. If he tossed it, he lost face. What else? But face was not a minor thing in this house. Remember Lyndon Johnson. Then he thought of General Hildebrand and his prescriptions, so antiseptic, so clinical, so deadly.

"I'd consider such a deal on one condition," he said.

"What's that?"

"That not another B.O.F. demand will be made on this government for a year." He would not trade for less. He could not govern under constant whimsical pressure.

"I'm not a leader of the B.O.F.," she said, "just one of the rank and file."

"I think you and Nicolet have a great deal of influence." The shoe was on the other foot now. "I want your promise that you and Nicolet will do everything in your power to prevent further B.O.F. demands for a year."

"That's a long time."

"Not so long. Anyway that's my condition."

"Okay. I promise."

"All right, then we have a deal," he said. "On Empire and the Truckers, I'll try."

"Try?" She was promptly suspicious.

"Miss Jones," he said patiently, "despite what you think, I can't command people who don't work for the federal government. I can only reason with them."

"A president can do what he wants."

"We'll see. Obviously I want this as much as you do. You have my word that I'll try." He stood up. "Where can I reach you?"

"I'm going to stay in Washington with a friend." She took her handbag from the coffee table and began exploring its voluminous contents. Randall went to his desk and returned with a pen and a note pad with presidential crest.

"Thanks." She wrote down a number. "That's the phone. I'll stay there until I hear from you."

He escorted her toward the French doors. She halted momentarily, noticing for the first time the President's seal woven into the green carpet. She inspected it, then looked up at Randall with mingled awe and helplessness.

"We got a long way to go," she said.

Randall said nothing, but he tightened the grip on her arm. He led her to the doors which opened on the colonnade.

"I do appreciate your coming here," he said. "The gap is awfully wide and maybe it can't be bridged in our time. But we've got to try."

She looked him in the eyes. "Naw, you don't. You don't understand what I've done to Danny Smith." She put her hand on the doorknob and suddenly her body tensed. "But someday, so help me God, Danny's goin' to win. . . . We'll have Gamal if we have to burn this house to the ground."

She was gone, a defiant woman marching determinedly through the rose garden. She did not speak to the Secret Service agent who fell in at her side. Randall stood at the door until she disappeared into the rear of the limousine.

He walked to his desk, flipped a switch on the panel box. "Emily," he said, "I want the names of all executive officers and board members of Empire Motors, also the same for the Truckers International. As quick as you can, please."

Within the next two hours, while members of HICOM waited in the basement situation room, President Randall made twenty-five telephone calls, most of them long distance. At times the switchboard girls had as many as four

men waiting like stacked planes over an airport. Near the
end the President was joined at his desk by Joe Voorhees.

"You heard that last call, Joe," said Randall. He replaced the receiver and leaned back in his swivel chair.
"I've got a deal with Empire and the Truckers. If Dittmar
agrees, two black men go on Empire's board—as something new, consumer representatives. If Tiegert agrees, a
black man goes on the Truckers' pension board."

Randall capsuled his conversation with Ginny Jones
without mentioning the word "Gamal." He had given his
word, and, he thought wryly, he would keep it even for a
woman who longed to burn his house down. Or did she?
He really did not know. Instead of explaining Gamal,
Randall told Voorhees of Smith and his plan to seize ten
thousand more homes under the fisted banner of revolution.

"What do you think, Joe?" He toyed with a brass letter
opener.

"Jesus, what am I supposed to say?" Voorhees was tie-
less and sweating despite the air conditioning. "If you can
buy your way out of this mess that cheap, you're a genius
—at luck. Thing is, will it work?"

"It's a gamble," said Randall, "but so is everything in
the last couple of days. What we don't know is the impact
of Nicolet and Ginny Jones as compared with Dan
Smith's voice. But if we can get a surrender of the six
homes before Smith speaks, maybe we can deflate him in
advance."

"Ask Hal Osborne. He'll know better than any of us.
He'll be for it, naturally. . . . But Lee, Edelstein, and Hildebrand? Brace yourself for some real static this time."

"I know." Randall stood up. "Well, let's go down and
face the animals."

They were back in the situation room at 12:40 P.M.,
more than an hour and a half after Randall's promised
return. In one quick glance Randall could tell that he was
being accorded the reception of an AWOL soldier who
wanders back to his unit. Only the machines seemed con-
tent, hammering away in indifferent concert.

"Anything new?" asked Randall.

Edelstein shook his head. "Nothing material."

"We believe the time for the assault plan is overdue,"

said General Hildebrand. He sat beside the gold phone to the Pentagon war room.

"The market's off again," said Lee. The Treasury Secretary's ashtray smoldered with half-smoked butts. "The silence from Smith is beginning to be ominous."

"I've decided to beat Smith to the punch," said Randall. "Walter, how much trouble is it to get messages into those homes?"

"No problem. Just use the bull horns."

"No, no. I mean a confidential message from me to the owners—say, Tiegert and Dittmar. Of course the B.O.F. men would read it too."

"Also fairly easy," replied Hildebrand. "We announce on a bull horn that a message is coming, then we can deliver by 'chute drop or by mortar. A mortar can be rigged to lob a canister with papers inside."

Randall nodded. "I've decided against an assault. I understand the desire for action, for major surgery, as it were. . . ." He paused.

"I'd hardly call it major," said General Hildebrand. "Surgery, yes, but neat and effective. Fast too."

Randall's sigh was an inward one. It was always neat, swift, effective for the military. He recalled the suggestion for a "surgical bombing" of Cuba, offered by a general during the Cuban missile crisis, according to Robert Kennedy's memoirs. Pluck the appendix, snip the cutaneous horn, slice out the goiter, and the body lives like new! No matter that the spirit curdles, the soul withers, and the patient flakes away to dust. The gun, that great healer, always cures, even as the last marching band of the victory parade echoes amid the drums beating for the next war.

"Unfortunately," said Randall, "Daniel Smith is ready to pounce on thousands of homes. Smith, I'm reliably informed, is ready to sound a desperate call for revolution. This is the time, gentlemen, not for the guns of the 82nd, but for conciliation and negotiation. Therefore, I—"

A gong sounded, a small, curt, urgent sound. An Army major hurried to a cream-colored machine resembling a large typewriter. The carriage gave a convulsive jerk and words spewed over white paper. The major ripped off a section and brought it to Randall:

Translation from Moscow hot line. Message received
7/10/1646 Z

    Philip G. Randall

    President of the United States

    I, together with the entire Russian people, applaud
your admirable restraint and sympathize with your dilemma. Please accept my most cordial good wishes.

                          Valadimir Zhudkov
                          Premier, USSR

"For God's sake!" Randall read the message aloud,
then handed it to Edelstein. "Now what do you suppose
that means?"

"The word 'dilemma' is probably the clue," said Edelstein. "It's Zhudkov's way of needling you for being saddled with a race problem he hopes you can't manage."

"Don't be so sure," said Lee. "I think we ought to take
the Russians at face value on this until they prove us
wrong. They're such hammerheads that you can usually
tell when they're dissembling. We know that millions of
Russians have been watching television for the American
news. Maybe Zhudkov senses that the people appreciate
the bind you're in."

The guessing continued for some time, the amateur
Kremlinologists fitting the pegs of haphazard insight into
the holes of speculation. There were but few good fits,
and Randall returned to the more assessable question of
trading the Tiegert and Dittmar properties for three black
members on boards of directors. Again without mentioning Gamal, Randall sketched Smith's blueprint for thousands of home occupations and the offer of Ginny Jones
and Alfred Nicolet to counter Smith's summons to revolt.

"Ah," said Lee, "then we finally know Nicolet's whereabouts. Good. I've got to talk to him."

"Sorry, Ed," said Randall. "Miss Jones didn't reveal
his location and I didn't ask her." Lee looked stunned.
"We can only assume he's somewhere in Philadelphia,
since that's where Miss Jones called from and chartered
the plane."

Randall explained to HICOM what he proposed to do.

As Voorhees had predicted, Hildebrand, Edelstein, and Lee promptly formed a phalanx of opposition.

"You'll be accused of yielding to blackmail," said Lee. "And with reason, Mr. President. You give in now and what prevents more seizures and more demands a month from now?"

Randall repeated Ginny Jones's pledge. A year of no demands by the B.O.F.

"Hardly a promise to be trusted," said Edelstein. "Anyway if you give in now, it's a sign of weakness. If Smith does rally his young troops for revolution, they'll rise all the faster, knowing that the wall has crumbled in one place."

"Right," said Hildebrand. "These are fanatics with guns, Mr. President. They intend to live by force and they'll be dissuaded only by force, swift and sure. We've got to show we mean business."

Osborne had a question. "What happens if, when you send in the messages to Tiegert and Dittmar, they refuse. No black men on the boards. Then what?"

"I don't foresee that, Hal," said Randall. "I've got majority backing from executives of the union and the corporation. If it does happen, well, I'll just have to try another tack."

"And the B.O.F.?" asked Edelstein. "After all, there's been no official word from the leaders. Suppose they decline to yield the homes on those terms?"

"I'm assured by Miss Jones that they will," said Randall. "Look, gentlemen, let's inspect this thing from the other side. Why in God's name shouldn't the blacks have a couple of Empire board members? They buy hundreds of thousands of Empire cars. And Tiegert's union has as many black drivers as the Army has black soldiers. This is a move that should have been made years ago."

"But at gunpoint?" asked Hildebrand. "We don't even negotiate with the Russians at gunpoint."

Osborne's quick smile indicated his awareness that General Hildebrand had conceded that the Soviets ranked higher on his scale of enemies than American blacks. "I think, Mr. President," said Osborne, "that we want to make dead sure that Alfred Nicolet appears on television with Miss Jones. Ginny Jones, for all her popularity as a

singer, is a woman, and young black rebels won't be likely
to pay heed to a female. But they do know and respect
Nicolet and his intelligence. As between Smith and Miss
Jones, it would be no contest. But as between Smith and
Nicolet, Nicolet might pull enough followers to break up
the revolt."

Randall nodded. "Good point, Hal. I agree. . . . Then
I'll consider it settled. Our next step is to write the notes
to Tiegert and Dittmar. Joe, a little help. Let's cook up
something that Tiegert and Dittmar can't refuse."

The two men seated themselves at one end of the long
table. The Marine sergeant unobtrusively placed some
paper and two pens before them. "Let's see, now," said
Randall. He gazed reflectively at the ceiling.

Ed Lee, who had been busy at the phones, appeared at
Randall's side. "Pardon me, Mr. President, but this may
be significant. The market is down only a few points. The
big investment funds are not selling. My best sources on
the Street tell me that many fund managers are hesitant to
sell, afraid they'll be accused of taking advantage of a national crisis."

Randall looked up with an ironic smile. "Patriotism on
the Street? Tell me another one, Ed."

Lee shook his head. "No, no. Apparently it's the children. I'm informed that several public relations firms that
handle some of the biggest funds are advising against
wholesale dumping. Their clients might be publicly
branded as bloodsuckers who intend to profit on the
plight of little children by buying back in after the market
collapses."

"Hard to believe. Madison Avenue to the rescue."
Randall put down his pen and eased back in his chair.
"You suppose that will hold long, Ed?"

"Frankly no." The Treasury Secretary was puzzled. "It
depends on what happens in this room." He glanced
down at Randall's work sheets as though they were pass-
ports to doom.

An Army major handed a yellow slip of paper to the
President. "A cable relayed from the communications
room," he said.

It was a message from the Prime Minister of Great
Britain, praising Randall for his "prudent course" and

wishing him well from the British people. The yellow paper was passed from hand to hand.

"Moscow and London," mused Voorhees. "Maybe there's a trend on."

There was. In the midst of speculation as to the implications of the British note, a cable arrived from the Chancellor of West Germany. It said the German people were united in their desire to see President Randall persevere on a course that protected innocent children. The Chancellor added his personal sympathy for Randall's predicament. Even though the wording smacked of a letter of condolence, Randall was cheered. The Chancellor was no sunburst of good fellowship.

They were still discussing the Chancellor and his sentiments when the Army major brought another cable. It was a friendly note from the Premier of Japan, expressing hope for the continued well-being of the captive children. Voorhees remarked that in times of stress old enemies seemed to rally round faster than old friends.

"I can't believe it." Randall heaved himself out of his chair and rubbed his hands together in excitement. He began pacing back and forth near the teleprinters, eying the machines as though they had been transformed into couriers of good news exclusively. The atmosphere in the room had a new crackling quality, the kind of electricity Randall had felt on election nights when sure losers began to sense the possibility of an upset in the rolling tide of votes. The proposed messages to the Tiegert and Dittmar homes were put aside for the time being. HICOM members crowded around the machines with Randall, provoking a glance of irritation from the Army major, who saw his private preserves being overrun by eager hunters. Then two more nations reported in to the basement command post. Messages from Egypt and Israel arrived almost simultaneously and were remarkably similar in their expessions of goodwill.

"You'd think the world was casting a vote of confidence in you," said Voorhees to Randall.

Spirits in the soundproofed room brightened by the minute. Secretary Edelstein, a model of funereal gloom for the past thirty hours, actually smiled. Ed Lee and Harold Osborne bantered with each other amid a ringing of phones. The Marine orderly grinned as he passed around a tray of soft drinks. Joe Voorhees suddenly remembered his growth of whiskers and went off in search of an electric razor. General Hildebrand broke out a cigar, his first of the day, and surprisingly offered one to Harold Osborne. The black cabinet officer not only accepted; he lighted the general's cigar for him.

Shortly after 2 P.M. came a print-out on the machine which carried secret documents, via scrambled xerograph equipment, between the White House and the Central Intelligence Agency. Under instructions from Randall, the CIA was making compilations of worldwide reaction every four hours. This latest digest said that much of the world was following the drama of the American homes on radio and television. People everywhere were caught up in the fate of the nineteen children, and even some of the names, such as Holly and Scott Crawford, were becoming known abroad. The anonymous author of the bulletin concluded: "Were it not for the critical nature of the situation, world reaction might be likened to that of a vast soap-opera audience."

A few minutes later an Army major who had been monitoring a muted television set whispered to the President, then turned up the volume. An NBC announcer, sitting before a huge map of the United States on which winking lights marked the locations of the six seized homes, was speaking:

In addition to the open expressions of support from a number of world leaders, we understand that some chiefs of state have sent private messages to President Randall which, it is assumed, will be announced in due time.

The latest public statement is signed by the heads of government of five West African nations, Guinea, Sierra Leone, Liberia, Ivory Coast, and Ghana. I quote:

"We, the undersigned leaders of West Africa, applaud President Randall and the government of the United States for their wise and temperate handling of this new American racial crisis. As heads of state of five black nations, we feel a strong bond of solidarity with the black peoples of the United States. We do not seek

to judge the aspirations of the organization known as
the Blacks of February Twenty-first, considering these
to be matters of internal concern to the United States.

"We do, however, deplore the use of children as instruments in achievement of political goals. We therefore call upon the Blacks of February Twenty-first to
release all children from the captured homes and to
send them forth under flags of truce. We hold that no
confrontation between racial groups should ever imper-
il innocent children."

Phone calls, cables, wire-service bulletins, and teleprinter messages now began to patter upon the White
House situation room like a soft rain on thirsty ground.
More nations expressed support for President Randall.
The only predictable off-key noise came from Peking.
The government of Communist China prodded black
Americans toward revolution without mention of the
youngsters. The Premier of Cuba was ambivalent. He
ended a four-hour television address to his people with
an enigmatic plea for safety for the children and the simultaneous crushing of Yankee racist imperialism. At
home a coalition of U.S. black leaders issued a statement
urging the B.O.F. to free the children. In Harlem more
than five hundred black mothers marched under homemade signs which proclaimed dual aims: release of the
children and satisfaction of B.O.F. aims, whatever they
might be. But some black men picketed this parade,
holding signs. One read: "THE CHILDREN BE DAMNED.
THEY'LL JUST GROW UP TO BE RACISTS LIKE THEIR PAR-
ENTS."

At home and abroad it was as though a worldwide
public opinion poll were in feverish operation with an international computer digesting and disgorging the people's
views minute by minute.

Elation gripped the command-post strategists at the
obvious trend, and amid the new ebullience a change of
attitude slowly manifested itself. The three champions of
the hard line—a prompt assault by paratroops—began
discussing the desirability of holding fast without an attack. Lee, Edelstein, and General Hildebrand debated

whether President Randall's initial course was not, after all, the wisest. Obviously the world was rallying to his support. Even though "holding fast" amounted to a do-nothing policy, there were times, as Edelstein admitted with a nod of his monumental head, when doing nothing accomplished much because of the enemy's deteriorating position.

At 4 P.M. the Vatican released a statement which quoted the Pope directly. His Holiness called on leaders of the B.O.F. to release all children forthwith. Children of whatever color should never become pawns in the great racial issues which so lamentably divided the world. The Pope closed with the anticipated quotation from Jesus: "Suffer the little children to come unto me."

Ed Lee, absorbed for ten minutes with one of his over-seas calls from Frederick Hochwald, the Geneva banker, turned from the telephone with a look of incredulity.

"What's the word from our Swiss skinflint?" asked Randall.

"I really find it hard to believe," said Lee. "Hochwald has canvassed central bankers around Europe. They're all but unanimous in their view that raids on the dollar must not be tolerated during our emergency."

"Good news," said Randall. "But why?"

"The kids."

"Again?"

"Yes. Those wonderful, damn children." Despite his praise, Lee seemed to resent this unbidden intrusion of small fry into the suites of high finance. "Hochwald says the bankers have all consulted their public relations advisers and the p.r. brains say the quickest way for a bank to tarnish its image is to fail to support the dollar when American children are in peril. However reluctant some bankers may be, they're going along."

"For God's sake," said Edelstein. "We're being saved by infants."

"No," said Voorhees, "by the public relations hotshots of the world. Show me a p.r. man and I'll show you a frustrated Dickens who wishes he'd been the guy to create Tiny Tim. But let's not knock it."

The bubble of excitement rose like a twinkling dome. Four men spoke at once. Edelstein thumped Voorhees on the back. Randall suddenly thought of his daughter Kathy, and their encounter project came alive again. Osborne told Lee a black political joke and the Treasury Secretary, usually the dourest member of the cabinet, laughed unnervingly.

The festive mood enveloped everyone but General Hildebrand. He slouched in his chair and stared at the large wall map with its bright cobwebs of ribbons. Randall rested his hand on the general's shoulder beside the four silver stars.

"What's the trouble, Walter?"

"I was just thinking," Hildebrand replied softly. "I suppose I command in dollars maybe a half trillion worth of planes, bombs, tanks, submarines, guns, and carriers. And yet it looks as though they're not worth as much as nineteen children. How much do nineteen kids cost? . . . Odd, isn't it?" He looked up at Randall and for the first time uncertainty showed.

"Odd, maybe," said Randall, "but good."

"Is it?" There was a breath of age on his voice. "I'm really not sure." The general shook his head. "The kids. The goddam kids."

Three hours had passed by the time President Randall returned to the messages to be sent to the Tiegert and Dittmar homes. He beckoned Joe Voorhees back to the chore and they settled down over the scratch paper. Secretary Lee cocked his head as he watched.

"You're still going ahead with that scheme to trade Empire and Truckers board seats for those homes?" he asked.

"Of course," said Randall. "I gave my word to Miss Jones."

"I think that's a mistake, Mr. President," said Lee. "The whole climate's changing. We can win this now without any concessions on the one hand or a troop assault on the other. I feel that in my bones. Now is the time to sit tight."

"You've switched sides, Ed," said Randall. "A few hours ago you were burning to send in the troops."

"I know that," said Lee, "but you've got the world behind you now. African prime ministers, black leaders at home, the Pope. You were right the first time. All you have to do now is wait it out. Those homes will break."

Osborne was listening to the exchange with a frown on his high black forehead. "What about it, Hal?" asked Randall.

"I disagree with Ed," he said. "You can't break your word to Miss Jones. But more, you've got to realize the tremendous appeal of Dan Smith in the ghettos. If he gives the signal to strike at a thousand homes, you could have revolution right now unless Ginny Jones and Al Nicolet can stop it, especially Nicolet. We're not out of the woods yet, Pope or no Pope. Believe me."

Edelstein, who had been busy at a phone during the discussion, interrupted from the other end of the table: "Bad news, Mr. President."

Randall eyed his Defense Secretary with a flicker of annoyance. Edelstein's inflection hinted that he rather welcomed this return of the more familiar brand of news.

"All right. Let's have it."

"That was the police chief in Philadelphia," said Edelstein. He looked grave, a repatriation of solemnity. "About an hour ago some B.O.F. men kidnaped a man out of a third-rate hotel named the Gaylord." He paused as though to bear the burden of solitude. "The chief's undercover black agents assure him that the kidnaped man is Alfred Nicolet."

Randall visibly winced. "Any idea where he is?"

"None."

There was a moment of stricken silence.

"The kidnapers have to be Smith's men," said Osborne. "We'll be hearing from Smith soon."

The Marine sergeant pecked at his typewriter. Hildebrand coughed and mashed out his cigar.

"And now?" asked Randall. He spread his palms in a gesture of need.

There was no answer. Only the machines talked, a gibberish of diligence.

Chapter Sixteen

Chili Ambrose kicked the base of the teakwood console. The color picture on the screen wobbled, collapsing a face like an accordion of flesh, then snapped back to normal focus. The sound guttered on, and a still-life picture of the Pope, a dim majesty of beatitude, appeared behind the broadcaster.

"Let the chil'ren go," said Ambrose, mimicking the announcer's accent. "Yeah, we let 'em go the day they elect a black Pope."

He turned to the young man who sprawled in a yellow slipcovered armchair. "That right, Jackson?"

"Chili, you kiddin' yourself." Jackson Dill measured his man like a physician scrutinizing a patient for telltale symptoms. Dill lay back in the chair, his long legs spread wide apart. Like Ambrose, he wore a pistol jammed behind his leather belt. His goatee only partially masked a look of weary cynicism. "In case you don't know it, we're losin', man."

"The hell we are."

Dill marveled to hear such virile dissent rise from such gullies of fatigue. He knew that Ambrose had not slept in more than forty hours.

"Chili, take them damn shades off. You been wearing them since morning." Dill spoke with impatient resignation. "You can't see what's goin' on around you anymore."

"I see what I need to."

Ambrose stood in the center of the room, an unsteady, quivering warrior, alert to every sound and movement, forcing himself to the limits of tolerance, commanding his muscles to endure for just a few more hours. His eyes ached despite the shelter of the purple sunglasses.

Fairhill's living room looked as though an earnest wind had hurried through it, clearing a passageway for sterner

269

gales. Tables, chairs, lamps, and bric-a-brac had been shoved against the windows. The dark-stained floor was bare, and the large carpet, a bright jonquil color, had been wadded between a chair and the needlepoint footstool to form a crumpled barricade at one window. An oak table, on which magazines once rested, had been dragged to the foyer and thrust against the front door. A highboy shouldered one whole window, blocking entry of the afternoon sun.

Chili had brought his radio transceiver from the woods, installed it behind the grand piano, and connected it with an outside antenna. Only the television console, now flawed by Chili's boot mark, remained in original position. Even the brass fireplace tools had been moved. They lay on the sofa like gleaming arms, the poker, the hearth broom, the shovel, the tongs.

Jackson Dill eyed the tools, his gaze lingering on the poker. He estimated the distance between the poker and Chili. He had been making similar calculations in recent hours. His man could not hold out much longer. Dill straightened into a normal sitting position, then slowly tensed.

"In case the ammo runs out," explained Ambrose. He had misinterpreted Dill's appraisal of the brass tools. "We gonna fight with what we can put our hands on."

"You maybe." Dill kept his voice intentionally low, forcing Ambrose to strain to hear it. Make him stretch to the outer borders with every sense, thought Dill. "I ain't in this thing for dying."

Ambrose lifted his right leg, swung it a few times. He had done this more than once recently, apparently to unkink a muscle spasm, and Dill surmised the kick at the console had been an effort to relax the leg as a gesture of contempt for the Pope. Dill expected to see a facial twitch at any time. Ambrose was becoming a raw nerve.

"Good man, but no brains," said Dill softly.

"What's that?" Ambrose roared at him.

"I said we could use some more bodies and brains around here," replied Dill. Weariness was his excuse for the faint tone. "You playin' it dumb, Chili."

Ambrose grunted an expletive. "You too young to be

givin' advice." He walked to the sofa and sank into the cushions. His fingers toyed with the smooth shank of the brass fireplace tongs beside him. Behind the shield of the dark glasses, his eyelids closed for a moment, an instant of luxury.

"You been buggin' me all day, Jackson," he said. "Time you quit. I brought the girl up to her mama, like you wanted. I gagged the fat broad in the tool shed so she'd quit hollerin'. And I locked Ben in the garage so we don't have to waste a man watching him. I done everything you bellyached about. Now I don't want to hear no more."

"I didn't say to lock Ben in the garage." Dill kept the pressure on unrelentingly. "I said you was stupid to waste a man guarding him. But why not let Ben walk around? He's got no gun, but he's a body. If shootin' starts, throw him a shotgun. But the way it is, you still got to watch the garage to make sure he don't bust out."

"I don't trust the bastard."

"The only smart thing you done all day is them Crawfords. At least you know where they all are."

And so, for his purposes, did Dill. The Crawfords had been confined to the rear of the first floor in a small area embracing the library, Liz's sewing room, and an adjoining toilet. The back door was locked and a chest of drawers wedged into the narrow hallway, barring passage to the rest of the house. Dill wanted to know Tim's exact whereabouts when the time came.

Holly had been reunited with her family in midmorning when Ben Steele was marched up the path from the stream and detained in the garage. Liz overwhelmed the girl with kisses and hugs, a damp demonstration that Holly deemed less a tribute than an ordeal. Adults were either too squishy or too forbidding. It was very difficult to make them behave properly, and Holly much preferred the predictable egotism and posturing of her brother, Scott. After all, what was all the fuss about? Of course she'd been scared when old Perly Wiggins grabbed her on the path, but then he apologized in his silly, squeaky voice, and after that everything was fun. She had a delicious time camping out by the creek. Ben Steele told her stories, she ate beans out of a can. Peter Wilson chased a frog and almost caught it, and at night she had snuggled in Mr. Marsh's sleeping bag and watched the gently swaying treetops and the strange searchlights sweeping across the moonless sky like ghostly brooms brushing the cobwebs of the night. She had slept next to Ben Steele, who had formidable fits of snoring, while Peter Wilson, grand and noble, stood guard over both of them. Ben Steele was more of a chum to her than anybody ever. In the morning she felt cheated when Harve Marsh brought her back to the house instead of putting her in the garage with Steele. Her daddy looked pale and defenseless after Steele's black face, which sprouted such a ferocious growth of whiskers.

She was surprised to find Scott so changed. Despite his ZAP T-shirt, he was buffeted by the same alarms and apprehensions that assailed her parents, especially her mother. Holly was warily mistrustful of Tim and Liz. First, Saturday night, they had told her the black men came to visit Fairhill. Now they changed their story and claimed the black men brought guns because they intended to take the house away from the Crawford family. The only half-good black people, they now said, were Ben Steele and the new one, Jackson Dill. That was hard to believe. Harve Marsh was great fun, and he had a way of sneaking around Liz's orders. Old Perly Wiggins wouldn't hurt a fly. So it was hours before Liz Crawford's contagion of fear infected Holly as well, and truthfully her new qualms were provoked less by what her parents said than by the irksome confinement to the library and the sewing room. Holly hated to be cooped up.

In the living room, this late afternoon of the third day of invasion, Jackson Dill maintained his psychological pressure on Chili Ambrose, steel wool on tender skin.

"You heard the news," said Dill softly. "The whole world's linin' up against us, heads of nations, the black leaders of West Africa yelling to let the kids loose, same with those coalition niggers and the black mothers marching in Harlem. And fifteen hundred troops with rifles around this place, when we ain't got but seven guns."

"All that gonna change, Jackson." Ambrose fingered the fireplace tools as though counting them. "When Danny calls for Gamal, thousands of cats will jump houses all over the country. The man's gonna be as busy as a dog with fleas. They ain't enough soldiers to go around. How they gonna fight for ten thousand homes at once? You so smart, college boy. Answer me that?"

"You think the whole B.O.F. will follow Danny after this kind of news, with everybody cryin' over the kids?" Dill snorted derisively. "I bet not more'n a third of the brothers stick with Danny. And them that does will be butchered like hogs. And that goes for us too."

"You stinkin' up the room with your fright," said Ambrose with disgust. "You scared to fight, why you come in here?"

"I came here to help you."

"Help! The way you talkin', if Danny was here, you'd be court-martialed."

"So when is Danny gonna do something? Tell me that. You ain't heard from Lion all day. . . . Chili, I tell you, you're losin'."

"Goddam you!" Ambrose bounded from the sofa, strode across the bare floor, and stood in trembling rage above Dill. "You keep talkin' like that and I'll send you down that hill and let them honky guns cut you up."

"Easy, man." Dill stared up at the purple glasses and the pitted face. He felt no fear. Dill knew that Ambrose desperately needed the extra body and gun. He forced a smile, framed in condescension. "You Number One. You better cool it." He lowered his voice to a whisper, and he could see Ambrose straining to hear.

"Yeah, I'm Number One and I'm ordering you to haul your fat ass outa the house. Harve needs to cop some Z's. You take his place by the big oak."

"Sure. Sure." Dill arose, stretched, yawned with exaggerated gaping, then patted Ambrose on the arm. "You too, Chili. You better sleep some too. Man don't sleep, he gets jittery."

"Don't handle me! Just go on out."

"Okay, Chili." Dill walked with a leisurely strut to the foyer, pulled back the oak table, and squeezed out the front door.

The late sun held Fairhill in a clutch of heat. Foliage drooped in thirst. It had not rained for a week across the entire country. A heat wave shimmered at the foot of the

meadow near the bramble-laden stone fence. Clouds
flapped like billowing sheets at the furnace of the sun. A
rumble of sounds came from the Great and Drakes
Corner roads where soldiers patrolled behind the thick
woods masking the highways. Harve Marsh rested his
rump against the huge trunk. His hand gripped a shotgun
barrel.

"Chili say for you to cop a nod," said Dill. "I'm supposed to take over here."

The look on Marsh's chubby, round face was a grateful
one. He wiped sweat from his forehead with the back of
his hand. "What's new?"

"The Pope says let the kids go." Dill condensed the last
several hours of developments for Marsh.

"I don't know," said Marsh equivocally. "It don't
sound so good." He handed his shotgun to Dill, and Dill
moved closer as he accepted the weapon.

"Harve," he said. "I'm worried about Chili. No sleep.
He's jumpy. Hard to tell what he might do."

"Yeah." Marsh looked unhappy. "Be too bad if Chili
done something to Holly or Scott by mistake. They nice
little kids."

Dill slid swiftly into the opening. "Could happen when
Chili's tired and mad. He so uptight, he hasn't got much
control."

"Chili ain't Ben," said Marsh morosely. He tapped his
head. "Chili not too quick up here."

"Then why you and Perly let Chili give the orders?
Wouldn't you feel better with Ben in charge?"

"Sure." Marsh brightened momentarily. "But Dan told
Chili to take over." Dan Smith's word was not to be challenged, Marsh implied. Marsh was a good soldier.

"But Danny's down in California, Christ knows where.
You for Gamal, Harve?"

"Yeah, sure." His tone lacked conviction.

"Even when it means shootin' and dyin' with the man
outnumbering us maybe a hundred to one?"

Marsh grinned, half fear, half bravado. "I like my
skin."

"Suppose we could get this house," pressed Dill, "and
walk out with the deed. Ain't that what you come for?"

"Yeah, I guess it is." Marsh was flattered to be consulted. Neither Steele nor Ambrose had so favored him.

"I think Steele could get us this house, if we let him out of the garage. Ben not doin' us no good, Harve, locked up like that."

"But Chili put him there."

"We need brains, Harve. You said yourself Chili don't carry too much in his head. What if you and me was to spring Ben?"

"Mmm. I dunno. Chili's Number One. Besides he mighty quick, that cat."

"But he's got to sleep," insisted Dill. "Sometime tonight he'll sleep. When he does, let's rap some more, Harve. Let's figure something."

"Okay." Marsh was dubious, torn between his loyalty to Chili's command and his hankering to be admitted to councils of strategy.

He moved off toward the house and Dill took over the guard duty. There was no breeze and the air had a dry, hot texture. Dill heard the sound of gears grinding on the Great Road, saw a mockingbird flutter from a hickory limb, and felt sweat trickling down his belly. He had a feeling of being suspended, as though on a huge spoon, over ominously calm tropic waters. Fairhill, so tranquil, was about to be lashed. Dill felt as he did in the last few moments before the onset of a summer storm.

And yet, four hours later, he was still beside the oak tree, though squatting now. Night had dropped slowly like a drifting tissue, and dark shapes began to fill the western sky where the sun, an orange disc, had just disappeared. A welcome freshness, damp and cool, touched his skin.

The front door sprang open. Harve Marsh ran toward the tree in his lumbering gait. "More news," he said, panting. "Chili wants you inside."

With Steele banished, thought Dill, Ambrose had only Perly Wiggins and Jackson Dill to lean upon. Dill thought it no great accolade to be preferred to the puttering Wiggins.

Chili stood in front of the color television console. He teetered slightly, and his arms were folded as though to lend support to his body. He nodded at the screen.

"They busted the Tiegert house." Ambrose was wrapped in sullen outrage, and his tone hinted suspicions of duplicity. "There's Ted Kent and Rube Claypool."

On screen a stout, scowling white man whose chest hair matted the V of his open sport shirt was speaking into a microphone held by an announcer. He was flanked by two black men wearing turtleneck sweaters, and a crowd of onlookers pressed closely about them. An Army truck stood nearby. Two bayonets glinted in the late California sunlight, and in the distance, across a lake, humped the bare granite mountains of the Carson Range.

"That's all there is to it," the white man was saying as though the words had been pried out of him. "The President asked me if I would agree to put a Negro on the Truckers' pension board. I said yes, if that's what he wanted. The B.O.F. said we were free. That's all I have to say."

He began to shove through the crowd, but the announcer followed him, holding the microphone between them like a chalice that must anoint both their lips. "But, Mr. Tiegert, isn't that duress? You were held at gunpoint?"

"That's all I'm saying." Tiegert glowered. "Except that they killed my dog. For the rest, go ask the White House."

He tore away from the mike and plunged into the crowd, clawing his way with both hands. The announcer quickly switched the chalice of universal communion to the face of a tall Negro. He was smooth-shaven and coffee-colored, and he squinted in the lowering sun.

"Mr. Claypool? Have I got it right? The leader of the B.O.F. force here?"

"Yeah," the black man answered easily. "I'm Rube Claypool."

"Will you please explain," asked the announcer hurriedly, "just what has happened, Mr. Claypool? We're confused. Has there been some deal imposed by the White House or what?"

"Nobody ever imposes anything on us," said Claypool. "We got what we came for. We won. So we're releasing the house and the Tiegert family." He exuded the quiet pride of a conquering general.

"How did it come about? Can you tell us what happened?"

"About an hour and a half ago a chopper dropped a can with something inside," explained Claypool. "I understand it was a message from President Randall to Fritz Tiegert."

"You understand? Didn't you read it?"

"Yeah, I read it. The President said the Truckers' board had okayed putting a black man on the pension fund. Tiegert asked me would we release the house and family if he agreed. I said sure, we'd been telling him that for three days. So Tiegert said okay. Then I asked the colonel on the bull horn did the amnesty deal still go? After a while the colonel—I guess he checked with the White House, you better ask him—the colonel of the 82nd said yes, it did. So we left our guns at the house and we all walked out here together, the Tiegerts and the six B.O.F.s."

"And how are the children?" asked the announcer. "I think I counted six children coming down the path. Those were Mr. Tiegert's grandchildren. Is that right?"

Claypool nodded. "We never touched the kids. They're all okay." He grinned. "In fact the two oldest boys were messengers between us and Tiegert, on account the ol' man wouldn't talk to us much until today."

"That would be Richie, twelve, and Tom, eleven?"

"Yeah. Those two great boys. We had twelve people to look after altogether, what with Tiegert and his wife, two daughters, and the black caretaker and his wife. We never laid a hand on any of them."

"What about the Labrador dog whose throat was cut?"

"Oh, now." Claypool smiled with a trace of guile. "You don't think I'd know anything about that, do you?"

"I see. . . . Twelve people freed here at Silver Lake, California, at 6 P.M. Pacific Coast time." The broadcaster beamed as though he himself were the agent of liberation. "And what does this mean for the other homes, Mr. Claypool? Can we expect their release soon?"

Claypool shook his head. "That's up to the national commander. We did our job. That's all I know." He moved out of range of the holy font that laved fifty million ears.

The camera caught a scene of milling confusion, gawking faces, people waving at the lens, helmeted paratroops trying to appear severe, a colonel giving orders, a knot of black spectators cheering, an ambulance with open doors but no customers. In the distance, across the shimmering lake, the rock mountains shouldered the sky.

The scene shifted to a studio where a somber commentator, seated before a large map of the United States, took up the narration.

"And so," he said, "two of the six homes are now released. The B.O.F. turned back the William O. Dittmar summer lodge on Angell Island in the St. Lawrence River twenty minutes ago. Unfortunately we have no camera facilities there as yet." The commentator's long, ravaged face brooded over this circumstance as though crisis, in resolving itself outside camera range, had somehow committed a breach of etiquette. "The Dittmars and the two children and five B.O.F. men came ashore near Alexandria Bay in two outboards. Mr. Dittmar, the president of Empire Motors, acknowledged receipt of a message from President Randall which was dropped by parachute. Mr. Dittmar said he had agreed to expand the Empire board of directors to include two new Negro directors, but like Mr. Tiegert, he refused further comment, referring newsmen to the White House.

"The Dittmar family was in good health, and the two children, Susan, twelve, and Henry, seven, said they caught a twenty-eight-inch northern pike this morning while casting from the far side of the island in company with two B.O.F. fishermen. Mrs. Dittmar praised the courteous treatment of the family by the invaders. Our Alexandria Bay reporting team had the impression that the white captives and their black captors had become rather good friends during the three days and nights on little Angell Island, which is only about eighty yards long and forty wide. . . . Of course we don't know what this portends for the whole operation. Commander Daniel Smith is still at large somewhere near the North Carolina mountains, and no word has been forthcoming from the four other seized properties. . . ."

Chili Ambrose stepped to the console and turned the volume down. "You kin say that again, whitey. Ain't gonna be no word either." He turned in fury, venting his chagrin on Jackson Dill. "Traitors! Turnin' them houses loose when we got a chance for Gamal. All those guys are following Nicolet. They double-crossin' Danny."

"How you know that, Chili?" Dill sowed doubt in the ruts of anger. "How you know Dan didn't order them to make the deals with Tiegert and Dittmar?"

"Because I know!" Ambrose thundered his faith in the black messiah of revolution. "Danny's goin' for Gamal."

"How you know?" Dill asked softly. "You heard from him?"

"What you say?" Chili's voice took on an edge of frenzy. "Speak up, goddam it, Jackson. You dyin' on the vine."

"Have you heard from Smith?" Dill raised the level only a notch.

"No, I ain't heard from him." Ambrose cast a forlorn look at his radio as though the equipment, by being moved from creekside to the living room, had somehow lost its potency. "But I will."

"I think Dan ordered them houses turned loose," said Dill quietly. "Something gone wrong with Gamal probably."

"Never." The disavowal lacked confidence. Another spasm seized Ambrose's right leg and he kicked out angrily.

"Dan probably told us to make a deal too, but you didn't hear it. Maybe your rig ain't working."

"Sure it is." Ambrose went to the long box, flicked a switch, turned several dials, and tuned one a hair to the right, a hair to the left. A moaning static, like the sough of branches in a high wind, issued from the set. "Right on," said Ambrose. He took the microphone from its bracket. "Position One. Position One. Come in, Lion. Come in, Lion." Only the moaning, a vacuum of hope, answered him. He repeated his instructions to the void. Again the static mocked him. He tried in vain for five or six minutes before replacing the mike and switching off the set.

"Nothing wrong with that rig," said Ambrose stubbornly. But his shoulders slumped, and he looked about erratically as though help might arrive from any quarter.

Dill put an arm around Ambrose's shoulder, guided him gently toward the sofa, and eased him down. Ambrose, pliant at last, did not resist. Dill squatted on the floor in front of him.

"Chili, you tired to death, man. Almost forty-five hours and no sleep." He spoke as soothingly as a nurse. "You got to get some shut-eye soon. Chili, take off them shades and look at me."

Ambrose did as bidden. The whites of his eyes were lusterless and flecked with red. His mouth hung open, and the single gold tooth stood out like a gilded sentinel. A jaw muscle quivered.

"Look, Chili," continued Dill. "Maybe they already took Danny and they keeping it quiet. Or maybe he's moving again. Maybe his rig is down. Maybe a hundred things. We got to plan what we're gonna do right here."

"Talk louder, Jackson," pleaded Ambrose. "You speak so low I can't hear."

And then, suddenly, Dill was enfolded in a wave of pity for this man. Chili Ambrose, the abandoned slum boy from Harlem, the nothing who learned radio and weapons in the Army, the decorated soldier in Vietnam who once crawled through paddy slime to choke a Viet Cong sentry to death with his bare hands, the jobless veteran who walked the Harlem sidewalks in a litter of shredded hopes, the empty shell who became a man again only when he joined the Blacks of February Twenty-first and Daniel Smith tapped him as a communications sergeant. Chili Ambrose owed his soul to Smith, and now Dill was wringing it like a chicken's neck. Where had honor gone, and was compassion but a weathered skull?

But Dill pressed on. "If we don't act soon, we could be rousted out of here with nothing to show for it. Chili, let me bring Ben from the garage. We need him bad. He's a thinker."

"No." It was a dull, reflexive answer. "I took over by orders, and I'm in charge until Dan Smith says different."

"Just to advise us. Ben's been sleeping. He's fresh. We need some ideas quick."

"No. Ben stays where he is."

Dill sighed, studying the man. Ambrose's bloodshot

eyes were glazed, and through their ache, Dill surmised, they were fastened on a far Gamal.

"Okay, then." Dill tried a new tack "Let me talk to Crawford. . . . Chili, we got to get something from that man. You ain't talked to him at all. Nobody's talked serious to him since you took over from Ben."

"What good that do?" Suspicion stirred again.

"What harm? Suppose I get the deed from him? Suppose we get the house? How would that hurt anything even if Danny calls for Gamal?"

"It's a nothin', Jackson." Ambrose was awash in disinterest. "So we get a couple of houses an' black flunkies on them boards. Hell, they could give us half Rockefeller Center and ain't nothin' changed. We still in hock to the man, pawnin' our soul for a tie and collar. No. Only one thing gonna raise us up. That's the black nation."

"But in the meantime? Why not? Think what we could do with this house and sixty-five acres. It might even be a division headquarters for you, Chili."

Ambrose gazed down at him, searching for faith in a forest of weariness. "Jackson," he chided, "you know that's foolish talk. Not gonna be no headquarters for Chili. All he good for is fightin' and gettin' killed for Gamal, so's you and Ben and Danny can run it someday."

Dill felt the surge of sympathy again, yet he pressed ahead, loathing himself. Forgive me for what I do, Chili Ambrose, my betrayed brother.

"So, okay if I talk to Crawford?" he asked. "No deal unless it's cleared with you. But let me put the arm on that honky. Squeeze him good."

"Okay. Okay." Ambrose sat in heedless torpor for a moment, then abruptly roused himself, as if bidden by sainted voices. He lurched from the sofa, brushed a hand over his revolver, squared his shoulders, and strode toward the barricaded door.

"You go talk to Crawford if you want," he said. "I'll make the tour, see if Harve and Perly at their places."

Ambrose slid into the night. Dill replaced the oak table against the front door, then walked down the hall toward the library. He pined for the shriveled hopes of Chili Ambrose, and never in his life had he felt such concentrated hostility for a white man as now possessed him.

Tim Crawford, the rich, weak honky, the hypocrite who lusted for Ginny Jones's black flesh in furtive shadows, would squirm until the alcohol was wrung from his soggy hide.

Chapter Seventeen

They had been closeted in the library for an hour. The house was so quiet now, Tim Crawford and Jackson Dill could hear the ticking of the ship's clock on the mantel. Across the hall there was no sound in the sewing room where Liz and the children slept on day beds brought down from upstairs. The time was ten-fifty and Tim wondered why the troops ringing Fairhill had not cut off the electricity. Had that been a detail overlooked, or did they calculate that a loss of power would hamper the Crawfords more than the black invaders?

Dill had played his hand with skill, converting his rage against Crawford into a strategy designed to force submission of the white man, to crowd him into a corner from which escape seemed perilous. Tim had been told only what Dill wanted him to know. Tim was unaware, for instance, of the release of the Tiegert and Dittmar homes. By Chili's orders the Crawford family had been denied use of the kitchen portable TV set and all radios.

Dill painted the threat of Gamal in bold, terrifying strokes: armies of B.O.F. guerrillas ready to seize honky homes by the thousand, the hot-eyed prophet, Daniel Smith, soon to utter a signal that would unleash revolution, bloody battles raging across the land until the nation of Gamal rose from the slaughter. Did Tim Crawford really want that? But if he yielded now, they might yet avert crimson-stained debacle and the stink of white and black bodies in a hundred cities. If Tim gave up Fairhill, Dill argued, it would break the back of the B.O.F. insurgency. Ginny Jones and Alfred Nicolet then could dangle a Fairhill victory before the blacks of America and Dan Smith's wrathful cry for Gamal would fall on less than fertile soil. The fellow invaders, disheartened, would release the five homes. Believe him, urged Dill, for he knew the mind and soul of the black man.

They had been interrupted only once. Chili Ambrose had appeared at the screen of the casement window and said in a spent voice: "You wastin' your time, Jackson. Whyn't you leave the honky sweat to hisself? Danny will give the signal soon." Ambrose stared at them a moment, a dark wraith of the shadows, then faded back into the night.

"I'll tell you the same thing again," Tim was saying now. "The house isn't mine alone to give. To make it legal the deed needs my wife's name on it. She refuses to sign. She's heard all the threats, and they don't impress her."

"But she doesn't know about Gamal," retorted Dill. "She doesn't understand about the killing that would certainly come." Dill had discarded the street idiom he used with Ambrose.

"So go over and tell her," said Tim. "See for yourself. She won't believe you. She doesn't trust the word of any black person on the place, not even Ben Steele. She'll say it's a story you cooked up to terrify her further. Go ahead, try." Tim motioned toward the door. "Be my guest."

"But you believe I'm telling the truth about Smith's plan." Dill watched him closely.

"Yes." Tim rubbed his cheek as he reflected. "Yes, I heard you and Ambrose talking last night outside the window. I misunderstood. I guessed that Gamal was a code word for an uprising. But the idea of a black nation fits Smith's character."

"You think I'm exaggerating the consequences?" asked Dill. "Blood in the streets, burning suburbs?"

"No. I suspect you're right."

"And you won't do a thing to head it off? What the hell would Fairhill be after months of race war? You think there's some kind of rabbit foot that covers this place?"

Tim shook his head. "No, I guess Fairhill's no exception."

"But you don't care?" Dill's hatred had long since

fragmented into a kind of gravelly rancor. He could not hate unless he saw the face of arrogance, and this white man was either too soft or too reasonable for arrogance. There was a blandness, yet a puzzling bent for accommodation, that exasperated Dill. Dialogue was not the meat on which enemies fed.

"Yes, I care," replied Tim. "You see, I've been doing a lot of thinking over the past few days. I've thought about everything Ben Steele said. . . . I like that guy. Do you believe that?"

Dill flicked his shoulders noncommittally. "I wouldn't know. What's more, I don't give a damn who you like or don't like."

"Ben reasons," continued Tim. "He makes a good case. He's partly right, you know. I didn't do a thing to earn this property. My father gave it to me. Ben says Tim, Sr., used profits made off poor blacks to buy this place. That's true. I just never thought much about it before. . . . On the other hand if the tables were turned, I'm sure Ben Steele's father would have done the same thing. Ben says no. An honest difference of opinion."

This dry, legalistic approach grated on Dill. Words, words, words. They marched from Tim Crawford like disciplined soldiers on a drill yard.

"For Christ's sake then. Give us the crib and forget it."

"I can't. My wife's signature, remember?" asked Tim dispassionately. He was back in the sparring matches he enjoyed. "No, I've thought of something else, a kind of compromise, we might call it. Seriously I've thought a lot about it, and I'd like to talk it over with Steele."

"That's out. Ben's locked in the garage. Chili won't let you near him."

"That's Ambrose's mistake. I know Ben would be interested. So would you."

"Crawford," said Dill, "I've told you once, but I'll say it one more time. Ambrose wants Gamal. He doesn't give a damn for this pad. He's so sold on Gamal, he'd give his life for it. In fact I guess he expects to die. He's seen Dan Smith's vision." He paused, a reflective interlude. "Sometimes I wished I had. . . . Chili's a real black man."

The talk lapsed while they brooded in their separate worlds, then Dill asked: "Is this a serious idea of yours?"

"Very."

"So tell me."

"No. Ben has to hear this."

"You don't trust me?"

"Not particularly," said Tim. "But that's not the point. This involves Ben, and we'd, well, have to work it out together."

The bronze desk lamp, its neck crooked low, threw an arc of light that left their faces in shadow. Tim sensed a desire by this young man to triumph where Steele had failed in the contest of wills at Fairhill. Black guerrillas were as vulnerable to ambition as other men. And curiously Tim knew that in any power rivalry among the invaders, Tim Crawford would never give comfort to a man who challenged Ben Steele.

"Let's have it, Crawford," said Dill. "Tell me. We haven't got all night."

"I think we have. At least until Ambrose falls asleep."

They sat without speaking. Tim lit a cigarette, smoked, and waited. He took wry pleasure in the thought that even a prisoner had his weapons, however fragile.

"Tell you what," said Dill at last. "You tell me your idea and I'll sneak over to the garage and tell Ben. If he buys it, you may have a deal." He paused. "Then the only thing left is to take Chili in his sleep."

"No. I've got to discuss it face to face with Ben."

"That's out."

"Why? If you can get to the garage without being seen, why can't you take me?"

"Is this compromise something we could take out of here as a B.O.F. victory?" Dill countered, detesting his own question. All his life, it seemed some white man held the key to tainted triumph or outright defeat.

"In a way, yes. Yes, I suppose it is." Tim sensed that Dill was weakening. "Who has my keys to the garage?"

"Chili." Dill hesitated, then added: "But I found your old lady's set." From his pocket he produced a ring with a half-dozen keys on it. "What's this compromise about?"

"You take me to Ben."

"You won't tell me?"

"After Ben hears it. Isn't he your commander here?"

"Sure. We're both with Al Nicolet, but Ben's my boss."

"All right, then," said Tim. "I want to talk to the boss."

"It's dangerous, man. If Chili saw you . . ." Dill pondered a moment. "Tell you what, Crawford. Let me go see where Chili is."

In Dill's absence Tim reflected on his own motives. Why was he offering compromise? If young Dill thought that the threat of bloody struggle implicit in Dan Smith's Gamal had frightened Tim into yielding, he was wrong. No. Tim could not conceive that any act of his would influence such vast tides as those on which Daniel Smith tossed. Rather, this was a private matter to be weighed on those small scales which gather dust in the attic of the self. On the one side, a few grains of Liz, several more of Holly and Scott, and many more of his own abiding respect for money and its comrades—ease, comfort, influence. On the other scale, three large grains of guilt, one for Tim, Sr., one for his own white indifference, and one for his lack of courage when Ginny Jones asked his help for this same abrasive Jackson Dill. Did Ginny herself balance Liz in memory's clutter of love, affection, yearning? No, Liz was too much a part of him, and the old Ginny was no more. Actually the largest weight that tipped the scales was as heavy as it was formless, a nagging torpor, a lassitude of the spirit. Jackson Dill could not know that, and Ben Steele could only guess.

They could not understand the empty shelves of Tim Crawford's life, the uncommitted yet obligatory and forever boring routine of the law firm, the Harvard Board of Overseers, the Brook Club, the commission in Washington, and those weekends at Fairhill as parched and as meaningless as sawdust. They could not know that Tim pined for the same fire and arousal that Steele enjoyed merely by a fluke of fate that stamped Ben as black, angry, and rebellious—and obsessed by all three. As a man of his time and class was Tim stricken by an apathy of affluence? Perhaps. All that he really knew was that his proposal involved working with Steele, and that the idea stirred him. In Steele, Tim saw strength, passion, grit, purpose. Somewhere there must be meaning for Tim Crawford too, a meaning derived of struggle. Money might not buy purpose, but perhaps it could buy access to the mansions of action.

Tim crushed out his cigarette and looked down at his uncallused hands, the manicured nails, the fingers which gripped nothing more challenging than a tennis racket. He smiled, mocking his own inchoate longings.

The back door creaked, then shut quietly again. Dill was back in the room. The arc of the desk lamp illumined only the lower half of his body.

"Ben says okay," said Dill. "Chili's in the front room watching television again. Let's go."

The night was somber. An overcast hooded most of the sky, leaving only a beleaguered patch of stars to the north. Two Army searchlights combed the low clouds as if seeking hidden fugitives. Tim followed Dill along the flagstones leading to the garage. The Jaguar still stood on the asphalt, and beyond it Tim could see a bulky figure on the driveway. He assumed it was Harve Marsh. Had Marsh agreed to permit this breach of Ambrose's orders? They walked swiftly past the tool shed where Dora had been held for so many hours, and Tim could only guess at the dimensions of her fear. Dill fitted a key to the lock of the garage door.

"You wait outside, Jackson." It was an order in Steele's low, casual voice.

Two stalls of the three-car garage were occupied by Liz's Lincoln and the Volkswagen bus which ferried Scott and Holly on their interminable missions. Although it was difficult to see in the gloom, Tim noted that Steele's sleeping bag was spread in the space where the Jaguar normally parked. There was no place to sit down. Steele slouched against the workbench, and Tim stood a few feet from him. He was unable to see Steele's expression.

"I hear you got a proposition," said Steele.

"Yes, I do."

"All right. Let's have it."

"Well . . ." Tim shoved his hands in his trouser pockets. "You see, your pitch got to me, Ben."

"So I'm Ben now," said Steele with quiet amusement.

"Yeah, I guess you are. . . . Anyway I think I know what drives you. If I were black, maybe I'd be a militant like you. I agree that whites have made life miserable for blacks for a long, long time. Still I think integration is the only way out. . . ."

"Integration!" Steele scoffed. "Man, you're ten years late."

"I don't think so. But even if you're right, at least we've got to work side by side with mutual, well, respect. It's the only way. As for Fairhill you may have as much logic on your side as I have. But you can't have the place. That won't go. . . . So I've been thinking. As you know, I've got some money. I'm willing to set up a foundation for black education or any similar purpose we can agree on. Two cochairmen, Ben Steele and Tim Crawford. We could work out the details later." He hesitated. "Well, I guess that's it."

"How much money?"

"Two hundred fifty thousand dollars."

Steele laughed derisively. "Come on, Crawford. Two hundred fifty grand? Why, you've got a cool million in government bonds, man, lots of other investments, and a helluva big income. Eighty thousand a year, isn't it?"

Tim felt a gush of anger. "The bonds belong to my wife as well. I don't consider I have a right to more than half of them."

"So why didn't you put up your half?" Steele folded his arms.

"Are you interested in this idea or not?" asked Tim with heat.

Steele considered. "Yeah, maybe. It depends."

"On what?"

"The bread, first of all. You could cough up five hundred and never miss it." Steele took a pack from his pocket and lit a cigarette. It was Tim's brand. The flare of the match briefly illumined Steele's bearded face. "You somethin' like yo' daddy, Crawford." The drawl was exaggerated. "Never offer more'n half what you should."

Tim winced. Ben was shrewd. Actually Tim had considered half a million, but he had sliced it down the middle because—well, because, dammit, that was the way business was done.

"You know two-fifty ain't no kind of money for a foundation." Steele, Tim knew, was using the idiom consciously now. "Hell, man, you can't hardly set up an office on the interest from two-fifty."

"All right," said Tim. "Five hundred thousand."

"I'll take it," snapped Steele.

"Then it's a deal?"

"Not so fast, man. What was that about cochairmen?"

"Yes, cochairmen," said Tim. "You and I. You're a reasonable guy. So am I, I think. We wouldn't have too many problems."

"No go," said Steele. "I swore when I joined this outfit that never again would I work for a white man. And none of that co-stuff either. If a honky's involved, either I'm boss or I'm nothing."

"Meaning just what, in this case?"

"That I'll be president or chairman or whatever they call it." Steele pulled on the cigarette, and it glowed like a coal for an instant. "I'll put you on my board of directors."

"Damn decent of you." Tim had almost said "white of you." In his flash of resentment Tim was on the verge of telling Steele to go to hell. Instead he searched again in the tangle of his own motives. His offer was sincere, but he had envisioned Ben and himself bargaining, discussing, planning as equals. Now Steele demanded his own version of equality—Ben's authority and Tim's money. Was Tim, indeed, ten years late? He sought Steele's eyes in the dark.

"Anything else?" he asked.

"No. But you got a right to know. If this thing goes through, we'll have an all-black board except for you."

When Tim did not answer, Steele continued in a more conciliatory tone. "This foundation would be for some kind of education, right? So you might as well educate yourself. See what it's like to be one white face among ten or fifteen black ones. See what we been goin' through a long, long time now. Do you some good." The cigarette glowed again, and Steele resumed in a subdued tone. "You see, I'm tired to my bones of these phony black-help outfits, dreamed up by whites, financed by whites, and run by whites. Honky knows what's best for us, always. That's over, man. From now on we're going to run it all or nothing."

"You sure you have enough experience, Ben? Finances, investments, all that. It's not simple, believe me."

"We'd rather make black mistakes than put up with

white mistakes," said Steele quickly. "All the years whites claim they've been helping us, things have gotten worse."

"But you don't mind white money," Tim retorted.

"Who said it was white money?" Steele's tone was harsh. "You ain't gonna trap me in that honky rhetoric. The way your daddy made his pile, it's more black than white, baby, and don't you forget it."

"This money came from Liz's father," said Tim.

"Don't bug me with what pocket you're takin' it out of." Steele lapsed into silence, waiting.

A minute went by. Jackson Dill opened the door. "Better move it," he said. "Chili's liable to be around soon." He closed the door again.

"How about it?" asked Steele. "We got a deal?"

"I don't like it." But Tim knew that if the situation were reversed, he would have made similar demands. He wondered if his rationality was a curse or a blessing. "All right," he said.

Tim stepped forward and held out his hand.

Steele shook his hand. "We don't need to shake. A white man's handshake don't mean nuthin'. . . . Mine don't either. . . . But I know you'll go through with it. You got no choice."

Steele moved toward the door. The time was up. "One thing bugs me. How come your wife went for this?"

"I haven't told her."

Steele whistled softly. "Mmm. You're a strange guy, Crawford."

Dill was waiting at the door. Steele put his hands on both men, drawing them together. "Now listen," he said. "Chili's bound to fall over from no sleep soon. When he does, you come get me, Jackson. And you be ready, Crawford. Meantime, Jackson, work some more on Harve. We can go without Perly, but we got to have Marsh. . . . Crawford, you tell Jackson about our deal."

Tim stepped into the night as Dill relocked the door behind them. They retraced their steps along the flag-stones. The night was black now. Even the patch of stars to the north had disappeared behind the overcast. Marsh was nowhere in sight. Dill entered the library with Tim. The desk lamp threw its low arc of light.

"What's the deal?" Dill asked.

Tim explained.

"Five hundred grand," echoed Dill incredulously. "Man, you're either crazy or scared to death." He eyed Tim with amazement, then shrugged. "I guess you're lucky Ben didn't make you cough up a couple of million."

"Thanks." The sarcasm vented, Tim stood in silence, speculating anew as to how he had arrived at his decision. He was not sure he would ever know precisely. For a brief span, curiously, he thought of Holly and of Ben Steele's tenderness with her. Tim had no regrets.

"He make you sign anything?"

"No. He takes my word."

"Goddam." Dill was further astounded, and Tim felt a quick glow of vindicated pride—until he thought of the spurned handshake.

"Will you tell Ambrose?" asked Tim.

"No. Waste of time. Chili's fired up for Gamal. . . . When the time comes, we all got to go after Chili. You afraid?"

"Some," admitted Tim. "But I'll do what I have to."

A loud guttural noise like a giant clearing his throat broke the night. They knew the sound. A bull horn, unheard for hours, was being tested on the Great Road. They waited.

"Members of the B.O.F." The voice beat through the room. "This is Governor Danzig. It is now 11:46 P.M. As you know, it has been more than two hours since the homes at Silver Lake, California, and at Alexandria Bay on the St. Lawrence River were released by your organization. All B.O.F. members freely left the scene. No one was followed or questioned by authorities."

Tim glared at Dill. The young black man's thin, superior smile held no apology.

"I'm once again renewing the offer of amnesty," continued Danzig. "You no longer have any chance of winning. The game is up. Come out unarmed and bring the Crawford family and Mrs. Dora Wilcox with you. You will be allowed to depart unmolested. Answer requested."

The sound echoed and faded. Then Chili Ambrose's amplified voice was heard from the front of the house.

"I tol' you once. This is the last time . . . no. Zero . . . you got it now, Guv? You un'stand me?"

The refusal rumbled down the slope and died amid the searchlights which spiked the sky.

"Tim! What was that noise?" It was Liz's sleepy voice from the sewing room across the hall.

"Nothing, Puss," Tim replied. "I'll be over in a minute."

Tim swung toward Dill. "You lied to me."

"Wrong. I told the truth. I just didn't tell it all."

"Why were the two homes released?"

Dill summarized what he had heard and seen on television, the intervention of President Randall, the agreement to put two black men on boards.

"And here it's the reverse," said Tim. "A white man goes on a black committee."

"Yeah." Dill grinned. "Now ain't that beautiful?"

"You told me you could be trusted," said Tim accusingly. "You know, Dill, I don't like you."

"Who cares? Christ, you still act like this was some kind of garden party. Crawford, you make my ass tired."

"From now on I'll talk only to Ben."

"Naw," said Dill. "You gonna do what I tell you on account of Chili. It's your neck same as ours. And you better screw up your courage. Them nice, smooth hands of yours liable to get smeared."

They stared at each other, and Tim, for all his anger, knew that Dill was right. The young black man turned and walked from the house.

"Tim!" Liz called again from across the hall. "Please come in here."

He entered the sewing room, still cluttered with Liz's belongings, skis, paintbrushes, portable typewriter, magazines, tennis rackets. Holly and Scott apparently had slept through the bleating of the bull horn, for they cuddled peacefully on their beds. He went to Liz's side. She reached up and pulled him down for a kiss.

"What's happening, Tim?"

"Come over to the study. There's a lot to tell you."

She threw a bathrobe over her nightgown, followed him across the hall, and seated herself in one of the armchairs. Although light from the desk lamp touched her but faintly, it revealed that three days and almost four nights as a captive had left bruising traces. Her tan had faded, her hair had a limp, disorderly appearance, and she blinked helplessly as though her own husband were an inquisitor bent on further persecution. If the invasion had alternately alarmed and exhilarated Tim, it had wounded Elizabeth Crawford, the beauty, depleting the wells of vitality that made her the envy of her friends.

He told her all that had happened in the hours since nightfall. She listened without interrupting and with only an occasional glance at him. Instead she fretted over the finger from which the roof sliver had been extracted, examining it with exaggerated concern.

"And so you gave away half our bonds to those people," she said when he finished, "without so much as one word to me."

"We'd always considered that money to be half yours and half mine," he said.

"Not one word." A footnote to his faithlessness. "And suppose I'd given half to a decent cause? I'd never have heard the last of it."

He straddled an arm of the big leather chair and lit a cigarette. "I might have questioned your judgment, but not your right to do what you wanted with the money."

"Those bonds were supposed to go to Holly and Scott someday." She said it spiritlessly as though she no longer had control over the baggage of her life.

"They'll inherit ten times more than most kids, maybe even a world they can live in . . ." He dropped the thought, unfinished.

"And you think some little foundation thing is going to change the world? Is that it?"

"It may help," he said a bit doggedly. He could see where the argument was heading, and he knew intuitively that he could be made to appear a fool.

She looked at him blankly as though he were an outsider whose impact on her life was, at best, minimal. She smiled wryly, shook her head, then inspected her torn finger again.

"It is really utterly absurd," she said at last. "Do you remember what we were arguing about when Steele showed up in that doorway Saturday night?"

He nodded. Steele's startling entry had nailed it forever in memory. Tim had accused her obliquely of being awash in liberal causes without an anchor of faith, while she countered that he was ignorant, indifferent, a shell of propriety.

"And now the roles are reversed, aren't they?" she asked with a drop of bitterness. "Now, I'm the mean, grasping, stingy white woman, while you scatter our largesse on noble causes."

"Well, no. It's not the same thing."

"You're damned right it's not," she flared with some of her old spirit. "And you know why, don't you, Tim? Because you caved in under pressure to a gang of thugs who clomped in here with guns, practically jammed them in our ribs, and demanded this house." The words rushed out. "I wouldn't sign, so to appease them, you handed over five hundred thousand. Five hundred thousand dollars! My God!"

He drew out his cigarette, flicked away ash, delaying his answer, hoping she would calm herself. But she glared at him, fully aroused now.

"Liz, I don't think you understand what we face," he said slowly, choosing his words. "Don't you realize what could happen if this house and the others aren't freed soon, if Dan Smith gives the signal for his black nation, this Gamal?"

He sketched the possibilities, the seizure of thousands of homes, the rattle of gunfire in the suburbs, the entire Army called up, burning cities. She heard him out.

"But, Tim, you would have offered that money to Steele anyway." She was sweetly insistent. "You'd have done it if you never heard the word Gamal."

"No. I'm not sure what I'd have done." But he realized that the idea had begun shaping as far back as Sunday.

"Of course you would," she said firmly. "And naturally you've given your word, so the papers are as good as signed. Isn't that right?"

"Yes."

"And you know that in the eyes of all our friends," she pressed, "you're going to look like a coward or an idiot?"

"I don't care about that." He had braved his way through that scene hours ago.

"I suppose not. Especially since they'll never know the real reason."

"Real reason?"

"Yes, dear." The tone was sarcastic. "That nice, little secret reason that only a few of our friends know—our fine new friends, Mr. Steele and Mr. Dill." She pronounced the names as though they were trademarks for plunder.

"Meaning what?"

"Her."

"Her?" Now he knew.

"Yes, Miss Virginia Jones," she said, dripping honey. "The lovely little package of soul, so exploited, so brave, so tormented. We think of her and we remember the soft nights in Acapulco, and we're so grateful to Mr. Steele for not telling our wife all about the beautiful romance that fills our dreams and—"

"Liz. Stop it!"

"And we can't leave our wife and our little children because we're not made that way. We're a poor WASP, you see, bound by all the old Puritan strictures. . . . And besides, maybe our little black songbird doesn't like our blanched skin anymore. So we set up a handsome foundation to the memory of what might have been."

As the mimicry went on, Tim stared at her through a haze of cigarette smoke, listening to the drip of acid in each sugary phrase. A swift emptiness engulfed him, a void in which Liz appeared as but a shadowy figure. Were there no bonds of speech for humans, no fragile bridges which could be thrown across the chasms of their loneliness? Was full understanding ever possible? The questions posed their own malaise. Here was his woman with whom he had shared a marriage for thirteen years. They had loved, conceived, molded a private world, yet they could not talk. No matter how they began, they ended by firing polished words like missiles. . . . How much had Ginny Jones weighed on the scales? Two grains, no more. For the Ginny of long ago was gone, and the new Virginia Jones was a fractious stranger.

"Tim?" Her tone had softened.

"Yes, Puss."

"Tim," she said with quiet resignation, "I don't think I'll ever understand you."

He mashed out his cigarette, walked across the room, leaned over, and gathered her in his arms.

"I love you," he said. And that simple statement, at least, was totally honest.

She kissed his cheek, then hugged him once, an urgent, desperate folding. "I know," she said.

The phrase made him think of Holly, and he wished that, like Ben Steele, he could purge himself with tears. Nothing else made much sense right now.

"Jackson!" A cry of triumph rolled down the hallway.

They heard feet pounding on the floor, the sound of the chest of drawers being shoved aside.

"I'm coming, Chili," called Dill from the rear of the house. He entered. The back door banged behind him.

"Jackson!" said Ambrose. "I raised Lion. He say stand by just a few more hours. He's gonna sound the word soon after dawn. He hopes by seven."

They could see Ambrose through the open library door. His stance was one of pride. His face was wreathed in exultation. The medallion of Frantz Fanon flashed in the tenuous light.

"You sure?" asked Dill.

"Sure as glory." Ambrose grinned like a boy. Weariness had fled as leaves before a storm. He raised a clenched fist.

"Gamal!"

Chapter Eighteen

Through the depths of sleep Tim felt the weight on his shoulder as though he were being dared to struggle upward. He surfaced slowly. The weight became a rolling motion, and then, as he opened his eyes, he could see and feel a hand prodding him. A man, etched in darkness, leaned over him.

"It's Ben Steele." The whisper was close to Tim's ear. "Get up."

Tim's eyes worked into focus. He saw the familiar outline of a dark face with mustache and goatee. Strange that
Steele, supposedly imprisoned in the garage, should be
here. But Tim felt warm breath on his cheek, and he
raised himself on an elbow.

"You awake?" whispered Steele.

"Yeah. I guess so."

"Come out the back door. It's unlocked."

Steele slipped out of the sewing room, the scuff of his
moccasins barely audible. Tim, who had slept in his
clothes, sat upright and looked about him. The family had
used four day beds, lining up like patients in a hospital
ward. Holly, next to Tim, was breathing evenly. Scott
stirred, thrashed about for a moment, sighed petulantly,
and curled up again in the snug position of a foetus. Liz,
a long, inert form, slept soundly on her side. Tim flexed
his arms, slid his feet into the pair of loafers, then tiptoed
through the open door and down the hallway.

In the drab predawn the sky was leaden. The garage,
tool shed, and trees were formless shapes, and the few remaining stars overhead had lost their glitter. To the south
the rays of two searchlights traced a pale cross. The air
was indolent, cool yet promising a lazy heat, and moisture
beaded the grass. Ben Steele waited with Jackson Dill beside the dogwood tree. Steele carried a rifle.

"Chili fell asleep under the big oak," he explained.
"Jackson let me out of the garage. Harve's with us. And
Perly, he wants to be on the winning side. . . . They're
waiting in front of the house."

Steele looked Tim over as though appraising him anew,
smiled, and offered his hand. The two men shook.

"I thought we ought to seal the bargain after all," said
Steele. His voice was brusque but friendly. "You know
what your first job is going to be, Tim?"

It was the first time Steele had called him by his given
name.

"No."

"Raise more money. I was figuring. The interest on five
hundred grand isn't a hell of a lot either."

"Come on, Ben," said Dill. "It'll be light soon. The
sun's liable to wake Chili." He jerked his thumb toward

Tim. "And you know I'm not for including this one. We don't need him now."

"Yeah, but maybe he needs some action." Steele exaggerated the drawl. He glanced at Tim with an amused expression. "Long way from Princeton to Newark. Right? How many years since you stuck your fist in some cat's face?"

"Not since high school, I guess." Then he added: "But I'm ready for whatever I'm supposed to do." The amendment sounded like boyish bravado, and Tim promptly regretted it. Steele merely grinned, but Dill moved into the opening.

"Whatever I'm supposed to do," he mocked with arch inflection. "Christ, Ben, send the guy back to bed with his old lady."

"Lay off, Jackson." Steele was curt. He turned to Tim. "Now here's the idea."

Steele outlined his plan and the reasoning behind it. He assumed, he said, as he had all along, that Governor Danzig would still grant amnesty this morning if they asked it. Danzig needed a chunk of the black vote in his reelection bid. If he failed to extend the amnesty deadline, he risked a racial gunfight—for he surely must realize that the B.O.F. men would not meekly surrender to face prison terms. And if blacks were cut down in a battle with paratroop sharpshooters, Danzig could kiss reelection good-by.

"So the first thing we got to do is take Chili while he's asleep," said Steele. "Then you get on the bull horn and parley with Danzig. If amnesty still goes, we all walk out of here together—lugging Chili if we have to."

"Why don't we just wake Liz and the kids," asked Tim, "release Dora Wilcox from the tool shed, and go down the hill while Chili's still asleep?"

"Never." Steele shook his head. "If we go down that hill right now, Danzig or the colonel are liable to open up on their bull horn when they see us. That would wake Chili. Sure as hell, that mother would start raising hell, probably shoot somebody. . . . Or maybe some nervous jump-boy might start firing when he saw blacks coming. Even if we made it down quietly to the road, Danzig could arrest us, figuring this morning he owes us nothing."

"Not much chance of that," said Tim. "What you're really worrying about is Chili." It came out as an accusation.

"You goddam right," flared Steele. "No honky soldier gonna get a shot at Chili. We takin' the black brother ourselves without hurting him—if we can."

The plan, said Steele, was this: Two loaded weapons, a shotgun and a revolver, lay on the ground at Ambrose's fingertips. Five men, Steele, Dill, Marsh, Wiggins, and Crawford, were to form a circle about thirty yards from the tree, then walk slowly toward the oak. Only Steele would be armed. If Chili awakened and grabbed a weapon, Steele could wing him without serious injury. Otherwise they would move on Ambrose, pinion him, and tie his hands behind him. Jackson Dill had the rope. With Ambrose out of action, Crawford was to ask the governor on the bull horn if the amnesty offer still held. If the answer was the expected "yes," they would leave. If it was "no," well, Steele would cross that bridge when he came to it. The first urgent step was to seize Ambrose.

"Okay," concluded Steele. "Follow me and no noise."

They skirted the house in single file. Wiggins waited on the path to the front door. Harve Marsh stood nearby. The gray of morning was flooding swiftly, washing the trees and shrubs and coursing over the lawn which sloped to the meadow and the stone fence beyond. At the base of the old oak Chili Ambrose was stretched out in slumber. The pistol lay within a few inches of his hip and the shotgun not more than a foot away.

At a signal from Steele, Wiggins went to the far side of the oak, Marsh took a position north of the tree, Dill moved to the south, and Tim stood to the east. Steele, a few yards from Tim, pointed his rifle at Ambrose.

The five men, treading softly, began to close on their target. Dawn blanched into clear daylight now, making plainly visible smudges of dirt on Ambrose's rumpled black sweater and olive-green dungarees. To his discomfort Tim saw that Ambrose lay directly in his path. If all closed at the same pace, Tim would reach Chili first. The thought was unnerving, and he welcomed the feel of solid ground beneath his feet. Also he felt faintly ridiculous, stalking a sleeping man like an Indian brave in a grade-"B" movie. He wondered what he would do if Ambrose opened an eye, saw Tim approaching, and swooped up the pistol. Would Tim have the courage to throw himself on Ambrose, or would he leap to one side and flatten himself on the ground? Or would some mysterious adrenalin take over, mobilizing his body to strike and relieving his brain of choice? If only Chili's weapons would vaporize before Tim took another step.

A shower of light fell abruptly upon the crest, and Tim knew that the sun had surged from the eastern horizon behind him. He was only about five yards from Ambrose now, and he swiftly resolved to dive on his man. He braced himself mentally.

"Daddy!" It was a gay, larking cry.

Tim turned. Holly was racing toward him from the corner of the house, her gray seersucker overalls flapping absurdly at her ankles and her small arms pumping like pistons. Holly was grinning, abrim with morning juices, and it was obvious she hadn't a clue to the situation.

"Get back!" Tim, Steele, and Marsh all shouted warnings at once. Holly halted, perplexed, then saw the rifle in the hands of Ben Steele, her friend. The grin faded and fright took over. Tim cursed himself for failing to relock the door.

From a corner of his eye he saw Ambrose lurch to his feet and scoop up the shotgun. Chili had come awake in an instant. Now he sized up the scene in one swift, feral glance. With two bounding steps he reached Holly, who stood frozen between the oak and Steele's raised rifle. Ambrose thew his left arm about Holly's shoulder and yanked the girl against his legs. The shotgun was clamped to his right side, aimed directly at Steele.

"Unh!" Ambrose grunted with surprise and outrage. Flung on the warming air, the exclamation was a fierce renunciation of trust.

Pushing the child before him while keeping her tightly clasped to his legs, Ambrose moved awkwardly toward the front door in the gap between Steele and Tim. He swept the shotgun's muzzle from one man to the other. When he came abreast of Steele, he turned with catlike speed and began backing toward the house. Now the sweep of his gun covered all five men. Holly had a look of terror, and she gasped for air as the arm encircled her neck. Chili crouched low behind her, yielding but a few inches of target for Steele's rifle.

"Drop that gun, Ben," he commanded. Then in a growl: "Ever'body put them hands up. You too, Crawford."

"Okay, Chili," called Wiggins. He raised his arms. Wiggins would waste no time debating a conflict of loyalties.

"Come on! Fast!" bellowed Ambrose. Tim slowly lifted his hands, noting that Marsh and Dill did likewise. Only Steele made no move. His rifle still pointed at Ambrose.

"Ben, I'm warnin' you," said Chili. "You don't loose that gun in five counts and you're dead. I'm counting. . . ."

"Look!" The shout of bewilderment came from Marsh. "My God!"

He pointed down the long slope of lawn toward the fence. Tim looked. The sight was so incredible, so alien to Fairhill's grim morning business, that for an instant his fear was gone.

Marching toward them from the fence, in the full glow of the swelling sun, came a line of young girls, perhaps a dozen. They advanced through the meadow, the timothy grass swishing against their skirts, and they all held hands as though in phalanx of virginal resolve.

Ambrose's initial count of one never left his lips. He and Holly were on the highest ground of the crest, and Ambrose could see the meadow without leaving the crouch in which he held Holly in locked embrace. Yet, as though drawn upward against his will, Ambrose raised himself to full height. He stood transfixed, a suspended moment in which he seemed to be waging some inner contest to understand. In that short span, perhaps no longer than a second, while Ambrose's eyes were fastened on the meadow, Steele dropped his rifle, took one long step, then hurled himself through the air in a flying tackle.

Steele crashed against Chili's chest and wrapped his arms around him. The shotgun was torn from Ambrose's arm. Both men fell to the ground, and Holly was sent spinning off to one side with a yelp of ignominy and pain. The two men rolled on the lawn. Jackson Dill and Harve Marsh ran over to them. Tim followed. Marsh and Tim pinned Ambrose's thrashing legs while Dill helped subdue their quarry from the waist up. Ambrose, all springy muscle despite his fatigue, was a difficult man to overpower. He cuffed Dill with a fist and kicked savagely at Marsh. But they finally managed to roll him on his side. Dill tied the hands with rope while Steele straddled the torso and kept Ambrose's mouth jammed against the ground. Only when the rope was firmly lashed about his wrists did Ambrose cease to struggle.

The panting men slowly rose, brushed themselves off, and looked again down the western slope. Holly ran to her father, sobbing, and held out a bruised arm for sympathy. But even Holly was overcome by the sight below her. The four black men and the white father and daughter stood in a numbed cluster on the rise and watched as the girls walked steadily upward toward the great oak.

They came from the meadow all abreast and they marched toward the rising sun, awash in golden light. There were short girls and tall girls, white faces and black, a billowing wave on the green lawn of Fairhill. They walked with a carefree lilt, just a shade off a skip, still clasping hands. Tim recognized the two girls in the center, white Bunny Jeffers and black Eileen Duncan, the swimming instructors at the weekly class that Scott and Holly attended. Now Tim could count the girls. There were fourteen, seven white and seven black. They wore bright summer dresses and looked as fresh as the dew beneath their feet. The men moved forward slowly to meet this strangest of Fairhill's invasions.

The skirted brigade, for the most part solemn but disrupted by several fits of giggling, came to a halt beneath the oak tree. Bunny and Eileen stepped forward.

"We came to take Holly and Scott to Wednesday morning swim class," said Bunny with rehearsed understatement. She spoke in her most honeyed voice, and she hoped that her cascade of blond hair looked as divine as it had in the mirror some hours earlier.

"I know," said Holly.

"We don't mean to mess with anything," said Eileen.

"We just want to take the kids to class." Her private glance at Steele, the obvious leader, implied that he could get on with his business as soon as the children departed.

Then the girls noticed Ambrose. He lay dumped on the grass like a sack, arms roped behind his back.

"A little disagreement," said Steele. "Nothing much."

The girls looked very serious now. The giggling had stopped.

"How did you get in here?" asked Tim. With fifteen hundred paratroops ringing the estate the feat seemed improbable.

Several girls tried to answer at once, but Eileen overrode lesser voices. "We came through the Peckinpaughs' yard," she said. "There was an Army captain there, and we told him we wanted to fetch the kids and asked permission to come up the hill. He wouldn't let us; then a major came up and some other soldiers, and while they were all talking, we ran through the lines where the soldiers were about twenty yards apart."

"We planned it yesterday," said Bunny proudly.

"There was two black soldiers could have stopped us," Eileen went on, "but they didn't. By the time the others realized what was happening, we were over the stone fence and they couldn't catch us. They yelled for us to come back, but we didn't pay any attention."

"Right smart," said Steele. He was as impressed as Tim.

"We got the idea because of all that fake crying over the children," said Bunny. "Everybody was wringing their hands over the kids. Yuck! So Eileen and I decided to show them that kids could do something, you know, besides stand around moaning."

"Weren't you scared we'd shoot at you?" asked Steele.

"At us!" exclaimed Eileen in a mock falsetto. "Naw, I knew you wouldn't. We're not even old enough for a white man to hurt us."

Her remark, so guileless and spontaneous, struck Tim with curious impact. It spoke of unknown but certain wounds to come, and he felt both despair and sadness. He had acted selfishly in his gift of money, thinking only of Tim Crawford, he knew, while out there were a million Eileens. Well, perhaps for many of the wrong reasons, he still had done the right thing. He had seen this girl a dozen times, yet now he looked at Eileen with new recognition.

"You ready for swimming class?" Bunny asked Holly.

Holly merely nodded, ashamed that she had shown her fear. Overwhelmed by the size of her feminine escort, she could find no words to surmount her unnatural shyness.

"Then go inside and get Scott," said Tim. "And wake your mother and bring her along."

"Can Peter Wilson go too?" asked Holly.

"Sure," said Steele. "And we'll fetch Dora Wilcox from the tool shed. We're all going to walk down the hill together."

"You are?" Bunny was stunned.

"Yes," said Steele. "It's all over."

Marsh came across the lawn carrying the loudspeaker. Steele took the bull horn and handed it to Tim.

"You might as well ask the governor, Tim," he said. "If amnesty still goes, we're all getting out of here. . . . Jackson, Harve, round up the guns."

Steele walked over and knelt beside Ambrose. Chili turned his head and looked up at his rival with a bleak, accusing stare of weary green eyes.

"You give me your word you won't make trouble, Chili," said Steele, "and I'll untie you. We're all leaving."

"So where's to go?" asked Ambrose bleakly. "You sold us out."

"That's not true, Chili." Steele leaned over and gave Ambrose a brief, whispered explanation of his deal with Tim.

"Same old nuthin', Ben," said Ambrose. "You sold out."

He turned his head away, his pitted cheek resting on the damp grass, his wrists lashed behind him.

"Can I let you loose, Chili?" asked Steele gently. "You gonna look funny, walkin' outa here with them hands tied."

"Do what you want." His voice was flat, lifeless.

"Promise? No trouble."

"You know I can't do nothin', Ben. You got my guns."

"That a promise?"

"Yeah." The spirit was gone. His eyes were closed and one leg twitched.

Steele undid the knot, then grasped Ambrose under the armpits and helped the exhausted warrior to his feet. Ambrose stood unsteadily, rubbing his wrists. He inspected the silent girls and appeared baffled by their presence. His gaze drifted beyond them, and for a moment the fatigue dropped away. He put his hand on the sleeve of Steele's black sweater, and he tilted his head as though straining to hear something.

"What's the matter, Chili?"

"I thought I heard Danny calling," he replied. His fingers trembled on Steele's arm.

"Danny's way south in Carolina."

Ambrose shook his head slowly. The pitted face had a curiously tormented look. Suddenly he gripped Steele's arm like a vise, freezing his restless fingers. "Danny!" he breathed. "He called for Gamal and nobody heard him."

A shivering overtook the body so depleted of sleep and so shorn of valor. Quickly Steele embraced Ambrose and began patting his back like a comforting father.

When Steele looked up at the hushed crowd, a peculiar assortment of ages and colors, his eyes met those of Tim Crawford, and for an instant bitterness warred with pity.

"Damn you, Crawford," said Steele.

"Ben, I'm sorry. I—"

"Shut up! Just lift that bull horn and get it over with."

The new chairman's first order to his board member fled across the crest of Fairhill. The eastern sun, huge and powerful, bathed the great oak in brilliant light. In the distance a siren wailed. Bunny Jeffers reached for the hand of her black friend. Eileen Duncan felt the touch— and moved away.

Dawn slid over the dry, crumpled fields, caressing the soil, laving the scrub pines and brushing the hollows where mist lay like pools of smoke. A wood thrush with speckled breast perched on a high maple limb and raised its flutelike call. A new warmth, full and fragrant, hugged the earth.

Inside the barn, there was a bustle of disciplined preparation. Men stacked guns in the van. Shorty tinkered with the engine under a lifted hood. Lothar washed tin plates in a leaking tub. Major Underwood bent over a map, making calculations with thumb and forefinger.

Daniel Smith strode about, the confident and sanctified commander. He held a tin cup of steaming coffee from which he took quick, nervous sips. His step was light, and a kind of radiance suffused the normal severity of his bearded face.

Dan Smith was tautly happy. Everything was going according to schedule. An hour ago, in the last shades of night, Shorty had returned from Greensboro in the old man's heap. Mission accomplished. Alfred Nicolet had been spirited away from the fetid Gaylord in Philadelphia and was now held prisoner in the basement apartment of Jimmy Fitt, who was poised to launch the great raid on two hundred Main Line estates. Commander Smith and his twelve men would lead the North Carolina B.O.F. in capture of fifteen homes in Raleigh, some eighty miles east of the farm. The investment of white homes in Raleigh was an act of deep symbolism with Smith, for Raleigh was the city of his birth.

In Dan Smith's mind visions of Gamal vied with grubby details of the military operation. He could see the teeming black cities, the long freighters gliding to the wharves of New Orleans, the proud black beauties walking the streets with stately grace, and the banner of the new nation, a crimson fist on a field of ebony, whipping from the flagstaff over the capitol of Montgomery.

There had been setbacks, true. The Tiegert and Dittmar homes, where the craven followers of Nicolet held command, had yielded to whitey's chicanery. But the four other homes held fast, and soon thousands of tough, silk-footed B.O.F. guerrillas would stream from the ghettos to seize the wealthy honky homes, ransom grist for the mills of Gamal. The call would be sounded in just a few minutes now. Smith was aquiver with the imminence of action, yet somewhat apprehensive, for he knew that last night's radio messages from the farm had been monitored. The van must roll out as soon as possible. Minutes counted.

Major Underwood arose from his crouch, folded the map, and tucked it in his hip pocket.

"We ready?" asked Smith. His eyes shone with the promise of the new day.

"Ready," said Underwood.

"Get set to go, Shorty," ordered Smith. "I'm goin' over to the house and give the signal on the radio. Then we bring the rig back here, stow it in the van, and shove off for Raleigh."

He drained the last of his coffee, raised the tin cup in a salute, tossed it to Lothar at the tub, and strode out the side door.

Behind the pines to the east could be seen the orange glow of the thrusting sun. The earth was gray and powdery, for there had been no rain for many days. Dust coated the leaves of the crab-apple tree in front of the sagging porch. The unpainted frame house, cracking as though from thirst, was clasped in the amber light of dawn. At an open kitchen window stood Jerry, the radio operator, and beside him a coffeepot simmered on a kerosene stove. Jerry grinned at his commander, a notice that the radio transceiver was in working order and ready to send forth the summons to a new nation.

Smith moved in great, long strides, his pointed beard thrust forward like a ship's figurehead, the medallion on silver chain thumping against his chest. He took in the sweet, fresh air in grateful gulps, and he was thankful to be alive.

"Dan!"

The piercing cry, startled yet filled with agony, came from Jerry. Smith caught the look on Jerry's face, instant and total pain as though his spine had been snapped. Jerry gestured weakly with an arm. Smith looked back across the cornfields.

They came slowly, inexorably, like giant driver ants intent on devouring the new corn and consuming any living thing in their path. They wore field jackets, dark trousers, and heavy work boots, and their tommy guns, held abreast at an angle, slanted upward like the antennas of insects. Some carried gas masks. The tramp of their feet on the powdered earth was the only sound to be heard save for a single a-olee, a note of liquid surprise, from the wood thrush high in the maple.

Smith revolved swiftly, sweeping his eyes around the

horizon. They came from everywhere, from the woods behind the barn, across the stubbled field beyond the house, through the corn rows, down the gravel road from both directions. They edged toward the house and barn in a slowly constricting circle, seeking temporary shelter from trees, furrows, and a hayrack. Smith knew them. They were federal agents, at least a hundred, perhaps a hundred more, and they obviously had overpowered his sentries before alarms could be raised.

Smith ran to the house, leaped over three wooden steps, pounded across the decrepit porch and through the doorway. He raced to the kitchen, shaking the house. Jerry, a stub of a man with heavy, brooding shoulders, shoved a rifle into his hands. Smith grasped it automatically and pointed the barrel at the waiting radio. The set rested on a table beside the lighted kerosene stove where the warming coffeepot stood.

"All stations," said Smith. "Quick!"

Jerry grabbed the microphone. "This is Lion. This is Lion. Emergency. Repeat. Emergency. This is Lion. Come in. Come in."

Through the window Smith could see the circles of agents halting some one hundred yards from the farm buildings. Some crouched. Others peered from behind trees or lay prone in the furrows. From somewhere behind them came the metallic boom of the inevitable bull horn.

"Daniel Smith! This is the FBI. All of you back out of the barn and house with your hands up. Leave your weapons inside."

The sound died away, trailing echoes through the scrub pines. Wavering static, scratchy noises, and sighing whistles came from the radio. Seconds ticked away in Smith's mind like the beat of a gong. The whimsical static, a medley of gurgles and piping sibilants, became a maddening sound. More than half a minute passed before a voice broke through the rattling void: "This is Position Three. Position Three."

"Stand by for Lion," ordered Jerry. He shoved the mike into Smith's hand. "This is the Lion," said Smith. "Can you hear me, Three?" There was no answer.